CRITICAL HIT

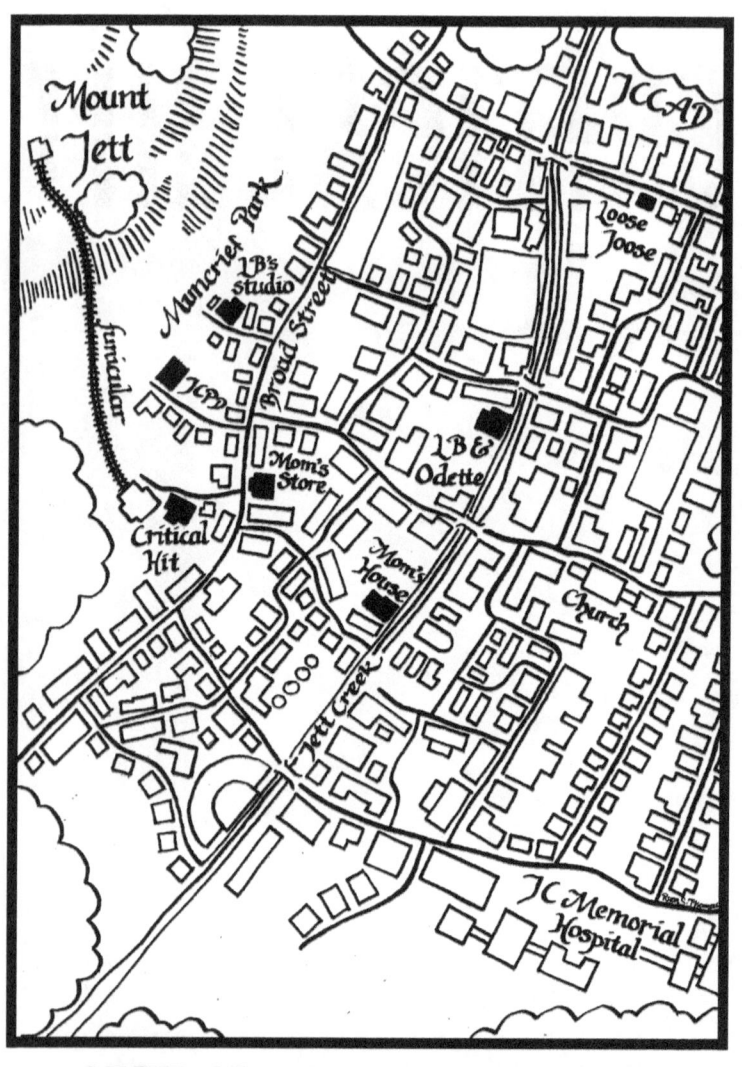

JETT CREEK, TENNESSEE
2003

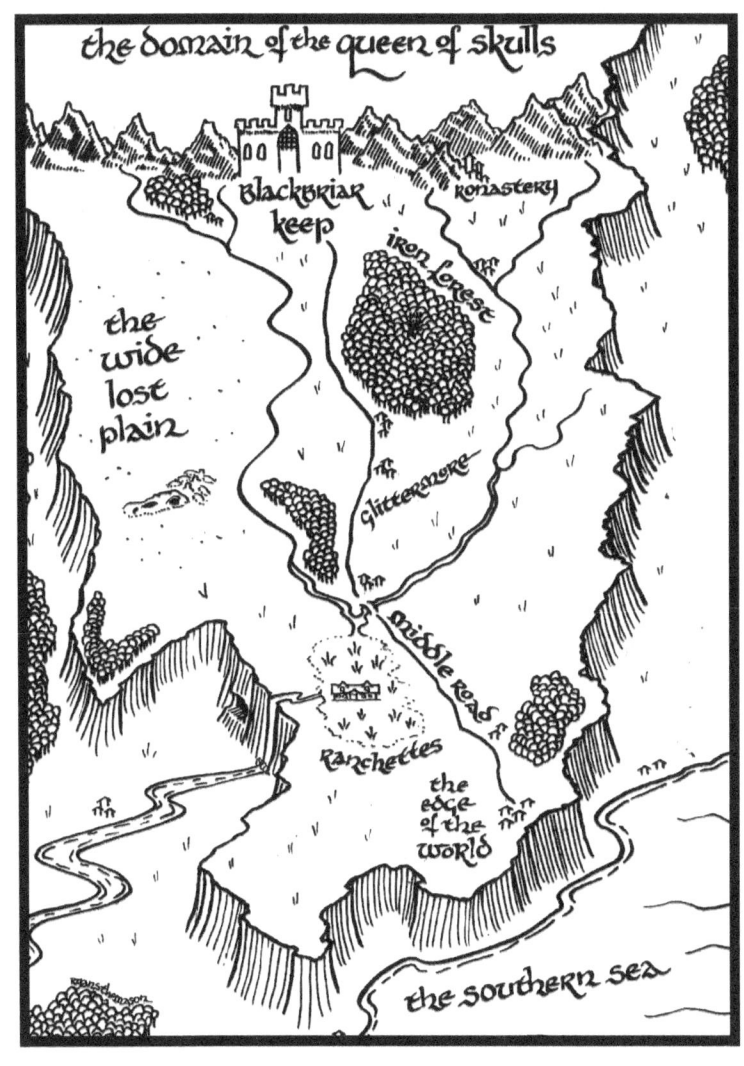

the domain of the queen of skulls

blackbriar keep

monastery

iron forest

the wide lost plain

glittermore

middle road

ranchettes

the edge of the world

the southern sea

THE WINTERWIND PLATEAU
YEAR 738

CRITICAL HIT

A GAMING MYSTERY

W.M. AKERS

WHAT HAPPENS NEXT PRESS
Philadelphia

Published by What Happens Next Press, a subsidiary of What Happens Next, Inc.

The What Happens Next name and logo are a trademark of What Happens Next Inc.

Learn more about What Happens Next and W.M. Akers' work at wmakers.net.

ISBNs
Paperback: 978-1-7373012-0-2
Hardback: 978-1-7373012-1-9
Ebook: 978-1-7373012-2-6

For my parents,
my brother,

and anyone who ever came to play

1

I LEFT MY FRIENDS BEHIND. THEY WERE FAR BELOW ME NOW—
thief, gladiator, bard, and mage—waiting on the frozen mud
of the Blackbriar courtyard, waiting for the gate to break, for
an army of thousands to pour through the door. I'd been with
them, but I broke and ran—not from cowardice, but because I
had a better idea.

Thud.

Wood splintered.

Thud.

Steel buckled.

Thud.

The doors exploded off their hinges. The Horde was inside.

I sprinted up icy steps, never doubting this was the only
way. Far below, the Heroes were surrounded. For the first time
in their lives, they looked small. I could not hear the battle. Up
that high, there was no sound but the roar of the wind and, far
above me, the creaking of bone.

I threw my bow over my shoulder and planted a foot on the
lip of the wall. A snowflake caught on my numb lips. It tasted
pure.

With a deep breath, I hurled myself into space.

The Hordesmen looked up. In their white armor, they were hard to distinguish from the ice on the ground. The ground that was, I realized, rushing up to meet me very, very fast.

If this doesn't work, I thought, I'm going to look like such an asshole.

And then a shadow swept out of the darkness: a massive, keening, riderless bird.

I crashed into its side.

My fingers clawed desperately at its bloody feathers. The great beast rolled, and the ground surged to meet me, and I was more certain than ever that death was coming tonight. I hung on tight, and when the roll stopped, I thudded into the leather seat on its back and did not let go.

"Thank you," I said, and the griffon screamed loud enough to knock a platoon of Hordesmen to the ground. I tugged on the reins. With a beat of its massive wings, it flung us into the clouds.

My breathing was steady. My hands didn't shake. I glanced over my shoulder and saw Blackbriar Keep, shrunk to the size of a child's toy. I wondered if any of my friends were still alive.

Didn't matter. The griffon crashed into the slushy, frozen clouds, which soaked me from head to toe. The sky went black. There was no sound but the occasional thump of the griffon's wings. And then we exploded above the clouds, where the Duke was losing the battle for the sky.

Of the hundred griffon-riders he had launched so optimistically before the assault began, only a handful were still in the air. In the light of a cold blue moon, they wheeled around their target: a hundred-yard long flying Horror made of sinew and bone. It snapped at the griffons and batted them aside with indifferent swipes of its barbed tail. The lances of the griffon riders clattered harmlessly off the beast, coming nowhere near their true target: the Queen of Skulls.

She was a smudge of green between the beast's shoulder blades, a warrior whose armies had broken a continent and slaughtered hundreds of thousands of innocents. Only

Blackbriar stood between her and Winterwind, and Blackbriar would fall unless she died. The griffon riders were never going to hit her. No one could make that shot.

No one but me.

For I was Arabeth of the Golden Mail. Arabeth the dead-eyed, Arabeth the level 12 marksman. Arabeth the best god-damned shot on the Plateau. I nocked an arrow, slowed my heartbeat, and lined up the shot that would end the war.

SOMEWHERE FAR FROM BLACKBRIAR KEEP, A BARRICADE OF EMPTY beer cans and crumpled chip bags ringed a plastic castle. On the white grid that represented its muddy courtyard, four one-inch miniature Heroes were locked in deadly combat with the dozen figurines that represented a Horde of thousands. They were beautiful little figurines, but all eyes were on the other end of the table. Nothing mattered but Arabeth.

She had one leg raised, her bowstring drawn taut, and a look of extreme do-not-fuck-with-me on her face. I'd spent twenty-two hours painting her, deploying all my tricks to bring her plastic to life. From her forest green boots to the curls of her rich brown hair, every millimeter was perfect. Tonight, perfect was what it would take.

It was April 2003, when tops were cropped and pants were cargo, when fedoras and trucker hats still seemed like good ideas, when America was already getting bored with its new war. More importantly, it was a Thursday, which meant the back room at Critical Hit was ours. Stale beer and smoke polluted the air. Imitation wood paneling peeled from a drop ceiling that was nearly as stained as the pea green carpet. The walls were close, or I guess the table was too big, because you couldn't shift your seat without banging into one or the other. Absolutely no breeze drifted through the little window on the far wall. Grimy lace curtains hid us from the rest of the game shop. It was a pit, but it had to be the happiest pit on earth.

The man who brought magic into that little room sat at the head of the table. One hand rested on his gut; the other twisted a beard flicked with red ale. His eyes—one bare, the other behind that ridiculous monocle—were slits. A playful smile drifted across his face as he tried to figure out what might happen next. He looked like a big, gentle grizzly bear. A stranger might have mistaken him for just another geek. They'd never have guessed that my big brother was the greatest gamemaster in the world.

"You sure you want to do this?" he asked.

"I think I already have."

He spun a die and stared at the ceiling, picturing another world, running the numbers to try to decide just how fucked I really was.

"You could back out," he said, finally.

"Yeah?"

"It's foggy. The Queen hasn't seen you. You want to bomb back through the clouds, get back to the main battle, back to the group, you can probably get away."

He squeezed my hand, real quick, like he used to do when I was a kid learning how to play. It wasn't often he gave us a chance to undo a stupid mistake.

"You know I don't mind if you go off the rails. I love when you go off the rails. That's where the best shit happens. But the Queen of Skulls is, shit, the Queen of Skulls. I certainly didn't expect you to face her alone. If you hit her and don't kill her, she's joining the fun right now. Y'all ready for that?"

I looked at the other members of my party. Across from me was Fale Mingori, better known as Doc. She wore a tattered blue JCCAD sweatshirt, thick red glasses, and a look of extreme displeasure. She popped a Milk Dud and chewed plaintively.

"If I can ask a slightly impertinent question," she said, "what the hell were you thinking running off from the group?"

It wasn't easy to explain. I was never the type to go it alone, but when LB set out his Horde figurines, they were factory gray. He hadn't even taken the time to apply a rudimentary coat of paint.

LB Kucek was a thousand things—thoughtful, introspective, flatulent, brilliant—but more than anything else, he was meticulous. If he wanted us to fight that Horde, he wouldn't have sent them into battle nude.

I knew all that stuff, but Arabeth didn't, so I answered like she would have—like I trusted my own decisions, like I wasn't afraid.

"They were going to kill us all."

"Maybe," said Doc. "Maybe if you'd stuck around, we could have killed enough to blunt the advance, turn the tide. Maybe we could have won."

The man sitting beside Doc leaned over the table to squint at Arabeth, so low that his rimless spectacles nearly slid off his nose. Matty Barber, a refugee from coal country who'd never attempted to shed his sorghum-sweet hill country drawl, was the strongest person I'd ever met. He was also a giant sweetie pie. He had a lank ponytail and thin lips and he brewed beer that was so good, it absolutely blew my mind. Tonight he was looking at me like I was crazy. No, not crazy—Matty never judged. It's more accurate to say he looked concerned.

"Am I missing something, or is this a real bad idea?"

"It was a trap," I said.

"It wasn't a trap," said Craig, the fourth member of our party, a deeply white juice bar owner who wore socks with his sandals and therefore merits no further description. "I know traps. I'm the king of traps. And if there are twelve extremely dangerous Hordesmen surrounding your party, it isn't a trap, it's a battle, and you need your marksman there."

He was right. Of course he was right. It's one of the first rules of roleplaying games, right up there with, "Don't eat the dice." Splitting up is a good way to get killed. I knew that rule better than anybody, because I always know the rules. Nausea swept up from my stomach—not the normal queasiness that comes from a dinner of Ruffles and High Life, but a dizzying gut-ache that got worse the more I dwelt on the fact that I might have just screwed up the battle, the campaign, my whole goddamned year.

"You said she can take it back," Craig said to LB. "She takes it back."

"Not your call," LB answered.

"Should we wait for Sondra?" said Matty.

"It's not her call, either. Arabeth—what's your move?"

I held his gaze for as long as I could stand. It was hard to tell beneath his beard, but I was pretty sure he was trying not to smile. I'd been following LB's cues my entire life, and they had never steered me wrong. He wanted me to take the shot.

"Y'all are right," I said. "This is probably a really stupid idea."

"Oh no," said Doc.

"Don't," said Craig. "Just please don't."

"If it were up to me," I said, "I'd be right there with y'all, but Arabeth is the one with the bow, and there's no way she could resist the Queen of Skulls."

LB clapped. Matty covered his face with his hands, knowing that when your GM is that excited, it means things are about to go straight to hell.

"Arabeth," said LB, "roll to hit."

The die squirmed inside my sweaty fist. I tried to play it cool, but I'm Callie Myles, not Arabeth, and cool is not exactly my thing.

I rolled.

And I missed. So, so bad.

"Shit!" barked Craig, smacking the table. "Total shit!"

"So let me guess," I said. "The arrow sails harmlessly past, she doesn't notice me, and I continue on my merry way?"

"You wish," said LB. "The arrow misses the Queen, but it smacks right into the shoulder of her flying beast."

"Fuck," said Doc.

"The monster wheels and charges, screaming in pain—a banshee shriek that spooks your griffon, which plunges into the clouds."

"Fuck," said Craig.

"It's pitch dark, sticky wet, and you can't tell which way is up. You hear the Queen's ride making this awful screeching noise. She is very, very close."

"Aw, heck no," said Matty.

"Gimme a DEX check to see if you hang on."

I rolled the die. This time it went better, allowing Arabeth to just barely avoid plummeting to a truly embarrassing death. The Queen's mount closed, its hot breath smelling like old hotdogs and slime. LB asked me to roll for Animal Handling, a skill that literally nobody ever uses, and I blew it. The Queen's bone-creature took a bite out of my poor griffon's wing. When we came out of the clouds, we were in a tailspin, falling fast.

My friends shook their heads, saying nothing, which was worse than if they'd been pissed off. Things didn't improve when Sondra slunk in, as sleek and indifferent as a cat.

"Did I miss anything?" she said.

"You missed everything," said Craig.

The newest member of our group, Sondra was a yoga addict from Maryland who simply creeped me out. Sitting next to her was like putting on a pair of wet socks. She sat in her seat and glared like she was trying to melt me with her eyes.

Flush with embarrassment, I ran a finger across Arabeth's golden mail, her hickory bow. As always, her posture was impeccable, her eyes unblinking. I tried to remember that as long as I was her, I had nothing to fear.

"You crash into the rampart," said LB. He was talking quicker now, the way he did when the story was really clicking, when he had so much good shit to throw at us that he could hardly wait for what was coming next. "The griffon rolls, throwing you from the saddle. You skid across the iron, cut the shit out of your arm. Mark seven damage."

"Gahhhh," I said. "Where's the Queen?"

"Coming in for a landing. Her beast grabs the wall. One wing bashes into the Slanting Tower and rips the top right off. You're right between its claws."

"Jesus Christ," said Doc.

"Yeah," said Sondra. "Nasty."

"It lowers its wing. It shudders with pleasure as the Queen descends."

I leaned forward. We all did.

Nobody moved. Nobody breathed.

Even the air was still. It was time to meet the Queen.

Moments like this were why we came here every week, why

we squeezed into this dank little room, why we stayed up too late eating so much junk food that we woke up with sodium hangovers. When LB was on his game, and my god that night he was on his game, there was no distance between us and our miniatures, and gray, pointless reality was infinitely far away.

"What's she look like?" said Craig. "What's she look like? What's she look like?"

"Shut the fuck up, Craig, that's what she looks like," said Sondra. LB gave her a nod of thanks and continued.

"She steps from her saddle and walks down the griffon's outstretched wing. She looks..."

He glanced at his notes and cackled, laughing hard enough to trigger the kind of coughing fit that only thirty-year-smokers enjoy. We laughed too, though we had no idea why. When he finished hacking, he wiped tears from his cheeks and said, "She looks like Danny DeVito."

"What?" I said. "I mean, what?"

"No shit! She's like, not quite five feet tall. Egg-shaped. Thin white hair, like the Crypt Keeper. Could be fifty, could be five hundred. She's dragging a sword that's twice as tall as she is—it's green, sharp as hell—and her face is hidden by a golden mask that shows a laughing skull."

He dug around in his bag for a plastic tray that held an assortment of miniature knights, wizards, bandits, and miscellaneous baddies. Finally, he pulled out a squat little woman with a colossal sword, a receding hairline, and skin as pasty as DeVito's Penguin. As always, the paint job was divine. He set it next to Arabeth.

"She hoists that sword above her head," said LB. "She's gonna disembowel you if you don't do something good. What's your move?"

I rapped a pencil on the list of gear in Arabeth's pack, considering something I'd been hanging onto for a long time. Something brilliant, a little stupid, and absurdly dangerous. I took a deep breath and said:

"I take off my pants."

For the last half hour, LB had been a motorcycle bombing

along at 100 miles-per-hour, every gear in alignment, every piston doing whatever pistons do. (I don't know anything about motorcycles.) My move sent him sprawling like a patch of black ice.

"What's that now?" said LB.

"You heard. Do I need to roll for it?"

"Uh, no. You're pantsless on a frozen battlement in the middle of the biggest fight in the history of the Plateau. You gonna attack or wait for frostbite?"

I sat up straight. Hopefully I looked like I knew what I was doing. It was the second time that night I'd taken a ridiculous risk. If it didn't pay off I would really look a fool.

"There's an arrow of lightning strapped to my leg," I said. "I yank it off and let it fly."

Flush crept in around LB's beard. Now that was something I hadn't seen in a long, long time.

"You can't just make stuff up," said LB. "You do not have an arrow of lightning strapped to your leg."

"Except, well, I kinda do."

I showed him the scribble on my inventory list: "Arrow of Lightning (in pants)."

"It's been there for months," I said. "I assume it's super uncomfortable."

"Where did you get it?"

"The session where we went rafting."

Silent and slow, LB flipped back through his binder. I couldn't see over his GM screen, but I knew he found the right page when he shook his head, smiling grimly.

"November 19. Morell's Rapids. Arabeth finds an arrow of lightning on the sunken barge. She hides it in her pants. Well. All right then."

"Well no kidding," said Matty. "No kidding!"

He smacked me on the shoulder. It hurt, in a very pleasant way. For a moment, I let myself believe that this madness might actually work out. Doc's smile suggested she was feeling the same. Even Craig and Sondra looked a touch less sour. LB tried to put some of the pep back into his voice. It didn't come through. I began to worry that I'd done something horrible.

"Come on Callie," he said. "Make the roll."

I reached for my sky-blue d20 and found my palms were dry.

"Shoot her in the eye," said Doc.

I held my arm high, turned my fist upside down, and dropped the die on the table. It bounced. It bounced again. It settled.

Twenty.

A natural twenty.

A critical hit.

"Right in the fucking eye!" said Doc, wrapping Sondra in an entirely unwanted hug. Matty and Craig shared an awkward high five over my head. I should have been on my feet cheering, but I was busy watching LB. He said nothing. He did nothing. But he squeezed that monocle so tight that the iron left a mark.

"Did she hurt her?" said Craig. "Did she kill her?"

"There's no way she killed her," said Matty. "Even with a crit."

"Roll for damage," said LB, almost too quiet to hear. "Let's find out."

I dumped a handful of dice across the table.

"54," I said.

"Damn," said Doc.

"It hurts," says LB. He was having trouble getting out the words. "Catches her right in the shoulder. Lightning races across her chest and neck like a web. Her flesh burns. It doesn't smell good, but she's far from dead. She rips the arrow out with one hand, and raises the Greene Blade with the other. She swings—"

"Wait," I said. My cheeks were flush. I couldn't meet his eye.

"What for, sis?"

"What about my modifier? I wouldn't bring it up except, well, rules are rules."

Craig sat back, puzzled. Doc and Sondra just stared. Only Matty knew what I was getting at. His famous smile broke across his face and he sat back in his chair, drumming his fingers on his belly, waiting for everyone else to see.

"What modifier?" said LB, truly off balance now.

"It's a lightning arrow. The Queen is wet. That's a 5x modifier. I don't mean to slow things down, but…"

"She's wet?"

"From the clouds. We're both soaked. You said, remember?"

"She's wet."

"The Queen of Skulls is wet," said Doc. I'd never seen her so close to awe.

"54 times five is…"

"270," Matty whispered. "Nobody soaks that."

"Is this war over or what?" said Sondra.

We looked to LB. We always looked to LB—that's what GMs are for—but LB wasn't there any more. Physically, yeah, he was still in his chair, but my brother had gone somewhere far away.

He dropped his pencil on the table, swept his papers carelessly into his binder, and shoved it into his bag. He picked up the minis for our characters, the Hordesmen, the Queen of Skulls and her mount, and packed them carefully away.

"You okay, man?" I said, soft enough that none of the others could hear.

He said nothing. He worked his way awkwardly around Matty and I and tried to pick up the model of the castle. The angle was awkward. It slipped out of his grasp and crashed to the table, rattling the battlements and sending the Horde sliding into a heap.

"Let me help you," said Matty. LB waved him away.

"It's cool. I'll get it tomorrow."

I'd never heard his voice so small.

"Six years," he said, and left the room.

Six years. He'd been building up to this moment over six years of campaigns, creating hundreds of characters and centuries of lore, putting it all together for our benefit after work and on weekends, when he should have been sleeping or eating or grading assignments. And I'd ruined it with one arrow.

We weren't laughing any more.

I followed him into the main room, a wide, cozy space filled with plastic folding tables and snacks and every game the world has ever played. A dozen drunk nerds and insufficiently-supervised teens looked up from dice, boards, cards, and meticulously-painted miniatures to watch LB lurch to the front of the store.

One of my fellow clerks, a hunched forty-something with thin legs and thin hands and thin hair named Diego, got up from a game of *Warhammer* and blocked my view of LB. He was a nice enough guy who had made the mistake, sometime the year prior, of getting a colossal crush on me. In my head, I called him Not Now Diego, because every time he tried to talk to me I said:

"Not now, man."

I pushed past him. He let me go.

LB leaned on the front desk. He didn't turn my way.

"Wait up!" I said. "I am sorry, dude. Just come back and talk about it. Let's finish the game."

LB handed his bag across the desk to a woman in soft white pants and a matching hooded sweater. This was Odette Sparks—his wife, owner of the Critical Hit Games Cafe and, for the last few, pointless years, my boss. She put her hand on his. He yanked his hand away.

"So is she dead or what?" I shouted.

At last, he turned my way. Christ, his face was red.

"She's dead."

"What happens next?"

With a shrug of his heavy shoulders, he left the shop. The bell tinkled. For a while, that was the only sound.

"Everything okay?" said Odette.

"I doubt it."

And Odette, because she is wonderful, didn't ask any more.

I grabbed two six packs from the fridge and returned to the back room. I didn't want to be there anymore, but I had nowhere else to go. This shop was my home, my hearth. That night I poisoned it. It would never be perfect again.

A LONG TIME EARLIER, I STOOD AT A CROSSROADS IN AN ANCIENT forest, not sure if I should walk to mountains or sea, castle or town. I rolled a gray, unpainted plastic figurine around my palm. She had a flat expression and lifeless eyes. I had no idea what she would want to do.

I was in my windowsill and LB was hanging off my bed, massive shoulders hunched, eyes inspecting the crumbs on my carpet. I was fourteen, a perfectionist who believed rules are made to be followed and who was just learning that such an attitude would make high school hell. LB was twenty-nine, failing to hack it as a sculptor in New York, and in the depths of what he would later describe as his "crappiest era." I spent all year looking forward to his rare trips home, even though afternoons with him were mostly silent—long awkward pauses interrupted by occasional awkward small talk. No matter how bored we got, it was an honor to have him in my room.

"So…" he said. "You're, like, fourteen."

"You said that before."

"Oh."

There was another long pause. He'd started to fidget, which meant he was close to slinking down the hall to his childhood room, whose door was an impenetrable force field that kept little sisters out, no matter how they begged. And so I tried something new.

"Why don't you show me that game?"

"What game?"

"The one you're always fiddling with on the porch. The one with the little plastic dudes and all the weird dice."

"You want to play *Winterwind?*"

He said it like I'd asked him to yodel.

"Why's that such a surprise?"

"I didn't realize today's hip young teens were into pen-and-paper gaming. I thought y'all were too busy with your MTV and your crack cocaine."

"I can't speak for the rest of the hip young teens, but I want to play."

"Well…well fuck yeah!"

And so he set up a session of the game he'd been playing my whole life, that mysterious thing called Winterwind that had pieces but no box, maps but no board, and nothing to govern it but glittering dice and imagination unbound.

"This is awesome," he said. "Just awesome. I can't believe I never thought to show you this before. You are going to have so much fun."

It's not an exaggeration to say I'd never seen him so excited. I was pretty excited, too.

There were countless RPGs out there, he gushed, but his was the best. It was a system of his own design, loosely based on a forgotten '80s gladiatorial combat sim called *Those About to Die*, which LB had hacked up and put back together until it was something only he could understand. The game was really just a conversation, a group make-believe where questions of chance were answered by bizarre dice of every shape and size. It didn't seem possible that so much fun could be spun from nothing but plastic and conversation, but that day I began to understand the holy secrets of the game.

"All right," he said, cracking his back. "Who do you want to be?"

The best I could do was, "Not Callie Myles."

"Why not? I always thought Callie Myles was a pretty cool kid."

"I'm not and we both know it, but cool is beside the point. I'm pointless. Boring. I want to be something more."

"You got it."

And so we rolled up my first character. She was tall, strong, fast, a defender of the weak, the scourge of evil men. She was as relentless as I was, as fiendishly principled, but with the strength to bring rule-breakers to heel. She was a lot cooler than Callie Myles.

When she was ready, LB put me at the crossroads and asked where I wanted to go.

"I can do anything I want?" I said.

"Anything."

"I could sit down in the dirt?"

"You could."

"I sit down in the dirt."

Laughter rumbled out of his chest like a brewer banging around inside a huge metal tank. It was the best sound in the world.

"Great," he said. "Now you're sitting in the dirt. You feel... dirty."

"But this isn't the story."

"No."

"How do I make you tell the story?"

"Start some shit. Roll high and things go well. Roll low and I'll tell you how bad it hurts."

"What if I don't want to start shit? What if I just want to, I don't know, go to the library and chill out?"

"Trouble will find you, even if I have to bend the rules."

That was what I loved about this man, my half-brother, who was so much older than me, who looked so different, but who was just similar enough that I couldn't understand him at all. Everyone on earth was bound by the rules, but he knew how to make them bend.

"Forget your instincts." He tapped the mini. "What would she do?"

"There are four paths?"

"Yep."

"I don't take any of them. I get out of the dirt, unsling my bow, and walk straight into the woods. Do I need to roll for that?"

"Nope," he said, screwing that stupid monocle in a little tighter, and I was on my way.

After he left, I stared at the raw plastic warrior until my eyes watered. There was so much detail there—from the hilt of her short sword to the folds of leather on her tunic. She just needed a little color to bring it out.

The next time I saw LB I asked him, "How do I paint her?" He put a brush in my hand, and I was hooked for life. I learned to clip out models and prep them for painting, to apply primer and acrylic in coat after delicate coat. I learned to make their plastic look flesh, to put life in their eyes. Once he taught me to paint, I never felt pointless again.

I spent the next decade following the rules. I worked hard, never complained. I went massively into debt for an English degree that proved even less lucrative than expected. I sent out hundreds of applications and got fuck all in return. When the world spat me out I landed in the only place I could live on the cheap: Jett Creek, Tennessee, where my mother had kept my bedroom just as it was the day LB taught me to play.

Shitty years passed. Life was gray, senseless, until the day LB came by the house to tell me a spot had opened up in his weekly game. One of his players, the notorious scumbag Randy Randy, had quit, and the seat was mine. In that filthy back room, I found friends, I found fun, I found a world where following the rules was the only way to win. LB convinced Odette to hire me to run the register, make coffee, serve beer, and teach people to play games—a menial job that would have been miserable if it didn't mean spending all day in my favorite place, a safe spot for weirdos, losers, freaks, creeps, sad kids, bad kids, rad kids, and anyone from ages eight to eighty who would rather save a pretend world than live in a real one.

I had the games, the table, the conversation, the paint, the dice. I wanted it to be enough, but all of it was plastic, and plastic just isn't that strong.

Two hours after LB sulked out, we were still in the back room. Matty was dozing off and Sondra was about to snap Craig's neck.

"Say it again, fucker," she snarled. "If you've got any balls, say that bullshit again."

"Leave it alone," groaned Doc.

"Hell no," said Craig, twisting the split ends of his ponytail. "I'm not scared of her."

"Then you're a moron," said Sondra. "Now let's hear it."

"*Daredevil* is the best movie made this century."

"Asshole."

"Ben Affleck is a major talent, and they will never make a

superhero movie as straight up awesome as—"

Sondra's hand smacked the back of Craig's head. His beer sloshed all over his shirt and fizzed away into the rug.

"What the fuck?"

"Talk shit, get hit," said Sondra. "Got a problem?"

"I can't believe we have to keep going over this," I said, slapping a fresh beer into Craig's hand, "but hitting is not okay and *Daredevil* was fucking terrible."

"She's right on both counts," said Doc. She pushed back her chair.

"Don't tell me you're leaving."

"I've got work tomorrow."

"So do I. Have another beer."

"Think it's at all possible that running a college requires more sleep than working the register at a games store?"

"Just siddown."

She sat. I slid her a beer. Matty snored, an incongruously cute sound, like a terrier's yap coming from the body of a Great Dane. Craig scooted as far from Sondra as the little room allowed, but he didn't leave, which was good. The longer they stuck around, the longer I could stay out. Home meant sleep, and sleep meant nightmares, and I was not in the mood.

"You're persuasive when you want to be, Callie Myles," said Doc. She burped thoughtfully. "You ever think about taking over the game?"

"It's LB's game, not mine."

"You think he's coming back?" said Craig. "He was pretty wounded."

"I'll call him tomorrow and tell him I'm sorry."

"What for?" burped Doc.

"I spoiled his ending."

"Fuck that. You won. Don't beat yourself up for being good at the game."

I wished it were that easy to let it go. But I'd seen the way LB slumped out of the shop, and hated myself for making him sad.

"I think you'd be twice the GM he is," said Sondra. "You

know every rule, even the stupid ones. LB is good, but he's not god."

"I've run games before. Back in college, a couple of times. It went bad."

"How bad could a session go?" said Doc. "Were there maimings? Did anybody bleed out?"

Worse. Even the thought of the heartbreaking multipurpose room I'd checked out for the occasion, where chipped dorm furniture sat on a mildewed gray carpet, made me sick. I'd gathered a handful of my fellow freshmen for what I promised would be, "the adventure of a lifetime." I gave them three hours of shuffling papers, halting storytelling, and incoherent chatter about rules they didn't want to understand. They looked to me, and I failed them. I didn't want to do that again.

I was cracking the last beer when Doc's pager blared. Matty's too. Without taking a second to smear the sleep from his eyes, he stood up fast, slamming his chair into the flimsy wall.

"Prewitt Road," said Doc, and they were out the door.

"The hell was that?" said Sondra.

"They're volunteer firefighters," I said. "They…"

And then I remembered.

Prewitt Road, a narrow street that twisted up from Broad Street and disappeared into the woods.

Prewitt Road, where LB had his studio.

Prewitt Road, where LB played with fire.

I swallowed a mouthful of beer, grabbed my hoodie, vaulted over Matty's empty chair, and slammed into the street. I turned away from the dead end, where the funicular railroad had closed down for the night. Down the block, Doc's car peeled out. I shouted for her, but she did not stop. LB had been my ride and he was long gone, so for the first time since I figured out how to cut gym, I ran. Chuck Taylors slapping on ragged pavement, I sprinted to the corner, turned, and charged uphill.

A liberal enclave perched on a mountaintop in country-as-hell East Tennessee, Jett Creek is a great place to get a cup of coffee. The little strip we call Broad Street is overrun with shops like Cup of Yo, Here's to Brew, and Holt's Roasting Co. If getting jittery on sagging couches isn't your idea of fun, it's a reliable destination for henna tattoos, bulk lentils, shitty paintings of the Smoky Mountains, essential and non-essential oils, and surprisingly acceptable sushi.

But most of all, thanks to the unique idiocy of building a town on a cliff face, Jett Creek is a horrible place to run.

I hauled my flabbier-than-I-would-like ass twelve blocks down and up and down those stupid goddamned roads. I kept running, forgotten muscles burning, until I smelled the smoke on Prewitt Road.

A Depression-era mechanic's shop, LB's studio was at the back of a sloping lot covered with garbage and twisted iron. It was just two rooms: an old forge on the first floor and a rat's nest of papers and art supplies on the second. It was where he went, he said, when he needed to make art that was too personal to make at the college, or when he just wanted the world to leave him be.

All of it was on fire.

It was hard to see where the building had been. It was curling in on itself, like a paper bag in a campfire. The fire truck was halfway up the hill, spraying water on the house next door. The studio, they'd quit trying to save.

Doc's car sat at the bottom of the hill, front doors open, engine running. I saw her, gray ponytail silhouetted by the flame, manning one of the jets. With what little strength I had left, I ran up the driveway. Matty leapt out of the truck's cab, fireman's coat still unbuttoned, and grabbed me by the shoulder.

"Is he inside?" I said.

"Get out of here."

"God damn it, if he's in there, we have to get him out!"

"It's too hot. Nobody's going near it."

Matty rested his hand on my shoulder, and I tried to keep still. I wanted to push him, to charge inside, to look for LB, but that would have been against the rules.

We were watching together when my brother's massive

body exploded out of the window, wrapped in a cloak of flame.

LB screamed something. Maybe it was words, maybe it was just pain.

It stopped quick.

I didn't flinch. I didn't run to him. Even from behind the barricade, it was obvious he was dead.

2

THE NIGHTMARES WERE USUALLY THE SAME. A WINDSWEPT WHITE church. A bare floor, cold whistling through slit windows. A ceiling of smoke. At the front, a long wooden table with LB at the head.

He rattled dice in one hand and lit a cigarette with the other. The flame geysered out of the Zippo, up his arm, and swallowed his head and chest. Blisters puckered on his skin. His beard burned away. He twisted, but found himself unable to get away from the fire. His skin peeled off but he did not die.

His lips moved.

No matter how close I got, I could only make out one word. "Fucking..."

The dreams quit the night he died for real.

AFTER IT HAPPENED, I STUCK CLOSE TO MOM, AND LEARNED GRIEF gets old fast. We cried, paced, fought, ate, forced laughter at bad jokes, ate some more, failed to sleep at night and dozed fitfully during the day. We had a few ups and a thousand downs. We hit rock bottom and found there was much farther to go. We broke and kept on. We shut down and started up again.

When we finally came up for air, it felt like lifetimes had passed.

It had only been three days.

The morning of the funeral, I found myself blocking the doorway to my brother's childhood room, refusing to let Mom inside. Behind me was a pile of pictures, trading cards, CD cases, shitty vinyl, and some of the gorgeous bits of metal LB spent his life heating and twisting into shapes that only he could understand.

It was impossible to think his hands would never touch anything again.

Mom was ready to say goodbye.

"I want that shit out of my house," she said. She clutched a limp garbage bag like a rapier, jabbing it at me with every syllable.

I stayed calm. She hates that.

"There are rules for this," I said. "We keep it for a year."

"I've kept it twenty years. Every Christmas, he said he'd clean it out. He never did."

She leaned back just long enough for me to relax my hold on the wood, then thudded past me into the room. Brilliant fake-out. Classic Mom.

Priscilla Myles is the fiercest person I know. She came to Jett Creek in the late '60s, drawn by promises of a hippie utopia and the kind of tolerance that, in the south, was at least theoretically possible in a college town. It turned out to be overrun with assholes, just like everywhere else, but she refused to leave. She's stubborn like that. So was LB. So am I.

A few years after LB was born, she got divorced, quit her accounting job and mortgaged herself to the chin in order to open a flower shop on Broad Street. It was the most magical place in Jett Creek. When LB was thirteen, to the shock of everyone concerned, Mom get pregnant with me. My dad was a visiting professor at the crafts college—a nice guy, Mom always said, but not worth marrying. His Scottish background gave me the unwieldy name of Caledonia, lighter skin than the rest of my family, and a fondness for rainy days. LB had Mom's beauty, her talent, and her smile. I will die jealous of all that, but I got to keep her last name.

She yanked a worn spiral notebook off of LB's overstuffed bookshelf and threw it in the garbage bag. I yanked it back out.

"Why?" she said.

"Notebooks are important."

"What's in it?"

"Presumably notes."

She grabbed it back and looked at the cover, which read, "Algebra, For Some Reason, Sophomore Year." Inside was a quarter-page of notes from the first day of class. The rest was empty. She threw it back in the trash.

"That's a perfectly good notebook," I said. "Everyone needs a notebook."

She hummed to herself, moving as fast as she could, fighting to avoid eye contact as she whipped around chucking treasure into the bag. She opened LB's closet and reached for his basketball trophy. I ducked under her arm and snatched it off the shelf.

"You're emotional," I said. "You're not thinking."

"For god's sake, it's not his award!"

She was right, in a way. The trophy showed a warped, pony tailed girl getting set for a free throw. Her white plastic skull showed through the flaking imitation gold leaf. At the bottom, a plate read, "Jenny Havermayer, 7th Grade JV. Gooooooo Tiger Sharks!" I'd bought it for LB at a thrift store and gave it to him for his thirtieth birthday. He laughed so hard, I thought he might die.

"It was a gift," I said. "He liked it."

"Didn't you ever wonder what happened to Jenny Havermayer that put her stuff up for sale at Good Will?"

"Let's discuss in a year."

She turned her attention to the part of the room I'd been avoiding: the hanging shelves above the bed.

"No," I said.

"Callie, this shit is rotting on the shelves."

She yanked on a stack of old legal pads, toppling the whole heap onto the floor. Dust bloomed. She shoveled them into the garbage bag. I pulled back as much as I could.

I flipped through a pad whose yellow pages were dry and pale. I saw places like Bleakrock, Wild Bay, Direhelm, and Farcall, villains like Izacar, Chraecula, and Hoviah, heroes like Mirella and Tinpot Tom. This was *Winterwind* before it was *Winterwind*, the holy books, the notes from the college sessions when LB was still figuring out the rules of the game.

"We might need them for the campaign," I said. I couldn't look up from the paper. I couldn't make my voice as big as it needed to be. Mom made the face she usually made when we talked about the game—something between polite indifference and an outright eye-roll.

"I thought the campaign was done," she said.

"Oh. Yeah."

The fight went out of me. I left the room and sat at the top of the stairs, digging my toes into the carpet, flipping through notes that meant nothing at all.

A while later, Mom came up behind me, dragging a bag that, just like me, looked ready to rip in half. The piles on LB's floor were mostly gone. Her eyes were red, but dry. We weren't crying so quickly anymore.

"Bobby was always trying to break his neck," she said. "He was always falling out of trees, leaping off ledges, dragging me to the ER. I spent forty years telling him to be safe and he never fucking listened. 'Accidents are something that happen to other people, Mom.' He thought that was hilarious. Now he's dead."

"Kids are a pain in the ass."

She laughed, because she knew she was supposed to. On the street, a car horn screamed.

"God I hate how Jill leans on that horn," she said.

"That's why she does it. Drive with us?"

"I'll meet you there. I have to get that room emptied or coming home will kill me."

"If you find anything special..."

"I'll put it on your desk."

But her eyes said that the only special thing that room ever held was not coming back.

I gave her a hug, which I needed badly, and walked downstairs. When the front door closed, she hadn't budged.

Jill Scarce was the only person I knew who still drove the car she'd had in high school: a cherry red Lincoln with saggy suspension and a bumper plastered with stickers for local bands that had vanished ten years before. Because Jill also still smoked like an eighteen-year-old, the Scarcemobile was as suffocating as a hearse, its scarlet leather stained with ash that she had never even considered scrubbing out. That week I was letting myself smoke as much as I wanted, and I didn't mind the stench.

She leaned across the squishy little armrests and popped open the passenger door. An unlit cigarette waited for me on the dash, neatly arranged beside my favorite lighter, which said "Pickle!" and had a pickle on it.

"Hey babe," she said. "You ready for this?"

"I am extremely fucking not."

"Yep. It's gonna suck. Glad I could give you a ride."

She didn't need me to tell her there's no one else I would have called. As she drove, she filled the spaces between the smoke with idle chatter.

"That guy Craig going to be there?" she said.

"Probably. He's hard to get away from."

"How single is he?"

"Profoundly."

"I was thinking he might be fun to fuck."

"Dear god, why?"

"He's so dirty, you know, and sad? I'd like to lock the door at that awful little juice shop and just yank off his shorts."

I snorted at the image. Jill said it like she was joking, but she was funny about lust. I could never tell when she was really into someone. It's possible she couldn't either.

"I'll check on it for you," I said.

"You're a peach."

She kept talking, serving up reheated gossip about the dumbest people we went to high school with, who had an embarrassing habit of getting married, having kids, and parading them around like they were something people wanted to see. I

33

was grateful for the noise, but I couldn't say a word.

The casket was open.

I hadn't expected that.

The entire town was crammed into the narrow stone church: gamers, students and teachers from the crafts college, and all the eccentrics, young and old, who had considered LB a stalwart in the fight to keep Jett Creek weird. None of them wanted to go near the body, but they forced themselves to walk down the aisle and shake Odette's hand, to hug her, to say something useless before sneaking a peek at the corpse and retreating to the pews.

Mourning be damned, Odette was still wearing the soft white pants and softer white sweater she'd worn every day since I met her, with a black band snug around her left arm. Matty was handing them out at the door. He pressed one into my hand when I crossed the threshold, sighed like he was going to say something, and teared up instead.

"Hey, buddy, it's okay," I said. "Everybody burns to death once in a while."

He pushed up his glasses to smear away the tears, then wrapped me up in the best hug in the world—a Matty Barber special, dizzyingly tight.

"I'm sorry. It's your day."

"Just like every little girl dreams of. Is there someplace I'm supposed to sit?"

"Up front, I think?" He read the disgust on my face. "But heck, sit wherever you want. They're not going to kick you out."

I decided I'd rather stand.

Jill and I huddled in the back corner, like we were planning to ditch a pep rally. We were right behind the university contingent, led by Doc, who had ditched the slouchy cargo pants for a shockingly well-tailored black suit. I'd never seen her looking so employed. She nodded at me, a little gesture that somehow managed to perfectly straddle the line between warm and reserved. Fifty-year-olds are good at going to funerals.

I looked for Sondra. I didn't see her.

Across the aisle, Craig fidgeted, hands between his legs, trying to act like he didn't mind being the only person there wearing tie-dye. Long and stringy, Craig had greasy curls and the worst beard I'd ever seen. It wasn't clear how long he'd lived in Jett Creek. No one remembered seeing him before 2001, when he opened a juice bar on the college campus. By itself, that wasn't a bad idea, but he named it Loose Joose, which was unforgivable, and decorated it the way he decorated himself: like the kind of dirt bag hippie whom JCCAD students quit imitating thirty-five years before. When he talked, I usually didn't listen, because he rarely said anything that didn't make my eyes roll.

"Fucking hippie," said Jill. She gave a lustful growl. I laughed, grateful for her bullshit, but then the room went quiet.

Mom came through the door.

For the millionth time I wondered how she had the power to make herself beautiful in ten minutes or less. She waved at me and sat in the front row. I felt like an asshole for not being next to her, but it was too late to move. Music started—something fuzzy, with enough distortion that I couldn't quite place it, even though I figured LB had been playing it for me for ten years or more.

People started making speeches. They were funny, wistful, melancholy, hopeful, and altogether sickening. Mostly they talked about how talented LB was with iron, how generous he was with his students. They'd asked me to speak, but I'd said no. Here's some of the stuff I might have tried to say:

1. When he felt like it, LB was the silliest person on earth, capable of poking fun without hurting feelings, of mocking himself without ever sacrificing his cool.

2. He loved music and shared it aggressively. If you complimented a record, he'd give you his copy. If you asked about a band, he'd make you a fucking genius mix showcasing them and their influences and three other bands who did what they did but better. Since before I could remember he'd been filling my ears with afro-funk and hardcore and dreamy, unintelligible shoegaze, and I would never be able to untangle where his taste

ended and mine started up.

3. He always had the best weed, and he liked to share that too.

4. He made good burgers. Not great, but good.

5. He was a beer nerd, but he wasn't a dick about it.

6. He was absolutely obsessed with French history—the Revolution, Napoleon, everything—but he never mentioned it. Unless he was drunk. If he was drunk, he wouldn't shut up about it.

7. He really, really loved to dance, and my god he could not dance at all.

Those are the things about LB that mattered, but nobody mentioned them at all.

At some point during the fifth or sixth speech, it became impossible for me to hear any more.

"I gotta get some air," I told Jill, and I fled to the steps of the church, where spring soaked through my sweater. Irritatingly, I found someone else lurking beside the door.

Shamelessly blonde and just as pretty as when I saw her beaming from the welcome desk on the first day of freshman year, Leah Sparks was one of those high school people Jill and I loved to bitch about. She had three or four kids, all as gorgeous as her, and looked ready to have three or four more without breaking a sweat. She wore a billowing black windbreaker, a gun on one hip and a gold badge on the other.

"I thought the fuzz only staked out mob funerals," I said.

"I'm sorry for your loss."

"No shit? You're the first person to say that today."

"Jesus, Myles."

She stepped out of the doorway. I followed her outside. The church was at the top of crumbling stone steps that led to a graveyard where no one had been buried since 1895. The sun was high and cold. Bare trees cast a weird net of shadows over the hill.

"What do you want?" I said.

She pulled a lump of black metal out of her pocket.

"Do you recognize this?" she said.

"It's a lump of metal."

"Very helpful, thanks. It was in your brother's hand when he died."

"Oh."

"Yeah. It's iron. Iron that melted in his hand."

"So what? LB had iron around him all his life."

"So what's weird is that—and I had to look this up—iron melts at like 2,800° Fahrenheit. That's way, way hotter than the average house fire."

I suddenly felt extremely thirsty. My palms sweated. My pulse picked up.

"So?" I said.

"It's just a question. Unusual deaths always throw up questions. When I can't answer them, well, it's annoying."

I looked past her at the headstones and monuments that sat unevenly on the sloping churchyard. As a child, LB and Mom and I spent afternoons walking those ragged rows, making etchings of lives that ended before our grandparents were born. LB collected strange names, and this patch of dirt housed hall of famers like Del Tutwiler, Biggs Works, Cozy Handiboe, and Delia Wambsganns. In high school, I came back a lot because they never locked the gate at night and it was a wonderful place to get high.

"Did Bobby drink a lot?" she said.

"I guess. His tolerance was insane. And he only let Mom get away with calling him Bobby."

"Was he drunk the night he died?"

"He'd had a couple of beers, but he was sober. Why?"

"The last time you saw him was at nine-fifteen? At the shop?"

"We talked about that before," I said. I was sounding pissy. I couldn't help it and, for that matter, I didn't want to.

She rolled the lump of iron between her fingers. The sun turned her hair into a blonde halo. Nobody deserved to look that good while they were at work.

"Bobby's blood alcohol content was .12," she said. "That's close to blackout."

"What's your point?"

"So if you could confirm he'd been drinking heavily during your game, or even that he was a heavy drinker by practice, it would make it easier for me to call this an accident and be done with it. Leave you alone."

Something about the way she said "accident" felt like an insult. Like because LB was an artist he'd had it coming. Maybe she didn't mean it that way, but in the moment, I didn't really care.

"If it wasn't an accident, what could it be?"

"Oh, it was, without question. He was working in a rat trap that should have been torn down thirty years ago. He was dead drunk. There was no one else there."

"But the iron, you said it yourself. It doesn't make any sense."

"Death isn't supposed to."

"Oh. Good to know."

"Anyway…I'm sorry for your loss."

She walked down to the street, forgoing the rocky path to trod on unkempt graves. She stepped out the rusted gate. I yelled after her: "He could have been murdered! You don't know!"

"He wasn't."

"People get murdered all the time."

"Not in Jett Creek."

"Well LB was very innovative!"

So I guess I delivered a eulogy after all.

I closed my eyes and waited until I stopped shaking, then went back inside.

The funeral dragged on. A lot of people said a lot of things. None of it mattered. I stayed by the door, staring across the churchyard, wondering when summer would save us from this spring.

When it was finished, I felt myself lifted into another of Matty's crushing hugs.

"Hell of a turnout," I said.

"He'd have liked it, except for the part about being dead."

"Yeah. Being dead was the kind of thing LB hated."

He sat on the steps and draped his massive hands across his knees. I sat beside him. An hour standing on stone had me aching all over. People steered clear of me on their way out, the same way they'd been avoiding me ever since LB died. It didn't bother me anymore. Matter of fact, I was getting to like it.

"How are you?" I said. "Having a fun week?"

"Feel like I got put through a wood chipper."

"What does this mean for your job?"

"My mentor being dead? It ain't good, but Doc says they'll keep me on for the year. There's a lot of paperwork and stuff that goes into having one of your star faculty burned alive."

"Are you taking over any of LB's classes?"

"Naw. You need a terminal degree for that, and I'm not even close." He shook his head, sick of whatever had been playing on a loop inside his head. Like me, he needed to hear about somebody else's pain. "And how are you doing? Terrible?"

"I aspire to terrible. I'm frozen. I want to do something, but everything I think of seems pointless or silly or selfish or impossible. I wish I was the kind of person who could throw herself across the coffin and scream. Doesn't that seem nice? Just scream out all the broken glass that's rattling around your stomach? I didn't even have the nerve to look at his corpse."

He gave me another hug. It didn't fix anything, but it didn't hurt. The back of my head got hot with his breath, and his glasses were foggy when he let me go. He wiped them on his shirt and said, "We were talking, before the fire—we were talking about you running the game."

"I thought you were asleep."

"A Barber never sleeps. He only rests his eyes. Do you think you're going to do it?"

"That was LB's thing. You'd have to love the spotlight. I'd wither."

"Don't you want to know what was going to happen?"

"Sure I do, but—"

"So I bet Odette would let you borrow his notebooks and see what he had planned for next week. Even if you didn't run a session, if you could just tell us what he had planned…"

"Why's it matter?"

"You ever hear of Irving, North Carolina?"

"Nope."

"No one ever has. You figure Jett Creek's nowhere? The place I grew up, electricity still felt new. Imagine being gay someplace like that."

"It's hard enough here."

"When I came here, I didn't know a thing except I liked bending iron. LB didn't just teach me my craft. He taught me I could be an artist. The game was part of that. It was… possibility."

That would have been a handy time to tell him how badly I was missing Arabeth, my plastic alter ego, my Hero, my escape. Matty would have listened. He would have understood. But all I could say was, "Yeah."

"If we're not playing every week, I just, I just don't know."

He looked sadder than I could take. I tried to change the subject, but didn't get far.

"LB was serious about safety, right?" I said.

"Militant. Why?"

"You know Leah Sparks, the cop? She thinks LB was working drunk, that he started a fire, that it got out of hand. You believe that?"

"I don't know."

"Why not?"

"It's not he wouldn't work drunk—he sure might—but that studio was for his personal work."

"So?"

"So he hadn't done any personal work in years. There's no reason, to my mind, that forge should have been hot."

I tried to keep talking, but he'd gone faraway, and it seemed better to let him alone. I went back inside, telling myself I'd speak to Odette no matter how sick it made me feel, but she was gone and so was everyone else. It was not a beautiful church. With the lights off and the pews empty, it was just a long gray room with something horrible at the end.

"Okay," I said. "Let's say goodbye."

The odd bowl smoked in an unlocked churchyard aside, I've never been much for trespassing. I get too nervous; I spend every second waiting to get caught. I felt that dread as I walked down the aisle, even though I knew I had a right—a duty, even—to be there. My feet got heavier with every step, and when I saw the thing in the coffin, I wanted to turn and run. But I did not.

It looked worse than I thought death could. I don't know what, if anything, the mortician did to clean him up, but it hadn't helped. The body was twisted, his beautiful skin bubbled and cracked. All his hair was gone.

They'd wrestled him into his favorite Stooges t-shirt, which he'd gotten at his first concert and hung on to even as it verged on disintegration. His hands were folded. The iron monocle peeked out from his ruined fist.

The monocle.

I don't know why I took it. Maybe I wanted a keepsake, or maybe it was just too special to bury. But before I knew it, it was in my hand. I sped out of the church, feet silent on the worn beige carpet, and I was surprised to find I didn't feel guilty. I almost felt free.

3

BACK IN MY BEDROOM, FOREVER IN MY BEDROOM, I CLIPPED ON the fierce white light above my desk, set out my colors, and tried to paint. Diego had given me $100 to paint a platoon of space marines—ugly little bastards with pinched faces. They looked like they were sucking on lemons.

"How bout we do the armor in teal?" I'd said, and he looked like he was sucking on a lemon, too.

"These are serious space marines."

"Are there any other kind? What about some nice soft pastels, y'know, for Easter?"

"I want grays and blacks. And little flecks of blood on their boots. Make the blood look good, or you won't get paid."

Normally, I love painting for the people at the shop, even when the client is a humorless jerk. It's good money, and the time melts by. But that night I felt every minute pass. My hands weren't steady, and the palate was bumming me out. There's enough gray and black and blood in the real world. Why add more?

I set down the brush. I flicked off the light.

LB AND ODETTE LIVED ON EDGEWATER, A TREACHEROUSLY STEEP street that wound up past the food coop into the trees. Their house was pure sixties: a box of wood, glass, and black steel that jutted into the forest on spindly stilts. It smelled of wet leaves and undisturbed dust.

As I turned my key in their lock—the key I'd been given for emergencies, or when I just needed a break from Mom—I told myself I was there to look for campaign notes, nothing more. I walked into the kitchen, which was filled with scummy takeout containers and coffee-stained mugs, and called Odette's name. She did not answer. I exhaled.

I didn't remember a time before I knew Odette Durand. She and LB were in the same year at Jett Creek High, where she was the only person who didn't laugh at the boy who came to class with a pocketful of dice. They used to argue about which of them introduced the other to *Those About to Die*, a grim, gloriously complicated little game whose manuals were printed in 9 point font. I'd always believed Odette when she said she found it first. They'd dated in high school and ended it, quite sensibly, when he went away.

While LB was washing out of the New York art world, Odette stayed here, taking a job as an essay coach at her old high school and starting an after-school gaming club for disaffected teens, most notably a young, beautiful, and profoundly unpopular Caledonia Myles. Three afternoons a week, over tap water and Saltines, she took us on adventures in every game she could get her hands on. We were warriors in ancient deserts, smugglers in distant galaxies, spies in East Berlin. Her sessions were airy and perfect and sweet, like a lemon meringue pie, and dreaming of them helped me survive Pre-Cal. LB had introduced me to the world of gaming, but Odette made me a citizen. After she quit the school to open Critical Hit, LB came home for good and she allowed him to marry her, and it felt like I was adopting the aunt I'd been waiting for my entire life. I couldn't bear to see her sad.

It was easy to tell which rooms belonged to Odette and which to LB. Hers were messy. His were vile, so crowded with books and papers and unfinished projects that a fire marshal would have condemned them on the spot. His study was worst of all, a square brown room packed with unwanted art, yellowing books, old notes, and banker's boxes collapsing beneath junk. The light was sickly fluorescent. The only window stretched from floor to ceiling, showing nothing but my ghostly reflection against the black of the forest night. I'd never been in this room without him. He would never be here again.

I sat in the cracked leather chair, which stank of the largely-ineffective natural deodorant he bought at the coop, and took in his desk. I nudged papers, looking for, well, I wasn't sure. I found the plans for his students' midterm projects, which were covered with encouraging notes in red felt tip: "Sublime!" "Astonishing!" and "Make this NOW!!" Wedged under the uneven stack was an oddly formal memo from Doc, reminding him of a meeting set for two days after he'd died. It was addressed to Robert and signed Dr. Mingori.

Nobody ever called him Robert. Nobody ever called her anything but Doc.

"Weird," I said to the dust. I felt like I was hiding inside someone's closet, watching their private life through the slats in the doors. It felt ugly, but I didn't leave.

In the drawers I found loose change, an empty pint of Dickel, scotch tape, a sheet of 1¢ stamps, and other junk. I also found LB's JCCAD ID, which made its way into my wallet—whether for sentiment or future use, I wasn't sure. If nothing else, it would be handy for sneaking waffle fries from the dining hall. Beneath it was an empty orange envelope. The return address was Campground 37 in Muncrief Park.

"Who gets a letter from a national park?"

This must be how it felt, I thought, when Leah's job asks her a question. It kind of tickled.

I put the envelope away.

I'm just here for his notes, I reminded myself. I'll take a look at what he's got planned. I'll see if I've got it in me to run the game. Probably I don't. Probably I lack something so profound that it will be clear instantly, and I'll be able to leave.

Just the notes. Nothing else.

LB's games books occupied a shelf in the corner. I shoved aside a pile of moth-eaten dress shirts and got close enough to the books that I could smell the paper. There were over one hundred, ranging from worn copies of '80s classics to shrink-wrapped editions of new games that Odette got for free, which LB absconded with but seldom read. Here was adventure at the edge of reality, at the dawn of time, in the farthest reaches of space, at the elbows of King Arthur or Luke Skywalker or the Ghostbusters or anybody else you dreamt up. A single book could keep a group entertained for a month, a year, a lifetime. Outside of wanton fornication or, like, going for a walk, table-top roleplaying was probably the cheapest possible way to have a good time. I didn't understand why it wasn't more popular.

I grabbed a book at random, an old campaign for *Those About to Die* called, "Terror of the Snake King!" The cover was a masterpiece of '80s cheese, showing a writhing beast with the body of a snake and the head of Chuck Norris. I flipped past intricate maps of dungeons I would never conquer, glossaries of languages I would never pretend to speak. I put it back on the shelf. It was the binders I'd come to see.

There were twelve of them, and he probably had others stashed at the games store. More than his teaching, more than his art, Winterwind was his life's work, and it had sprawl. The freshest D-Ring, which Odette must have brought home from the shop, had a label tucked into its plastic: "WW / 12/19/02-_____" I tugged it off the shelf and made room for it on the desk, ash in my mouth as I violated my brother's holiest text.

On the first page, an ink drawing showed a squat little woman slouched on a simple wooden throne. Her hair was thin; her face hidden behind a mask decorated with laughing skulls, and at her side was a sword that must have been twice her height. The Queen of Skulls. She really did look like Danny DeVito. Goddamn, could LB draw.

The next page was filled with LB's cramped, elegant cursive. After twenty years, I still had to squint to make it out.

"Here begins the saga of Lomella, daughter of a shopkeeper, child of the farthest reaches of the Winterwind Plateau, whose mother Summer burned to death one morning in the fall of 544..."

"Who the hell is Lomella?" I said, and read on. Anyway, I tried to. The language was florid, the detail numbing—LB described practically every leaf on every tree. I flipped forward. Lomella was learning magic. I flipped again and she was at war. I thumbed through the pages until I got to the end of her story, which wrapped up with her crowning herself the Queen of Skulls.

"Jesus," I muttered.

Hundreds of hours of prep just to build up background for the little speck flying on the griffon, laughing while men died. Good god. He was even better than I thought.

I pulled back my shoulders and threw up my chin, trying to think how it felt to stare down at five people hanging on your every word.

"You guys think you're ready for Blackbriar Keep?" I growled. "Think you're a match for the Queen of Skulls? Sure. Sure. Take a fucking shot."

I felt an embarrassingly powerful urge to cry. I fought it off.

Inside his backpack, I found our character sheets. Even if they weren't labeled, I'd have recognized everyone's at a glance. Doc's was pristine. Sondra's was a mess of geometric doodles. Craig had a bizarre habit of fraying the corners of his papers until they curled inward, while Matty's was crammed with session notes and salsa stains. And here was mine. Here was Arabeth.

I'd rolled her up about a year prior. The heat was out at Critical Hit. We could see our breath. At our last session, a fluke encounter with a basilisk had led to a total party kill. The group was near mutiny—a TPK will do that—but LB brought us back to earth.

"Well that was a total goddamned mess," he said. "But that's okay. If they could live forever, they wouldn't be Heroes, right? Tonight, we're rolling up a new party, and I want you to roll high. We'll meet in an inn at the Edge of the World. We're going the whole length of the Plateau on this one and we're taking aim at the Queen of Skulls."

For fourteen months, we fought our way north. We grew stronger, learned new skills and spells, amassed untold treasure and found weapons so rare, the gods must have been jealous. LB had never been in better form. No matter where we wandered, he had trouble in store. No matter how weird the story got, he always knew how to bring it back and tie it up. Every session was a brilliant surprise. Fourteen months of work led to the fight with the woman who had been Lomella, an encounter that should have been properly epic, and I'd wrecked it with a single roll.

No wonder he was so sad.

I thumbed the exquisitely-detailed biography of the Queen of Skulls, and knew I could never match him. I was an idiot for even thinking I might try.

I popped open the plastic case that held our miniatures and took Arabeth in my hand. Magnificent warrior. She had no idea LB's death had killed her, too. I set her on the table. She stood tall, ready for anything, never going to fight again.

I went to rub my eye. I was wearing LB's monocle. It was heavy, and keeping it squeezed into my eye socket was giving me a headache.

I did not remember putting it on.

I reached to take it off. Right at the top, I felt a bump, a little wart, so small I had never seen it from the table. As I ran my finger over it, it moved slightly, and I realized it wasn't a bump at all, but a button.

I pressed it. What are buttons for?

The room got still. Dust held steady in the air. The monocle grew hot, too hot to touch, but I couldn't get it out of my eye.

I couldn't move at all.

And then Arabeth looked at me.

She cocked her head, brown eyes wide.

She looked at me.

"What," I said, but no sound came from my mouth.

The monocle got hotter. My skull scorched. My eye was

frozen open, and I could only watch as molten iron dripped out of the glass, puddled across the desk and spilled toward my lap. I wanted to twitch, to run, to throw myself through the window, or simply to scream, but I was paralyzed.

The bubbling metal dripped onto my knee.

I expected it to burn. I never felt it at all.

The instant it touched my leg, metal screamed and I tumbled forward, spilling end over end faster and faster until the world was a blur and I had to shut my eyes or puke. I landed on my back, felt the wind go out of me, and knew I was breathing again.

Water stains covered the ceiling, wet and brown. I looked at them for a long time, and once I was sure they weren't moving, I attempted to stand.

Every part of me cracked. It didn't hurt, exactly, but it was so loud it hurt my ears. I reached for something to lean on and found my hand pressed against a gleaming green boulder with figures scrawled on it that I had to turn my head to recognize.

They were numbers, and it wasn't a boulder.

It was a die, a d20, half the size of me.

"Something has gone wrong," I said.

My voice was not my own. It was smoother, deeper, operatic. And my hands were wrong, too.

My feelings about my body are, let's say, complicated, but one area I've never taken issue with is my hands, which are the closest any of me comes to delicate. The tangled network of veins and bone I'd spent my life taking for granted was gone. Instead, I found two perfectly smooth fists, which cracked horribly when I opened and closed them for the first time. My skin was utterly without blemish, without detail. There were no veins. No hairs. The flesh shone like…

Like plastic.

I looked up and saw Callie Myles—the classic edition, with hair and pimples and soft human skin—sitting in LB's chair, staring like a zombie. And if she was there, and I was here…

"Oh my living god," I said.

I threw open my cloak—I was wearing a cloak?—and saw

what I hoped for, what I had dreamed of in my sleep and at the table for over a year: minute rings of plastic chain, painted to glow brighter than gold ever had. My wrists wore matching +1 bracers, and in their reflection I saw bright eyes, razor-sharp cheekbones, perfectly sculpted hair and skin any human would kill to have. My dagger was on my hip, my bow and quiver crossed on my back. I even had my dainty little Ring of Wayfinding on my hand and my Stargazer's Cap perched on my head. I rolled up my sleeve and flexed, just a little.

I had a bicep. I'd never had one of those before.

"Okay," I said, wondering how long it would take before I started saying something useful. "Okay. What? What!"

Later it occurred to me that I should have been afraid. I should have been puking or sobbing or shitting or screaming with fear. But the moment I saw that golden armor, all the fear and hurt and indecision drained out of me, and so I did not panic when the world above began to dim.

Something flickered beneath my feet. The ink on LB's map writhed like snakes. I filled my lungs and let the air out, and watched the office fade away. I closed my eyes.

I smelled boiling oil.

Snow melted on my lips.

I opened my eyes and saw Blackbriar Keep.

You'd think there'd have been some uncertainty, but I knew right away. Take the wall, for starters. You find yourself standing at the corner of a colossal iron wall, that's usually a tip-off you've left East Tennessee behind. Then the guards on the rampart below—we don't have soldiers patrolling the streets of Jett Creek, at least not yet, and if we did they'd probably sport camo and M-16s, not the signature hooked dagger of the Blackbriar Guard. There were subtle things, as well. The night was quieter than we really get in the 21st century—no humming heaters, no chattering TVs—and the wind carried the smell of campfires and shit.

But the biggest thing is that it was all made of plastic. It gleamed, weightless, like some perfect toy.

The snow fell in a perfect line, in flakes big enough to

see every detail—like the snow in the old claymation specials LB and I used to watch every Christmas—dusting a castle that looked extremely *Scooby-Doo*. Think tilty towers, uneven windows, and identical soldiers moving in tidy rank and file. North of the wall, the fires of the Queen's Horde burned in perfectly ordered rows. South, I saw the glowing lights of the castle, Blackbriar Town, and the flares that marked the path down the mountains. All the pointless details that give reality texture—light bouncing off a far-off window, a half-seen animal darting through a bush—were gone. Everything was very clear.

Mom likes to tell a story about when I was a kid, in the narrow window between when I learned to talk and when I learned to doubt. She asked me, "Callie, how does Santa Claus do it? How does he get to all those houses, all over the world, in one night?"

I answered without hesitation:

"Magic."

Here, the answer was the same. I'd always assumed my big brother was magic. Now I knew.

"Okay," I said. My voice snapped through the frosted air like a whip. "Cool."

I was inside the greatest miniature ever built, and I felt no fear. The ease of being at the table was back, and it was on steroids. I stared up at the perfectly-spaced pinprick stars and felt that somewhere, just past the sky, Callie Myles was watching to make sure nothing went wrong. I peeked through the monocle and saw LB's study in full, non-plastic reality, where the dust hung frozen and the clock's second hand was stuck between ticks. My old-fashioned human hand was poised beside the d20, waiting for my move.

I hopped. It was the best thing I could think of. I hopped onto the parapet, which was no wider than my hand, and balanced on one foot. I hopped back and forth—left foot, right foot, left foot, right foot—landing squarely on the frozen iron, never slipping an inch. This was insane, pointless, exhilarating. It was also too easy.

And so I ran. As fast as I could go, fast enough that the world slipped into motion blur and there was no sound but my sharp breath and the thudding of boots on skinny iron. I didn't miss a step. The wall curved and I curved with it until we reached the ruins of the Slanting Tower, which the Queen of Skulls' mount had crushed with a single beat of its wing. I was out of runway, and so I leapt, hurling myself forward, flipping end over end in a perfect triple whatever twist, and somewhere, Callie rolled a die. The sound echoed off this plastic world like distant thunder. I guess she rolled well, because I stuck the landing.

"Take that, Kerri Strug."

I was shimmying and laughing and rejoicing in the absence of pain when a roar tore through the sky like an elephant being ripped in half. The Queen's bone beast, even uglier than LB had made it sound, swept across the sky, blocking out the moon. It wheeled around the castle, neck twisting like it was searching for something. It dipped a little lower, and when it banked for the next turn, I saw something on its back. A silhouette, egg-shaped and squat, with a colossal sword strapped to its side. The Queen of Skulls.

"Hang on," I said. "I killed you."

I rolled a twenty. A crit, plus lightning damage. I saw the electricity race up your body and stop your heart. I saw you crumple. I saw you die.

Only, I didn't. I only heard what LB told me.

I charged up the tower, not smiling anymore. The third step was missing from the first flight of stairs, and the second, and the third—one of those little details in a plastic model that looks cute the first time but gnaws at you the more it repeats. The air was numbing. The higher I got, the steps grew icy, but my feet stuck to them like glue. The staircase ended at the next landing, where the top of the tower had simply been brushed away.

One of the Duke's workers was in the corner, tapping use-lessly at the wood. He had a Friar Tuck haircut, a circular face and a round nose to match. Three long nails dangled out of his mouth. When he saw me, they popped out like they were spring loaded.

This poor dude. He had scrub written all over him, from the smudges dancing around his mouth that were supposed to be dirt, I guess, to the way he hunched to pick up his nails. Knowing LB, he probably didn't even have a name—in this world, non-player characters only got a name if they were integral to the plot. Minions, villagers, workers, soldiers, guards, and any other cannon fodder didn't rate.

"Arabeth," he said. "Thank god you've returned."

"Never mind me. What the fuck is the Queen of Skulls doing flying around all, like, alive?"

"Where else would she be?"

"I don't know if you missed the news bulletin, but I shot her. She died."

"You are…you are wrong." He croaked out the words like they hurt to say. "You wounded her. Her cries rent the night, and so frightened her soldiers that the assault stopped dead. But then you disappeared, and her Horror flew her to safety. The siege goes on."

"Well that's bullshit."

"Yes. Yes it is."

I leaned on the broken tower wall, staring at the mountains that stabbed into the air and vanished into the moonlit clouds. I wondered how far this game would go. All the way to the Edge of the World, I imagined. Maybe farther. God damn, it would be fun to find out.

And then the Horror screamed again.

"I'm sick of that sound," I said. "Are you sick of that sound?"

He nodded, not sure at what I was getting at but certain he didn't like it. I whipped my bow off my shoulder and slid an arrow against the string, as casually as I'd tie my shoes. It felt wonderful. I lined the Horror up with my arrow. Without thinking, I tracked its flight, predicting exactly how hard I'd need to pull the string to put an arrow right between the Queen's eyes. I drew back.

I did not fire.

"What is wrong?" said the repairman.

"I tried going it alone before, and everything went wrong. You have no idea how wrong it went. I don't even have an arrow of lightning this time."

"But if you can't do it…"

"It's okay. I know folks who can."

I put a chummy hand on his shoulder. It might have been comforting if the Horror hadn't chosen that moment to let loose another of those eardrum-splitting screams. The repairman blanched. If I'd had any hair on my arms, it would have stood up straight.

"Oh no," he said. "Oh, by the Gray Lord, no."

He held up a shaking hand. The monster had seen us. It screamed again, flapping its bone wings, and went into a vertical dive.

"Crud," I said.

The repairman bolted for the trap door. I just stood there, clutching my bow.

It was close. It was closer. It was almost on top of me, and I'd forgotten that I was supposed to be Arabeth. I was Callie Myles, and I was fucking afraid.

"Nope," I said.

It roared again, stinking of corpses, spraying blood.

Its jaws opened wide.

"Nope, nope, nope, nope."

I jabbed at the button on the monocle. The beast froze. Snow held in the air. Molten iron slipped forth. It pooled in the air, rushed down the wall, and sucked me back into the dark, all the way back to real life.

It was like I'd spent too long on the bottom of the pool. Like I'd been down there watching the other swimmers' legs kick, enjoying the weird distortion of their screams, ignoring the pressure in my ears and lungs. And then panic hit and I kicked off the bottom, exploding through the surface to find eyes and lungs burning, ears ready to pop.

For a long time I didn't move. Then I ran my hand across LB's armchair, tracing every crack to confirm that it was real. I plucked the monocle from my eye and set it on the desk. My mouth was cotton. My heart throbbed in my ears. I sat until the fear seeped away. I looked at the clock. Less than a minute had passed.

Our little adventure had not disturbed the plastic mini of Arabeth. She was as she'd been before—alert, eying the table for something to shoot—but her position on the map had shifted from the wall to the tower. Had I moved her while I was in my trance? Or had she moved herself?

"What other secrets do you have?" I asked. Her face gave nothing away.

I decided to focus on simpler questions. I flipped through Lomella's endless biography until I found stats for the Queen of Skulls. My extremely cunning, extremely brilliant arrow of lightning had tagged her for 270 damage. It was the single greatest attack I'd ever made.

But as written, she had 350 hit points.

In the margins was a little note from LB:

"Get QoS & Arabeth alone. Callie will use lightning arrow. (It's in her pants.) If she sells it, let her kill the Queen."

I laughed, a chuckle that turned into a chortle that erupted into a full-body gigglequake.

"LB!" I shouted. "You shifty bastard!"

He had played me perfectly. I'd been holding that arrow in reserve for months, waiting for just the right moment to spring it. I thought I was so clever, and he knew what I was doing all along. He faked it all—her death, his tantrum—just to give his little sister a win. I spent a good five second imagining how I was going to thank him for that ridiculous performance when I remembered I would never see him again.

I quit laughing.

And there was the power of this game. It took us from where we did not want to be. It let us forget. And that magic, it finally dawned on me, did not die with LB.

The Queen of Skulls lives. The campaign must go on.

I closed the binder. For the first time in a while, maybe ever, I felt in control. I didn't want to let the feeling slip.

I ducked under LB's desk and tore a sheet of paper out of

his printer. I snatched one of his red pens and shoved enough shit off the desk to give me room to write. At the top, as neat as my shaking hands could manage, I wrote: "How It Works."

After all, even magic has rules.

1. *Pop in the monocle, press the button, and you open a gateway to the game.*

Clear enough so far.

2. *Do it with a mini on the table and you can inhabit them.*

I gnawed my pen, wondering what might happen if you went in without a mini, the way that LB had every Thursday night. Would you just be yourself, human and frail? Or would you be something more?

3. *The rules still apply. Do something dangerous and the dice determine the outcome. This works because magic.*

4. *While you're in the game, time in the real world holds still. Almost.*

I was still chewing that pen when steps sounded in the hall. I stuffed the monocle in my pocket. Odette came around the corner and I put on the face you make when you haven't just gotten back from a magical adventure.

"Hi," I said, extremely normally.

"Hey."

"I'm sorry for just, like, showing up."

"You never need to call. That was the deal when we gave you the key. That isn't going to change."

"Thank you."

She leaned on the door frame and smiled. The effort seemed to take most of what she had left. She squeezed her hand on the back of her neck, trying to rub away stress that could not be dislodged.

Overwhelming grief-fatigue aside, she looked the same as when I was in high school. Even then, she'd always worn white: soft cotton sweaters and billowing pants that glowed against her dark skin. She looked like she knew secrets, and I wanted to know them, too. Every day I'd find an excuse to drop by her office, which was really just a desk crammed into the back of a library study room, to show her something I'd found in one of her game books—a badass drawing or particularly nasty trap—that I thought she'd enjoy.

Tonight I had the secret to end all secrets. I wanted to drape the monocle around her neck and show her what I'd found. It had made me happy for a few minutes, and I burned to share it with her.

Odette picked up Arabeth and turned her in the light, squinting like a jeweler inspecting a gem.

"Nice paint," she said. I blushed, and looked at my hands.

"It's the best I've ever done."

"Don't sell yourself short. This might be the best anybody's ever done. How'd you get the wood grain on the bow?"

"Scratched it up with a wire brush."

"It looks like you actually chopped down a tiny tree."

"That probably would have been faster."

She walked around his desk, trailing her finger through the dust, and looked at the open notebook. I felt the stolen monocle in my pocket and imagined it was scalding me again.

"Matty asked me to keep running the game."

I said it like I was asking for permission, which I guess I was.

"You sure you're up for that?"

No.

"Of course I am."

"Bobby spent too much time on this game. I always told him, there are like 5,000 RPGs out there. Life is too short to get stuck on one system."

"When I'm looking at these notes," I said, "it's like he never left. I can't throw that away."

She shrugged her hand out of her long white sleeve and put it on mine. Tell her, I thought. Tell her and she'll help you. Tell her and she'll know what to do.

"I'm sorry I missed you at the funeral," I said. "I should have been up at the front with you and Mom."

"Nobody needs to apologize for staying away from an open casket. Especially that one."

"I should have said hello."

She gave me a close look, the same one she'd given Arabeth.

I doubt I looked as good.

"You okay?" she said.

"Oh yeah. Best week ever." She said nothing, and I hated and loved her all at once for refusing to let my bullshit slide. "I'm okay. Not good, but okay."

"Your hands are like ice."

I put them in my pockets. She was right, I realized. They had been cold for some time.

4

THE NEXT DAY, I WORKED MY FIRST SHIFT SINCE THE FIRE. WASHING mugs, making panini, restocking shelves, and teaching after-school groups the intricacies of *Carcassonne* proved a special torture. The teens were particularly shrill that afternoon, and their endless bickering gave me a headache no amount of Tylenol could break. Diego was off that day, which would have been a relief except it meant I was working with Karina, my nemesis, a spunky board game expert who was quite unashamedly twenty-one. Every time I passed her, she gave me a sickly pitying smile. I didn't break any of her teeth, and I think that should have earned me some kind of award.

The school kids' sugar high peaked at 4 p.m., and the noise in the shop turned deafening. I dug my knuckles into my temples, trying to drive out the ache. When I opened my eyes, I saw Karina and Odette huddled at the front desk over a sheet of paper. Even on busy days, Karina was always dragging Odette aside to "pick her brain," part of her self-declared ambition to "learn the ropes" at the store. But today they kept glancing at me. Finally, I went to see what was up.

"What's going on?" I said. I tried to sound friendly, but I

don't think it worked. "You know I hate to miss a team meeting."

"Hey Callie," said Karina. "Is this yours?"

She showed me the paper: a photocopy of a photocopy of a photocopy covered with so many blotches and streaks that you could hardly read my brother's handwriting. But I'd seen the originals, and I'd filled out plenty of my own. At the top it said, "Hero of Winterwind—For LB's Crew ONLY." The sight made my stomach lurch.

"This is one of our character sheets, but I didn't print it." I looked at Karina. She shrank away. "Did you?"

"No, no, of course not. I'm a board game geek and that is it. RPGs go right over my head."

She illustrated that by whipping her palm over her tidy little braids. It was awfully cute.

I glanced at Odette. She shook her head.

"You know I don't play anymore. Could it have been someone in your group?"

"I don't think so. It's been a while since any of us needed a new character. Can I see it?"

The sheet wasn't totally blank. It had been halfway filled with what looked like the makings of a mage, specifically a dazzler—a class whose strength lay in glitter and illusion, making them lousy in a fight and historically unpopular with our group.

Karina drummed her fingers on her cheek.

"What about that guy, the creepy guy with the goatee who used to play with you?"

"Randy Randy? He hasn't played with us in forever."

"That's so funny. I could have sworn I saw him around."

"Where?"

"I don't know. Just one of those places. Like, around."

"Very helpful. Thanks."

I folded the character sheet and slid it into the pocket of my loose, fraying jeans. I spent the rest of the shift scanning faces, wondering who might have been trying to intrude on my game, but my gaze kept returning to the human puppy who followed Odette around. When the front counter was unoccupied, I slipped behind it and typed Randy's name into the membership database. He was marked as inactive due to lack of payment, and he hadn't bought anything at the shop in five years. His address was 347 Collins Place, walking distance from the shop. I wrote it down. I'm not sure why.

I said goodbye to the last of the school kids at six, which gave me an hour to nurse a beer while I waited for my players. My mouth was dry. The beer didn't help. I tried to focus on how pleased the group would be when they found out that LB's campaign wasn't finished, that the Queen of Skulls was ready to be killed again, but the joy I'd felt the day before had hardened into fear.

Monday nights were slow. The only regulars were an old Pakistani couple who came to play chess and grumble at each other. Odette offered us the back room, but I didn't feel worthy of LB's scarred wood table. Plastic was good enough for me.

"Want me to hang out?" she said.

"I'm good," I said, which felt like a lie. I waited until she'd vanished upstairs to place the monocle behind the GM screen I'd bought that afternoon, which featured a big tacky dragon that was extremely wrong for a game LB had always kept pointedly dragon-free. I arranged my reference sheets. I rearranged them. I was still fussing when Craig Upshaw's head poked up from behind the screen.

"I'm first," he said.

"You're always first."

I handed him his mini, a shadowy figure who held a poisoned dagger at his hip. The paint job was gorgeous, because I'd done it myself. Craig had paid me, even though he said it was selfish "to ask money for doing something you obviously enjoy." Fausto was the vainest thief on the plateau, and his obsession with gold had never quite fit with Craig's anti-materialist vibe.

"I want to go somewhere with treasure," he said over the GM screen.

"Of course you do. You're a thief."

"Not like, an ordinary amount of treasure. I want, like, a lot. Fausto is sick of scraps, Callie. Fausto is sick of being a joke."

"But he's the best joke we have."

Ever since his first session, when he blew a charisma roll trying to seduce a tavern keeper and she dumped a stein of ale down his pants, we had been laughing at Fausto. If Arabeth botched an athletics check, she'd fall and hurt herself. Fausto would fall, get stuck in a tree, and hang upside down, twisting slowly in the wind, until we cut him down. If that sounds cruel, it wasn't. Fausto attempted ridiculous shit and endured ridiculous shit in return. We all laughed at him, but Craig laughed, too.

He crept awkwardly around the corner of the table and knelt beside me. I used the GM screen to cover my notes.

"What, dude?" I said. "You're not supposed to be back here."

His voice dropped lower.

"I want you to kick Sondra out of the game."

"Why?"

"Because...she's...a...bitch."

If I hadn't reprimanded Sondra for smacking him the other night, I'd have hit him myself. Instead I jabbed him in the poncho. He tumbled onto his ass.

"You don't get it, man. I can't say anything without her jumping down my throat. It sucks, okay? Like last week I just mentioned that I dug *Daredevil* and she hit me in the face. That's not cool!"

I slapped Fausto's character sheet onto the table.

"Quit bitching and play the damn game," I said. I picked up my screen and busied myself with my notes until he quit sulking and took a seat.

After several long minutes, Doc slumped into the chair closest to me.

"Thanks for calling the session," she said. "This has been a brutal week. The metalworking department is an absolute disaster. Matty pulled LB's lesson plans for me and I can't even tell you what a mess they are—mostly hand-written, with so much shorthand that it seems like a foreign language."

"Artists."

"If I could find a way to run an arts college without them, I would. Matty's trying to translate them so we can hand them off to whoever we find to replace LB, which is its own headache, and...wait a minute. I promised myself I wouldn't bring work to the table."

"You did."

"Got my bard?"

I handed her the plastic model for Billiam Fakebeard, a crooning magician who wore a patchwork rainbow coat, a plumed hat, and an outrageously fake-looking beard. I'd painted him for Doc—she had neither the time nor the inclination to waste on the hobby—and I'd used his guitar to try out the wood graining techniques I used on Arabeth's bow. It was a nice piece.

"Before I joined the game," I said, "y'all played with a guy called Randy, right?"

"He was a scumbag," said Doc, "and proud of it. Grabbed tits like he thought he'd find a prize inside."

"LB put up with that?"

"Not officially. He always told Randy to knock it off, but Randy never did, and LB never kicked him out. He should have. Randy was not a good dude."

"Why'd he leave the game?"

"They had a fight about, I don't know. Something."

"No, it wasn't that," said Craig. "Randy got a job in California selling auto parts or vacuum cleaners or, I don't know."

"How would you know that?" said Doc. "You didn't even live here then."

"I just, I guess I heard."

"Well, that might be right. I don't know. Why?"

"No reason," I said.

I looked over Craig's shoulder to the board game wall, where Karina was animatedly pitching a young couple on the delights of a game called *Puerto Rico*. I didn't even realize she'd been working here when Randy Randy had been around.

Weird.

Sondra arrived and sat as far from Craig as the table allowed. She said nothing, staring at me like she was waiting for me to fuck something up. I lowered my head behind the screen, silently mouthing to myself: "They're going to love it. They're going to love it. They're going to love it."

My stress mantra was interrupted when Matty appeared and started passing out beers. Just having him there took my blood pressure down a tick. The man was a human sunbeam.

"That's an IPA for Doc, Blue Moon for Craig, cider for me, stout for Sondra—."

"Thank you, Matthew," said Sondra, drinking deep enough to give herself a Guinness moustache.

"And oh hell, Callie, your glass appears to be empty. What are we going to do about that?"

"You're so cute I can't stand it," I said. "What gives?"

"How about we pour you a pint of…" He dug into his messenger bag and withdrew a dusty black bottle capped with wax. "My October ale."

I gasped. I couldn't help it. He tore off the wax and tipped the beer into the glass. It was the color of paprika and smelled like crunching leaves.

"I thought you finished the last of it at New Year's."

"I was saving a bottle. Going to give it to LB as thanks for, well, it's not important. It's yours."

"I can't."

"Come on. It means a lot just being here, and the fact that you called an early session—I couldn't have waited 'till Thursday night."

"You make the game sound like therapy."

"Well, yeah."

I took a long sip.

"You fucking bastard," I said. "That's the best beer in the world."

Matty smiled. He knew.

I slid Sondra the mini for Phælandro, a skeletal elemental mage who specialized in drowning their enemies in mud, and gave Matty the figure for Zircon, a gladiator who was as big as

Matty but a hell of a lot more mean. At the sight of him, Matty clapped his hands and let out an unfiltered North Carolina whoop.

"Who's ready to play a freaking game?!"

I sat behind the GM screen and found I couldn't see the table. I stood up instead and said the words I'd been rehearsing all day long, the words that would let them know that nothing had to change, that LB's campaign would go on forever, that would make us whole—or at least less broken.

"You stand in a courtyard at Blackbriar Keep. From the sky, you hear a bestial scream."

"Don't you mean beastly?" said Sondra.

"She means bestial," said Doc. "It's a word."

"I don't think so."

"It is. It means beastly."

"Y'all hush," said Matty. "I want to find out what's screaming."

"A hideous beast made of sinew and bone whose screams sound like sheets of metal being ripped in half," I said. My description was accurate. I'd heard the thing myself. "In the light of the Blackbriar moon, you can see it is being ridden by...the Queen. Of. Skulls."

There was a long, unimpressed pause, and I was back in the multi-purpose room freshman year, dying slow.

"Bullshit!" said Sondra. "You zapped her, remember? Right in the fucking eye?"

"She survived."

"This is not LB's greatest hits. She's dead. Let's move on."

By their faces, the others agreed.

"You don't get it," I said. "The only reason I killed her was because LB cheated."

"So what?"

"So it wasn't fair."

She let out a long, irritated sigh. I'd been telling people things weren't fair my whole life. This was about as well as it ever went.

"Fuck it," she said. "Fine. Let's kill her again."

It wasn't exactly St. Crispin's Day, but it was the best rallying cry I was going to get. I laid out a map of Blackbriar Keep and asked how they wanted to proceed.

"Some stuff that might be helpful," I said. "There's an old barracks about three hundred feet north where you might take shelter. There's a retired monster hunter at the House of Kerr, south of Blackbriar, and if you're in the mood for a two week walk, you maybe could—"

"Politely," said Sondra, "no."

"Let's just kill her," said Matty, sliding into character. "Kill her with hammers and things."

"I just stick my knife in the air," said Craig, "she'll impale herself on the blade."

"I don't think that will work," I said. "If you take a little time to plan—"

"I made a plan. Fausto wants treasure. If you need me to kill the Queen of who gives a shit first, let's get it over with."

I gave some papers a meaningless shuffle and muttered, "Okay. Let's start."

I put on the monocle. Sondra scoffed.

"Thought we'd seen the last of that fucking thing," she said. Probably Matty glared at her, or stomped on her toe, or stuck her with a quick elbow to the ribs. I don't know. I couldn't meet their eyes.

LB had a ritual for the start of sessions. He settled back, cleared his throat, and rapped his fist three times, like he was calling a court to order. I forced myself to do the same. On the plastic table, my fist barely made a noise. The metal folding chair dug into my butt. I was not comfortable. I was not ready. But I had magic on my side.

Pretending to straighten the monocle, I pressed the button on its top. The clock stopped. The world did, too. The iron poured out and touched my leg and my first session was underway.

I DON'T KNOW WHY I THOUGHT IT WOULD MAKE SENSE. I ASSUMED I would understand how to run a session from inside the damn game. But LB made this without instructions and when I came back to it, the only clarity I got was a Horror screaming about two feet from my face.

I slammed into the creaking plastic of the Slanting Tower. The air split above my neck as the great beast tore past. I swear to god, I felt its claws scrape my back. My ribs hurt like hell, and my feet were stupid and slow. I had no golden mail, no bow, no quiver. I was Callie Myles, flesh and blood gone all shiny-plastic, wearing a cable knit sweater and tatty knockoff Levis that did nothing to keep out the cold. I rolled over and heard the Queen screaming for the Horror to make another pass. Its wings flapped mechanically, like none of it had ever been alive.

"Callie? You there?"

The voice was Matty's. It came in, tinny as a transistor radio, from the monocle. I popped the lens into my eye. Through it, I saw my players staring at me like they were afraid I was asleep or dead. I'd thought time would stay frozen at Critical Hit while I got my shit together. I guess I'd been wrong.

"Yeah!" I said. My voice echoed through the glass. "Yeah, yeah, I'm just, uh, just getting my bearings."

The Horror screamed again. I scurried for the exit. I'd never felt so slow.

"Where did you say we were standing?" said Matty.

"Hold on," I said, struggling for a grip on the trap door. "Just one sec. Let me, uh, let me look at my map."

Another scream. Closer now. Much closer. The Horror plunged through the air. I couldn't see anything of the Queen but the silver light that glinted off her massive sword. The ring that opened the door slipped through my whitening fingers.

"You said we were in a courtyard, right?" said Doc. "What do we see?"

I got both hands through the ring and pulled hard. I didn't dare look back, but I knew the beast was too goddamned close.

"Callie?" said Sondra, snapping her fingers in my face. "What do we see?"

"Just gimme a fucking second!" I barked, and dove through

the open door. The Queen's blade exploded through the wood, stopping an inch from my face.

"You take your time, honey," said Doc, uneasy. "Just take your time."

I ran down icy steps, gripping the handrail rather tighter than I had on my way up, grateful my old Chucks still had a whisper of tread on their soles. At the next landing, I looked through a slit onto the muddy castle yard.

"Okay, okay," I said. "I've got it. You stand in a courtyard at Blackbriar Keep."

And then the sky tore in half.

Orange light poured through the shredded clouds, followed by earsplitting thunderclaps—*boomboomboomboom*—one for each Hero floating to earth.

They landed in the courtyard posed for battle: Billiam with his guitar across his crotch; Fausto clutching his poisoned dagger; Phælandro with their strange, thin hands over their heart; Zircon standing like a goddamned refrigerator. They looked like plastic and flesh all at once, stiff and supple, dead and alive. They were ready for battle, but doing nothing at all.

The fiery orange faded. The Heroes just stood there.

"And what do we see?" said Craig.

"Right!" I said, and clattered down the stairs, splitting my focus between what I'd seen of the courtyard and the delicate work of not falling to my death. "You see, well, there's a lot of mud. And rats. And it smells so much worse than you'd expect. Like, really really bad."

"I quit fighting rats at level two," said Sondra. "What about the Queen of Skulls?"

I was still two flights from the base of the tower. I tried to stall. It went not good.

"Yeah! Yeah, the Queen of Skulls. She's the Queen all right, big nasty Queen. Well not that big, you know, since she really does look like Danny DeVito, and not young handsome DeVito like in *Taxi*, but—"

"Young handsome DeVito?" said Doc.

"Yeah, I mean, I think he had a certain something to him,

a kind of Jersey flair—"

"God damn it, Callie," said Sondra, "get to the fucking game."

I leaped over the last three steps and landed awkwardly in the mud. I slammed open the door and saw the heroic quartet perfectly posed in front of the recently-repaired Spur Gate.

"Okay! You're in the courtyard—"

Zircon rested his war hammer on his bare shoulder and waved. His bangs dangled, boy band perfect, from a tidy center part, and his chest shone with something that looked like baby oil, but which I recognized as a gloss I'd loaned Matty when he was painting Zircon's mini. If I'd been into seven-foot-tall muscle-bound action figures, well, this one was awfully cute. His face wasn't Matty's, exactly, but his smile was, and so was the voice that came from his neatly-drawn lips.

"We know about the courtyard."

"Of course, yeah," I said, tired of sounding so lost and dim. "You're in the courtyard and the Queen of Skulls is..."

I scanned the flat black sky for the woman who had just come so close to separating my head from my body.

"Gone."

"What?" said Matty/Zircon.

"Gone. She's gone."

The snow fell as hard as ever, in flakes so big and perfect that they looked cut from construction paper. There was nothing else in the sky.

"Hell of a twist," said Sondra/Phælandro. "So what are we doing here?"

"I don't know," I said, pressing my hands to my eyes, hoping to hold back the tears. LB would have known how to handle it. If something he planned didn't come off, he had ten more ideas waiting. In moments like this, when the party spun its wheels, he knew how to get them back on track with a challenge, a threat, a taunt.

"She's laughing at you," I said.

"What?" said Sondra, or Phælandro, or—good god, I thought, just pick one! I let the monocle drop away from my face. As long as I was here, I would talk to Phælandro, not Sondra; Fausto, not Craig; Billiam, not Doc.

"As she flew away, the Queen of Skulls was laughing at the Heroes, cackling because they fell for her trick, howling because they were not strong enough to kill her all the way."

"As far as I'm concerned we already killed her."

"Try again."

Phælandro scowled. They were good at that, as good as Sondra. They made me feel small.

"Nobody laughs at me," they said, and I exhaled. Now we had somewhere to go.

"This isn't going to be easy," I said, channeling every inspirational halftime speech I'd ever seen on TV. "There's thousands of Hordesmen between you and her. You'll have to strike under cover of darkness, sneak or tunnel or magic your way past an entire army, and prepare for the greatest battle of your lives. You'll need to be subtle, quiet, artful, cunning, and—"

Zircon threw his hammer over his head and bellowed the war cry that had made him famous up and down the Plateau:

"Zircon crush!"

"Excuse me?"

"Zircon crush," he said again, quite polite. "What more is there to say?"

He jogged across the courtyard, mud slurping at his boots, and leaned back on one great leg, ready to stomp. The thunder of dice boomed across the sky. The iron gate crumpled beneath his foot.

"Oh," I said. "Or you could do that."

"The gate is open," said Zircon, bowing to his friends. They leapt through the ruined door and charged into danger, and everything got simpler until it all went to hell.

At first it was easy. I led them down the path to the edge of the Horde camp, where a gang of archers attacked us, just like bad guys are supposed to do. Once we were in combat, things went as they're supposed to. Zircon was a spinning, deadly top. Fausto danced in and out of the shadows, poisoning everything he touched. Billiam switched seamlessly between singing for his fellows and cutting throats, and Phælandro stood back from the pack, grinning as their earth magic crushed the life out of the dying soldiers. Every burst of sorcery was accompanied by an explosion of color; every clang of metal threw up glittering orange sparks.

I handled the GM side of things okay, and for a while there my friends even seemed like they were having fun. And yet I hung back, uneasy, wondering why I wasn't enjoying the show. Finally, I put my finger on it. At the edge of the clearing, there was a greasy shimmer in the air.

When the last body fell, Billiam threw his guitar onto his back, straightened his false beard, and said, "I think that's the last of the bastards."

"That's all the archers, yeah," I said. The wind picked up, cutting deeper into my already numb hands. Over the stench of death, I caught a whiff of sage.

"Awesome," said Zircon. "Easy peas."

"Whole lot of army between us and the Queen," said Phælandro. "Shall we get to it?"

"After we loot," said Fausto. Phælandro nodded, and the gang got down to an adventurer's true work. They stole boots off the dead soldiers, ripped off their armor, emptied their pockets, tossing aside the junk and pocketing the rare gold coin or useful potion. It was strange to watch. Loot collection was routine—something to be breezed through in a minute or two. In the game, it took a lot longer. I couldn't tell what that meant for the passage of time back in reality—everything about time here was dizzying, and easier for me to just not think about— but watching my friends try on the dead Hordesmen's bloody armor, well, they didn't look so heroic anymore.

As they sorted their winnings, I walked away from the increasingly-nude corpses, following the smell of herbs. The field was slick with corn syrupy blood. As I got closer to the little patch of shimmering air, my ears rang. My lips and eyes burned. I pressed my hand through the haze and was only half-surprised when it disappeared.

Oh boy, I thought. That's not good.

I reminded myself that the GM should be decisive, fearless, omnipotent and omniscient and omni-everything else all at once, but as I stepped into that haze, I was scared shitless.

I emerged into a pocket of darkness. Before me, a sweaty young mage stumbled through an incantation, trembling as he traced runes in the air with a bunch of burning sage. The bubble of invisibility popped. He stared at me, puzzled and terrified, but did not stop writing with his smoke.

I sprinted back to the Heroes, who were almost done stripping their vanquished enemies. I slipped in a patch of mud and gore, staggered to my feet, and shouted:

"There's a mage."

Phælandro, busy tugging on a dead man's glove, did not look my way.

"You said we killed everybody," they said.

"He was invisible. He's not now. He's—"

"Really, Callie, this is the kind of stuff to show, not tell," said Billiam.

"If you're just making this shit up to fuck with me—" said Fausto.

"I'm not! He's right there, getting ready to—"

"I've got it," said Zircon, and did what gladiators do. "Zircon crush."

He ran across the field, preposterous chest still glistening despite the cold. He raised his hammer, took a flying leap, and swung it into the mage's chest like the kid's sternum was a croquet ball. He crushed the boy into the ground and sent the sage spinning out of his hands to trace little spirals in the air.

The mage wrapped a skinny hand around the gladiator's mighty ankle and ended his life with a smile.

"You got him," I said, that sick fear still swimming in my stomach.

"I grab the corpse by the ankles, like I just caught a fifteen-pound bass, and wiggle him around. I spin him over my head like a slingshot and hurl the body into the woods. And now I do my little dance."

Matty's voice was still coming through the monocle, but

the gladiator wasn't talking any more. Inky black spread across Zircon's eyes. His mouth went slack. As Matty narrated his elaborate victory dance, Zircon pounded across the clearing, heavy footsteps shaking snow from the trees. He leapt through the air—not in slow motion now, just fucking fast—and swung his war hammer at Fausto's head.

The thief didn't duck. He didn't even flinch. He just stood there, the handsomest man on the continent, grinning serenely as the hammer connected with his temple.

Zircon's blow tore Fausto's head from his body. It landed at my feet. I didn't want to look at it, but it was my job.

Fausto died smiling, too.

I jammed the monocle back into my eye, pressed the button, and came back to see Matty, half out of his chair, doing a little shimmy that had all of them—even Sondra—laughing.

"Uh, guys?" I said.

"You digging my moves?" said Matty.

"He's dead."

"We got that," said Sondra.

"No, fuck, no..."

"What is it, sweetie?" said Doc. "I know you're trying here, but we're all just a little confused."

I stared at the mass of dice behind my screen.

"As he died," I said, choking down a sob, "the mage cast mental transference. He stole Zircon's body."

"What did he make me do?" said Matty.

"Attack Fausto."

"Okay, great," said Craig. "I'm gonna drain that healing potion I found last time and whip out my knife, then—"

"It already happened," I said. "It happened so fast."

"Did he hit me?"

"Yeah."

"For how much?"

I checked the dice, rechecked them, wanted to lie and knew I never could.

"It was a crit," I said. "He severed your head."

"Can anybody heal me?"

"He took off your head, Craig. That's it."

I was conscious, suddenly, of feeling very sweaty. I gripped the table with both hands.

"That is fucking bullshit," Craig said. He wasn't looking at me. He was staring at his character sheet, carefully embellished for over a year, now nothing but scrap paper.

"This is just your first go," Doc said. "Things got out of hand. We can walk it back. Try again next week."

"There's no walking it back," I said, staring at my lap. "Rules are rules."

"You didn't have to kill him," Craig said.

"I didn't kill him," I said. "Zircon did."

"Please don't bring me into this," Matty whispered.

"Your brother," said Craig, "knew how to give a character a good death."

He crumpled up his character sheet. I thought he was going to throw it at me, but he just dropped it on the table and walked away. Matty and Sondra went after him.

"Aren't you going to close the Spur Gate?" I said. "The keep is wide open. The whole goddamned army is about to come pouring through! They'll take the keep!"

"Let 'em have it," said Sondra.

Doc reached for the ball of paper. She unwrapped it. She smoothed it out. She shook her head.

"He was a really good thief," she said. "I usually hate thieves, but he was a good one."

I had nothing to add. I stuffed my papers back into my accordion folder and slammed my GM screen shut. I took the monocle off my neck and dropped it deep into my bag. Only Karina watched me leave.

5

A WOMAN CAN ONLY DRINK SO MUCH SLEEPYTIME TEA BEFORE SHE starts to retch. I pushed away my cup and watched the trees wave in front of the streetlight. I had been sitting in this window my entire life.

Tonight I'd learned I wasn't ever going to hack it as a GM. I'd botched things so badly that, I figured, the group was done with *Winterwind* for good. They might be done with me, too. But somebody had to close that gate.

I looked down at my notebook, where I'd been adding to my list of rules.

> 5. *In GM mode, you're just Callie. No powers, no armor, nothing to do but watch and talk. Stay out of the way.*
>
> 6. *Time goes a lot faster when other players are there.*
>
> 7. *You suck at this and should never do it again.*

I picked up the mini for Arabeth, who was, as always, leaping into battle with her bowstring taut. If she was disappointed, she didn't look it. Everything about her said, "Let's fucking go."

"All right, girl," I said. "We've got a castle to save."

The monocle was finding its way into my eye easier now, even as I accepted that I didn't deserve to wear it. I set Arabeth on the map and pressed the little iron button. The world froze. Iron poured forth. I left my windowsill behind.

I appeared at the clearing's edge, outside the shattered gate, standing over Fausto's head. Even with his body halfway across the clearing, he was smiling still. The sight of it made me want to cry, but Arabeth's courage settled on my frayed nerves like a lead blanket, and spared me the embarrassment of mourning a broken toy.

Deep in the woods, men shouted and metal clanged. A Horde was coming to life.

I loped back to the castle wall, where a few dozen guardsmen—anonymous hunks with identical tunics, identical faces, identical everything—frantically patched the ruined gate. They hadn't gotten far. I grabbed the nearest and asked who was in charge. He pointed a shaking finger at a catwalk that crossed the courtyard, where the captain of the guard gawked at the mess Zircon had made. He just as blandly sexy-tough as everyone else there, but I could tell he was the captain because he had a bigger hat.

I vaulted up the slick iron steps to the catwalk. The captain's eyes went wide as I loped toward him. Before I really knew what I was doing, my fingers were wrapped around his neck. For a moment I was horrified by the feel of his squishy-hard skin underneath my fingers, but then I heard LB reminding me to stay in character. This was just what Arabeth would do.

"Why...why did Zircon smash the gate?" he said.

"It doesn't matter. Are you ready to fight?"

He shook. The castle did too.

"I'll try. I'll try."

And try he did. He rang a bell and shouted for his men to quit wasting time on repairs. They formed into ranks, taking positions behind overturned wagons and piles of wood and all the other meaningless junk that crowds fantasy landscapes. There weren't many of them, but they were brave, and they would fight to the last.

The earth rumbled as the Horde rushed toward the broken gate, screaming grisly war cries. There were too many of them to count. I'd seen LB's minis, so I wasn't surprised by their gleaming armor and razor swords, but I hadn't expected them to be so goddamned big.

Beside me, the captain quivered. I wanted to tell him that it would be okay, but, well, that would have been a lie.

The Horde swept over the Duke's guards like onrushing surf. As the guards scattered, the Horde fought as one, weaving and spinning and plunging steel into every bit of flesh they could find, filling the air with bloody mist.

I fired an arrow into the crowd, catching a Hordesman in the throat. I fired and fired and fired again. For every Hordesman I killed, there were a thousand waiting to take his place.

The catwalk rattled. An arrow whipped past my ear and buried itself in the captain's eye. He slumped over the railing. I tried to grab him, but he slipped out of my grasp and fell to earth.

"Shit dude," I said. "I'm sorry."

I'd have liked to give him a decent eulogy—even cannon fodder deserves better than that—but it seemed smarter to deal with the bastards that killed him before I caught an arrow of my own. There were two Horde archers on the catwalk. They were as big as tanks, their white armor shining in the moon-light, their skull masks barely big enough to cover their huge, boxy jaws, and they were closing quick.

I nocked an arrow. I was the best archer on the Plateau, firing at short range against a fat target. I should have buried the arrow in his throat, but as the dice echoed across the night, my shot sailed high.

Their turn.

The enemy archer fired. His arrow sliced into my left wrist.

For a second, I wondered how many hit points I'd just lost. Then the pain crashed over me, and I couldn't think of anything else.

"In this game, pain hurts," LB had said once, had said a thousand times. This was like pressing my arm against a hot iron. The blood washed Arabeth's fearlessness away, leaving nothing but Callie Myles from Jett Creek, Tennessee, trapped like a rat with nowhere to run.

The other archer fired. His missile sliced into my calf. I fell to one knee screaming every curse I knew. It was like no pain I'd ever felt before, and I really wasn't into it.

They dropped their bows and drew short swords. I scrambled for my knife, ripping it off my belt and fumbling to get it pointed the right way. I stabbed the first archer in the crotch. He must have been vain, because his codpiece was as thick as a brick. My knife bounced off.

Their turn again, and they made it count. One stuck me in the back, the other in the gut. Even with the golden mail, blood poured freely. I couldn't handle any more pain.

I looked over my shoulder. The ground was very far away, but I didn't have anywhere else to go.

I leapt, grabbed hold of a dangling chain, and swung through the rising smoke. It was as close as I'd ever come to flying, and for a long moment, the pain floated away. Then the boys I'd been fighting got their parting shots. One arrow sizzled across my neck, the other added to the rapidly-growing number of holes in my back.

"Fuck!" I said. "Don't these assholes ever miss?"

My bloody hands lost their grip. I crashed into the stables. Horses screamed. Smoke bubbled through the thatch, followed by fire. I limped across the roof, trailing blood across the straw and trying not to choke on the smoke. When I ran out of roof, I dropped to the dirt.

A patrol of guardsmen nearly bulldozed me. The one bringing up the rear was a carbon copy of the captain who'd caught the arrow in the eye—big hat and all. The sight of him made me dizzy.

"Arabeth," he said. "Where are you going?"

"Battle's over, pal. Today is a stupid day to die."

He looked at me all disappointed. I didn't care. I limped down the alley, hoping the guards' heroic last stand would give me enough time to get away. For a second I wondered what LB would say if he saw his bravest hero retreating like a coward. I decided I'd be better off leaving such thoughts behind.

Because every corner of that plastic castle looked the same, I got lost immediately. Luckily, I had my Ring of Wayfinding—a magical trinket available in armories, trading posts, and village fairs up and down the Plateau—to show me the way. With every step I took away from the battle, its little white rock glowed brighter, pointing me down an alley that led to a tunnel that led to the sewer. I dropped underground and followed icy shit downhill.

Anguish drifted down from the surface. The Horde was not holding back. I heard people choking, buildings burning, the thump of corpses on pavement. I stopped for a moment, trying to get my bearings, and heard the clatter of steel as a guardsman threw down his sword. He started to say, "I surrender," but his words were interrupted when a Hordesman cut his throat. Blood spilled through the gutter. I ran on.

Jesus, LB and sewers. They were one of his favorite tropes—an easy way to whisk a party past an impenetrable fortress wall, or to give a way out during a prison escape. He loved describing the rushing water, the eerie echoes, the one-eyed beasties swimming through the muck. Also I think he liked forcing our gleaming heroes to get shit on their shoes. The filth in the Blackbriar sewer smelled just as bad as it did in real life, and each new stench reminded me that this was LB's story. No matter how nasty it got, I was lucky to be hearing it.

The sewer opened at the base of the keep's southern wall, where its stream splattered against the frozen canal that separated castle from town. A bridge stretched across the ice. The town, which sloped sharply down from the keep, was a mystery to me: a place to stock up on potions and armor, to pick up a side quest, to sleep. The first time we came here, Billiam left his pipe burning in the library of the inn. The books caught fire, and half the town went up in smoke. (Billiam felt awful—he wrote a song about it called, "Oops," and gave a charity concert that raised quite a bit of money, most of which Fausto stole.) Tonight the town was burning again, and I had no idea how I'd get through.

The Horde had seized the bridge, so I slid onto the ice. The canal dipped and swerved under bridges, past burning houses, and into a slum graffiti identified as Pigshit Corner. A flight of steps led me up a side street, but I hadn't gone fifty feet before I smacked into another brick wall.

I took a deep breath, and every wound screamed. I needed rest. During sessions, there was always time to take a break, to heal, think, re-arm, sleep, breathe. Eight hours around the campfire cured all wounds. As the city burnt around me, I realized how silly it was that LB's heroes could always find time for a nap.

I looked for an exit, a ladder, a hidden door. Nothing.

At the mouth of the alley, footsteps broke through the quiet. They were Hordesmen, tall, burly, white armor, skull masks. I'd have been bored if my wounds weren't still dripping blood. I didn't have the appetite for another fight, but I doubted these guys would take a rain check.

"See that golden armor, boys?" cried the captain. "That's the one tried to kill our queen."

"What do we do?" said the Hordesman nearest.

"Rip her head off at the stump."

Yeesh.

I wondered what level these guys were. Five grunts and a mini-boss. A standard encounter for the full party, but alone, well...it was time to start rolling better.

I leveled my bow and shot the captain through the heart. He fell without a sound. I was kinda hoping that would spook his cronies into a retreat, but it just made them angry. The bricks of the alley shook as they charged. I reached for my dagger. I stabbed the first one in the gut, tossed him aside and tried to guess which one would come next. They attacked all at once, like they'd forgotten we were supposed to be taking turns. I dodged one blow and deflected another, but the third soldier, whose face was just as square and featureless as all the others, found a gap in my armor and took out a chunk of my shoulder.

It was like sticking my tongue in a light socket. I threw up in my mouth but stayed on my feet. I grabbed the soldier by his wrist and squeezed until it snapped, then buried my knife in his throat. It wasn't enough.

The three survivors formed a circle and raised their swords high. I spun, pointlessly. The circle closed.

For the first time I wondered what would happen to real-life me if Arabeth didn't make it out. If you died in the game, would you die in real life? Surely not. That would be so fucking stupid.

Right?

Fuck it. No matter what happened here, it was more fun than I'd been having in Jett Creek.

"Come on, grunts," I said. "One of you is going to kill me. The rest will die. Let's find out who's who."

They took the final step.

Three swords plunged toward my golden mail.

White light filled the alley, as bright and startling as a nuclear bomb.

Trumpets blared so loud that there was nothing else but the sound.

I know that spell, I thought. Blinding Glare. Who knew it would be so obnoxious?

I kept my footing. I don't know how. Blood sluiced down my arm as I stumbled blindly over the quivering, fallen soldiers. One of them grabbed my ankle. I stabbed until his hand fell away. I bounced off the walls of the alley, trying to find a way out, but my eyes were useless and my feet weren't much better. I tripped over something—a body?—and was trying to remember which way was up when a firm hand seized me by the wrist. I lashed out with my other hand and, for my trouble, got punched in the jaw.

My teeth felt loose.

I quit fighting.

The hand dragged me to my feet and shoved me forward. I staggered across a threshold. A door slammed. A lock fell.

When the white light burned away, I found I was lying on cold tile. My ears were still ringing. The lobes felt moist. At first I thought they were bleeding but no, it was just sweat. I was, improbably, fine.

I looked up and met the NPC who'd saved my life.

She wore heavy green pants tucked into thick leather boots that had been patched and resoled until it was impossible to tell what their original color had been. Many-layered robes twisted around her chest, exposing arms blanketed with tattoos.

Her square-ish face was dark brown; her lips were two red slashes; her hair was short and perfect, giving her the robotic beauty of mid-70s Bowie, when his personality had been smoothed flat by cocaine. Her eyes shifted from blue to green to dusty red, and it might have been the light, but I swear her ink was dancing.

I guess my point is, she looked cool.

"You fight like an idiot."

Her voice was flat, cynical, bored with me already. I felt a horrible desire to impress her, like I was a freshman in high school and she was the hardass punk smoking behind the gym.

"I'm not rolling well tonight."

"That supposed to mean something?"

"Just that I'm having a rough time."

"So's everybody. The Horde took the Keep?"

"They did."

I thought she might flinch, or sag, or even cry, but she stood perfectly still, staring through me, considering her options until she landed on the inescapable conclusion:

"We're fucked."

"Don't quit yet."

I tried to sit up, to look inspiring. I didn't get far. When I finished coughing, I opened my watery eyes and saw her with a pack over her shoulder, halfway to the door.

"Wait!"

"I saved your life once. That's all you get."

"What's up your ass?"

"Excuse me?"

Smart NPCs didn't talk back. Just ask the shopkeeper in the Silver Valley who got his fingers ripped off for refusing to sell Zircon his belt, or the family of seven whose barn burned down after they told Billiam they, "didn't care for bards." For an NPC in a Heroes' world, refusing to help was suicide. So what was her deal?

"You're a mage, aren't you?" I said.

"A dazzler." She snapped her fingers and a tiny fireworks display exploded out of her hands, filling the crude stone room with color that quickly faded away. "I know a few tricks, nothing more."

My mind snapped back to the dazzler I'd seen sketched out on the mystery character sheet back at Critical Hit. It might mean something. It might not. I was hurting too much to care.

"Don't you have any healing spells?" I said.

She gave another long stare. The way her eyes changed color made it impossible to look at her for very long, but I did my best to ignore the pain in my back and sides and, well, everywhere and hold her gaze. She shoved me against the wall. Pools of white light formed in the crooks of her elbows, dribbled down her arms, and collected in her fingertips. Even through my cloak, I could tell her hands were fiery hot.

She unbuttoned my cloak, tugged it open, and let out a sharp, dry laugh when she saw my golden mail.

"What's the joke?" I said.

"I knew you looked familiar."

She slid up her left sleeve. A portrait of Arabeth stretched from her shoulder blade down across her bicep, showing me with six arrows nestled in my bow and a mound of corpses at my feet. LB's other heroes filled out the rest of her arm. Phælandro, hands bright, summoned death from the mud. Fausto lurked in the shadows; Billiam wailed on his guitar; Zircon held his hammer high. But Arabeth was the biggest, the most beautiful of all.

She poured her light into the wound on my shoulder. Her touch burned in a very pleasant way. She ran her hands down my back, down my legs, sealing the wounds and dulling the pain. When she was finished, I could stand. Healing Touch, I thought. A stalwart level two spell.

"I guess you don't remember me," she said.

"Give us a hint?"

She clapped her hands. A light show glittered out of her palms, showing five Heroes strolling down a city street. The ground split, and a few dozen Hordesmen poured forth. Phælandro called forth a mudslide, and just before it smashed into the Hordesmen, a girl staggered into its path. Arabeth grabbed her by the wrist and dragged her to safety, looking even more heroic than I'd imagined.

"You were the girl," I said.

"Yep," she said, her voice still as flat as a frozen lake. "That was a big day for me. Not just 'cause you saved my life—although yeah, thanks for that—but because until then I'd never really believed in the Heroes. I'd never believed in anything. You saved me, saved all of us, and then vanished back into the sky."

I ran my hand over the places where my wounds had been. My skin was, once again, perfectly smooth.

"Thank you," I said. "I guess this makes us even?"

"Not even close."

With the pain gone, I had a chance to look around the room. It was a stark, undecorated box. A few rickety benches were scattered across the packed earth floor. At the end of the room, something hid under a sheet. Something big and, somehow, familiar. I grabbed hold of the coarse fabric and yanked the sheet away.

What I saw knocked the wind out of me. I gasped for breath and tried to make it make sense.

The statue was twelve feet tall, cut from coarse gray stone. It was carved by an amateur, but the likeness was clear. From the belly to the beard to the eye squinting behind the monocle, this blocky behemoth could only be LB Kucek.

"My god," I said.

"Mine too."

"Excuse me?"

"In Blackbriar, we call him the Gray Lord. In the south, he's the Strider, the Chuckler, the Walker of the Middle Road, the Heavy Iron. He is our past and our future and where he goes, miracles follow. Why are you looking at me like that? This is stuff you've heard before."

"Yeah. Of course I have."

I turned back to the statue. I placed my hand on top of LB's. When I was a kid, he would take to the bakery and buy me sticky buns the size of my head. As we walked home, he was so worried about crossing the street that he would squeeze my hand until it hurt. I didn't mind. I loved the way his fist swallowed mine.

"How are you handling it?" said the dazzler, snapping me out of my fog.

"Handling what?"

"I mean, how are you doing since he died?"

I stared at her. She held my gaze, her eyes a heavy purple, like the pansies at Mom's shop.

Through the cracks in the boarded up window, there came the ugly percussion of marching soldiers. One of them laughed a ragged, bloody laugh. They weren't rushing anymore. This was mop-up.

I squeezed the dazzler's shoulder.

"How could you possibly know that he's dead?" I said.

"Easy. I saw the whole thing."

The doorknob rattled. A fist banged on the door.

"Shit," she said. "We need to—"

The door exploded. Five soldiers burst through the door. Their white plate was splattered with blood. I was about to be afraid when I remembered I had no reason to be.

My first shot cracked one of their skulls like an eggshell. The second drifted, driving deep enough into my target's chest to hurt without killing. He should have run, but instead he showed the suicidal tenacity common to all low level baddies, and ran straight at us, screaming incoherently about his devotion to a faraway queen.

My dazzler pulled her hand back like she was drawing a bowstring. Golden light spun out of her fist, tracing an intricately wrought bow that looked, for the second or two it existed, a lot fancier than mine. She let fly, and the incandescent arrow exploded into the soldier's chest, dropping him to the floor.

Arrow of Light, the preferred attack of level one mages everywhere. I'd heard it cast a thousand times. I'd never imagined how beautiful it could be.

She saw LB die.

Our turn was finished. The surviving soldiers charged. I shoved the dazzler aside and let the soldiers come to me. The first blow missed; the second bounced off my golden mail. The third caught me on the arm. Once again it hurt, so, so bad, but I soaked it. I jabbed with my dagger, which got jammed in his plate. He pulled away, tearing the knife out of my hand. I lunged for it, and one of his friends bashed me across the skull.

I fell to my knees, spitting blood.

The knife had fallen at the foot of LB's statue. I scrambled for it, but it was too far. One of the Hordesmen kicked me in the gut. I rolled onto my back. He stomped on my chest. I clutched his ankle and was wrenching him to the ground when a roar came from the corner of the room—a guttural, anguished howl that sounded like a momma bear who'd caught someone messing with her cub.

It came from the dazzler's throat.

Her shoulders swelled and her robes split. Hair sprouted all over her face. Bone cracked as she bulged to three times my size. She fell onto her newly-grown paws and roared again, spraying spittle across three men who so recently thought they were tough.

The Hordesmen formed a rough line, weapons out, hands shaking.

The beast took a step. Its breath, hot and sweet as garbage in July, filled the room.

One of the men ran.

It took another step. It sniffed the face of the man who'd stomped on me. It licked its lips.

Those guys ran, too. The door slammed, and I was alone with the beast.

No, but seriously, how did she see him die?

I grabbed the knife and got to my feet, trying to find a middle ground between nonthreatening and on guard. Hideous noise poured out of the beast. I was about to bolt when I realized it was laughing. It lowered its head. I gave it a scratch, expecting coarse fur. The instant I touched it, the illusion snapped. The dazzler was back. She took a bow.

"God damn," I said.

"Just a few cheap tricks."

"I'd clap, but I think we should get the hell out of here."

"Sure."

"We can follow the boulevard to the South Gate."

"Nope."

"What's that now?"

"You're a heavenly creature. You take the high road."

"So what?"

"So when an invading army is going house to house cutting throats, the high road will get you killed. Follow me."

At the risk of repeating myself, how the fuck did she see him die?

She bolted out the front door, around the corner, and down a winding alley that ended at a high whitewashed wall. I helped her vault over, then scaled it myself. I leapt down, feeling as heroic as I had all day, and landed in an ocean of shit.

"Excuse me?" I said.

"Welcome to the stockyards."

This was LB all over. He loved to lift us up and knock us back down, letting us feel heroic and goofy all at once. For a moment, her laughter sounded like his.

We waded through shit until we reached a ladder. We climbed to a catwalk that wound between the pens. The pigs were mad with fear. Their screams drowned out those of the people outside. It was not the most pleasant arena for a conversation, but I couldn't wait any longer to say the words that had been thudding against my skull.

"So what do you mean, you saw him die?"

"I have trouble sleeping. Always have. When I can't sleep, I walk, and that night I was by the Old Citadel. The weather turned sour and I felt a storm coming up. I made for home and saw the top of the First Tower burst into flame. A second later, the Gray Lord exploded out of the window and fell to earth, screaming. His corpse burned for twelve hours. When the fire went out, nothing was left. It was magic unlike anything I've ever heard of."

I'd seen him burn outside his studio and at the table in my dreams. I'd watched his lips moving and didn't hear a sound.

"Did he say anything?" I said.

"It didn't make any sense."

"Gods never do. What did he say?"

"'Fucking avenge me. Ron will find a way.'"

"No kidding."

"It's meaningless. I mean, Ron. What kind of name is Ron?"

I stopped. I looked up at the endless black sky and felt I could see Callie looming over us, her dice guiding everything that happened here. For a moment, I fancied I could see LB, too. The big dude raised a beer and smiled.

Fucking avenge me. Ron will find a way.

Now I knew the point of this NPC. She wasn't just here to heal me; she wasn't just here to fight. Even in his last moments, LB had been thinking of me. He knew I'd take the monocle; he knew I'd find the dazzler, and he'd used her to give me what every Hero needs.

A quest.

Only a genius could run the game from beyond the grave. Only the best big brother in the world would think to give his sister a Get Out of Grief Free pass. As long as I followed his story, everything would have meaning. The game wouldn't end and my brother, no matter how dead he happened to be, wouldn't be gone.

The dazzler kept walking. The fires of the burning town made her skin glow orange. The color of her eyes shifted again—from pale blue to solid black—and I knew I'd been stupid to think she was just another NPC.

"You have a name, don't you?" I said. She looked at me like I was crazy, but I didn't mind. Demigods are supposed to be mad. "What is it?"

"Myantha."

"Cool. You should know, Myantha, I'm really fucked up right now."

Her left eyebrow popped up. Very Spock.

"Fucked up how?"

"Every minute since, uh, since the Gray Lord died, I've been holding back a scream. I want to kick shit, hurt shit, break shit. Instead, I can't do anything but sleep and eat and cry. It's bullshit that he's gone. It's bullshit how he died. He was my entire world—he was there before I was anything. He taught me what to be, who to be, what to do. Whenever I was lost, he found me, and he made me laugh. I just assumed it would be like that forever. I haven't told anyone else this, but I guess it's okay telling it to you."

"Why?"

"Who are you going to tell?"

She lunged toward me. For a second, I thought she was going to break my neck, but it turned out it was for a hug. By the way she gripped me, I guess she needed it, too.

"So are we avenging him or what?" she said.

"Yeah."

"I don't know where the hell we're going to find someone named Ron. Weirdest name I've ever heard."

"Don't worry about that. Ron and I are old friends."

The catwalk led through the slaughterhouse, which stank in a way I cannot describe, to a small plaza where a circular staircase twisted down to the South Gate. I dragged Myantha through the thickening crowd. The ignorant cursed me for pushing ahead. The clever got out of my way.

The gate was twenty feet tall and, like so much in this world my brother had crafted, made of iron that looked as light as lace. It was held shut by a fabulously ornate chain and guarded by ten or eleven terrified guards whose spears barely held the mob at bay.

"Back to your homes!" begged their captain.

"Our homes are burning," cried the stooped old man at my elbow. "Open the fucking gate!"

"The Duke gave no order. I can't open this gate until day-break. It would be treason."

I'd had enough of this shit. I loosed my cloak. Myantha flicked her fingers, spraying a beam of pure white onto my famed golden breastplate. It was like turning on the sun. I brushed the gawking guards aside and hefted the chain. It was strong. I wondered if I was stronger.

I twisted the chain around my knife. I pulled hard, and that beautiful iron tore like wet cardboard. I kicked the gate open. The crowd flowed out and we went with them.

"They would have unlocked it if you'd asked," Myantha said.

"Who has the time?"

I took a last look at Blackbriar Keep and the burning castle that sat above it, as useless as a boil. Somewhere up there, the Queen of Skulls tore across the night.

She could wait.

I cinched my cloak, certain for the first time that night, that month, that lifetime that I was going the right way.

6

WHEN I MET RON, HE WAS HIDING FROM A MURDEROUS GOAT.

It was just that kind of day.

LB called a session on a Saturday morning—the first time in ages we'd played during the day. I met him outside the shop. He slouched against the front door in a t-shirt and shorts, monocle around his neck, cigarette hanging from his lips. He looked like a lemon with the juice squeezed out.

He handed me a cup of gas station coffee. I savored the way it burnt my tongue.

"Why the morning session?" I said.

"Thought we could use a field trip."

"Why?"

He dragged on the cigarette, shaking his head. LB never liked to spoil a surprise. While we waited for the others, I asked about work, music, what he'd been watching on TV. He didn't give me anything there, either. He spoke like each word hurt. I hadn't struggled so much to make small talk since he initiated me into the game.

It was a miracle, I realized, that LB and I had any kind of relationship. I knew a couple other people whose siblings were way older, and they were lucky to see them once a year. LB was more than some haggard stranger who surfaced at the holidays. He was one of my closest friends, and we had five hours of quality time every week. I knew him as well as I knew anyone else on earth, but when he looked worn out, I didn't have the words to ask why.

Before I could find a way through that wall, Craig and Matty and Sondra and Doc arrived. LB led us to the cul-de-sac at the end of Carriage Street, where the ancient proprietor of Jett Creek's funicular railway welcomed us to our town's one-and-only tourist attraction. Built in the '70s by an overly-optimistic chamber of commerce, it took its few daily visitors on a slow climb to the top of Mount Jett, where an observation station offered astonishing views and disappointing hot dogs. We each paid a buck and took seats on the benches at the back of the boxcar. We were the only passengers. LB passed out our minis, dropped a dice bag on the seat beside him, and nestled the monocle into his eye.

He rapped his fist on the wooden seat.

"Let's play," he said. The tension in his voice had disappeared.

The funicular's narrow track cut through dense birch, buckeyes, and magnolias, whose leaves ranged from pale gold to the red of a dying sun. On summer days it was sweltering, but that was one of those perfect fall mornings that I guess will always remind me of September 11, as crisp and sweet as a graham cracker. As the car lurched along, LB took us on an adventure.

Eyes half closed, hands draped across his chest, LB played that morning without notes, improvising brilliance without breaking a sweat. He told us of the fanatic monks who lived on the mountaintop. They had a library, he said. They were wise. They might know how to kill the Queen of Skulls. Anyway, it didn't hurt to ask.

The session got silly quick.

We'd just entered the monastery when the goat attacked, screaming curses in whatever language sentient goats use. It took a bite out of Phælandro and was coming after me when Zircon crushed its head. We found a monk hiding in a wooden chest. LB said he looked like "Friar Tuck after a bender." I asked if he had a name.

"Uh, no," said LB. "What would you name him?"

This was an unusual question. LB never asked our input on anything, especially character names, because whenever he did the results were usually as stupid as what I blurted out.

"Ron," I said. "Father Ron. Of the Ronastery."

Normally, LB would have politely requested that I try again. That day he let it stand. Ron was utterly charmed by the ruthless marksman who'd saved his life, and offered the freedom of his library if we could deal with those damned goats.

On the slopes below the monastery, we found the rest of them: a few dozen goats with sharp fangs and a thirst for blood who had been granted intelligence by…I can't even remember. Something that seemed very funny at the time. We had a lovely time slaughtering them. Playing outside was an unexpected pleasure. I sat with my back to the visitor's center, soaking in a view I'd always taken for granted, pretending Jett Creek was Blackbriar Keep. I felt closer to Arabeth than I ever had.

When the last goat's skull was split, we entered the Ronastery's library.

"What brings you here, travelers?" said the grateful scribe.

"We come to learn the weakness of the Queen of Skulls," said Billiam.

"That's easy. She has none."

"None at all?"

"None at all."

"Well. Damn."

The session had been a perfect waste of time. As we trundled back down the mountain, no one complained. I sat beside LB, saying nothing, marveling at how well he ran his game. He had never seemed so unlikely to die.

On the mountain south of Blackbriar, Myantha and I ascended a set of weather-worn steps that had been hacked into the slope long ago. The landscape was flat, gray, and endless—an unbroken expanse of featureless rock. It was as dull as the surface of the moon. I didn't want to be anywhere else.

After untold hours trudging up the crumbling steps, we passed into the clouds. Damp weighed down my cloak. The taste of rain clung to my lips. I could see Myantha and the steps ahead and nothing more. When Myantha slipped on a loose stone and smashed into the mountainside, I helped her up. A perfect trickle of blood ran down her chin. She breathed hard.

"Need a rest?" I said.

"What do you mean, rest?"

"Make camp. Find shelter, build a fire, forage, recharge. Sleep for eight hours and wake up healed."

She looked at the barren slope, the ancient stairs cut into the rock.

"If we slept here, we'd die," she said.

"Oh. Good point."

She dragged her wrist across her mouth. We kept climbing.

"So what's your deal?" I said.

"My deal?"

"Where do you come from? What's your lineage, your back story, your motivation? What's your deal?"

"Do you really want to know?"

"Maybe we can figure out why the Gray Lord brought us together. Or maybe not. Either way, it will pass the time. You got parents?"

"A mother."

"That's all you need. What's she like?"

"Cheerful. Clever. A healer in a small town, respected by everyone. Loved."

LB had done his homework, as always. If you want Callie to vibe with an NPC, give her a working mom.

"So you're not from Blackbriar?"

"Almost no one is from Blackbriar. It's a place for people with nowhere better to go."

"What brought you there?"

She stopped, took a deep breath, and clapped her hands

three times. A trio of iridescent butterflies dripped from her fingers. They fluttered away into the mist, which quickly swallowed their neon glow.

"Butterflies?" I said.

"Magic. Ever since I was a kid, I've lived for it. My mother feels…differently."

"Why?"

"She believes the Gray Lord created magic for his Heroes and nobody else. I believe no god worth a damn could be so selfish."

"Do you miss her?"

"Only every day."

We kept climbing and I kept digging, trying to figure out how she fit into whatever LB had planned for me. She told me that all the women in her family—and there were mostly women in her family—were healers, trained to walk among the sick without fear. When she refused to join the family business, she was kicked out. She was fourteen. She made her way to Blackbriar, hoping for an apprenticeship at one of the ancient magical guilds, but found that such positions are reserved for children of the inbred, wealthy, and corrupt. Since then, she'd lived on the streets of the city, picking up scraps of magic where she could, using it not for war or science but simply to charm crowds into giving her coins. Until she saw me in action, she'd never believed in anything but herself.

This was all lovely stuff, but it was just like the binder about Lomella: back story. Filler. None of it connected to me.

Gray mist gave way to white. My ears popped. The clouds drifted away and through icy, thin air, I got my first look at the Ronastery. It was how LB described it: a stone pile with a single tower and three tiny windows clinging desperately to the mountain's peak, with gardens and a few outbuildings nestled behind a dry stack wall. Unlike Blackbriar, it didn't look like it had been constructed from a model kit. It looked like it had been carved into the stone.

Myantha's pace picked up. I held her back.

"One more thing," I said.

"Fuck! Can you quit with the questions and let us do what we came here for?"

"I know it's obnoxious, but there's something we're missing. Something vital."

"Isn't it possible the Gray Lord put us together for no reason at all?"

"That's not how he works."

"Worked."

"Yeah. Worked."

The past tense is a bitch.

I paced. It didn't really help, but it made me look like I was about to have an idea.

"What's your birthday?" I asked.

"The eighth day of the second harvest month."

"Doesn't mean anything. What about…what's your favorite food?"

"Griddle cakes."

"Favorite color?"

"Turquoise."

"Me too!"

"So what?"

"Well…I don't know."

"As a rule, I don't argue with demigods, but my clothes are wet and my legs ache and I've got a blister that's about to bleed through my boot. Can we go inside?"

She threw her hood over her head and approached the monastery gate, where a figure in purple robes waited under a low arch. He didn't move. Didn't wave. Just waited. When I got close, he gave me a fierce hug. When he pulled away, tears hung in the corners of his eyes. His head was as round as a tomato, completely bald save for a patch of hair above his forehead.

"Good to see you, Ron," I said.

"We prayed you would come back."

"Can we take this reunion inside?" said Myantha, pushing past on shaky legs. "Some of us are cold."

The stench of hand-made candles and rendering fat filled the monk's low-ceilinged dining hall. A pale blue sideboard held a crooked stack of wooden bowls and a pot of congealing lentil stew.

"I count extra bowls," I said.

"Our numbers have thinned. Even above the clouds, war touches everything."

"I'm sorry." I wanted something better to say—once you saved an NPC's life, LB made sure you cared about him, even if he did look kinda dopey. "Will you keep going?"

"Have we any other choice?"

He slopped out soup. Myantha snatched her bowl and shoveled it down.

"Good soup," she mumbled around a mouthful. "Real good."

I was about to eat when I heard a noise from another world. It was earthly, familiar. It made my stomach flip. It sounded far too much like home.

Dice. Dice falling to a tabletop. A sound that could entertain you for an evening. A sound that could create a world.

Someone was playing a game.

In the corner of the room, four monks—all exactly as pudgy as Ron, with the same triangular patch of curly red hair—huddled around a table, scratching at paper and whispering. I got closer. They stared at a map of the Ronastery, as lavishly illustrated as any medieval manuscript, where painted figurines stood in a circle. And by their wrists, each of them had their own die.

In a severely nasal voice, one of the monks squawked, "I recite the blessing to greet a new dawn."

"Do you have your prayer book equipped?" said the monk at his left.

"I know it by heart."

"Roll for memorization."

"It's a common prayer. I shouldn't have to—"

"Take a plus one modifier, but you still have to roll."

Huffy, the nasal monk picked up his die. Before he could throw it, I plucked it from his hand.

"Excuse me!" he said.

"You're excused," I murmured, turning the die in my hand. It was dark wood, polished to a shine. Its sides weren't quite even—nothing beats plastic for that—but it was a beautiful d10.

"This is very nice," I said. The monks hunched over the map, trying to hide it. I bent to look at their figurines. "And the paint on the minis is good, although your flesh tones are a little uneven. I could help with that. Mind if I join the game?"

"This is no game," said the GM.

"Okay, whatever, just teach me how it works. I've always got time to learn a new system."

"Women have no place in our prayer."

"Oh, well, if you're going to be an asshole about it."

I set the die back on the table, thudding it down just a little harder than I had to. The GM picked it up, sneered at it, and chucked it in the fire.

It crackled.

"It's a sin to waste a die," I said. The monks scowled at me the way that only monks can.

"We're not the sinners here."

I could have smashed their game to dust, but I learned a long time ago that dudes who are too shitty to share their toys aren't worth playing with anyway. I walked away.

Myantha approached, smirking. There was a streak of lentil stew smeared across her chin.

"Did I mention the soup is good?"

"I can tell." I wiped her chin clean. "Do you know what they're doing?"

"Looks like prayer."

"Is that the normal way?"

"Nothing about what these monks do makes any sense. A d10 system is absurd. Even the most ignorant gutter rat in Blackbriar knows the Gray Game only works with a twenty-sided die."

"The Gray Game."

"Don't tell me you haven't heard of it."

"No…no, but I think I understand."

Games within games. I was laughing when I sat down beside Ron. This was all so extremely LB.

Myantha was right. The soup tasted better than it looked. She drained her bowl and went back for another.

"What brings you here?" said Ron.

"I'm here to learn about the Gray Lord."

Ron scowled like he was trying to ignore a fart.

"That's what your tattooed friend calls him?" he said. "City cults. Blasphemers. We call him by his right name, his old name, the Starlighter."

"How long have you worshiped him? Five years? Ten? How long has he been, like, a thing?"

Ron snorted.

"The Starlighter was first spotted in Year One."

"And, uh, what year is it today?"

"738."

You know when you're on a plane that's about to take off, and the jets kick in and you feel all that pressure shoving you backwards into your seat? That's how the idea of 738 years made me feel.

"Impossible," I managed to say. "There's no way he's been hanging around here for 738 years. "

"The impossible is his specialty. He was there for the climax of every war, famine, flood, or plague—to bring relief, to ease suffering, to make broken people smile. And he has been here for the good times, too—marching across open country, inspecting his territory like a mad count, making notes, laughing at unknown jokes, and simply knowing all."

"Where does he come from?"

Ron shrugged, palms up, and smiled at the beams above his head.

"Where does he go when he's not here?" I said.

"Every sect has a theory. They say he melts into the earth or steps into the sky. They say he retreats to a hollow tree on the Wide Lost Plain, or dips his toe into any body of water to be swept south to the Edge of the World, where he turns into the bubbles on the sea."

"What do you think?"

"That he never really goes away."

"Does he have any enemies?"

"Does the sun have enemies? Does the wind? All righteous people worship the Starlighter, all evil men fear him."

"What about weaknesses?"

"I don't understand what you're asking."

I looked at the little bald men in their little purple cloaks. Their fingers were dirty. Their cheeks were stained with lentil soup. They had given up their lives in service to a god—a god with a beer belly, a lifetime of unfulfilled promise, and tenure at a largely unknown crafts college—and now their god was dead.

"If someone wanted the Gray Lord dead, how could they kill him?"

Ron pushed his soup away.

"You've been spending too much time around back alley priests. That question is insane."

"Why?"

"The Starlighter is all-powerful. Immortal. Even in Blackbriar, they must know that means he cannot die."

"You're an arrogant buffoon," said Myantha, without looking up from her bowl. I put my hand on her arm, trying to steady her. It didn't help. "And your hair is stupid."

"Excuse me?"

"What's the point of you? Sitting on top of your mountain, scribbling in your books, making up theories about shit you could never understand, while down in the city, people starve. You think you're serving the Gray Lord? You're a fucking parasite."

"His name is Starlighter."

"He's the Gray Lord!" she muttered. Ron spluttered something, but she kept on. "Even your calendar is a joke. 738 years? The Gray Lord has been here since before the world was born."

"Our histories show no mention—"

"Then your historians weren't paying attention. He created this world—"

"He was *given* to this world—"

"Your god is dead!" I shouted.

It's the kind of thing that gets a monk's attention. They quit talking, quit eating, quit rolling dice. Even the soup seemed to quit bubbling.

"Impossible."

"Like you said, it's his specialty. The Gray Lord, the Starlighter, whatever—he's dead and we are trying to avenge him and you are wasting our time."

I'd never seen anyone swoon before, but Ron basically did. He grabbed me by the arm.

"How?" he wheezed.

"Fire. Unheard of magic. He burned to death in the middle of Blackbriar Keep, burned for twelve hours. Myantha saw the whole thing. We want to know who did it, but first we have to know how it was even possible. Your library is the only place on the Plateau that might have an answer."

"The skies should have split. The mountain should have crumbled beneath our feet. How...how did we not know?"

"Yeah. It sucks for everybody."

"What of Blackbriar?"

"It fell. Somebody, uh, somebody left the front door open."

All the red drained out of his face. His brother monks looked just as pale. The nearest grabbed Ron by the collar and said, "Brother, brother—what will we do?"

"Barricade. Repent. Pray."

Myantha scoffed as loud as a person can. When it was clear no one cared, she left the room in what can only be called a huff. Ron scowled as she left, as though all of this were her fault.

Outside, a bell rang low and loud, sending out a rumble like the building was in pain.

"I have to see your books," I said.

"Books will not help us now. Our gates are closing. Go with your gutter priest and leave us to pray."

The monks barred the gate behind me. I found Myantha stomping along the wall, carving a trench into the dirt. I wanted to hit her. There's nothing so galling as an NPC who fucks up your game.

She wasn't looking at me. I fixed that, grabbing her by the shoulders and shoving her into the wall.

"Get your book?" she sneered.

"I might have, if you hadn't pissed him off."

"I'm a woman of faith."

"And that excuses your behavior?"

"It demands such behavior. It doesn't matter if the Gray Lord created the world or was given to it or if he shit it out of his divine ass. It's his teachings that count, and those are simple enough that anyone can grasp them. Murder is wrong. Liars are as bad as killers. And you honor your god by helping people, not hiding in the clouds."

I threw my shoulders back and let my cloak fall open. I looked every inch a demigod. She tried to pretend she wasn't scared.

"I am Arabeth the Dead-Eyed. I have saved your life. I have served your god. I order you to go back inside and grovel until he gives us what we need."

"No."

She was as stubborn as a shard of popcorn wedged between your molars. She was as stubborn as me.

"If you won't apologize," I said, "what the hell are we going to do?"

"All you've done since I met you is bleed, beg, and whine." She jabbed at the portrait on her bicep. "This bitch doesn't ask for permission."

When we were playing the game, if LB ever saw me hesitating or overthinking, he would lean over and whisper, too quiet for the others to hear: "Don't think, Arabeth. Just stay in character." And now here was his dazzler, telling me the same thing: this was a game, and I'd been playing like a loser.

Three minutes later, I was dangling a librarian out a window.

He looked just like the other monks—shiny head, quivering jowls, wet eyes, terrified.

"I need a book," I said. He screamed as loud as the wind.

"A book about other worlds. A book about deicide."

"Blasphemy!"

I let him slide a little farther out the window. It works in action movies, I figured. It did the trick.

"Sweet mercy, pull me in!"

"Have you got a book like that?"

"I have!"

I dragged him back into the library and dropped him on the floor. He wheezed for a few moments while I savored the intoxicating taste of adrenaline and cruelty. For the first time since she rescued me in the alley, Myantha looked impressed.

The librarian dabbed his forehead with his sleeve.

"I thought you were our friend," he said.

"I was, until y'all got in my way." It was a nasty thing to say. It was also perfectly in character for Arabeth. "The book. Quickly."

He fished a heavy key from beneath his robes. He trudged to a gated section at the back of the room.

"Blackbriar has fallen?"

"Yes."

"Then why aren't you down there fighting?"

"Shut up is why," said Myantha.

For the moment, he did. The key clanged; the door swung open, and we stooped into a dim little room where the books were chained to the shelves. The walls were filled with lewd engravings and portraits of the Gray Lord.

"My private collection," said the librarian, waiting for us to be impressed. When he got tired of waiting, he went on. "History, theology, poetry, erotica, arcana. All the collected knowledge of the continent. If the Queen of Skulls' armies get their hands on it, it will be a blow from which Winterwind will never recover."

"Thousands died when the keep fell," said Myantha. "I'd burn every book here to bring one of them back."

"Well, not everyone is a reader."

"Quit needling him," I told Myantha. "Where is it?"

"You seek a volume titled *Being an Exploration of the Planes of*

Life, From High to Low and Elsewhere, and Theories on the Beings that Walk Between."

"Catchy."

"Profane. It describes Winterwind as the Starlighter's playground, a place created for his Heroes to wage war."

"That's preposterous," said Myantha.

"There we agree," said the librarian. I just smiled.

He ran his fingers down the leather cases. He pulled one down and unlocked it.

Empty.

"It must be here," he said. "It must!"

Even when I'd had him dangling out the window, he hadn't looked so scared. He shoved the neighboring books aside, finding nothing, kicking up enough dust that my eyes watered. He slid down the shelves, clutched his shins and cried.

There was a message carved into the empty case: "I'm sorry."

"Who wrote it?" I asked.

"The fool."

"His name, or you're out the window for good."

"It's all over. You don't need to threaten me anymore."

"But she's so good at it," said Myantha.

"Brother Fisher," said the librarian. "The youngest of us, here just a few seasons. He disappeared during the last snow. Thirteen brothers went with him. The others wrote them off as apostates, but they had been confiding in me."

"What about?"

"Dreams, every night the most hideous dreams, of the Starlighter seated at a table in a white chapel."

A white chapel. LB at a long table. I'd seen that dream before. I took off my glove and squeezed the back of my neck. My fingers were icy, and the cold kept me from swooning.

"Dying in fire?" I said, voice barely there.

"How did you know?"

He looked spooked. He had no idea how I felt. Myantha looked at me like the color had run out of my plastic skin. Maybe it had. I tried to get it together.

"Any idea where these runaway monks might have gone?"

"They didn't tell me. I knew they were unhappy, but I didn't think they would really go. And to steal such a terrible book..."

"Why did he want it?"

"He was obsessed with it. He would appear at night, begging to read it again and again. I never asked why."

"You've read it?" said Myantha.

"Once."

"What does it say?"

"It imagines a spell that could open a door between the worlds. The author calls it Astral Leap. It suggests the Starlighter and the Heroes are weaker in their world than in ours—that magic they shrug off here might kill them there, if only they could be reached."

"How does the spell work?" I said.

"It states clearly that—"

Voices came from outside the library. A fist pounded on the door. Ron shrieked from the other side: "Brother, are you all right?"

Myantha chuckled. Deadly light collected in her arms.

"I'll hold them off," she said. She looked happy to have something to do.

"Don't bother. We're almost done."

I snatched a book at random and held it over the candle. The flame leapt a little higher, hungry for vellum.

"Please," the librarian whimpered.

"What else did the book say?"

"Astral Leap cannot be fully imagined here, because this is the lower world. Only a traveler from the higher plane could teach it to us. Only the Starlighter, or..."

"Or one of the Heroes?"

"That's right. No one but a Hero could kill this god."

The door exploded open. The librarian covered his perfectly round eyes, and Myantha jumped into a fighting pose. Seconds earlier, this had all felt like life and death, but the suggestion that one of my friends might have killed LB left this feeling like nothing but a silly, pointless game.

"Explain yourself," shouted Ron, "or face the wrath of—"

He stopped talking when I smacked him in the face. One of his buddies, who looked as soft and dumb as everyone else, thumped me in the shoulder with the bench they'd used to bash down the door. I shoved it back into his chest. He crumpled.

"Got a message for your runaway monks?" I called back to the librarian.

"You can't go after them! They've tasted power you can't understand, terrible power..."

He kept talking, but once we shoved our way out of the library, I couldn't hear him so well anymore. If there were other monks, I guess they scattered. At that point, I didn't particularly care.

"Where now?" said Myantha, skipping to keep up.

"Down the hill."

"It's a hell of a climb. We need water, food—"

"We don't need shit. We're catching a ride."

EVEN ON SUNNY DAYS, IT'S COLD ON MOUNT JETT. BY THE TIME we'd finished saving the Ronastery from the goats, I was shivering under my hoodie. We slouched across the splintered picnic table, voices hoarse, surrounded by litter. I was contemplating an afternoon nap when LB announced we had to get our Heroes back to Blackbriar before we could quit for the day.

"Next week the real war starts," he says. "The siege comes down. I know you're all wiped out—I am too—but I want to make sure we can start next session right."

"So we hike back down," said Doc. "Easy. Done."

"It's a bitch of a climb. You've gotta play it out."

"I've got a better idea," said Craig, and he told us what he had in mind. It was deliciously stupid—the sort of thing that LB would normally laugh away—but that day was special, and LB let it pass. His eyes were squeezed shut and he was rubbing his temples hard, but he nodded and said, "All right, Fausto. I'll give it to you."

When his eyes opened, he shook his head and smiled.

"The shit I let you idiots do."

CRITICAL HIT

Myantha and I plunged through the Ronastery's garden, stomping runner beans and collards, a pack of angry monks on our heels. Myantha slipped on a heap of compost. I yanked her back onto her feet. She laughed as she ran.

"Whatever you've got planned," she said, "please let it work. Torn apart by monks is not how I want to die."

"Don't worry. I've always got a way out."

When Myantha and I rounded the Ronastery's garden wall, we saw a whitewashed gazebo where a wicker basket sat anchored by sandbags, attached to a line that stretched out of the rocky earth, straight off the mountain and down into the clouds. A thick chain stretched across the opening, inscribed with all manner of holy symbols that amounted to a big "DO NOT TOUCH."

"What the hell is that?" she said.

"A zipline. You like heights?"

"Not particularly."

"Well, you're gonna hate this."

We leapt over the chain just as Ron rounded the corner. When he saw what we were doing, he turned white.

"Blasphemy!" he shouted. "That basket is our holiest relic, a miracle placed by the Starlighter himself!"

"Sorry, dude."

I almost felt bad for him, but if you're gonna chase me, I'm gonna run. I hopped into the basket and dragged Myantha after me. There was ice on the cables and fuzzy blankets on the seats. I batted the sandbags aside. We lurched into thin air. Wind caught the basket, knocking it so hard that Myantha nearly tumbled out. I grabbed her, forced her onto the bench, and tossed a blanket over her lap. In a breath, the monastery was far behind us, as perfect as a child's model. Then we were in the clouds and it was gone.

"Where did this come from?" hissed Myantha, as though speaking too loud might snap the cable.

"Like he said—a gift from the Starlighter. Sorry, make that the Gray Lord."

For a long time, there was no sound but the wind. Finally,

I broke the silence.

"What the librarian said about a Hero killing the Gray Lord. It's absurd."

"It's the truth."

"Bullshit."

"If that's what you want to believe."

"How about you quit smirking and tell me what you know?"

"Just before the Gray Lord's tower caught fire, I heard a thunderclap and saw orange across the sky."

"The herald of the Heroes."

My stomach hadn't lurched when we zoomed off the cliff face into the clouds, but it turned now.

"Why didn't you tell me that before?"

"Because it's a shitty thing to hear. I mean, those are your friends."

Yeah. They were.

I squeezed the basket, pleasantly unafraid of the drop, remembering how tired LB had looked when we came back down the side of Mount Jett. When I was driving away, he was back outside the games store, looking even more worn than he had that morning. I rolled down my window and bummed a cigarette.

"You okay?" I said. Two words. Hard to say.

"Never okayer."

"You know, if you ever want to talk to me…"

"Callie, I just talked to you for five hours. What more could there be to say?"

I laughed like it was a joke, rolled up my window and drove away. That's the day I realized you could use games to bring people in, but you could also use them to shut people out. I didn't know him like I thought, and if I didn't know him, I sure as shit didn't know the other people who shared our table. It broke my heart, but it was entirely possible that one of them had killed my brother, Myantha's god.

For a long time, we were in the clouds, which were infinite and wet, and we forgot our speed. Then we burst through. The mountains were behind us. Ahead, sludgy rivers cut through bare forests and untamed beasts dotted wide, unkempt fields.

"I can see my house from here," said Myantha.

"Ha ha."

"Honestly, I can. That town in the valley, there in the foot-hills? That's Glittermore. I grew up there."

That name tickled something deep in my brain. I wasn't sure why. As the foothills flew toward us we saw that what we'd thought were animals were refugees fleeing south. Behind them, so much was on fire.

7

It was morning at the Jett Creek College of Art & Design and I was overdressed. It was spring's first warmish day, and the students had welcomed it with spaghetti strap tanks and irrelevant shrug sweaters that only covered their shoulders. I trembled beneath my two ugliest flannels and a winter coat. The light was too bright, the lines too sharp. Not even the backdrops stood still. Reality was a headache.

After leaving Winterwind the night before, I found time in Jett Creek had slipped forward only fifteen minutes during my two days in the game. My desk was covered with scraps of notepaper on which zombie-Callie had scrawled crude maps of Blackbriar pass, the path up the mountains, and the Ronastery. I crumpled them up, put Arabeth in her plastic case, made some phone calls and crashed headfirst into leaden sleep. I woke sluggish. Coffee didn't help.

Now I was parked illegally in the student lot outside of Loose Joose, waiting for my friends. My car was a 1990 Acura Legend—champagne gold with a sunroof that worked almost half the time. The back seat was all Wendy's wrappers and crumpled napkins. Jill said it smelled like a hamburger on wheels. I'd never minded the clutter, but after two days immersed in the severe beauty of the Plateau, it seemed pretty gross. I resolved to give the car a solid clean as soon as I'd found a killer, avenged my brother, and slept for a week.

Craig showed first. He scrubbed some scum off his shop's bright yellow sign and unlocked the front door. He took a deep breath, put on a painfully fake shopkeeper's smile, and went inside. Harsh lights flickered on. Next came Doc, then Matty. The number I had for Sondra had been disconnected. I'd asked all of them to try getting in touch with her. Looked like they'd struck out.

It was easy to picture their characters killing LB. They were killing machines. Any one of them could have picked up a scroll or learned the incantation necessary to burn him to a cinder.

It wasn't so easy when the suspects were my flesh and blood friends.

"This shit is outrageous."

LB wouldn't have died any other way.

I drummed on my steering wheel cover, looking for an excuse to quit. I didn't find any. LB had used his dying breath to start me on this quest. I'd spent my whole life following LB's suggestions, and I wasn't going to quit now.

This was gonna suck.

I walked into the juice bar and remembered how much I hated it in there. There were too many wobbly tables and too many wobbly chairs. Three walls were wasted on a painfully cute stoner-themed mural—think zucchini and collards in tie-dye and dreadlocks—painted by high school arts students whom Craig tried to pay with gift certificates for discount juice. The whole place was bullshit. It suited Craig perfectly.

I locked the door. Craig made the kind of face he usually made.

"What's this about?" he said. "I'm supposed to be dicing mango right now."

I did a kind of smile thing—the kind you do when you're not about to accuse your friends of murder. Craig looked like I was about to bite him.

"First of all," I said, "I'm sorry for how shit went at the session last night. I bit off more than I could chew, nobody had any fun, and that was my fault."

"Not everyone's meant to be a GM," said Doc. She said it like she was letting me down easy, but it hurt like a broken bone. I smiled bigger.

"Does Fausto get to come back to life or what?" said Craig.

"I mean, no."

"Why not?"

"Dead is dead, dude," said Matty.

"It still sucks."

"It does," I said. "And I'm sorry. But before we can close the book on it, I've got a couple of questions. Y'all know how I hate loose ends."

"Go ahead," said Doc. She was wary, and I guess she was right to be. I'd try to make this quick.

"Any of y'all know a spell called Astral Leap?" They looked at me like I'd started singing in Dutch. "What about that session at the Ronastery, right before Blackbriar, with the goats? Did any of you talk to the librarian?"

"That was a while ago, Callie," said Matty.

"Feels like yesterday. Have any of you been dabbling in trans-dimensional magic of any kind, in the game or elsewhere?"

"I run a juice bar and that's kinda it," said Craig.

So far, I felt as stupid as I had the last time I got the group together. I pressed on anyway.

"Do y'all remember a session in a town called…" I groped for the name. "Glittermore?"

"You mean Gutterbog?" said Doc. "That village in the bog? That place sucked."

"Y'all are both making shit up," said Craig.

"They're not," said Matty. "We did a full session in Gutterbog and that place did suck. And we went to Glittermore, too, but I think we just passed through."

"Anything else happen there?" I said.

"A fight, maybe. I don't know. You're being real mysterious, Callie. You gonna explain what's going on here or do we have to guess?"

I'd run out of friendly questions. From here on, it would be unpleasant.

"Okay. Okay, okay. Craig? Can I have some juice?"

He fixed it. It used too many machines, made too much noise, and took too long. I watched my reflection in the table.

"I love talking about the game as much as anyone else," said Doc, "but couldn't we have had this chat over the phone?"

"You caught me. It's not just about the game."

"Strawberry soy wheat bran," said Craig, like a sommelier presenting a $3,000 bottle of pinot. "On the house."

It tasted like the inside of a lawnmower bag. I choked down as much as I could, wondering how they would react if I told them the truth of the monocle, the game, and everything Myantha and I had uncovered there. They already looked worried. Honesty would probably just get me committed.

I set the juice down.

"Y'all know Leah Sparks, the cop?" I said. "The way LB died, it bugged her. The fire was too hot, something like that."

"So what?" said Craig.

"So she thinks he might have been murdered. And, well—there's no polite way to say this—she thinks one of us killed him."

"That's the silliest thing I've heard all morning," said Matty. "And I watch cartoons."

"I know. I know! I didn't kill him, and obviously none of y'all did and neither did Sondra, but I thought it might make sense to talk about why she might think we did."

"You're talking about interfering with a police investigation."

"I guess? I was thinking of it more as a GM looking out for her players."

I hadn't planned on lying. I'd wanted to handle it like Arabeth—by pressing an arrow to their foreheads and ordering them to confess or else. But I didn't have any arrows, so lying was the next best thing.

"Let's think out loud," I said. "LB was an amazing guy."

"Yep," said Matty.

"Talented. Imaginative. Thoughtful, warm."

"Indeed."

"But you ever go on a road trip with him?"

Matty pulled off his rimless specs. He shook his head.

"He'd make a different tape for every hour of the drive," I said. "Song after song, curated to fit the landscape, the time of day, how far we'd be from the nearest Waffle House. Those drives were amazing—unless you tried to switch to the radio. He'd lose his shit. I'd never known a car could feel so small."

"So what?" said Craig, who could always be counted on to miss the point.

"So he wasn't much fun when he was grumpy."

"Nobody is," said Matty.

"Was he easy to work for?"

"Once you knew him, yeah."

"Leah sees it differently."

"Oh?"

"She says LB wasted your whole career."

I hadn't wanted to start with Matty. Matty was my favorite, and now he looked like a lion who'd stepped on a thorn.

"Why would she say that?" he said, hand tightening on the side of the table.

"Seven years is a long time for an apprenticeship. You've got the experience, you've got the degree. She thinks you should be teaching somewhere, or working for a commercial firm or, I don't know, something. She had the feeling LB wouldn't let you go."

"She doesn't know what she's talking about."

"Oh?"

"LB was my mentor, not my owner. I'd been with him eight years, which is a long time, but I came in pretty raw, and he had a lot to teach. End of last semester, he told me it was time to move on. He got me an interview with a jewelry firm in New York. Gave me a hell of a reference. That man wasn't holding me back."

"See? I'm glad I asked. That makes perfect sense, and when you tell it to Leah, she'll get it, too. No problem."

Doc scooted her chair around until she was close to me. She smelled like rose water.

"This really coming from Detective Sparks?" she said.

"Yeah."

Doc was the adultiest adult I knew. In front of her, I felt like an impertinent child. But just like Leah had said, these questions were bugging me. From my coat I took the memo I'd found in LB's office—the invitation to a meeting that sounded like a threat. Doc recognized it. She put on a scary-polite smile, the way only Southern ladies can.

"She gave me this, too," I said. "Wanted me to ask you what it's about."

"This is official JCCAD correspondence. Strictly private. Where on earth did the detective get her hands on it?"

"LB's office."

"And just why did she find it so unusual?"

"She thinks, well, you must have been pretty angry to call him Robert."

She folded the memo and dropped it into her purse. Her face was stainless steel.

"I get you're hurting, Callie," she said. "Losing family will do that, and I'd never seen a death as…tough to watch as LB's. But if you're gonna accuse your friends of murder, at least have the decency to come right out and say it."

"Accuse us of murder?" said Craig.

"The police aren't in the habit of using games store clerks as proxies, and they don't just give away evidence. Callie's got her own theories."

"You didn't get that?" said Matty. "I thought we all got that."

"I got it," said Craig. "Of course I got it."

He sat on a stool behind the counter, just out of sight. Doc and Matty turned back to me. I felt like I'd been sent to the principal's office. This feeling, this trapped, shameful feeling— this is why I don't break the rules.

"What are you holding back?" said Doc.

On another day, I might have spilled everything. Even if

Doc didn't believe me, she'd have been nice about it. But a thunderclap had sounded in Blackbriar the night the Gray Lord died, and that meant I couldn't trust any of them any more. I kept my mouth shut.

As pissed as I'd ever seen her, Doc pulled on her sweatshirt and threw her purse over her shoulder.

"It's always wonderful seeing you on campus, Callie," she said, "but I'm afraid I've got another, more conventional meeting to get to. Try to get some sleep today."

"I'm sleeping plenty."

"Nobody's ever sleeping enough. And leave the balance of this to Detective Sparks."

She unlocked the front door and left. I felt like I'd been punched in the stomach, but I tried not to let it show.

"Is this really what you think?" said Matty, whose lips shone like tulips against his increasingly pale face. "That I killed him?"

"I don't know. Did you?"

"Do you really think I'd just come out and say it?"

"It would save a lot of time. So did you kill him? If so, why? Please show your work."

"How could I? We were all at the game store, same as you."

I kept talking, because I was afraid that if I stopped, I would hyperventilate or puke or something similarly embarrassing. I got close to Matty. His breath smelled like Cheetos.

"There are lots of ways to set a fire, even far away. You could have rigged something up that afternoon. Where were you before the session started?"

"I drove there with LB."

"A dead man's not much of an alibi."

"Stop it."

"Or what?"

"Just please, stop it."

"Cheetos for breakfast, man. You're a mess."

He dragged his hand across his mouth. His knuckles came away orange. He sighed, stood up, and was halfway to the door when Craig spoke up.

"Four twenty-five," he said.

"What?" said Matty.

"For the Bran With a Plan eye opener. It's four twenty-five."

Matty slid a five across the counter and left his change behind. As he closed his wallet, he turned to me.

"The next time you want to talk to me," he said, "I'd rather maybe you just didn't?"

If he'd punched me in the stomach, I don't think it would have hurt more.

Matty left. Craig's hands shook as he picked up the remaining cups. He stared into them. They were both nearly full.

"Come on," he said, not glancing up. "It's my turn now. Matty killed your brother for fucking up his career; Doc did it because of some mysterious JCCAD business. Why did I do it?"

"Forget it, man. I'm sorry for wasting your time. I'm going to go home and go to sleep."

"You sit down. If you're going to accuse anybody of murder at Loose Joose, I want to be included."

I had to stare at him for a long second before I realized he was kind of joking. I'd never seen Craig make an actual joke before. Suddenly I felt even worse for how much I hated his juice.

"LB laughed at you," I said. "Every week, he got you stuck in giant glue traps or chased by bees or impaled on an umbrella. You were his favorite joke."

"Fausto was the joke."

"But we were laughing at you."

"You think I'd kill him for that?"

"An hour ago it kind of made sense. Now…"

"And how about Sondra? Has she got a motive, too?"

"I don't want to do this anymore."

He sat down across from me like he was going to make some meaningful eye contact, but he got distracted by a piece of gum that was stuck to the chair. As he scraped it off with his fingernail, he said, "I was mad last night, because last night was bullshit, but driving home I felt the funniest thing."

"What?"

"Free. Fausto sucked. He was clumsy, stupid, a show-off.

That makes a shit thief. Since he died, I've just about been walking on air. Thank you."

"You're welcome, I guess?"

"If we ever start playing again, I want to be somebody like Zircon. Somebody who just rules, who everybody likes."

It didn't seem the moment to tell him that he could never pull it off.

"You don't get to quit," he said.

"Excuse me?"

"Your brother is dead. If you think he was murdered, you gotta follow through. Talk to Sondra next. She and LB had some shit."

"How do you know?"

"We talk sometimes."

"I thought y'all hated each other."

"That doesn't mean we can't talk."

He scratched his beard like a dog trying to get at a flea. "What was that spell you asked us about?"

"Astral Leap."

He opened my bag and pulled out the D-Ring. I wanted to smack it out of his hands, but that morning I was moving slow, even for Callie. He flopped it open and pulled out our character sheets.

"Check our spells. Most of us only have four or five. Fausto had extremely cool shit like Shadow Walk. You've got nature girl magic—Wolf's Breath and Death Rain and Lunar Touch. Billiam has all his cringey bullshit like Wailing Ax."

"I hate Wailing Ax."

"It's the worst. And Zircon's spells are basic gladiator stuff—Ring of Blood and Deadly Rage and Mighty Roar. But Phælandro..."

He flipped over their character sheet, where the spell list spilled out of the small box provided to occupy every blank corner of the page. Even more than your average sorcerer, Phælandro hoarded spells. Craig tapped the top right corner, where their names wrapped around like a line of marching ants.

Astral Leap. Phælandro knew Astral Leap.

Fuck yeah. I felt giddy, almost lightheaded. I don't think it was the juice.

"Do you know where I can find her?" I said.

"Muncrief Park."

"Like, in a ranger's cabin?"

"Not quite. She's got a yurt at Campground 37."

"Campground 37. My, my."

I remembered the orange envelope on my brother's desk. I should have recognized Sondra's sloppy cursive. I still had no idea what the letter could have meant, but the thought of finding out had me trembling.

"Why are you being so helpful?" I said. "I hijacked your shop, caused a scene, halfheartedly accused you of murder. Why not throw me out?"

"Because it sucks when your brother dies."

"No shit."

"No, I mean… My brother was, like, the seventeenth American to die in Afghanistan. Right at the beginning, back when every name made it on the front page of the paper. Twenty-two years-old."

"Oh my god."

"Yeah. It just…it sucks. Bush called me. At least you don't have to deal with that. The whole conversation was like, it was supposed to be some big honor, and I'm thinking I'm still pretty pissed off that my brother is dead."

"I'm sorry."

"So's everyone. So what?" He tossed the barely-touched juice in the trash. "You know I hate all this hippie shit?"

"I thought you were all this hippie shit."

"Then I'm a better actor than I thought. I got my MBA at Emory and my market research suggested a guy could make a mint selling juice to burnouts as long as he looked the part. Grew out my hair, boxed up my suits, started dressing like an asshole. So far, it hasn't worked."

"Maybe it's cause the juice tastes like shit. Or maybe your customers smell the lie."

"I fooled you." He had a point. I tried to picture him with a business school cut and clean-shaven cheeks. I couldn't make it fit.

I put five bucks in the tip jar and was halfway out the door when I remembered I had some good news to give him.

"You know my buddy Jill Sparks?" I said.

"Pink hair, works at the thrift store?"

"Yeah. She wants to jump your bones."

His face turned the color of Jill's hair. I smiled like a rascal.

"When she says it, she means it, dude. You want me to give her your number?"

"No, uh, no. No."

"You sure?"

"Extremely."

"Your loss."

He was still blushing when I left.

Driving off campus, I saw Doc crossing the quad. I slammed on the brake and rolled down the window. I was going to scream that I was sorry, but then I noticed the woman she was talking to: a blonde in a windbreaker with a gun on her hip. They walked into an administration building. I smacked the steering wheel. My hand was numb enough that I didn't feel a thing.

A MOUNTAIN OF DIRTY SNOW FILLED THE CORNER OF THE MAIN LOT at Muncrief Park. I nosed my car right up against it. Staring into the wall of grayish-white, I felt for a moment that I was back with Myantha on Blackbriar Peak. I flexed my hands, which weren't plastic at all, and shook off the dream.

On the bulletin board by the trailhead, a map with frayed corners showed happy cartoon hikers enjoying all the park had to offer. I was trying to decipher the route to Campground 37 when my cell phone rang.

Matty.

By the time I got the phone to my ear, he was already mid-apology.

"And the fact is that no matter how upset you make me,

we're still friends, close friends, like I consider you one of my closest friends in town, and you just suffered a grievous loss, and you deserve slack, even at eight in the morning when you're accusing me of murder and, well—"

"Hush."

"What?"

"I'm the one who fucked up. You don't need to apologize."

"It's the Barber family version of conflict resolution. Always be sorry, even when you're right."

"Mom always told us that guilt is a wasted emotion. When you fuck up, just keep going and hope that if anybody notices, they're too awkward to say anything. It works pretty good."

He chuckled. I watched a pair of hikers in day-glo fitness gear unload packs and head off, looking even more chipper than the doodles on the park map. How could anybody look so eager to exercise?

"Anyway, I'll take a page out of your book," I said. "I'm sorry."

"You seriously think LB was murdered?"

"Yeah."

"You gonna do like Doc said and leave it alone?"

"I'll do my best."

I sighed. Lying to Matty was worse than anything. He was always ready to believe. Even over the phone, I heard his forehead unfurrow and his smile break out.

"Thank you, Callie. LB was a good man, but he had his stuff. That's another Barber family tradition. Once a person's gone, let their stuff alone."

We said goodbye. I trudged up the hill after the day-glo dopes, wondering just what stuff Matty wanted left alone.

Campground 37 was far from the parking lot, and I was wheezing before I'd climbed halfway. It was hard to believe that the night before, I'd scaled a mountain that made this hill look like a mosquito bite. The air was soft, with just a hint of damp. Birds sang annoying songs. Nothing was silent, nothing was still. It was way too much to take in, and I found myself missing the stark perfection of LB's world.

Nature's racket kept me from noticing that I was being followed until it was too late to do anything about it. I was wheezing against a yellow birch that was older than my grandparents, making renewed promises to give up cigarettes completely, when a shadow flitted through the trees. It was smaller than a bear, bigger than a wolf, and fast enough that I didn't have a chance.

I reached for the arrows in my quiver before I remembered this version of me was completely unarmed. I slowed my breathing and walked off the path. My feet churned up sulfurous rotting leaves. I looked this way and that way and this way again. The shadow was gone.

A firm hand grabbed my shoulder.

Like a true hero, I yelped loud enough to startle every bird on the mountain:

"Jesus fucking Christ!"

It was Sondra, of course it was Sondra, wearing a poncho that was equal parts black, brown, and stain. I'd never seen her so amused.

"Sorry for the scare," she said. "I thought you were the rangers. They are sick of me, let me tell you."

"Nope. Just me."

"What brings you up my mountain, Arabeth?" she said. Her accent, purest Baltimore, twisted the word "you" into "yew." I put on a big grin, like we were really friends, like I wasn't afraid.

"Me and everybody got together at the juice bar this morning to talk about LB. I tried to invite you."

"I know. Matty called. I just didn't want to come."

"Oh."

She started uphill, striding like her legs were trying to swallow the mountain whole. I kept up, but it wasn't graceful.

"I wanted to ask about Astral Leap," I said, between gulps of air.

"What?"

"It's a spell."

"Oh. Yeah. I took it when I hit level 11. It sounded kinda

spacey, kinda cool. I never used it."

"Why not?"

"What's the point of a spell that lets you walk from dimension to dimension when all the other players are stuck back on earth?"

We crested the hill. As the trail leveled out, Sondra walked even faster.

"You didn't haul yourself up this mountain to ask me about my spell list, right? I mean, that would be really fucking dumb."

"I didn't."

"So have you just now figured out LB was murdered?"

I stopped walking. I stopped everything—thinking, seeing, breathing—for just a second, as I processed what she'd just said. The sound of a woodpecker going to town on a nearby spruce brought me back to earth. Sondra was far down the path. I ran until I caught up. Her face was red, but nowhere as red as mine.

"What makes you think he was murdered?" I said.

"Because he was. Duh."

"Why?"

"Because he was such a huge dickhead. Again, duh."

"My brother was not a dickhead."

"Tell that to my yurt."

I was about to say something clever—like "What?" or "Huh?"—when we broke into a muddy clearing littered with ramen wrappers and empty packs of clove cigarettes. There was a picnic table, but it had been smashed and flipped on its face. The yurt, a heavy tent whose thick violet canvas looked lovingly hand-dyed, sagged on its frame. One side was tattered, streaked black by smoke and fire. The spring air should have felt pleasant, but there was sweat on my neck and bug bites all over my wrists and churning terror in my gut.

"Oh shit," I said.

"Welcome to Campground 37."

"What happened here?"

"Your brother."

My brother.

I wanted to slide down that mountain like spring runoff. I

did not want to be here. I did not want to hear her story. But it was too late to run.

"I'm not explaining shit until we have tea."

"Okay."

I lowered myself onto the driest looking rock. Sondra pulled on an oven mitt and lifted a speckled steel coffee pot off the fire. She poured steaming tea into a Sierra cup and stared at me when I cupped it in my palm.

"Doesn't that hurt?" she said.

"Oh. Yeah, I guess. Ow." I shifted to hold it by the handle. "So what…what happened? Did he leave a joint burning in the tent? Did he knock over the stove?"

"In a way, yeah, you could say that. In another more accurate way, you could say he set my yurt on fire while I was sleeping."

"My brother, my brother would never…"

"Except he did. Sure, he said it was an accident. Said he kicked over a lantern in his sleep, like Mrs. O'Leary's cow. But when I woke up, fucking gagging on smoke, he was safe outside with a big ass grin."

"He was sleeping here?"

"That's the part that surprises you?" She laughed and coughed at the same time. "Was he ever a Boy Scout?"

"He made Star, not Eagle."

"Figures. It was very tidy, for a fire."

I looked around the ruins. There was no way LB could have done this. But if he had, well, it would be tidy.

"You don't believe me," she said. "Whatever."

"Because it doesn't make sense. My brother could be moody but he wasn't, like…"

"An arsonist? A murderer? Funny what people do under pressure."

I tugged the orange envelope from the hip pocket of my parka. Sondra ran her tongue across her teeth.

"Is this the pressure you're talking about?" I said.

"You read the letter?"

"No."

"I guess he burned that, too."

"Are you going to tell me what it said, or—"

"I was blackmailing him!" She screamed it, but her gaze was flat, like she was bored with the whole thing. She was seeming less and less like someone I wanted to be alone on a mountain with.

"I usually expect people to be a little more circumspect about that kind of thing," I said.

"I didn't get anything out of him. I was just trying to. That's not a crime."

"It definitely is."

"Fuck it. You're not a cop. He had a secret and I knew it, so I blackmailed him. That's what you do, right?"

"I guess, if you're a...certain type of person. How much did you want?"

"I didn't want money. I'm not a scumbag. You know those big sculptures of his outside the admissions office?"

Lilies. Ten feet tall, twisted and alien but lilies nonetheless. He'd done them after he came back from New York as a Mother's Day present. When she saw them, Mom cried for a half hour.

"When I first toured JCCAD," said Sondra, "they blew my mind. Stared at them for hours. Memorized every curve. I'd never fallen in love with a sculpture before, but there you go. I decided that whoever sculpted them was going to do a statue of me. That's what I asked for to keep his little secret safe."

"What was the secret?"

"If you don't believe me about the yurt, I'm not telling you shit."

"So make me believe. As far as I know, you and LB didn't have anything to do with each other. You took a couple of his classes; you played in his game. What else was going on?"

She tugged her cloves from the big square pocket on the front of her oversized L.L.Bean shirt. She lit one, handed it to me, and lit one for herself. The cigarette tasted like sawdust. I was very grateful for it.

"I've always had a weakness for gurus. In high school, it

was my art teacher. In college, this anthro adjunct. After college it was one, two, three, four viciously manipulative yoga instructors. The last one brought me here and left me behind when his studio got nailed for tax evasion. I was fucking lost, so I did what I've always done: I went back to school. Thought learning to work iron would help me get a grip on life. Turns out I suck at iron working, but when I met LB, I felt that old pull."

"To what?"

"To follow him around, to impress him."

"Why didn't you fight it?"

"I never have."

The more she talked—and man, could she talk—the harder it was to believe she'd lied.

"So, like," I said, "when he died, were you, were you..."

"Fucking? No."

"Good."

"We had fucked, but we weren't presently fucking. One of us lost interest around the time he set my house on fire. Is this really the shit you came here to ask?"

The clove hit my stomach hard. The image of LB and Sondra writhing in her sleeping bag didn't help. Whatever control I had over the conversation would evaporate if I threw up, so I fumbled my way through a less nauseating question.

"After what he did, why did you keep playing with us?"

"To show him I wasn't afraid."

"Did you kill him?"

"Nah. But fuck, I wish I had."

"Did he ever talk about the game?"

"He talked a lot about a town called Glittermore."

My stomach twisted harder. I felt Myantha's shifting eyes staring at me, full of hope and misplaced trust. I didn't know what it meant but I knew that every time I heard that word I wanted to retch.

"No shit," I said, trying to sound not crazy. "I was thinking about that session yesterday."

"LB was obsessed with it. He thought we'd fucked it up really bad. He said we'd sinned. I thought that was an odd word for a dude who thought all churches should be converted to public housing. Was he, like, sneaky religious?"

"No." Although, now that I thought about it, he might have been. There was lots about LB I didn't know. "Do you remember anything that happened there?"

"How could it possibly fucking matter?"

Damp seeped through the toe of my shoe. I looked down and saw that my hands were shaking so much, I'd spilled my tea. I let the cup drop. The tea made a little mudslide in the dirt. Sondra stiffened. She looked like she might pelt her cup at me.

"You gotta be really fucking spoiled to waste good tea," she said.

"Our GM is dead. He burned to death. Am I the only one who gives a shit about that?"

"After what he did to my yurt, I gotta figure it's poetic justice."

"Oh come on. LB didn't set your tent on fire."

"It's a yurt."

She said the word like she was a Mongol, born and bred, with the kind of misplaced authority granted only to overeducated white people. I was sick of her, so I said something stupid:

"It's bullshit, same as you."

She jumped at me like her legs were spring-loaded—all that yoga was paying off, I guess—and had me in a headlock before I could move. Her bicep felt like a lead pipe.

"Are you fucking crazy?" I gurgled.

"Apparently."

She dragged me into her tent. All her stuff, and there wasn't much, had been consolidated into a single corner where a limp tarp dangled over a scorched hole in the canvas. She threw me to the dirt. I landed face first.

"Jesus Christ!" I said. "What the fuck is wrong with you?"

"You were fucking with me. I went for your throat. Wouldn't you do the same thing?"

"Of course not!"

I tried to stand up. She prodded her boot into my chest.

"That's where he lit the match. Right where I sleep. Right by my head. He knew what he was doing and he didn't care. Believe me now?"

I nodded. I hated it, but I believed. She removed her boot. Her face was sunburn red.

I got to my feet, wiping the dirt off, trying to decide if I'd rather scream or hit her or cry. I held myself together and, instead, did nothing at all. She wanted a big reaction and she wasn't going to get it—not until she told me what I wanted to know.

"So are you going to tell me what you were blackmailing him about?"

She lit another clove and breathed deep.

"Nope."

I walked out of the yurt. Sondra followed, took a long swig of her tea, then clasped her hands bent into a question mark. Her back cracked like someone stepping on a bag of chips.

"Craig was right," I said. "You're awful."

"I don't care what you think about me, Arabeth."

"Oh, go fuck yourself. You cannot touch people like that. Ever. You're out of the group."

She rolled her eyes.

"There's no point fucking with you," Sondra said. She stood as tall as she could, which was plenty. The sun was right behind her head. I had to squint to see. "I've had my tea, which is some seriously heady herbal stuff that is about to commit extreme violence on my GI tract. I've had my cigarettes. I'm about to go take a shit and things up here are gonna get really earthy. You might want to find a bathroom yourself."

She waved bye-bye, tipped some water into her cup and hurled the tea leaves into the woods. She walked up the hill toward her slit trench.

Arabeth would have cut Sondra or split her throat with an arrow or just laughed and walked away. I had no weapons, no armor, so I just slunk down the mountain, hoping I could find shelter before the tea hit.

8

EVERY SUMMER, THERE HAD BEEN LILIES. THEIR VARIETY WAS AS-tonishing, like a family reunion so sprawling that some of the cousins bore no resemblance to each other at all. Before I was old enough to read, LB taught me their names: water lilies, trout lilies, avalanche lilies, and the glorious, early-blooming daylily, whose burnt orange streaked across our front porch like a tropical sunset.

When the lilies were blooming LB always dropped by Mom's shop to water them, deadhead, whatever the plants re-quired. His fingers were thick but graceful. As he reached down to pinch off a spent bloom, it was easy to see how he could work wonders with iron. It was always a treat when he showed up at the shop—he was looser, sillier there than at Critical Hit. As I emerged from the store bathroom, where I'd taken refuge when Sondra's tea came for me, it occurred to me that I hadn't seen him tending lilies in years.

The shop was had a pebble floor and a glass ceiling that let in crystal blue light. I stopped at a particle board table covered end to end with succulents. I ran my fingers across the sage green leaves of some alien plant. I did not know its name.

Mom leaned against the table eating peanut M&Ms. She was wearing her work clothes—a floral headband, an old men's button down and billowing orange pants. She and Odette were proof that if a woman wants to dress comfortably at work, she'd better own the place.

"You okay?" she said.

"Better now."

"Do I want to know what happened?"

"Bad tea."

She rubbed her thumb across the scrape where Sondra had thrown me to the dirt. It stung. She kissed it. It stung less.

"Did LB ever talk to you about sin?" I said.

Her face was tight. Mostly we hadn't been talking about him, and mostly that had been working. I didn't want to keep asking these questions, but they were gnawing at me, and if I didn't get them out I was afraid they'd chew right through my chest.

"Bobby and I hadn't traded two words about God since he was six, when he woke me up at three a.m. to tell me he'd figured out that Santa Claus was a hoax and Jesus was, too."

"So he never said anything to you about, like, being born again?"

"Even if he got religion, he wouldn't have told me. He didn't tell me much of anything."

"When you were going through LB's room, did you find any other games stuff?"

"Just what you saw."

"What about the basement?"

"Nope. What're you looking for?"

Proof that he wasn't as bad as Sondra thinks. Proof that I wasn't wrong to love him. Proof that there was some kind of reason, no matter how awful, behind the way he died. I could have said any of those things, but I was trying not to make Mom cry, so instead I said:

"A couple of pages out of one of his binders, about a session we played last year. For the campaign."

"You try his office at school? Doc was always on him for

tinkering with the game while he was supposed to be working, although I think she kinda liked it, too. I'm sure Matty would let you in."

I gave her a hug and she gave me a handful of M&Ms, a fair trade, all around. Moms—there's nothing they can't do.

THE BONFIRE STANK OF ARMPIT. THE DRUM CIRCLE WAS WEARING out the canvas and the fire burned twenty feet tall. Figures thrashed in the smoke, mostly underclassmen whose enthusiasm for the annual ritual was still as fresh and firm as their skin. The older kids stood apart, staring with glassy drugged eyes at their younger classmates, wondering where the years had gone. Faculty, staff, and townies formed a ring around them, sipping beers and enjoying the spectacle of bonfire night, when the past burns.

When I was in high school, this is how I'd imagined college. Instead, I'd ended up at a liberal arts school that was older than the United States and a hell of a lot more uptight than JCCAD. Instead of bonfires and orgies, I got four years of sitting in circles on dorm furniture, sipping cheap red wine and politely agreeing with whatever bullshit the person closest chose to spew. Kids at JCCAD were full of shit, too, but they looked like they were having fun. I wish I could have gone here, but arts school demands either talent or confidence, and I'd had neither.

A girl with brutally straightened hair and a skinny choker pushed past me. She hurled a pair of spiral notebooks into the flames.

"Fuck you, Spanish requirement! Fuck you too, introduction to basketry! Baskets are fucking dumb."

I tapped her shoulder. She spun around.

"Isn't burning stuff the best?"

"Oh, totally. An unrelated but cosmically vital question: which way is the metalworking building?"

She pointed over her shoulder and wiggled back into the crowd. Eyes watering from the smoke, I left the party behind. I slunk through a patch of well-manicured woods, where every shadow made me flinch, to the two-story brutalist pile that housed LB's department. It looked just like all of the other viciously ugly buildings that made up the campus. Only the chimney rising from its middle hinted at the magic inside.

The door was heavy steel, but LB's ID unlocked it. In the hallway, tall windows overlooked the field outside. With the lights on, I couldn't see anyone out there, but they could see me.

LB's office was all the way at the end. It was locked, too, but *sniiiick*, the ID popped that door, too. I turned off the hall light and shut the door. My hands shook like autumn leaves. The rest of me wasn't too steady, either, but I'd come too far to turn back, and anyway, I'd already paid for parking.

"Come on bro," I said. "Show me something to believe in."

This room featured no game books, no teetering fire hazards, no mold. The only thing that distinguished it from any other faculty office were the four pieces of delicate iron art, one for each wall. They were faces. They looked sad.

Campus IT had taken away LB's computer, but I don't think I'd have found anything there. A proud Luddite, one of LB's many mottoes was, "analog 'till I die."

"Good job, dude," I said. "You won."

The rusted green filing cabinet was locked.

"Fuck that."

I kicked the drawer. The clang echoed like cannon fire. Adrenaline filled my mouth. Every inch of me swelled with anger. It was an ugly sensation, but it beat being numb.

Kicking that harmless old filing cabinet felt so good, I decided to do it again, and again and again. I kept stomping on it until the drawer bent and my sneaker's heel split and I fell onto my ass, cursing and laughing through a mouthful of bitter spit. I tugged on the drawer. If anything, it felt more locked than before. Didn't matter. I had a lot more kicking in me.

Before I unleashed the next assault, a hand fell on my shoulder, as warm and heavy as a porterhouse steak.

"That's JCCAD property," said Matty Barber. His eyes were red behind his glasses; his fingertips were Cheeto orange. "What brings you here?"

"Didn't I tell you? I'm moonlighting for Consolidated

Filing Cabinet, doing stress tests all over campus."

"Mmm-hmm."

From his pocket he pulled a grimy JCCAD lanyard, from dangled keys of every color. He spun it around his finger.

"You wanted to look inside, you just had to ask."

"I'll remember that next time."

"What is it you're after?"

"Glittermore."

The lanyard stopped spinning. Matty's face suddenly looked very hard. His biceps, too.

"You said you were going to lay off this murder stuff," he said, so quiet I could barely hear.

"What makes you think Glittermore has anything to do with the murder?"

He slumped onto the floor, arms across his legs, fingers trailing through the carpet. I sat beside him. The crisp smell of bonfire drifted off his army surplus jacket.

"Why do you keep pushing this," he said, "if you know it only hurts people?"

"I never liked walking away from a quest."

"Cute answer. Why not tell the truth instead?"

"It is the truth. I know it sounds silly, but he was the greatest GM in the world, right? How can I walk away from his last campaign?"

"The best in the world, huh?"

"Yeah."

He knelt before the filing cabinet and forced his key into the battered lock. The drawer popped open. He pulled out a notebook marked "Glittermore." Looping calligraphy danced across the cover: *"Thoughts For the Campaign. Do Not Open, Fucko."*

It felt heavy. It felt real.

"You don't need to open it," said Matty. "Drop it in the drawer, kick it shut, and I'll chuck this key into the gorge. I promise you'll be better off."

I ran my fingers along the warning. When I was a kid, if LB told me not to touch something, I dropped it like it might scald. But this was my campaign now. I trembled as I flipped back the cover, frightened and eager at the same time. Whatever he'd had waiting for us, it was going to be goddamned good.

There was no map in there. No traps, no treasure. No monsters to fight or battles to be won. Instead, there were just two sentences, scrawled out in LB's perfect script.

"All Sins Will Be Forgiven. No Sins Will Be Forgiven."

Those two sentences, repeated endlessly, filling every inch of the first page and its back side and every sheet after that.

All Sins.

No Sins.

All Sins.

No Sins.

What. The. Fuck.

I dropped the notebook like it was going to bite me. Matty tossed it back in the cabinet. I tried to picture LB hunched over his desk, scrawling those meaningless words over and over again. It wasn't an easy fit.

"What *is* this?" I said.

"Glittermore."

"What the fuck was Glittermore?"

He took a deep breath. Looked like it hurt.

"No surprise you don't remember. We were barely ever there. Stopped for food and a night's sleep, reupped on potions and arrows and field rations on the way out. Ten minutes tops, in real time. Wouldn't have mattered at all except that while we were walking out, you asked me to make you a poison arrow."

"You made me those all the time."

"Yeah, but that session I'd learned the recipe for a really nasty new poison and we wanted to try it out. I collected herbs, ground em up, and smeared the paste on one of your arrowheads. It was rust red. You remember any of this?"

Almost. An image of Zircon bent over his mortar and pestle floated across my mind, but I had no idea if it was real or fake.

I shook my head.

"You loaded up the arrow," he said, "and shot it at a chipmunk. You missed. The arrow sailed off into the woods and we went on our way."

"So what?"

He rapped his fist on the filing cabinet door.

"Six weeks back, LB gave me a call. It was 2:15 in the morning. He was fully freaked. Said your arrow had flown through the trees and landed, splash, in the town well. Poisoned the water supply. Hundreds died. The rest moved away."

I remembered the light that flashed across Myantha's face when she caught a glimpse of her town. It did not feel good.

"If he wanted to make that part of the campaign," I said, "why'd he only tell you?"

"He and I were doing…I guess you would call it a solo campaign. Only not by choice. Every few nights, around three a.m., he'd call up sounding drunk or I don't even know, and he'd tell me where Zircon was. 'You're strapped to a rock, naked and cold. The wind cuts your skin.' 'You're alone on a raft in the middle of a sludgy lake.' Stupid stuff like that. He'd make me play until he fell back asleep."

"And he made you go back to Glittermore?"

"No. He made me confess."

"What precisely did he say?"

Matty twisted the ring on his right hand, a plastic bauble engraved with his high school's name. He dropped his voice an octave and did an entirely convincing impression of LB.

"There's a conspiracy in Glittermore, Matty. A bunch of crazy ass monks. Stupid looking little fuckers, but smart and mean. They're trying to kill the Gray Lord. Fucking hell, they're trying to kill me. You gotta tell em it wasn't my fault. I didn't make you craft the arrow. I didn't fire it. Tell them it was you."

I let that soak in. No matter how often I turned it around in my mind, I couldn't imagine why LB would come up with something so gloomy, so weird.

"What was your answer?" I said.

"That I was going back to sleep. So he held a gun to my head. I told you he was writing me a reference to St. John's Jewelers, up in New York? Very prestigious firm."

"You mentioned it."

"Well he wrote it for me all right. Nicest letter you could ever get. All sorts of five syllable words that all boiled down to, 'Hire this man.' But that wasn't the only letter he wrote."

"What did the other one say?"

"'Matty Barber is a half-witted hillbilly refugee who I keep around for laughs.'"

"Fuck me."

"'His mind is clumsy. His fingers, too. Even his fried chicken sucks.'"

"Your fried chicken is great, dude."

"Don't you think I know that?"

He dropped into the wooden chair opposite LB's desk. It was college grade—cheap and flimsy—and his bulk nearly finished it off.

"He told me to write out a confession or he'd send the nasty letter. So I wrote it, just the way he told me to. 'I am Zircon the Shirtless Annihilator and I have sinned oh lord I have sinned, I harvested the herbs and I ground the poison and I anointed the arrow that killed this town, it's my fault, all, all my fault, the Gray Lord is faultless, the Gray Lord is immortal, the Gray Lord is good…' Went on like that for a while. He made me write until my hand cramped. I gave it to him the next day."

"And he sent the nice reference letter?"

"Course not. He sent the mean one. You won't believe it, but I didn't get the job."

Okay, Callie. There's your proof. At best, LB was a dickhead. At worst…good god. I couldn't even put words to it.

"But it wasn't your fault. You made the poison, but I fired the arrow."

"He told me to leave you out of it. I have no idea why."

A question shot across my mind—a question that would wound him as sharply as breaking a bone. There was nothing in the world I hated more than hurting Matty Barber, but I said it anyway.

"If LB sent that reference letter, if he really did that…there are worse reasons to kill."

He clasped his hands behind his head and sucked in air like

he was trying very hard not to scream.

"Why would I kill him now? He treated me lousy for years, you know that? Made me clean toilets. Called my art trash, then put his name on it. Called me useless every dang day, then threw a fit if I tried to leave."

"Why didn't you quit?"

"I quit every three months. Each time, he broke down, begged, told me it'd be different. And I'd remember how he was when I first came here, when he was actually worth looking up to, and I'd back down."

"Maybe this time you didn't."

"And just how did I do it? I was half a mile away. I was with you!"

"A long fuse. A bomb. You're a volunteer fireman—you must know a few tricks."

"You overestimate me."

"Then maybe it was magic."

He stared at me for a second, waiting for me to laugh or grin or wink. When my face didn't give him what he wanted, he broke the tension with a laugh.

"You and your brother, I swear to god, were put on earth to torture me."

I gave the filing cabinet one last kick.

"What if the game really did want him dead?" I said.

"'Scuse me?"

"What if he needed our help? How could a person ask for something like that without sounding insane?"

"I can't even engage with that question."

"But if there really was a conspiracy in Glittermore to kill him, that would prove—"

"Come on, Callie. That wouldn't prove nothing at all. Now let's go, all right? I'm supposed to be at the bonfire."

"I know. It's late. You're tired of being accused of murder. Can I use your bathroom before I leave?"

He escorted me back to the hallway, where a unisex bathroom waited beside the front door. The floor was black and white tile—a perfect game board. I dug Arabeth out of my sweatshirt, popped her out of her little plastic case, and set her down. I was going back into the game, and I was going to stay until I figured out what had pushed LB over the edge. Here, every question brought more pain. Maybe in Winterwind, I'd find answers instead.

I locked the door, pulled the monocle out of my pocket and slid it into my eye.

MYANTHA WAS RIGHT WHERE I'D LEFT HER—SHE WAS HANDY LIKE that. We'd camped beside a crystal clear stream that flowed along the base of a towering, perfectly flat cliff face. It reminded me of Campground 37, and that made my cheek ache. We were wrapping up breakfast—field rations, woo!—when I told her we were paying a visit to her hometown. Her eyes flashed red, then settled into a pulsing sage. She wanted to run, but I couldn't tell if it was back to Glittermore or far, far away.

"Why?" she said. "Why there?"

"I think that's where we'll find our mad monks."

"How could you possibly know that?"

"Check out these cheekbones. I clearly know everything."

"I'm serious, though. We were in the zipline. We landed. We slept. Did this shit come to you in a dream?"

I sat beside Myantha.

"This isn't the only, uh, plane I'm operating on," I said. "I'm a demigod, right? I go high, I go low, I go in between."

"And which one is Winterwind? High or low?"

The sky was flat and clear and ice blue. The cliffs were featureless. The creek flowed as straight as a highway, its banks unmarred by scrub or moss or deer shit. There were no distractions here, nothing to get in the way of the game.

"As far as I'm concerned," I said, "this is the highest plane there is, because the Gray Lord made it. Everything here has meaning. Whatever we're looking for, the Gray Lord will make sure it's there to find."

"Sounds good. But brace yourself for my mom. She's the worst cook on the Plateau. Nothing the Gray Lord taught you will prepare you for that."

I didn't know what we'd find when we got to Glittermore, but I didn't think there'd be any home cooking. I should have gone ahead and warned her, but I didn't. I told myself I was just staying in character, but the truth is I was bitterly afraid.

It took a day and a half of tough hiking to get to Glittermore. The monotony was punishing. Spot an interesting rock, and you'd be sure to see it again fifteen seconds later, and then again, and again. Same for every gnarled tree or unusual cloud or the haggard, identical citizens of Blackbriar fleeing the conquest of the Queen of Skulls. LB had always let us fast forward through this stuff. I understood why. It was almost enough to make a girl doubt her brother's creative genius. I might have lost faith if it weren't for the Iron Forest.

The trees looked like apple trees, trunks stretched and twisted, branches plunging into the ground, but they were made of matte black metal, so dark it seemed to suck the light from the air. It was not an inviting place, but my Ring of Wayfinding insisted we press on, and so we stepped into that dead forest, where no birds sang and nothing grew at all.

"I've heard of this place," said Myantha. "I didn't think it was real."

And yet, it was realer than everything else in this flimsy world, because of all the thousands of warped metal trees, no two were alike.

After six hours picking our way over the treacherous roots of the forest floor, I heard hissing steam. In the distance, my marksman's eyes picked out the faintest glow—the first sign of light, of heat, this place had provided. I approached on silent feet. The trees stopped. The ground fell away into a deep crevasse. High in the sky burned a ball of molten iron—a miniature sun, hung by a god. Every few seconds, it dripped, loosing a loogie of boiling metal that tumbled slowly through the air to splash, splatter, and cool in the rent in the earth below.

A stalagmite had formed there: an iron shard that reached up from the earth like a witch's finger. A bridge stretched over the crevasse. As we crossed, we looked down. The shard could have been a mile long, maybe more, and it would keep growing until its airborne forge died.

"Welp," I said. "That's the coolest thing I've ever seen."

"Yeah," said Myantha, wonder in her eyes. She knelt on the bridge and opened her bag. "Could you give me a few minutes? I need to pray."

She tugged open a drawstring bag, withdrew a little stone die, kissed it, and let it fall. She traced a circle on the ground and whispered to the sky. I was deeply curious about what LB put into his liturgy, but even I wasn't enough of a creep to eavesdrop on prayer. Instead, I walked down the lip of the crevasse and stared at the sizzling iron, wishing I could crouch at her side, wishing I had the strength to pray to her god.

Even if I could, I don't think I'd have had anything to say.

She put her die away and coughed to let me know she was done.

I watched the iron drip one more time. No wonder LB had abandoned his studio—this was his canvas now. Here was proof of the Gray Lord's power, which Myantha never doubted, and of his genius, which Sondra made me question. An artist who would make something like this would never hurt his friends.

I mean, right?

We worked our way back to the middle road. It was clogged with old men and mothers, children and shamefaced teens. They were hungry, cold, cheeks rough with dried blood and dirt and tears. All of them looked the same.

WE FOUND GLITTERMORE NESTLED AGAINST THE WALLS OF A sheer rock canyon. Myantha had told me that when she left, it was a boomtown, where merchants gouged miners and miners made too much money to care. It was clear the boom was dead. Myantha's running commentary on the countryside—"I got drunk there," "I had sex there," "I got drunk and had sex over there,"—stopped. She began to walk very fast.

Garbage filled the road and fine rock dust caked everything. The banks of the creek were stained rust red. If it weren't for the monument, I wouldn't have believed there had been a town here at all.

Whoever carved the statue had talent. It showed the Gray Lord in the heat of battle—when did my brother ever dirty his hands with battle?—smashing a spear into the deformed head of a twisted, overgrown dog. LB's mouth was open in a hideous scream. His eye sockets were oddly deep, like they had once held jewels. Whatever filled them was gone now, replaced with painted red Xs. He looked devilish.

"Is he supposed to look so evil?" I said.

"Of course not. Someone has stolen his eyes."

Past the monument, skeletons lay in tidy lines, head to toe in every street. Rats had gotten to them. Myantha gave each one a close look, inspecting their jewelry, their boots. If she recognized anyone, she didn't say.

I should have called her back and told her what I knew, but everyone in the real world was so angry at me, I couldn't bear losing the only friend I had here. If I felt silly for developing such affection for an NPC, well, that was just a testament to how well LB shaped his game.

The town was in bad shape. Doors were missing. Every window was shattered. The buildings were all stone, with walls as thick as Zircon was wide. They were all coated in a thick layer of rock dust and grime, and anywhere water dripped, the poison's ochre stain marked the stone. Glittermore sloped up toward the canyon wall, growing steeper the deeper we went. Before long, Myantha was breathing hard. There was no other sound.

We turned down an alley so narrow that the sun disappeared. Dust churned like a motorboat's wake. Stained curtains hung in glassless windows. I nudged one aside and saw a low couch, a doll, cheery pictures on the walls. I let the curtain fall.

For the first time, Arabeth-me felt the same way Callie-me had felt all week: like my legs were lead, like if I sat down I'd never get back up. I pushed those feelings aside. Callie had completed the first stage of grief—being told by everyone you know that, "Grief just takes time, sweetheart,"—and gotten off to a flying start on the second: accusing half your friends of being murderers. But Arabeth mourned no one, and that meant I could postpone Stage Three—figuring out what the fuck grief actually is—as long as I was her.

Stay in character. Stay in character. Stay in character and it will all be fine.

Myantha was at the end of the block, leaning on a broken fence, staring at a faded pink cottage whose once-lavish garden was desiccated and gray. She didn't have to say it was her house. I put my hand on hers. It was cool, like plastic is supposed to be. She did not pull away.

"What happened here?" she said. "What does it take to kill a town?"

There was a well on the corner. We leaned inside to see the ring of rust above the waterline.

"Poison," I said.

"From where?"

"I don't know," I said. The lie came easily, and that just made it worse. "When we find the monks, we'll make sure they explain."

"I don't want to go in the house."

"That's why we've gotta."

Glass crunched under our feet. The house was cozy, with low ceilings and whitewashed adobe walls decorated with the prints of tiny hands. Myantha moved slowly, righting the upended furniture and straightening the rugs that covered the floor. I wanted to promise that her mother was okay, but I knew that would be a stupid thing to say.

When she had everything in some kind of order she took a deep breath and called, "Zara? Hey! It's your kid. I'm home."

The words died without an echo. No answer came.

"Come on," she said. "There's just a few more rooms."

We searched them. It didn't take long. The kitchen was empty. So were the bedrooms and the store room. Aside from the art on the walls, there was no sign anyone had ever lived here at all. When we were done, she leaned on the front window, staring into the deeply shadowed street.

"There's nothing," I said.

"God. It's hellish, isn't it, seeing the place you grew up

stripped down to bare walls? Like your whole childhood was just…nothing."

Her eyes were flat, her hand pressed tight against her forehead. It wasn't pleasant, seeing her so close to breaking, and so I told her what she wanted to hear.

"Maybe it's empty because they packed up and ran."

"You think that's likely?"

"Why not?"

She wanted to believe it, and so she did. By the time we reached the street, the idea had taken firm root. Her step was light and her eyes were a blue as pure and uncomplicated as the sky. She smacked her hands together.

"All right!" she said. "Let's find some evil monks!"

It got me moving. We tore through the ghost town, searching every house, every shop, every alley, every gutter, every heap of bones. I rapped floor boards, massaged the mortar between bricks, flipped mattresses, and nudged books. I found no hidden compartments, no tunnels, no messages, no sign of the path LB had left for me to follow. When we reached the last house on the last street, the sun was low and my quest was as dead as the town. I sat at the table in the back room, tracing figures in the dust—Zircon, Fausto, Phælandro, and the bard—as Myantha opened and closed cabinets we'd already searched twice. The room was filled with a vanished family's junk—old furniture, paintings, wadded bedding and summer clothes. Beside the back door was an altar—a few delicately painted figurines showing two mothers and two children, and a steel twenty-sided die.

"In the Iron Forest," I said, "when you prayed, what did you ask for?"

"The Game doesn't grant wishes. It's an opportunity to prove yourself to the Gray Lord, to show him that you're clever, that you're lucky, that you deserve his help."

"Does it work?"

"If you're asking to pray with me, the answer is no."

"But we've looked everywhere. We haven't found shit. No signs. No secrets. No story. I can't think of any other way forward, and we have to move forward, because if this is another dead end…"

I'd have to go back to the real world.

Myantha shook her head.

"I've been playing solo for a long time. And the idea of playing with you…"

Without knowing she was doing it, she rubbed her bicep, where Arabeth looked more heroic than I'd felt in a long time.

"It scares the hell out of me."

Once, I might have eviscerated an NPC for being so unhelpful. Today, it was easier to say okay. I stood up, ready to keep trudging forward, to crisscross the Plateau for as long as it took to find the missing monks, the answer to LB's riddles. I was bracing myself for an epic journey. I should have been watching my head.

The shutters above the table were open. My head smashed into the corner hard enough to shatter the wood. I don't care what level you are, that shit hurts.

"God damn it!" I said. I smacked the shutter closed—a feeble gesture, because it just bounced open again.

Myantha grabbed my hand.

"Do you see that?" she said.

"Huh?"

She pointed out the window, over the hedge to the shack in the neighbor's back yard.

"A shack," I said. "Did we search that shack?"

"We did not," she answered, and my skull didn't hurt anymore.

We hopped out the window and bounded across the back yard. As I vaulted over the hedge, I felt weightless, almost like I could leave my guilt behind.

The shack was unpainted and windowless, sagging wildly to one side. Myantha tore open the door. I followed her into a workroom decorated with a bench, a pile of rusted metal, and a rack of unfamiliar tools. We took tools off the wall at random, hoping they might open a secret compartment. None did. We poked around the fireplace, finding no secret messages or half-burned letters. The only interesting thing in that bleak little room was a door, about knee high. When Myantha nudged it open, we shared a look that told me she understood—whatever we were looking for was in that room, or it was nowhere at all.

We dropped to our knees.

"If there are any evil monks in there," she called, "watch out, 'cause we're coming in!"

We crawled into a store room where crooked shelves held canned fruits, jellies, and veg. Myantha snapped her fingers and clear white light floated up from her hands like smoke. It was just enough light for us to see the person in the corner of the room.

It had been a woman. An arm, a leg, and most of her face were gone—eaten by rats or something worse. Her fist clutched a jar of preserved meat spotted with mold and stinking of what I assumed was botulism. Her skin clung to her bones like saran wrap. She had been very hungry when she died.

"Oh my god," I said.

Myantha's eyes turned black. I'd never seen that before.

"Mom. It's Mom."

"Oh fuck. Oh god, Myantha, I'm sorry. I, I…"

All my words slipped away. I was left with nothing but the countless clichés I'd been subjected to since LB died.

I'm sorry for your loss.

They're in a better place.

Oh, honey. Grief just takes time.

I knew everything not to say, but it took me a full minute of clammy silence before I thought of the one thing that she—that I—might have wanted to hear.

"Would you like a minute alone?"

She nodded, lips pulled tighter than ever. I retreated to the workroom and shut the door behind me. Through the wood I heard her rolling her die. LB had put that body there for a reason. I had no clue what it was. He'd introduced me to Myantha for a reason, but I couldn't see that either. Ever since he died, he'd been wasting my time, and the only result was that this very kind NPC was hurting as bad as I did, and that made me hate him for the first time.

She was in there for a long time. Long enough for me to rehearse six or seven different ways to tell her the truth. Long enough for me to settle on the simplest one, the one that would make me look exactly as guilty as I was.

The die stopped rolling. Myantha crawled out of the storeroom.

"I need to tell you something," I said.

"We've got work to do first."

She yanked a pick-ax off the wall and chucked it at me. She grabbed a shovel. I followed her into the backyard.

We hacked a hole in the dirt. At first, it was easy, but the soil got rocky quick. For the first time since I'd slipped into this magnificent plastic body, I felt myself losing steam. Myantha did not slow. She dug fast and silent, and in no time at all we had a perfectly tidy grave.

We slid her mother out of the store room. Her skin was slippery and cold. She weighed almost nothing at all. We placed the body in the grave and piled in the dirt, working by the light that streamed from Myantha's hands. Burying this woman did nothing to unlace the knot of guilt in my stomach, but it was better than doing nothing at all.

When we were done, we put back the tools. I cracked my knuckles, trying to remember how my mea culpa was supposed to begin. Myantha stared at the empty hearth.

"The poison," I said.

She crouched in the fireplace and ran her fingertips across the stone. They came back clean.

"Have you ever seen such a tidy hearth?" she said.

"I haven't. The homeowners must be very proud. Can we talk now, please?"

"Whatever it is you're so hot to tell me, can it wait?"

"Why?"

"The chimney's bricked up. Not even, actually. It's like there was never a chimney at all."

"So what?"

"So lighting a fire in a workroom with no ventilation is a

quick way to die. Hand me the pick-ax."

I passed it to her, feeling my confession slip farther away. She reared back with the ax and smashed it into the bricks. She hit it again and again, chipping away but revealing nothing. I clenched my fists, desperate for there to be something hiding there, for all of this shit to mean something. But she found nothing. When she slumped backwards, panting and red-faced, and let the pick-ax drop, she looked beaten. I was not. I snatched the pick and smashed it so hard against the hearth that the handle splintered and the head went flying.

The bricks broke, too.

The dust cleared slowly, drifting across the room, sinking down beneath the level of the hearth—down into the hidden passage below.

Myantha clapped, and golden fireworks exploded out of her palms. By their light I could see that she was almost smiling. It felt good.

"Not bad," she said.

"You softened it up for me."

I kicked bricks until the entrance was wide enough, held my nose and jumped in. I didn't know what the hell we'd found, but it was something, and that was enough.

9

THE TUNNEL WAS MUDDY. THE SUPPORTS WERE SPONGY WITH ROT, and the air stank of dead plants.

"Light?" I said, and a long thread of liquid silver unspooled from Myantha's fingertips, just bright enough to show that there was nothing in here worth seeing. After a few minutes splashing through the muck we came to the main shaft. The tunnel stank of standing water. Far down the shaft, there was a soft orange glow. We followed it until it resolved into flickering light. The chanting of the faithful drifted up to meet us.

"Cultists," I said. "Classic."

Myantha jogged ahead. I hissed and she stopped. She stood not quite still, straining like an unhappily leashed pet. I'd never seen her so angry.

"Got a plan?" I said. "That sounds like a dozen monks, maybe more. The Gray Lord intended this battle to be fought by the entire party of Heroes. Instead it's just me."

"And me."

"Yeah." I cracked both wrists and slid an arrow into my bow. "I don't want you to die."

She chuckled. I tried to remind myself that she was just a

handful of numbers jotted down in one of my brother's note-books, but it was getting harder and harder not to care.

"If you think I'm going to stand back and let you do all the avenging, you're wrong. I lost my mother. I lost my god."

"And I know grief makes people do stupid shit. You fight as hard as you want, but when we're in there, leave the risky shit to me."

"Come on. Let's fuck 'em up."

We slipped into a cavern whose ceilings were high enough to hold a cathedral. Two dozen monks in purple robes knelt around a tower of glistening rock whose base had been hollowed into a forge. They all had the same round face, thick unibrow, and quivering jowls. One manned the bellows. Another read from a massive leather book that would have fit snugly at the Ronastery library. I guess that made him Brother Fisher.

"Twenty-four mad monks is no joke," I said. "They're going to have hooked daggers and wild spells and I don't even know what, and Fisher is going to outdo them all. This is going to be a bitch."

"I'm ready."

"Make me a promise."

"Yeah?"

"If I die, run."

She nodded. White light flowed from her fingertips to her elbows. I pulled my bowstring tight. We stepped out from behind the rock. Fisher's head snapped up. His eyes were sharp. He gave a little smile.

"I told you, brothers, the Heroes would come to disrupt our work."

"Sorry to disappoint you," I shouted, "but it's just me and my friend."

"It doesn't matter. The others will come in time."

He raised a pudgy finger. The monks stood. The light in Myantha's arms began to spin into the shape of her magic bow. It was too beautiful for this dismal room.

"We trained for this, brothers," said Fisher. "We prayed—"

It sounded like he had a whole villain's monologue prepared. I didn't have the time.

"Watch this," I told Myantha, and pointed my bow at the sky. "Pointed Rain."

I launched my arrow.

The shaft split into ten slender arrows that plunged into ten soft throats. The monks gurgled as they died.

The survivors charged—all but Fisher and the monk pumping the bellows. Myantha was about to loose an Arrow of Light when she saw what the monks had in their hands.

Nothing.

Well, that's not entirely true. A few had rocks; one guy had a pocketknife. But otherwise, they carried no weapons at all.

Myantha fired her arrow at the ceiling. It sprayed little tufts of flame across the ceiling.

"Your aim's getting worse," I said.

She tried to force me to lower my bow. I didn't let her.

"They are unarmed."

"I saw."

They were also almost on top of us. One of the guys with a rock had his eyes on Myantha. He raised his weapon high.

"So let them live," she hissed.

"That's not how this works."

"Arabeth—"

"Think of your mother."

It wasn't a gentle thing to say, but I guess by then I was playing dirty. Myantha fell back and I emptied my quiver, scattering a few more corpses around the wide stone room. Blood flowed like a dam had burst. The rest of the monks continued their charge. Maybe these scrubs couldn't hurt me, but they would tear her apart. I couldn't have that.

I swapped bow for knife and flung myself into the mob, so happy to have no more questions to answer, no more feelings to feel, nothing to do but fight.

I spun through them like a tornado. I cut a throat. I sliced a belly. I rolled on the slick red rock, severing tendons as I went, then leapt up and slashed their wrists, just to be sure.

I'd never felt so one with Arabeth. This was her, this was

me, both of us doing exactly what we needed to do. The monks were terrified, and I was as calm as bedrock—just like a marksman should be. At least I thought I was, until I heard myself scream.

"Fuck you!" I shouted.

"Fuck you for making me love you!"

"Fuck you for having to die."

So maybe I wasn't quite as cool as I thought.

The guy with the pocketknife came for me. I saw what he was planning and leaned into it, inviting him to bury his blade in my side. A long second before he made contact, I swept my arm up and smashed his knife into his heart. That was the closest any of them came to dealing damage.

Suddenly, there was only one left, on his knees, fat little hands covering fat little eyes. He was talking, but I didn't have to listen any more. I stabbed him in the back of the neck as I walked past. He fell, but there were so many corpses that he didn't even hit the floor.

Blood dripped down my arms. Once I was reasonably sure none of it was mine, I glanced back and saw Myantha at the mouth of the cavern, slouched against the wall, still looking like the coolest girl in school. She didn't step forward or back. She just stared.

I was about to go to her when Brother Fisher coughed, and I remembered I was in the middle of a boss fight. Feelings could wait.

"It's the book you want?" said Fisher. His voice was hoarse, like a telethon host sagging across the finish line. The acolyte at his feet did not let the bellows rest. His sweat glowed orange in the light of the forge.

"I hear it's a hell of a read."

He closed the book. Grinning like we were chummy co-workers, he offered it to me. The veins in his arms bulged with the effort of holding it. Shadows danced wildly across his face.

I reached for the book. He hurled it into the fire. It hissed, almost like it was screaming, burst into flame and was gone.

"Well jeez," I said, "you don't have to be a dick about it."

"You think we don't matter," he said, rubbing his hands like he was warming up for something big. "The Gray Lord thought the same. We taught him otherwise."

"So you did kill him."

"We helped. Many from our world collaborated, and one from yours."

"Matty Barber? Doc Mingori? Sondra? Craig?"

Fisher just smiled. Oh well. If this were easy, it wouldn't be any fun.

"Are we fighting or what?" I said.

The man on the forge snatched something from the fire and dropped it into a bucket. Sizzle.

"Our work is done," said Fisher. "And you're done, too."

He raised his hands and gave his nastiest stare. His veins glowed neon. Red light collected in his hands. His minions had been nothing but a warm-up. This guy had power, and he wanted me to know it.

"It's awfully rude to kill your gods," I said.

"You are no god of mine."

I wrenched an arrow out of the nearest corpse. My mouth ached. I was thirsty, honest to god thirsty, to find out what he'd throw at me. I was ready to finish this. I was ready for a fucking fight.

The pressure dropped. My ears popped. Bloody light swirled from his fingertips as my blood-slick fingers struggled to cozy the arrow against my bowstring. I wasn't going to make it. I braced for pain.

"Feel our wrath!" he howled, and drew back his arm. The light from his fingers scribbled out the shape of a bow and arrow. The missile struck me in the chest.

It hurt.

Almost.

I'd guess two, maybe three HP.

"What?" I shouted. "That's your opener? Arrow of Light! That's your fucking move?"

He didn't answer. His face was blank. I couldn't tell if he was disappointed, if he really thought that starter kit trash would bring me down.

I took my shot.

Fisher's skull burst like a rotten plum. His body crumpled. A crit, maybe. Or maybe this dude just sucked.

As his blood sprayed across the forge, the last monk finally got the message that the fight wasn't going his way. He bolted, but there was really nowhere for him to go. I grabbed him by the jaw and let his own momentum snap his neck. It made a very small sound.

The water in the bucket quit steaming. At the bottom, I found a hunk of iron, a little bigger than a walnut, covered in tiny facets. There were no numbers on it, but I didn't have to count to know how many sides it had.

"A d20. Weird."

It went into my adventurer's bag.

Something smelled wrong. This fight hadn't just been easy—it was a joke. I tried to picture LB leaning back in his chair, holding back a smile as he waited for us to put the pieces together, to spot the trap, the ambush, the twist. I was better than anyone at guessing what he was thinking—he loved it and it drove him nuts, all at once—but in that moment I had nothing.

Myantha put her hand on my shoulder. It was as cold and soft as silk.

"Who's Matty Barber?" she said.

"You wouldn't know him."

"Doc? Sondra? Craig? What are those names?"

"Give me ten minutes, okay?"

"For what?"

"There's something else here. There has to be."

I looked around. Saw nothing but her flickering, furious eyes.

"Those monks were unarmed," she said.

"I thought you wanted vengeance. Did you think it would be pretty?"

"I came for a fight. Not a massacre."

I knelt beside Fisher, pulled open his robe, emptied his

purse. I found nothing but a few stray coppers and a scroll containing his pathetic final spell.

Myantha watched me go down the line, rooting through pockets and purses, finding a healing potion, some herbs, a few more pitiful coppers. The bodies stank of shit. Everything I touched was covered with viscera, gristle, and flecks of broken bone. I ignored it. My hands moved automatically, snatching what was valuable and tossing the rest. My brain was replaying Fisher's pathetic Arrow of Light, his lame ass death. That was no way to end a campaign. LB was fucking with me again.

"What the fuck is wrong with you?" said Myantha. She smacked her bicep. Her tattoo flushed red. "She protects the weak. She doesn't kill them."

I pushed past her. She tried to stop me, but I wasn't having it, and level 12 means I can do what I fucking want. I had one more body to search. This guy's purse contained the same junk as everyone else's. His face was just as flat; his eyes just as dead.

"This is bullshit," I said. Myantha just stared. "God damn it, there has to be another clue, another lead. I cannot take another dead end."

As I said it, I tore off the monk's sandals, gave them a quick glance and tossed them aside. He had warm wool socks that told me nothing in particular, and coarse, oft-patched pants belted with a thin brown rope that didn't mean anything either. I ripped them off his corpse and threw them on the pile. I flipped him onto his face—they were so light, all of them, so easy to toss around—and yanked off his robe. I dug my knife into its seams and pulled, splitting the fabric like it was wet Kleenex and revealing absolutely fuck all.

"What's next?" said Myantha. "Cut his gut open and search his stomach?"

"God damn it," I said, and chucked the robe to the floor. It landed on the corpse, half covering it and offering no dignity at all. Whatever. The light of the forge was just bright enough, though, that I saw something stitched into the collar.

The thing I'd been missing.

The thing I hadn't wanted to see.

It said, "Zeg."

"What's a Zeg?" I said. Myantha didn't answer, which was certainly for the best.

Zeg

I went down the line, jerking their robes back and checking inside the collar. Every one bore a different word.

Ralno.

Mankin.

Carn.

Delaga.

Shach.

Xail.

Names.

"Oh fuck," I whispered. "Oh fuck, oh fuck, oh fuck."

I looked back at the cannon fodder I'd cut down so easily. Their blood dripped down my forearms. The odors of their death stung my nose.

Not monsters. Not bad guys. Not NPCs. Just people.

They all had names.

Of course they did, because this wasn't a game. This had never been a game.

Myantha stared through me, worshipful no more.

I whipped up the monocle up and slammed the button down.

I CRASHED BACK INTO THE JCCAD BATHROOM. MY HEAD CRACKED against the paper towel dispenser. I fell to my knees, pressed knuckles into tile, and filled the toilet with vomit. I spat a wad of puke-flavored phlegm into the bowl and wiped away hot tears and hot snot on my hoodie's sleeve.

Twenty-four dead. Twenty-four by my hand.

Oh fuck oh fuck oh fuck.

Matty banged on the door.

And that was only tonight. How many had I killed since I rolled up Arabeth? How many soldiers, how many bandits, how many hapless scrubs who just made the mistake of getting in my way?

There was the session we tricked a family of farmers into setting their own house on fire because we needed light to cross their field. We promised them money to repair the damage, but when we were clear of their crops, we ran.

I'm a monster.

There was the time we snuck into the encampment of the Army of Skulls, and Fausto tricked a soldier into placing a deadly curse on his unit's food supply, killing dozens. When he saw what he'd done, the man cut his wrists.

We are all monsters.

There was the unforgettable evening Phælandro botched a fireball, blowing up an enchanted swamp and coating an entire valley with thousands of gallons of toxic sludge.

Sin, folks. That's the only word for it. Irredeemable sin.

"Oh, man, fucking hundreds of people are going to die because of this," said LB. "There's gonna be birth defects, cancer, all kinds of shit for, like, generations. A lot of birds will die, too."

He had to fight to be heard over the table's hysterical laughter. He was grinning, too. He loved when we fucked up, and we loved it even more.

All sins will be forgiven. No sins will be forgiven.

LB knew. He must have known, and he let us play. He encouraged us to stay in character, rewarded us with XP and gold. He made it fun. The best GM in the world.

He was so, so much worse than we could have known.

"You dying in there or what?" said Matty.

"I'm fine," I barked, and threw up quite a bit more. When there was nothing left to give, I slumped between toilet and wall. I blew my nose and spat until my mouth was dry.

I reached for the ChapStick that lives in my right pocket. My fingers were numb, and I had to stand to get them into my pants. They found something. It wasn't ChapStick. It was the cast iron d20, a souvenir from another world.

Another mystery. Who fucking cares?

I put it back, sorted out the ChapStick, and tried to pretend properly moisturized lips made me feel less vile.

Matty waited in the hallway, huge hands in huge pockets, wearing a tortured smile.

"What happened to you?" he said.

"Poor decisions."

He led me to the vending machine and bought me a ginger ale. I could not feel the metal can. My puke-coated mouth couldn't handle the sugar. I took a small sip and let the drink dangle at my side.

"You all right?" he said.

"I thought I was doing okay, but I'm a fucking mess. Probably have been for a long time."

He gave me a hug. The man had arms like freight cars, and the weight of them crushed me into his chest hard enough that for a moment I could not feel anything else. I could have suffocated in there. I wouldn't have complained.

"I'm sorry," I said, "for, well..."

"Saying I murdered my boss?"

"Yeah."

"Still think I did it?"

"Who knows? But you can suspect someone of murder without being a pill about it."

"I'm going to stitch that on a sampler for you."

I padded down the thin gray carpet, looking out the long line of windows into the invisible night. The light was as cold as I was. It seemed grossly unfair that I was allowed to pass through this extremely normal hallway after what my hands had done.

Matty held the door open for me, just like he always did, letting in the tang of bonfire, the sweet stink of mulch, the murmur of one of the waterfalls that littered the campus. I deserved none of it.

His little round glasses fogged up. He was ready for me to leave—had been for a while—but I was not prepared to face night in Jett Creek.

"Did we do good?" I said.

"What?"

"In the game—we were heroes, but did we do good?"

"We killed a lot of monsters."

"We killed a lot of people, too. Hundreds of them, and we were laughing the whole time."

"But none of them were real."

"What if they were? What would that make us?"

"War criminals, I guess."

For a second, he felt doubt. Perhaps he thought of Glittermore, of what we'd done there. Perhaps he remembered the words he'd written in his confession and considered the hell that would await if what he'd put down were real. Such thoughts cannot be endured for long. He put his smile back on.

"Does this mean you want to keep playing?" he said.

"I'm through with games. For good."

I dug into my pocket for the iron d20.

"Can you check this for me?"

"Check it? For what?"

"Just...what kind of iron is it? Is it, I don't know, weird?"

"Sure," he said, chuckling. "I'll run a full battery of tests. Break out the crime lab and everything. I love you, Callie. Go home."

I unstuck my foot and the door swung shut. He turned toward the forge, and I tried to find the strength to walk to my car.

The lock clicked.

Behind me, Matty screamed.

I spun around. His eyes locked with mine. I'd never seen anyone look so afraid.

His hip was on fire. He smacked at it, and the flames spread up and out. He tried to tear off his pants, but his hands were already burning. He got one into his pocket and pulled out the d20, which burnt like a tiny sun, pouring flame down his arms, around his chest, and to his beautiful heart.

The door was locked, of course. Campus security is very strict these days. I fumbled for LB's ID, but my numb fingers were too stupid to swipe it cleanly. It fell to the ground. So did Matty. He got up on his elbows. Even through the thick glass, I heard him call my name.

I had Arabeth in my back pocket and the monocle around

my neck. I pressed that button and his agony stopped long enough for my molten portal to take me somewhere I had the power to save this man's life.

I WAS RIGHT WHERE I'D BEEN A FEW MINUTES EARLIER, STARING into Myantha's icy eyes. Before she could continue laying into me, things began to change.

A fireball belched out of the forge, wrapping the oven in a column of flame that went all the way to the cavern's roof. And there I saw my friend.

Matty hung in mid air—not Zircon, who was built for punishment, but sweet, gentle Matty Barber, who was not made for this world. He writhed in the fire, trying to crawl away but finding no purchase, still screaming Callie's name.

Myantha raised her hands for Arrow of Light. I batted them down.

"Just run. Seriously, get the fuck out of here. Go!"

She'd never heard panic in my voice. It got her attention. She ran.

At the bottom of the forge, Brother Fisher's headless corpse was on its knees, fire pouring out of his shattered jaw. I put an arrow in his chest, and another, and another, but still the fire spewed and still Matty howled my name. He burned, hot enough for his glasses to burst and his skin to melt, still alive.

"Let him go or let him die!" I said, and the flame began to shift. The jet of fire that held Matty in the air bloomed across the ceiling, dripped down the walls, and flooded the floor like spreading cement. Little pops sounded as the corpses burst, one by one, into flames. I raced ahead of the liquid fire and took shelter on the little platform that surrounded the forge. Fire lapped over the edge. I would not be safe for long.

I tried to breathe, to remember how easy this had felt when it was just a game. I opened my eyes and recognized where I stood.

The bare floor.

The slit windows.

The long table.

The intricate carvings on every surface.

The fire had formed itself into the church from my night-mares, ten times bigger than was sane. At the head of it sat a monstrous image of my brother's corpse, which looked quite at home among the flames.

More fire billowed out. It flickered into the shape of a woman, twenty feet tall or more. She wore an eye patch and a ponytail, and her arms looked big enough to choke out the world. She strode across the floor, each step sending up the crackling stench of burnt flesh, and drew a knife of flame from her hip.

I fired an arrow through her heart. It exploded into dust and fell, sparking, to the floor.

She looked down at me, her one eye an orange, pupil-less wall, then slashed her colossal knife into Matty's gut. His screams became inhuman. She worked it up his chest, shattering bone and shredding what remained of his skin, until she sliced him in two.

He fell, a cinder. I ran to his side. There was nothing left. I retrieved one of my arrows from Fisher's corpse. The woman sneered, and she said my name. My true name.

"Callie Myles."

The arrow fell out of my hand. I tore open my adventurer's bag, looking for a spell or potion or anything that could save me from what was coming. Her blade swept down from the ceiling. It split me. The stink of my own scorching flesh filled my nose.

That was the first time I learned how it felt to die.

I woke on the cold wet grass of the college campus. I could barely breathe. Across the lawn, LB's building burned. Somewhere, too far away, there were sirens. I twisted against the unyielding earth, trying to crawl inside it, looking for anything that could keep me warm. The world was on fire and I had never been so cold.

10

FIVE STRANGERS MEET IN AN INN AT THE EDGE OF THE WORLD.

Mage. Thief. Gladiator. Bard. Marksman.

Over hot sausages and cold ale, they pledge to fight their way north to battle the Queen of Skulls, righting wrongs as they go. The thief attempts to charm the innkeeper into giving him a kiss. She answers by dumping a stein of ale down his pants, fixing him as the butt of the group's jokes until the night he dies.

While the new friends cackle at the sodden thief, bloody screams come from outside the inn. The newly-minted Heroes snatch up their weapons and charge outside to fight.

Nasty little cliff-men with squeaky voices and beady eyes swarm the village square, trilling a bawdy war song as they slaughter the innocent. With mud and steel, arrow and knife, the Heroes fight them off. When they are done, they loot the corpses. The marksman finds a Ring of Wayfinding, which they use to track the cliff-men to their beach-side caves. The villains beg for mercy, but it is too late. The Heroes kill them all. They head north and never look back.

Arabeth killed four cliff men that day. I know because I put a tally at the top of the sheet for each victim. By the time our second session was done, I'd quit counting my dead. In the year and change that I'd played her, there had been hundreds more.

War criminals.

I reviewed session after session in my mind, trying to picture those I'd killed. When I finished, I went back to the top. It didn't take long to replay the tape. You can think pretty quick when you're flat in a hospital bed, hooked up to enough cables and monitors and little dripping bags that you couldn't move even if you had the life to do so.

I'd been there about three days. A parade of weary residents expressed horror at a body temperature so low, I should be dead already. They treated my burns, but they wouldn't let me leave until my temp went up and I remembered how to talk. They put medicine into me. I slept.

You know you're doing great when you hear doctors throwing around the word catatonia. I think they were being a little dramatic. Yeah, I looked right through them, and did the same to everybody who came to say hello—Jill and Doc and even Craig and my poor fucking mom, whose eyes were as rough and dark as the pit of a peach, and who just stared until she had to leave.

I wanted to tell her I was okay, but that was a lie. I don't know precisely what kind of daughter she'd planned on raising, but I didn't think she was going for mass murderer.

But it was LB's fault.

It was your fault.

But it was Arabeth.

It was you.

So I'm not a doctor or anything, but I don't think I was catatonic. I was busy. Busy remembering the smell of the corpses in the cavern. Their blood, their shit. The sounds they made when they died. I was trying to add up all the lives Arabeth's arrows and knife had converted into XP, all the monsters and demons and bandits and guards and goons and ordinary fucking people whom I'd murdered just for fun. I tried to pay my respects and let them go. I tried to do the same thing for Matty, that poor dope, for Myantha's mother, even for LB. But no matter how often I impaled myself on my guilt and my grief, I never felt ready to stand.

When I slept I saw the woman with the eye patch, human-sized and fully flesh. She chased me through the hallways of Jett Creek High and over the ramparts of Blackbriar Keep, along rocky ridges that alternated between stunted Winterwind evergreens and towering Smoky Mountain spruce. She gave no clue as to who the hell she was, where she came from, or what I'd done to make her hate me so bad.

Finally, my dreams brought me back to the white church on the hill. As always, I went inside. As always, someone I loved was burning at the table, but this time it wasn't LB. It was Sondra, Doc, and Craig. It was Matty, too, still twisting in the agony that I had dropped into his hand.

The woman with the eye patch sat me at the table. She handed me the lighter. I flicked it and guided it to my chest. The fire was licking the zipper on my sweater when she smacked me in the face. The lighter skidded across the floor. The woman shouted: "Caledonia Elizabeth Myles, get out of that goddamned bed or you're going to miss the bus."

"I'm up!" I said, and the dream was gone, and I was back in my hospital bed, watching Mom clap her hands and cry.

"I knew you were in there," she said, and she gave me a hug that didn't stop until my hospital gown was damp with her tears. "Never again, kid, never do that again."

"I'm sorry."

"Don't be, baby. It's been a shitty couple weeks. We could all stand three days in a vibrating bed."

"It doesn't vibrate. It just goes up and down."

"Then what the fuck are they charging you so much for?"

No wonder both her kids turned out to be assholes—Priscilla Myles could joke her way through hell.

I tried to sit up. What muscles I had hurt like crazy. I matched Mom's fake smile.

"They decide what's wrong with me?" I said.

"Shock. Say it's normal when people keep burning to death

in front of you. I say it sucks."

"And Matty?"

"DOA, same as Bobby. Funeral's tonight."

Her forehead tightened as she pushed back against however that made her feel.

"I should be there," I said. "It's my fault he's—"

"Bullshit. And even if it weren't, well, guilt is a wasted emotion. Now cheer the fuck up. I've got magazines."

She pulled out a stack of supermarket tabloids. Brad Pitt and Jennifer Aniston beamed at me from the top of the pile. I couldn't match their enthusiasm.

"What do the police think happened?" I said. "They get that it was murder, right? That LB and Matty were killed by the same person?"

"Now how would I know what those detectives think?"

"Moms know things."

She let out a Mom-grade sigh and quit trying to be fun.

"Doc gave me the whole story," she said. "The police say accident, no question. Blame the whole thing on shoddy safety standards in the metalworking department. That detective girl you went to school with?"

"Leah."

"She called that forge a fire waiting to happen."

"But the fire didn't start by the forge—we were at the front door."

She shrugged, which was her way of telling me to shut up. I suddenly felt crushingly hungry. A craving for peanut butter and jelly flashed across my brain, and I remembered the first time I ever met Matty, when I made an off-hand comment about how I'd never have any real problems as long as I didn't run out of PB&J. The next time I saw him, he gave me a peanut butter and jelly sandwich made of iron, small enough to fit in my hand.

"Now you'll never have to worry about running out," he said, and I knew he was too good for this world.

I wanted to tell Mom about that. I wanted to tell her a lot of things. But if I said one more word about Matty I would start to cry, and neither of us could stand that, so I submitted to her attempts to make me feel better and tried to forget about friends and food.

We spent an hour flipping through her magazines, cackling at the stupid shit famous people wear on the red carpet. By the time my mom blitzed through the People crossword puzzle, visiting hours were just about closed. She left the magazines and slipped my cell phone into my hand.

"You're not supposed to have phones in here. Nurses think it'll mess with the equipment, like one plastic telephone is going to break all this high tech shit. Fuck 'em. If you need me, if you're lonely, if it's three a.m. and the machines' beeping is driving you crazy, you call and I'll make you feel better."

I kissed her. She left.

I imagined my rules for the monocle, composed so confidently just a few days before. I slashed out Rule Number 3—the one about how Winterwind was "just a game"—and added two more.

5. It's not a game, dipshit.

6. But it is trying to kill you.

I looked at the clock. The second hand rounded the twelve. I gave myself one more minute to wallow.

"You're a killer," I muttered. "A monster. A sociopath. A war criminal and a sloppy dresser, too."

That ate fifteen seconds.

"Matty Barber was the sweetest man to ever come down from the mountains of North Carolina. He burned until his skin melted and his organs burst. If you hadn't given him that iron d20, he'd be alive."

That brought the second hand past the six.

"If there's a hell, you're in trouble, because for what you've done, you don't get forgiven. But you've still gotta atone."

Fifteen seconds left. Make it count.

"There's a wizard with an eye patch that's killing your friends. You gotta find her and stop her before anybody else dies. You gotta finish this quest. Wake up, Callie. Get the fuck out of bed."

My minute was done.

I poked Jennifer Aniston in the face. She kept smiling.

"Well, Jesus," I said, "if rich white celebrities can be that happy, maybe life is worth living."

I dialed a number and said, "Meet me in the hospital parking lot in twenty minutes. Bring clothes and chips."

I got up. My legs felt like jelly. I walked anyway, out of the room and down the hall, ignoring every nurse who yelled at me and every doctor who gave me the stink-eye until I got downstairs, where a chinless administrator screeched "Ma'am!" loud enough that I had to stop.

"Yeah?"

My voice was a little bit slurred. I couldn't tell if it was from the effort of walking on dormant legs or if there had been something heavy in those IV bags.

"You can't just walk out of the hospital."

"But I'm all better now."

"You haven't been discharged."

"Mark it on your form. Callie Myles discharged herself."

"We have to talk about your bill."

"Oh, don't worry about that. I don't have insurance, so I was definitely never going to pay. Goodbye."

He started to get out from behind his desk. I pointed a finger as straight as one of Arabeth's arrows, and bellowed: "Sit the fuck down."

He sat. Nifty, huh?

"I've killed at least five hundred people. With bow, knife, magic, my bare hands. You do not want to mess with me today."

I don't know what he did next. I strutted out the sliding doors and felt cold spring air dancing up my far-too-exposed thighs. The Scarcemobile screeched up. A pair of sweatpants thudded into my chest.

"Put those on," said Jill, "before you drive me into a frenzy of ill-advised lust."

I pulled on the pants, climbed into her car, and put on a faded UT basketball t-shirt that was so big it must have belonged to her dad. Four bags of Ruffles waited on the dashboard, alongside my pickle lighter and a Camel. I lit it, dropped the hospital gown out the window, and told her to drive.

"Matty's funeral?" she said. "I guess I didn't dress you for church."

"I'm maxed out on funerals. I need to talk to the police."

She shrugged like that was normal. Waiting for the light at the edge of the parking lot, she drummed on the steering wheel.

"You ever talk to Craig?" she said.

"What?"

"I was thinking about seducing the dirty hippie."

"Trust me, you don't want to. He's a total poser. I don't even think he's that dirty. He went to business school."

"Oh, that's disgusting." She swung into traffic. "I can work with that."

In the stained concrete rectangle that housed the fearless Jett Creek PD, I found the leading light of our detective squad investigating a takeout salad. She picked out a piece of steak, ate it, and went looking for more.

"You're supposed to eat the vegetables," I said.

"Vegetables suck."

According to the rules, murder was Leah's problem, not mine. It was hard to believe this woman could help me, but before I pushed on alone, I wanted to see what would happen if I tried telling someone the truth.

I took a chair. I would have put my feet on her desk, but I'd forgotten to ask Jill for shoes, and I didn't need Leah Sparks judging my toes. She scowled at my shirt.

"Go Vols," she said.

"Rah rah."

"Are you the same Callie Myles who just skipped out on a freaking huge hospital bill, threatening staff on the way out?"

"I only threatened the one guy."

"What are you doing here?"

"Did you find it?"

"Did I find what?"

"The thing in Matty's fist."

With an extremely cop-like grunt, she pulled open a squeaking metal drawer. Inside, among a mess of plastic silverware, tampons, kleenex, snack bars, hair ties, newspaper, and badly rumpled spare clothes, was a flat disc of iron, just like she'd found on LB's corpse.

"Do you want to know what that is?" I said.

She snatched one more piece of steak out of her salad, pushed the rest aside, and picked up a legal pad.

"Fire away."

"My brother was killed by a secret society of mystical monks." I waited for Leah to laugh. When she didn't, I kept going. "They were in league with, maybe even working for, a woman with an eye patch. I don't know her name."

"Where are these monks from?"

"Good question! It's not our reality—it's in the game we play. Only, guess what, it's not a game. That monocle LB wore is magic—it takes him to this other world, which looks like a plastic model but is actually real."

Leah wrote "Magic Monocle" in big letters and drew a box around it. I wasn't sure if that was good or bad. I pressed on.

"LB set himself up there like he was a god. *Apocalypse Now* shit."

"I never saw it."

"It's about this soldier who—nevermind. Some of the people—"

"The monks?"

"Yeah, and other people too I think, they got sick of him and used magic, powerful magic, to kill him in their world and in ours. One of the people I play games with, either Sondra, Craig, or Doc, helped them do it."

"Not Matty?"

"Whoever killed LB killed Matty too, but I think I was the target. That metal disc used to be an iron d20."

She made the face people usually make when you say "d20."

"A twenty-sided die," I said. "I traveled from their world to ours, and it came with me. I think it serves as a kind of homing beacon for their spell. I know this sounds, like, less than sane, but it's the truth. You're not writing this down."

"It doesn't seem worth the ink."

"You and I were never friends, Leah, but I always thought you were smart for a cop."

"Fuck you."

In high school, Leah had been threateningly beautiful: the kind of pretty that was hard to look at, like the sun. For the first time maybe ever, I took a long look at her. Her hair was greasy, and it was weeks since her blouse had seen an iron. She looked as tired as me.

"I see two possibilities," she said. "One is, you're right. A magical conspiracy is killing the roleplayers of Jett Creek. It'd take a great wizard to solve that kind of problem, and that ain't me. Or you're nuts, like your brother, and I need to have you taken back to the hospital for an intense psych eval."

"Two close friends died in freak fires. Isn't that enough to start asking questions?"

"If you want me to rip up our coroner's reports, call this a murder, and start from scratch, I can. But in a typical investigation, you know who'd be the natural suspect? The girl who was at both fires. Is that how you want it?"

I shook my head. She shrugged. It was a very cop gesture. I wonder if they learned it at cop school.

"A few days ago," I said, "I saw you and Doc talking on JCCAD campus. What was it about?"

"Private cop stuff."

"Tell me anyway?"

"I can't comment on open cases."

"You said these are accidents, no question. Doesn't that mean case closed?"

She chuckled. Either she was a little bit impressed or she realized I wasn't going to leave until she gave me something useful.

"The afternoon before Bobby died," she said, "a gardener on Prewitt saw Doc at the studio. I went to ask what she was doing there and why she'd kept it to herself."

"What'd she say?"

"She wouldn't answer."

"So why didn't you make her?"

"This isn't *24*. If someone won't answer a question, there's not much I can do."

"I had no idea our local cops were such wimps."

She put her pad back in her desk and renewed her attack on her salad. I didn't blame her for skipping the veggies. The lettuce was far past dead.

"I always wanted to play games with you, you know that?" she said.

"Yeah?"

"When all the other kids were doing homework or eating lunch or rushing off to get to, whatever, soccer practice, you and your friends were taking up half the hallway, rolling dice and laughing your asses off. It looked fun."

"Why didn't you ask to play?"

"Because I knew that no matter how fun it looked, none of it was real. Go home, Myles."

"Think you could loan me a pair of shoes?"

She pulled one from the lost and found: oversized men's sneakers to go with my circus tent shirt. I trudged toward home.

THE HILL WAS SLIGHT, BY JETT CREEK STANDARDS, BUT IT MADE my atrophied calves scream. I turned onto Collins Place, a sleepy one-way street that runs past the long defunct Mickelthwaite-Collins Mill. I turned a corner and was treated to one of those miracles of Jett Creek: a skinny waterfall slipping from a crack in the rocks to crash into the icy pond below.

It had been a while since I thought about high school. I never saw those kids anymore, but I remembered every character they ever played. The games felt fresh then and life did too, like the crack of a book when you open it for the first time. We didn't know what idiots we were.

Somewhere, far away, people wanted me dead. For my crimes, they had every right. I watched that ceaseless water and felt the spray on my face and knew that no matter how much I deserved to die, I did not want to leave this behind.

I walked home thinking about level 1, about the first characters I created, the first villains I killed. There is nothing like learning a new game, when the rules knit in your mind and what had been an impenetrable wad of text becomes a system, spinning as elegantly as the stars in the sky. If I wanted to make up for what I'd done—if I wanted my friends to live—I had a quest to finish, and I'd have to start from scratch.

ARABETH'S FACE SHOWED NO GUILT. HER SHOULDERS WERE straight; her brown eyes shone brightly, and the edges of her mouth still curved upward to make the faintest, coldest smile. I'd put a lot into this mini. So many coats of paint, so many hours with my finest brushes, finessing detail after detail until my eyes watered and my hands cramped and I pressed on because I knew that the more real I made her, the better the game would be, and the game was all I had.

I'd fallen into her all the way. When I needed to feel nothing, she let me. When I needed control, she gave me power no person deserves. I had killed with those tiny plastic hands. From the moment I stepped into her body at Blackbriar Keep, I was choking guardsmen and dangling librarians out of windows. I couldn't do that anymore.

I brought the hammer down hard. She exploded into shards, the smallest of which fell to the carpet, where they would stay for all time.

I put on a tape of dreamy '80s synth pop, snapped on the bright white light above my work table, and set out my paints. From the bin under the table I took an unopened mini. I clipped her out of her plastic frame, glued her together, and got to work. I forced myself to work fast, painting with a fat brush, laying on paint so thick that it pooled in her eye sockets, in the tops of her boots, in the crooks of her arms.

While I was waiting for her to dry, the tape ran out. I flipped it over. Once again, there were LB's slanted Ls and cramped little Os. "For Callie. Real good shit. 8/8/99."

I put the tape away.

When the paint was dry, I looked at what I'd done. The bow in her hand looked like a kids' toy. Her hair was a cheap wig. I wanted to strip the paint off and start again, but there wasn't time for that. As a concession to my perfectionism, I reached for one of my finer brushes, dipped it in my light brown, and touched up her eyes. Two quick strokes, and there she was. She was everything I loved about marksmen, everything I'd made Arabeth to be: decisive, dangerous, silent, the type who got shit done without anyone ever knowing they were there. She was Arabeth's little sister. She'd be just as tough, but with a pure heart. I named her Arabelle.

I placed her on a map of Glittermore, squeezed the monocle, and said a prayer to the Gray Lord. I pressed the button. Hot iron swept me into another world.

11

THE SCENE WAS AS I'D LEFT IT—A CHURCH OF FIRE, AN EVIL ONE-eyed inferno-lady, a couple dozen senselessly murdered corpses burning on the floor, etc.—but only for a moment. Before Arabelle could take her first breath, the cavern sucked back the fire like someone swallowing a burp. I was in a large, empty kiln, and the heat fled fast.

I flexed, and found my new body less ostentatiously muscled than Arabeth's. I might have been an inch or so shorter, too. The leap into this form wasn't as seamless as the first time I'd gone into Arabeth. That made sense, I guess—I'd been pretending to be Arabeth for so long that when I finally got the chance to do it for real, I anticipated the tension in her shoulders, the way her fingers danced up and down her bow, the ease with which she slipped a knife into a stranger's windpipe. Arabelle chafed like a new pair of boots. Maybe it was the quickie paint job, or maybe it was because this time I knew it wasn't for pretend. I was here to do whatever I could to save my tattered soul.

I forced myself to march over to the heap of massacred monks, whose bodies had melted into a mess of plasticky flesh, like when you put Barbie in the microwave. I tightened my gloves and dragged one of them—Carn? Ralno?—shoulder to shoulder with the one beside him. The fire had softened their flesh, and my fingers sank into them like I'd grabbed a fistful of silly putty. Nausea and guilt—two things Arabeth had never bothered feeling—swept over me, and I gripped them tight. Feeling like shit was the right thing to do.

I kept going until my victims made a ragged line. I lifted the remains of Brother Fisher and the forge-tender and put them with the others. I wanted to cover them with rocks, but level 1 was wimpier than level 12, and I was winded. Instead, I crossed their arms and put a single rock above each of their heads. It looked like shit, but there you go.

When the fire dropped him, Matty fell to a heap beside the unlit forge. His corpse was mangled, and it took everything I had to straighten him out.

I'd spent three days in the hospital trying to say goodbye to him. I still wasn't ready to let him go, but now was the time. I kissed my hand and forced myself to press it to the lump of charcoal that had been Matty's sweet face.

"I'm sorry I skipped your funeral," I said. "That was shitty of me. I'm sorry that you died."

The words left my mouth and vanished, and he was still dead.

Arabeth got the same treatment she'd given so many others. I pulled off her boots, her bracers, her golden mail, her cap, her adventurer's bag. I even took her rings. I did not kiss her. I did not say goodbye. Mostly, I tried to not look at her face. She looked too much like Callie Myles.

I walked until I reached the false chimney. I dragged myself out of the hole. I knew that on the other side—if I was lucky—I'd find the person I'd hurt most of all. In the back yard of the abandoned house, Myantha sat with her knees pulled up to her chin, rolling a die beside her mother's grave. I'd buried a brother and it hurt like nothing I'd ever known, but as I watched her toss her d20, I felt Mom's hand squeezing mine. I was the reason this girl's mother was dead. I couldn't make up for everything I'd done to this world, but maybe I could do something for her.

"I can't believe you're alive," she said, "and I don't fucking care."

"You're right to hate me."

"You could have subdued them, asked questions, let them go. What was the point of all that blood?"

Six or seven handy lies popped into my head. I stomped them back down. The truth, when it came, fit as awkwardly as Arabelle's skin.

"There are things I haven't told you."

"No shit."

I took a step back. The moon was gone now, and she couldn't tell that I had changed.

"Matty Barber is, or was, one of my closest friends. An ironworker with big arms and a bigger heart—an artist who comes from the mountains. That's who he is in my world. Here, he's named Zircon. Doc, Craig, and Sondra—they're Billiam, Fausto, and Phælandro. And the Gray Lord, well, that's what you call him. I grew up calling him LB. He's not just your god. He's my brother."

I heard the gears whirring in her head as a new cosmology whirred into place. Someday all of this would be written down and chained to a shelf in the Ronastery's collection of apocrypha.

"Your brother," she said. She was still pissed, but her fury had been corrupted by the faintest hint of awe. I didn't care for it.

"Half-brother, if we're being technical."

"Your half-brother is the divine force that was given to us to fashion order from chaos, light from darkness, joy from misery. Your half-brother is the most powerful being to ever walk the Plateau. Your half-brother...no wonder you're such a pain in the ass."

"Yep."

"Did he create you?"

"It might be more accurate to say he molded me into what

he needed me to be."

"Why did he bring you here?"

"To fight for him. Only…"

"Only what?"

I had to tell her. If I were ever going to be worthy of this woman's friendship, I had to force her understand that I was no god, no Hero, nothing but an underemployed fool from Nowhere, Tennessee, who had committed sins no person gets to come back from, who had poisoned Glittermore, who had driven her mother to death. But she got close to me then. Her eyes lit up hot yellow and burnt my new face like the sun.

Myantha clapped. Bronze sparks exploded from her palms and she got her first look at Arabelle.

"You've changed," she said. There was the awe again, the wonder that I needed so badly to kill.

"Heh. Yeah. I was building up to it but, I guess you could say I kinda sorta came back from the dead."

As she admired me, I took a new look at her. She was more tired than I'd realized. Circles as dark as wet clay rimmed her eyes; weary lines stretched out from the sides of her flat mouth. She was too young to look so worn, but LB's world—or rather, the world he'd abused—made her that way. She'd lost her god, and I knew how bad that hurt, because I'd lost him, too. I could destroy her faith, or I could give her something to believe in. It would be better—it had to be better—to lie.

"Are you still named Arabeth?"

"No. No, she's gone forever." Shattered into a thousand pieces on my work table—and both worlds better off for it. "Think of me as her sister—Arabelle."

By the sparks smoldering in the dirt, I could see she wanted to believe. I let her.

"I'm still me. The same memories, the same blind spots, the same weaknesses. But I'm raw. This conspiracy—whoever those monks were in league with…they killed my brother. I can't let that go."

She squeezed my biceps. Her hands felt rough against my smooth, untested skin.

"You're not as strong as before. You need me, don't you?"

"If you'll have me."

"Are you done killing people for no reason?"

"Yes. Yes I am."

Pink light filled her fingertips. She rubbed her hands together, and the light smeared across them like day-glo paint. Then, with a weary smile, she patted my cheek.

"The shit I do for the Gray Lord."

She said goodbye to her mother's grave. We walked through the empty house and down the hill out of town. At the monument to the Gray Lord and his Heroes, she stopped walking. In the dark, LB's massive bulk reared up like a true monster.

"What now?" she said.

"We find the woman with the eye patch."

"How?"

I held up my Ring of Wayfinding.

"It's never steered me wrong before."

She lit up the tip of her finger like E.T. and held it over my ring. The stone was dark. I stepped forward. It stayed dark. I stepped back. It did not change. Either its magic had died with Arabeth, or there was nowhere in this world it thought it safe for me to go.

"Huh," I said. "Shit."

"I have a better idea, but we have to get away from here."

"Where to?"

"Literally anywhere. This place is fucked. I never want to come back."

And so we left that dead town. The going was tougher than on the way in. My legs were as wobbly as a foal's. The cold cut through my golden mail. Most of me hurt, and the rest of me was numb. It was like every hike Mom had ever dragged me on, only Mom always helped me up when I fell.

As we walked, she hammered at the story I'd told her, demanding every detail I could give about the faraway world called Jett Creek. I told her of the wonders of the peanut butter and jelly sandwich. I told her of the ambrosia known as Dr. Pepper. I told her of telephones, airplanes, email, the Smoky

Mountains, the funicular railroad, and the magic of compact discs. I did not mention cars, TV dinners, payday loans, the hole in the ozone layer, weapons of mass destruction, boy bands, or the swing revival. I sold it so hard that I almost forgot how crummy life on planet Earth can be.

After a few hours, we made camp just off the trail, behind a mound of fallen rocks. I lit a fire and bolted down some field rations while she told me her plan.

"I'm going to teach you the Gray Game."

Warmth surged through me, the same as when she healed me back at Blackbriar, the same as when LB put the first die in my hand. I almost thought I was going to cry, but that wouldn't have helped anything, so instead I said, "Are you sure?"

"Always."

"That's your private prayer thing. I really don't want to intrude."

"Games are meant to be shared."

"Thank you."

With a shrug, she emptied her leather bag into the dirt. The black die swallowed the light from my little fire. She unwrapped a vellum scroll, which was covered edge to edge with numbers and words written in a microscopic hand.

"My oracles," she said. "They'll tell you whatever you need."

I reached for the die. She smacked my hand away.

"Slow the fuck down. This isn't back alley fortune telling. This is the Gray Game. If you want your prayers answered, play like you mean it."

I fought the urge to smile. For just a second, I was back at LB's table, and everything was simple again.

"Do I need a character?" I said.

"Can't you play as yourself?"

"I've been a killer for a long time. I'd love to be something else."

She reached into her bag. After a long breath, she withdrew a polished wooden figurine that showed a woman kneeling with her hands crossed over her face. It was heavier than it looked.

"She's beautiful," I said. "What's her name?"

"Cerena. She's a healer."

"Your family trade."

"It's the only way I could ever be who my mother wanted me to be. Keep her safe, okay?"

"I will."

You'd think it would be intimidating, running a session for a demigod, but she showed no nerves as she rapped her fist on the dirt and started the ride.

"You're outside a fort at the edge of a great forest. Death hangs in the air. A sign warns of plague. What do you do?"

"I walk inside."

We played all night, the way I had when I was a teenager, when there were no snacks I couldn't metabolize and nothing wrong with sleeping deep into the afternoon. I healed the sick. I tracked the disease, following its path to the spring that supplied the fort with water. At the bottom of the crystal pool, I found a water nymph whose throat had been cut ear-to-ear. Back at the fort, I found the man, a magistrate, who'd killed her. My impulse was to decapitate him, but Cerena was just, and I wanted to honor that. I dragged him home and let his neighbors decide his fate. They banished him. The fort was saved.

Easy.

Myantha was like no GM I'd ever had. The story spat from her like paper rattling out of a dot matrix printer, dragging me deep into the game. She never looked up from her dice, her oracle, and the maps she sketched in the dirt. This was not a performance. It was a trance, and it was sublime.

When the sun kissed the mountains, Cerena was in a temple, kneeling at the altar, prepared to ask her question at last.

"To whom do you pray?" said Myantha.

"The Gray Lord."

For the first time in hours, she met my eye.

"The Gray Lord is dead."

"Still."

"Ask."

"I'm looking for a white church on a hill where the wind

blows hard. There is a woman there, a woman with an eye patch who wants me dead."

Myantha rolled the die, grimaced, and rolled again. She rocked back on her heels, laughing like mad. The trance was finished. I picked up the oracle.

"Bad?"

"So bad."

"Tell me."

"If I'm reading this right—and I've never made a mistake before—the oracle says your church is waiting for as at the Edge of the World. You're not going to believe it, but it's fucking far. Ten months. Maybe more."

"I know. I've been there before."

We started walking, and I told her about the day Arabeth was born: the beer in Fausto's lap and the cliff-men and everything else. No matter how many times we went over it, we couldn't think of anyone we'd met who might want me dead.

"What about the cliff-men?" she asked. "Maybe one of them survived."

"Knowing my party, we killed them all."

The road was so clogged with refugees that we had to walk in the ditch. Here were people who had lost everything but hunger and fear. I cinched my cloak tight to hide the glittering golden mail. I did not need them knowing how little I could do to help.

"I haven't run the Game for anybody since I left home," she said. "You're not bad at it. For a beginner."

"Thank you."

"Not everyone would have let the magistrate go. Killing is easy. Mercy is hard."

"If I had killed him…

"Yeah?"

"Do you think that's as bad as killing someone in real life?" She laughed.

"People have been debating that as long as the game's been played. Some people kill as much as they can, as a tribute to the Gray Lord's strength. Others play more gentle than they live their own lives, in honor of the Gray Lord's mercy. Some people think how you play the game is more important than how you live. Others think all that shit is stupid, because it's just a goddamned game."

"What do you think?"

"I think…I think you can tell a lot about someone by how they treat an NPC."

We kept walking. The sun rose but warmed no one. The trail was wrecked and the going was hard. Up ahead, the road wound around a stumpy hill whose base was fringed with gnarled trees. The shadows shifted. I saw something breathing in the woods.

I knew what it was: a random encounter. You can't walk half a day in this kind of countryside without being set upon by bandits or raiders or some magical beastie—faceless villains who attack senselessly and die readily, providing cheap thrills, a bit of treasure, and XP. When we had new characters, LB would toss us a few of these pointless scraps to help us get comfortable in our new plastic skin. But these were real bad men lurking in the woods. Blood flowed in their veins; dreams of home flickered across their minds. I did not want to die again, but more than that, I did not want to kill.

I pointed the raiders out to Myantha.

"Good eye," she said. "Do we attack head-on or work our way around the back?"

"I was thinking…what if we avoided them altogether?"

She cackled.

"Don't be silly You're a Hero, aren't you? If we don't stop those bastards, they're going to rob these refugees, kill them, worse."

I sighed, missing Arabeth's easy confidence, feeling nothing but fear.

"Let's go head-on," I said, trying to summon up a little bravado. "Evil doesn't wait. Neither do we."

"Fuck yeah."

She darted ahead. I dropped my cloak. Beneath the gray sky, the golden mail hardly sparkled at all. The first raider stepped out of the trees. Magic danced along Myantha's hands.

I drew my bow.

It was heavier than I remembered, and running made it nearly impossible to aim. I missed so badly, I didn't see where the arrow came down. Myantha blinded the raider, then laid him out with an Arrow of Light. I followed her into the trees. My boot caught on an unseen root. I went sprawling across the dry dirt of the forest floor.

"God damn it!" shouted Myantha.

I rolled onto my back and saw we were surrounded by five of the biggest, ugliest bastards to ever suit up for the Queen of Skulls. Two were on horseback. The others ran our way. I scrambled halfway to sitting, drew a bead on the biggest bastard's forehead. I had my shot. Before I could take it, I saw this dude as a baby, as a kid in muddy shorts, as a gawky, hopeful teen who'd first put on this uniform because it made someone proud. I just, I couldn't.

I aimed for his leg instead.

Another miss.

Before I had time to curse my luck, that sweet little boy brought his ax down on my skull.

My head went crunch, and for the second time, I knew what it was to die.

12

I SUCKED IN AIR, TRYING TO FILL LUNGS THAT WERE SHRUNKEN AND stiff. I was slumped across my window seat, face pressed into the glass, limbs numb.

I couldn't move.

My breath grew quicker, helping nothing. My heart raced.

I closed my eyes and tried to slow down. I counted to fifteen, willing my heart to slow. Feeling returned along with memories I did not need. Myantha kneeling by her mother's grave. Refugees fleeing the Queen of Skulls. A world broken by me and my idiot friends, a world I had to repair.

Arabelle, bless her, had been a big goddamned flop. If I was going to get through this, I'd need the rest of the party.

I crossed the floor on tingling feet and lifted my phone from the cradle. Craig, bless him, answered on the first ring.

"You know how late it is?"

I looked at the clock. In all that time, not five minutes had passed. "I do."

"Then why are you calling?"

"We're meeting at the store when it opens. We've got to play the game."

"The campaign is over."

"It doesn't have to be. It can't be. I have to talk to y'all—I know some stuff about Winterwind, about how LB and Matty died."

"Like what?"

"I can only explain at the table."

There was a long pause. His breathing was heavy. I wondered what he was doing. I'd never seen his apartment, never heard him talk about other friends. It was impossible to picture him anywhere but the juice bar or Critical Hit. I felt ashamed. I hardly knew him at all.

"Doc's coming?" he said.

"She's bringing muffins."

Another pause. Craig liked muffins.

"What about Sondra?" he said. "It's stupid playing with just two people."

"You're bringing her."

"Are you kidding?"

"I haven't made a joke in like two weeks. You guys are such good pals—drive out to Campground 37 and get her. The sun will have her up by dawn."

"Why can't you do it?"

Because I can hardly walk. Because if I try to climb her hill, my heart will stop. Because if anyone sees me looking this weak, they'll take me back to the ICU.

"I've gotta prep the session. It's all you, Craiggy boy."

"She's gonna ask why."

"Tell her about the muffins."

More silence. My cheek was sweaty from having the phone pressed against it, and my arm ached. I needed sleep or I was going to drop dead, and this son of a bitch was still thinking.

"I'm supposed to open the juice bar tomorrow morning," he said, with a heavy sigh. "And I don't even have a character. I really can't come."

"Nobody cares about the juice bar, Craig."

"Fuck off."

I wanted to tell him to fuck off right back, but that didn't seem constructive. I took a deep breath and tried to remember what sweet sounded like.

"You need a character? Play as Zircon."

"Yeah?"

"Think of it as a tribute to our fallen brother."

That got him. He said, "Yeah" about fifteen times and hung up, so eager it hurt. I called Doc on her cell, her house, her office. I called her office again. She picked up, pissed off.

"What?"

"You're working too late."

"One of my buildings burnt down. I had to close a whole department, and now I've got 33 kids halfway through a semester with no classes to take. I'm pulling stuff out of my ass over here. You got any interest in becoming an adjunct professor? Want to teach a class on, fuck, I don't know—silver smithing?"

"Kinda. But that's not why I'm calling. You need a break."

"Correct."

"What are you doing tomorrow at 8 a.m.?"

Papers shuffled. A lighter flicked. Doc was the only person on campus who could get away with smoking in her office, and she saved it for when things were truly fucked.

"My current plan is to spend the next ten hours banging my head against this course schedule, pass out for thirty minutes, then rip it up and start over again."

"How'd you like to play Winterwind instead?"

"That's a lousy idea. I'm in."

"Fantastic. Bring muffins."

I hung up before she could argue. My legs were bags of waterlogged sand. I flopped into a half-sleep. I had vague dreams of night on the Plateau: the cold, the howling wind, a warm bedroll, the firm ground beneath my back. Finally, I abandoned the down comforter and plush mattress. I threw open the window and slept naked on the window seat. There were no more dreams.

I WOKE BEFORE MY ALARM, SHOWERED, AND FORCED MYSELF TO eat. My stomach rebelled against the coffee, but I choked it down and felt a measure of triumph that I was able to get out of the house without gagging.

I wedged Arabelle's clumsily-painted mini underneath my Acura's front tire. She looked so hopeful, poor thing, so excited for her shot on the big stage. I'd done nothing with her at all. I shoved my car into drive and heard the plastic shatter.

My skull ached as I remembered how it felt when she died.

I drove through empty streets with the windows up and radio off, flinching at every jogger, dog walker, or passing car. If some magic broke through from the other world, I didn't think I'd get any warning. If I did, my only chance would be to run.

I parked by the funicular, whose wizened operator was already opening for the coming trickle of tourists. I trudged to the store, where the lights were on and fresh coffee perfumed the air. Odette was behind the bar, hanging mugs on hooks. She didn't usually open, and it occurred to me that maybe she just didn't want to be at home. I dropped my bag on the nearest folding table, sat, and tried not to stare at the clock.

Once, I'd have passed the time flipping through a manual for a new game or an old favorite, dreaming of campaigns I would never have time to play. Now I saw those books and thought of Myantha, of my victims, and tried not to wonder if *Winterwind* was the only game where the dead were real.

"Coffee?" said Odette.

"Another cup would make me throw up."

"That's the kind of thing you love to hear from your employees, thank you. Are you okay?"

"Not particularly."

"Need to go home? You don't look like you're here to work."

"I'm running a session. I'll be fine."

A glass of ice water appeared at my elbow. Odette sank into a chair and peered into my open bag.

"I know those D-Rings," she said.

"Figured I should get in another session while some of my players are still alive."

I drained the ice water. I'd needed it more than I thought.

"Why not play something else?" she said. "We've got, like, a lot of games."

"We've got unfinished business on the Plateau."

"Who gives a shit? RPGs are about escape. Does *Winterwind* help you get away from anything?"

"You'd be surprised."

She took a long, unsatisfying breath. Her skin was gray and the dark circles under her eyes were threatening to spread to her entire face. I wanted to comfort her, but I'd never learned how.

"Did LB ever talk about someone wanting to kill him?" I said.

"I heard you've been asking people that. I thought Matty's death might make you back off, but I guess that was naive."

"Why?"

"You're obsessive. LB was the same way. It's why you drove him crazy at the table. You never let him get away with anything."

"Which is why I haven't forgotten that you didn't answer my question."

That made her laugh, which felt precious.

"He had black moods. Weeks where he drank too much or didn't sleep or got tripped up by a disagreeable new drug. Weeks with all three. When he got like that, he thought everybody wanted him dead."

"I never saw him like that."

"He was good enough to hide it from everyone but me."

"I'm sorry you had to deal with him alone."

She slouched down in the plastic chair and threw her hood over her slowly graying curls.

"It's all right. Most of the time, we had fun."

"How often was he at the studio on Prewitt?"

"He slept there a lot. I didn't mind."

Arabelle had spent a full day on the Plateau, and only five minutes had passed in Jett Creek. How many months could LB live on the Plateau in one night of Earth time? How many years had he lived as the Gray Lord? Could it have really been 738?

Could it have been more?

"Did he ever say anything concrete, anything outside of the usual ravings, that made you think he could really be in danger?"

"From who? I know you've got suspects. You wouldn't operate any other way."

"My first thought was Matty but then, y'know, he died."

"LB broke Matty's spirit a long time ago. If he was going to lash out, it would have happened already."

"What about Craig?"

"Craig? Really? He's such a nice guy."

"Aren't they the scariest ones? He's the fragile type of nice, the kind who could turn true psycho if you poked him the wrong way."

"Yeah, okay. And LB made fun of him a lot, but as far as I know Craig never threatened to do anything about it."

"Could you see Doc killing him?"

"Yeah. Maybe."

I sat up straight.

"How come?" I said, trying to underplay it, as though that were something I actually knew how to do.

"Doc loved LB when she needed him to attract new students or alumni donations, and hated him when it came to the actual business of, y'know, teaching sculpture. There are worse ways to get rid of a tenured professor."

She cracked up. Her laugh was like the sun breaking through on a cold day.

"You know I'm joking, right?"

"Oh yeah, of course. Me too. But you got any idea what they were talking about at his studio the day he died?"

The question made her flinch. I almost regretted it.

"I didn't…no, I don't." She forced a smile. "Why haven't you asked about Sondra?"

"You think she had it in her?"

"Well, she was blackmailing him."

"How did you know?"

"She sent me a note that said, 'I am blackmailing your

husband,' in bubble letters. She never really asked for money. I think it was about attention, or fun. She's odd."

"They were also..."

"Fucking?"

"Yeah."

"A lot of people can make that claim. Do you think it bothers me?"

"No."

"Hm." She took my empty cup and wiped the ring off the table with her sleeve. "It's almost time to open, and since my star clerk is playing games instead of selling them, I guess I should get behind the register."

"I'll start working again soon."

"Don't worry. We give one week off for the death of friends or loved ones. As long as your people keep dying, you're on leave till Easter."

"Paid?"

"Go fuck yourself."

She took her spot on the high stool behind the register. The bell chimed. I looked up, adrenaline churning, and saw it was only sweet, pointless Karina. She beamed at Odette and Odette beamed right back. The golden girl of board games peered at my notebook. I slapped it closed. She smiled bigger than I had in my entire life.

"Aren't you off today?" she said.

"I'm running a session."

"Oh. Cool."

"Yes. Games are really cool. What do you want?"

She sat down and put her hand on mine—it felt so hot, she might have had a fever—and gave me a look that I'd guess you'd call sisterly.

"I have a confession."

"Did you murder my brother?"

"Uh, no. But that character sheet Odette found in the printer, for the mage? It was mine. I was too embarrassed to say so the other day."

The few parts of me that still had warmth went cold.

"Who gave you permission to do that?"

"Nobody. I just found the file for the blank character sheets on the computer—I guess LB left it there?—and his notes for creating characters. I had to try it out. That game is just so different, y'know? I'm early today and I was gonna ask if maybe I could play?"

I grabbed her wrists. She pulled back, but I held tight.

"What made you create a dazzler?"

"It just seemed cool."

"Did you take Arrow of Light as a first level spell?"

"What does it matter?"

I squeezed harder. Her wrists went all purple.

"Is your mage a Black woman with short hair and eyes that change colors?"

"You're hurting me."

"Does she come from Glittermore? Is she a born-again Hero worshiper? Can I trust her?"

With some force, she ripped her wrists away. Red ringed the bone. I wondered if they would bruise.

"I don't know what the heck you're talking about," she said, the lilt gone out of her voice. "Nevermind, okay? Just forget I asked to play."

She retreated to the board game racks. I threw on my hoodie and went outside, hoping there'd be someone on the sidewalk who could bum me a cigarette. There was nobody. I pressed my cold hand against my neck, trying to slow my breathing, and saw Craig's car by the dead end. He wore a sharply-pressed tie-dye t-shirt, and Sondra was there too, in unicorn pajamas that were big enough to swallow her. She had him pinned against the hood, kissing him like she was trying to swallow his head. My stomach lurched. This was way more than I could handle.

"What the fuck," I asked the universe. The universe did not reply. They fucking hated each other, so maybe it made a kind of sense. All I knew is that Jill would be pissed. Or she'd think it was hilarious. Maybe both.

Someone tapped me on the shoulder: Diego, whose eyes

were red and whose lips were wetter than ever.

"Callie. Do you have a second for me to—"

"Do you have a cigarette?"

"I don't smoke."

"Then leave me alone." I turned away, then turned back. "Sorry, I know that's an extremely rude thing to say. But also, I need to be alone. Thanks."

I went back to my table and buried my head in my hands. The door opened. Craig and Sondra made their entrance screaming.

"You're a fucking idiot," she said. "No good music has been made since 1997 and no good music will ever be made again."

"That's insane. Insane! Music is better now than it has ever been."

"Shut up before you embarrass yourself."

"Never! There are bands out there doing incredible stuff. Blink 182, Sum 41, Good Charlotte—I could go on."

"Please don't," I said softly. He shut up. I had no idea if their fight was fake or real, whether it was meant to cover up the hideous display of affection I witnessed outside or if it was some kind of foreplay, but if Craig liked Good Charlotte, he really might be capable of murder.

"Come on," I said. "We're in the back room."

They followed without saying hello. As we walked, Sondra got close. I flinched. I wished I hadn't.

"Boo," she said.

"Do I look scared?"

"A little. I thought I was 'out of the group.'"

"Yeah, well, I decided we'd all done worse shit than shove somebody into the dirt."

If that bugged her, I didn't notice. I really, really didn't care how Sondra felt.

No one had been in the little wood paneled room since LB's last session. I cleared our trash off the table and made a show of straightening the chairs. Doc entered, muffinless, and Craig scowled like a pre-teen. I tossed a bag of dice on the table. My players didn't move. They looked pale and sluggish, like people who have been too sad for too long. I found myself hating them—for betraying my brother, for disrespecting me, for being ignorant of the blood on their hands.

I squeezed the back of LB's old chair and tried to keep the tremor out of my voice.

"Okay. Before we get started, let's have a quick refresher on morality."

"Fun," grunted Sondra.

"Murder is A: Right or B: Wrong?"

"A," said Craig. "Wait, no, shit. B. I meant B. Murder is wrong."

"Very good, Craiggo," said Sondra, patting him on the head.

Doc made a big show of checking her watch.

"Can we move this along? I really should be back on campus, trying to keep the rest of my college from burning down."

"Just a couple more questions, real quick. If murder is wrong, is pretending to murder people A: Right or B: Wrong?"

"What do you mean pretending?" said Craig, thinking harder than he was accustomed.

"Like in a game."

"If nobody actually gets murdered, then no. It's B."

"You mean A," said Sondra.

"Fuck! Yes, A. Right."

"What if the game is all about getting lost in your character, immersing yourself until you forget the real world is out there, coming so close to what's happening that you can taste the blood? Is roleplaying murder A: Right or B: Wrong?"

"Still A," said Craig. "I got that right, right?"

"Right," said Sondra. "Everything's cool as long as nobody dies."

"And what if somebody does?"

I set their minis on the table. The paint glinted in the sickly fluorescent light.

"Go ahead," I said. "Take your guy."

They didn't. I pushed Zircon, muscles bulging like overfilled balloons, to Craig.

"Come on, Craig," I said. "I thought you were psyched to be Zircon."

"And I thought there were going to be muffins, so I guess we're both disappointed."

He sulked into a corner. Sondra leaned across the table until her face was uncomfortably close to mine.

"You were going to let him play as Zircon?"

"As a tribute to Matty."

"All of this is bullshit."

"That's no way to talk to your GM."

"You're not my GM."

I pulled the monocle out from under my sweaters.

"I've got this," I said, "and that means I'm in charge."

I thought she might hit me. Instead, she just stood there. I felt like a trapped animal. Doc put her hand on my shoulder, warm but firm.

"It's been a rough couple weeks. A lotta trauma. You ever wonder if maybe you'd be better off—"

"Back in the hospital?"

"I was going to say in bed."

I threw myself into LB's chair.

"Y'all said you wanted to play."

"And after we talked," said Doc, "I called Craig and we agreed that, well, that you didn't seem like you were at your best."

"I said you sounded crazy," said Craig.

"Very fucking helpful," muttered Sondra.

"Not at my best how?" I said.

"A touch erratic," said Doc. "Like maybe you're not reacting to things precisely how you'd prefer. Like maybe you need a rest."

I wanted to scream. I chose not to.

"I'm going to say this as politely as I can," I said, soft enough that they all had to lean in. "Sit in your fucking chairs."

"Hon," said Doc.

"Matty's skin bubbled until it popped. He screamed like an animal. I was there. Y'all weren't. Now sit down so I can tell a story that will save your lives."

They sat. For the first time, they were listening to me. I allowed myself the faintest measure of hope.

"Once upon a time, a mage named Phælandro asked a general store clerk to give them wine for free. He said no, and so they summoned a mudslide with their hands and buried an entire village alive."

"In my defense," Sondra said, "those guys were dicks."

"Once upon a time, a bard named Billiam hypnotized a group of retreating bandits and forced them to run off a cliff. Their bodies burst on the rocks and their entrails mingled with the sea."

"What's your point?" said Doc.

"Once upon a time, a thief named Fausto tested a new invisibility spell by sneaking into a barnyard and slaughtering every animal he could find. He returned covered in blood and feathers, and his friends laughed like it was the funniest joke in the world."

"You're on my ass for killing animals now?" said Craig.

"What about the farmer? What about his family?"

"They don't exist?"

I leaned back as far as LB always had. I'd never realized how comfortable this seat could be.

"What if they do?" I said.

Craig pulled a face that said something like, "This bitch is crazy." He looked at Sondra and Doc, waiting for one of them to meet his eye and match his expression, but they were looking at me.

"What if every person, every beast, every soldier we killed at this table was a living, breathing thing? What if it was real? I asked Matty that question, right before he died. He said we'd be war criminals."

"And we would be," said Doc, "only, sweetheart...it's not."

"But what if it is?"

I unrolled one of LB's private maps. Drawn in hair-thin India ink, it showed every inch of the Plateau, from Blackbriar in the north to the Edge of the World at the southern tip. As pissed as they were, this caught their eye. They leaned over the map, tracing its unfamiliar contours with their eyes, and looked the same as they had every Thursday night for years. They looked like my friends.

"Here's the thing," I said. "Winterwind is real. The Keep is real. The Plateau is real. The Queen of Skulls is real, and her armies are tearing this continent apart because you assholes let them in the front door. LB knew all of this. He wasn't a great GM—he was just an asshole who'd stumbled onto a little piece of iron and glass that let him leap from our world to theirs and back again. His sessions seemed so goddamned real because they were."

"You're talking about magic," said Sondra.

"Yeah."

"Keep talking. Magic is cool."

"It would be, only somebody down here got sick of LB farting around their continent like he was a god. They killed him. They killed Matty. If we don't stop them, if we don't fix what LB fucked up, they are going to kill us all."

And one of you is helping them do it, I thought, but we'll put a pin in that for now.

"I'm not a murderer," said Craig. "Not in real life, and not in this stupid game."

"Fausto killed a shitload of people," I said. "That means you killed a shitload of people, mostly for no reason at all."

"So fucking what?"

"Even if it was real," said Sondra, "LB didn't tell us. We didn't know what we were doing."

"It doesn't matter. It's still murder."

I tossed the monocle on the table. It skidded across the map. No one reached for it.

"See for yourselves."

"Fuck this," said Craig, shriller and shriller. "I'm sick of you and your brother telling me what to do. I'm sick of getting laughed at in this shitty little room. I was told there would be muffins, god damn it, and even that was a lie."

He leaned across the table and tore LB's map in half. I felt about ready to rip, too.

"Fuck this family," he said, "and fuck this game."

"They're going to kill you," I said, softly.

"Let them try."

He left, finally getting to look as tough as he'd always wanted this game to make him feel. Sondra glanced at the door.

"So...he's my ride," she said.

"Just go."

"Magic *is* cool, y'know. Leave it to you and your brother to suck the fun out of it."

And she left, too.

"You walking out too?" I asked Doc. She sucked in a long, angry breath.

"I know you're going through some ugly shit," she said, "and nothing I can do will ease your pain, but no matter how bad you hurt, it is unconscionable to lash out at your friends."

"I'm trying to save your lives."

She jabbed the ruined map.

"You need to live in this fantasy for a little while, go ahead. I'm the last person who's going to tell you how to grieve. But if you get nasty any time anybody tries to help—"

"If you want to help me, play the game."

"Give me a call when you're ready to quit fucking around and start to heal. I can't babysit you anymore."

"I know that you lied."

That stopped her.

"Scuse me?"

"You saw LB at his studio the afternoon of his death. You lied to the cops about it. They caught you. What were you doing there?"

She pressed her knuckles into the table. Very board room. I think she thought she had me frightened. She didn't come close.

"Sondra sent me a letter. The envelope said, 'Blackmail Materials.'"

"Bubble letters?"

"Yeah. Fourteen pages of meticulous documentation

showing every time LB came to class drunk, every time he fucked a student, every time he said something nasty about me. At the end of it she'd added a sticky note that said, 'And when I threatened to send this to you, he burnt my fucking yurt!'"

"You believed it?"

"Some of it? I knew he slept around and talked shit about me, but that's not a crime. Arson is another thing. I asked him if he'd set Sondra's yurt on fire because she was blackmailing him. He said, 'Absolutely not. I set her yurt on fire because she's the most powerful wizard in Jett Creek and I do not trust her anymore.' That, well, it surprised me. He spent an hour jabbering about how Winterwind was real, how we all had blood on our hands."

"What did you tell him?"

"I asked him if he'd thought about getting help. He told me to shut up and come to that night's session on time. I came to keep an eye on Sondra, make sure she was okay. If he hadn't died, I'd have fired him."

"If you thought he was losing his mind, why didn't you tell me?"

"You were the kid sister. What could you have done?"

"Did you tell my mom?"

"No."

When she said it, she glanced down. A lock of silver hair escaped her ponytail. She brushed it back and put her hand on mine. I waited as long as I could before pulling away.

"I'm sorry," she said.

"Everybody is."

I watched her exit the shop. Without looking up from her book, Odette shouted: "That's the thing about other players. They're a pain in the ass."

I returned to the back room and drew the stained lace shut. I rolled up the halves of my map and collected the blank character sheets. I sat at the table and watched LB's empty chair.

Long before, after the total party kill that set the stage for the birth of Arabeth, LB leaned back in that chair, one hand clutching a warm beer, the other on his gut, and got real.

"I'm sorry folks. It's not my fault you're dead."

"That was a bullshit encounter and you know it," I said.

"Quiet."

"You be quiet. I've been listening to you talk for four hours. This session started with us chasing an elemental mage who'd kidnapped a hunter's daughter."

"Yes."

"Thanks to Billiam's incompetent wayfinding, we got lost in the woods."

"So you did."

"I heard a noise in the trees. I went after it."

"Like the stalwart hero you are."

"But it wasn't an evil mage. It was a basilisk, and it fucking tore us apart."

He chuckled—not malicious, exactly, but like a god who can't believe what fools these mortals be. The rest of the party slouched against the table or the wall.

"So what's the basilisk got to do with the evil mage?" I said.

"Nothing."

"And that's why it's bullshit! You can't kill the entire party on a random encounter."

"I didn't kill you. The basilisk did."

"But you put it there."

"It was there the whole time. That clearing is its home. You were the one who wasn't paying attention. You didn't look for its tracks, its odor, the fucking bits of bone and flesh that littered the area all around its nest. All you knew is you heard an interesting sound and just had to check it out."

He drained his beer and set it among the empties collected on the floor.

"It's still bullshit," I said.

"Keep telling yourself that. But if your GM warns you and you don't listen, you deserve to die."

What an asshole. Even dead, he was always right.

I scattered dice across the table. I picked up my sharpest pencil, grabbed a blank character sheet, and created someone invincible, unfeeling, who didn't need anyone at all.

13

I WANTED TO BE TOO STUPID TO THINK. AN OGRE. A BRUTE. A brick with legs. She would have no family, no friends, nothing that would make her feel real. She would be as alone as I had been this entire time.

I started by snatching up a trait, "Reckless Fighter," that doubled my chances to crit. LB had long considered striking it from the game, as it was totally unfair, but had never gotten around to it. Even so, he didn't like people taking it at level one. If they did, he'd hold them to it, forcing them into situations so dangerous they rarely made it to level two.

Next, I ran my finger down the list of starting gear. I knew what I wanted. On LB's oft-photocopied list of, "Fabled Magical Items of the Plateau," there was a two-handed blacksmith's hammer called Vingram's Mallet of Extreme Incapacitation. It was marked XFR, or "Extremely Fucking Rare," because in addition to doing a hideous amount of damage, it had a feature that had until that moment seemed dull: instead of killing, it knocked enemies unconscious for a solid ten hours, meaning I'd be able to fight without getting any more blood on my hands. I might break bones, I might cause pain, but nobody would die.

Basically, I'd be like Batman, only really ugly and really dumb.

Except the dice did not cooperate. No matter how many times I rolled, they spat back stats so low they made me want to scream.

I pushed the character sheet away. My numbers were cramped, almost illegible, and some of what I'd written had already smudged off on my heavy, nervous wrist. This was unquestionably the shittiest character I'd ever created: a min-maxed mess with no personality, no grace, nothing that would make her fun to play.

Which would be a problem if I were still playing a game.

"You little fuckers," I said to the heap of six-sided dice. I found my fingers walking across the table. I flicked one die so that it showed a six. I did it with its sisters, too.

I braced for retribution. This was cheating, and I'd never been able to cheat without instantly getting caught. I expected the skies to tear, the table to catch fire, the dice to melt in my hands.

Nothing happened.

I cheated until I had my fighting machine: long on strength and health, short on charisma and smarts. I was reaching for the monocle when I remembered I needed a mini, too. I rooted through my bin and ripped open the package on a screaming, deformed orc-type who wielded an ax that was taller than her. Close enough.

I didn't paint her at all.

I put on the monocle and pressed the button. The hot iron flowed. I touched it and dropped onto the Plateau. I was done with feeling, done with thinking. I wanted an ending, and I would hurt whoever it took to get there.

THE FIRST THING I NOTICED WAS MY ARMS. THEY WERE PAST ripped. They were knotted, twisted, hard as oak. Veins bulged, blue and red and seriously unhealthy looking. The slightest movement of my bicep threatened to shred my overtaxed yellow tunic, and I was about to make some serious movements indeed.

I stood astride the corpse of poor, pathetic Arabelle. The raider who killed her was halfway through a victory cry when I appeared. He staggered back, mouth open, looking me up and down like he wasn't sure if he wanted to run or beg for sex.

"I know, right?" I said. "I'm a fucking cartoon."

The words came out like they'd been fed through a shredder. I don't think he understood me, and it didn't really matter, because he was always going to swing his weapon and I was always going to swing mine.

Vingram's Mallet was a long black monstrosity. It was heavy, but I swung it like it was tinfoil, slapping his blow away with my first swing and knocking him thirty feet backwards with the second. He sat up, for just a second, and then he slumped to the ground, still alive but definitely unhappy about it.

"What the fuck!" shouted Myantha. I guess nobody in this world was ready for Callie Myles, muscle mag babe.

"It's me," I said. "Arabeth, Arabelle. Don't be afraid. I'm here to protect you."

At least, that's what I tried to say. It came out like, "Aggggggggghraghhhhh," and didn't reassure her one bit. I wanted to comfort her, but instead I found myself sprinting to take on the remaining raiders by myself. Somewhere deep in my muscle-bound brain, I thought, so this is reckless. It was terrifying.

It was also kinda cool.

They waited in a ragged line: riders on the flanks, grunts in the middle. If I were smart, I'd have knocked out one of the mounted baddies and stolen his ride. Instead I charged right at the boys in the middle and let them surround me.

It was a death trap.

Whatever. I'd died before.

The tallest soldier stepped forward. He was stupid handsome—truly square jaw, a tidy beard, a nose straight and strong enough to build a house on—but he looked scared enough to puke. That little glimpse reminded me of LB, of the tiny details he always had on hand, no matter how fast the game was going, and it made me very sorry I had to do what I did next.

My not-quite-deadly mallet smashed him into the nearest tree. His bones cracked horribly, but he kept breathing. I felt impressive for about half a second, until I felt the rumble of two charging horses about to run me down.

I dodged the first one—I was a fucking acrobat—but I couldn't escape the second rider's lance. My armor might as well have been plastic wrap, because it stuck deep and stayed buried. I yanked it out, doubling the length of my wound, and hurled it after him. It clattered harmlessly against a tree. Sweat clouded my eyes. I wiped a hand across my brow, streaking my vision with blood. Through the red, I saw the surviving foot soldier make his move.

He advanced slowly, a small shield covering most of his face, ax steady at his side. I might have looked for a weakness or higher ground, but my mind was branded with a single word: "DESTROY." I threw back my shoulders and gargled out something like, "Come and get it!"

I'd have looked awesome on the cover of a third-rate metal album, but as a defensive pose it wasn't ideal. He lunged and I dodged, taking his blow on my wrists. My mallet slipped out of my hands. An ugly little thought skittered across my brain: "These fuckers are going to kill you again."

I scrambled for my mallet. I couldn't see much and my hands were too bloody to be much good.

A woman screamed.

It was Myantha, whom I'd honestly forgotten about, doing something really weird with her hands. If I'd been thinking clearly—if I'd been capable of thinking at all—I'd have recognized her warm up to Blinding Glare, but in the moment I thought she was just waving hello.

I waved back.

From her fingers came the flash of a hydrogen bomb.

For a minute or two, I was nowhere at all.

When I could see again, I found the foot soldier, half-dazed, squeezing his hands around my throat. He'd lost his sword, and was about to learn that going hand-to-hand with my wonderful brute was not a good idea. While he struggled for purchase on my blood-soaked neck, I clamped my hands onto his skull. It would have been wonderfully easy to snap his neck. Just a flick of the wrists and the problem would be solved. Instead, I bonked him on the head. He slid off me, eyes rolling back in his head. An ugly sound roared out of my mouth.

I was laughing.

The horsemen came around for another charge. The rider who'd lost his lance was drawing a short sword when an Arrow of Light knocked him off his mount. The other guy flew in at a full gallop, lance leveled at my heart.

I was on foot, unarmed, and out of ideas. I just stood there. At the last moment, I stuck out my arm. I did not flinch when the lance bit into my shoulder, and I gave no ground when the mount slammed into my wrist. The horse's windpipe crumpled. The beast crashed to the ground.

"I just clotheslined a horse!" I screamed.

Myantha gave a look that might have been awe but was probably closer to fear.

The rider's leg was shattered. His partner helped him up. They were weak; they were frightened; they were trying to get away. I wanted to turn them into ground beef. But instead I picked my mallet off the ground.

They fell to their knees, more from exhaustion than surrender. I pressed the mallet against the nearest man's chest. He bawled. I liked knowing they were afraid.

Myantha looked at me without expression. Even I wasn't dumb enough not to know what she was thinking.

"Run," I told the raiders, and they did as they were told.

I put my hand on my shoulder. It came away sticky.

"I'm hurt," I said, and sank to the ground.

I must have bit my tongue when I passed out—it was so bulbous, it was hard to keep it out from under my teeth—because I woke up with a mouth full of blood. Myantha grunted like she was hefting a sack of potatoes and flipped me onto my back.

I tried to force myself onto my elbows. She pushed me down. Her hands scalded my flanks. The last time she'd given me her healing touch, she was gentle. Today, she was not. She dug her fists into me, crushing my wounds shut and making me scream like I did not know a person could. When the burning stopped, she cinched a bandage so tight my eyes bulged.

"Ow," I growled.

She smacked me.

"Anyone who stands still for a horse charge ought to be cut in half."

I sat up, fighting a hideous urge to smack her back. My blood stained her robes.

"Gonna strip," I grunted. Shaking her head, she turned away.

I shrugged off my tattered armor and stripped Arabelle's corpse. Squeezing into the golden mail was like trying to fight my way into my high school jeans. The gold dug into my armpits and the clasps barely shut. I nearly broke the bracers trying to force my obscenely muscled wrists through them. Even the Ring of Wayfinding was a tight squeeze. The boots were hopeless. I tossed them into the woods. I checked on the soldiers whom I'd knocked unconscious. None of them looked good—the guy I'd knocked into the tree was in particularly poor shape—but they'd live. I was trying to be proud of that when Myantha interrupted me.

"So you're back from the dead. Again."

"Hrmph."

"You keep grunting and I'm leaving you here. What are you supposed to be?"

I kicked Arabelle's corpse onto her face. I was through looking at it.

"She was weak. She died. I'm stronger. Strong as I need to be. Strong enough to fix shit."

"I just don't see why you had to be so ugly."

I twisted the bracer, which still shone brightly even though its wearers kept dying horribly, until I could see my face. It looked lumpy, overripe, like a vegetable left in the crisper until you couldn't tell what it used to be.

"Pretty doesn't win," I said.

"What's your name?"

"Huh?"

"I like to know who I'm traveling with."

I fumbled for the monocle. My brow was so heavy, my eye so beady, it barely fit. I peered onto the table at the games store and saw that in my frenzy of minmaxing I'd forgotten to give this character a name.

"The nameless one," I said, and marched south. I don't think she liked it, but she followed. We rejoined the parade of refugees. Even if they'd known we saved their lives, they looked too numb to care.

We walked until my legs collapsed. Myantha built the fire. She laid her bedroll on the far side of it. Before I slipped into sleep, I called to her: "For you—that's why I let them live."

She did not reply.

In the morning, my wounds were healed and my step was light—it's amazing what eight hours sleep does for a Hero—and our trip really began. It was easy to quit wondering who killed LB and whether or not they were going to kill me too, and focus on finding the white church and the one-eyed wizardess. We were at the start of a very long road, and I was thankfully too dumb to think of anything but putting one gnarled foot in front of the other.

We walked ten days, always south, across a cracked, gray waste. Every time we stopped, I peered through the monocle at Callie's torn map and was furious at how little of it we had crossed. Travel was so much easier when you had a GM to fast-forward through the boring bits.

Of course, it wasn't all dull. Once or twice a day we came across what LB would have stridently refused to call a random encounter. Usually, Myantha hung back while I hurled myself into the fray, absorbing stabbings, beatings, magic, and fire as I bludgeoned strangers into unconsciousness. For the first few days, it was easy to walk away while they were still breathing. The more I fought, the harder it got to let the vanquished go. Most of the time, I was able to believe every life I spared was a credit to my spiritual account, but I so enjoyed the crack of bone and flavor of blood that I often felt I was back at the table or in Arabeth, killing for laughs.

Being the nameless one was like having a brain wrapped in lard. If I forced it, I could put a couple of thoughts together. Anything more brought on a migraine that could only be washed away with blood. But once, as I fought one of the Queen of Skulls' finest, the battle slowed, and the relentless pounding in my ears faded away. The clouds broke. Golden light fell on the riverbank. I saw every drop of sweat on my enemy's brow. I counted every grain of rust on his blade. I heard his heart thud, pulling blood in and then out.

I clonked him on the side of his head. He collapsed into a heap. His heart beat slower.

The golden light faded. I felt skill I hadn't had before.

"I just leveled up," I muttered, forming words with the kind of clarity I thought I'd left behind. The shackles on my brain loosened. For a moment, I felt feather light. Then I saw the dent in the side of his head, another person crippled by my hand.

He was killing innocent people, and so I stopped him.

It's not okay to hurt people.

I didn't kill him!

This ain't much better.

But they're bad guys! They have helmets and axes and honest to god skulls on their shirts!

Sure, they're bad guys. But what the hell are you?

For the first time in days, I remembered how LB and Matty crackled as they died, and I knew nothing I was doing could make up for what I'd done. There was no story here. No progress. Only an endless grind. LB wouldn't have let a quest go so stale, but LB was dead.

And then the fog came down and, gratefully, I was stupid again.

The herd of refugees broke up as the middle road dissolved into a delta of nameless paths. We kept heading south, each step a little closer to the Edge of the World.

On a steel day, walking along a barren field, I noticed a little trail branching off the road into the trees. It was nothing, not even a deer path, but it spoke to me, somehow, and I could not pass it by.

"What is it?" said Myantha. It was the first thing she'd said all day.

"That way."

"Hell no. We lost half the morning so you could chase down those bandits and beat them till they cried. We have to keep walking or we'll never get anywhere."

"That way."

"I'm not taking directions from a creature too stupid to tie her own boots."

It did not occur to me to be insulted. I was straining my brain to find a non-violent way to persuade her when I noticed something glinting on my swollen finger. The Ring of Wayfinding had come back to life. Silver glowed deep within the round stone. I took a step down the rocky path, and it glowed brighter.

"The ring," I said. "Let's go."

Myantha did not argue.

The path sank into a dense forest whose spongy ground melted into swamp. It wove through sunken trees, keeping us a few inches above water the color of red wine. Finally, it faltered. I stood at the trail's end and squinted into dim woods, seeing nothing of what lay ahead. I kicked a rock into the water. It sank slowly.

"Let's turn around before we lose the last of the light," said Myantha. "I'm not sleeping here."

I held up the ring, which burned brighter than I'd ever seen.

"We go on," I said. "Ride on my back."

I didn't mean it to sound like an order, but everything I said came out that way.

"You're a Hero, not a pack animal."

"I don't want your robes spoiled."

"Then stop getting blood on them," she said, and stepped into the goo.

We waded up to our knees, our hips, our chests. Even with

my strength, it was hard pushing through the slime. The sucking feelers of some unseen creature danced across my feet. I could not tell if they belonged to many small things, or one large beast. I never considered stopping. Arabeth would have pressed on because she was brave. This creature I had become was just too senseless to care.

Night fell like a curtain. Myantha's fingers lit up the dark, but her magic only cut a few yards into the gloom. As we pressed deeper into the swamp, her light faded until it was little more than the glow of a dying match.

"Tired?" I said.

"No."

She was lying. I was about to throw her over my shoulder when a light flickered in the fog.

Our pace picked up; our legs felt lighter. The ground grew firm, and we found ourselves on an island covered in wet, rotting leaves. For the first time in hours, I saw my feet. I tried not to wonder how many leeches, or worse, covered my much-abused skin.

We picked over fallen trees and hanging vines. I stepped onto something uncommonly hard, so familiar that I flinched. It was black, cracked, and it stretched on into the dark.

Pavement. A mailbox. A number.

"4404," she said. "What does that mean?"

"Home."

I rumbled up the driveway. At the top sat a wonder of modern engineering that would have mystified the most brilliant designers ever employed by the Duke of Blackbriar.

A ranch house.

A 1962 special, to be precise, clad in shit brown siding, with a concrete patio and a single light burning out front. It was built on the fringes of Jett Creek as part of a development called the Ranchettes that was demolished in the mid-90s so that newer crappy houses could be built instead. LB was born in its living room. Mom stayed there until I was five. I didn't really remember it, and no matter how often I'd squinted at blurry pictures of our lives there, the ranch's plush shag and oppressive wood paneling never felt like where I belonged.

I guess LB felt differently.

Weeds sprouted through the cracked patio. The screen door hung loose. The front door was unlocked. I nudged it open, but did not step inside.

"Where the hell are we?" said Myantha, inspecting the concrete. Her cheeks were streaked with dirt. Her robes were a total loss.

"A house from Jett Creek. The Gray Lord's. Mine."

"Then this is holy ground. I can't cross that threshold and neither should you—not with so much blood on your boots."

I scraped my feet on the welcome mat. Some of the filth came off. She followed me inside.

It was like falling backwards in time.

Vases of flowers—all symmetrical and bright, just like in the drawings on the seed packet—occupied every shelf and sill. Above the mantle were framed posters from an impressionist art exhibition that had come through JCCAD. Those posters, faded like crazy from the sun, were still hanging in the office at Mom's shop. I felt her here, in the art books and the stacks of *National Geographic*, in the tchotchkes crowded around the fireplace, but I didn't sense LB.

Two dying couches stared at each other across a coffee table that, like so much furniture in the house, had "LBK" scratched into its wood. I slid my fingers along the deep grooves of the letters and tried to remember the boy who put them there. Nothing came back.

I twisted on the TV. It hissed out static. I turned the knob until I caught a signal, broadcast from god knows where, a story painted in colors bright enough to make the impressionists sick.

He-Man. Of course.

I slapped it off.

"I don't get it," I growled.

"What's not to get?"

"Huh?"

She picked up a magazine, flipped through it, and put it down.

"I don't know where the Gray Lord came from. I'm not worthy of such knowledge. But his origins were clearly humble. When he wanted to remember what it felt like before he knew he was a god, he came here."

But that simpering nostalgia was the sort of thing LB hated most. Any time I tried to talk about the tiny segment of our childhood that overlapped, he shut me down. He built this place for something else, and if I could understand that, maybe I would understand what he'd become. Maybe I'd find a reason to forgive myself for loving him.

At least, that's what Callie was thinking, somewhere far away. Rather than tire herself untangling that wad of emotion, my nameless fighter grunted and moved on.

A long carpeted hallway served as the house's spine. Family pictures filled its walls. LB at the beach, eating sand. Mom in high school, dressed for marching band. Mom in college, smoking on a rooftop and acting like she didn't know the camera was there. Little baby Callie, stone-faced and fat. The three of us, in a park I didn't recognize, with LB holding me by the ankles and me grinning like the happiest gremlin on earth. They meant nothing to the character I'd become, and I passed them by.

The hallway ended at a wall, clad in the same peeling wood paneling that decorated the rest of the house.

A wall where a bedroom should have been.

"Huh."

I thumped it. It felt more solid than the concrete outside. I pressed my ear to it. Somewhere, deep inside whatever this wall hid, I heard the whisper of a song I could almost name.

"Looking for a hidden switch?" said Myantha.

"No."

I wrapped my hands around the base of the paneling and tore it off in one ragged sheet, exposing scum-slick stone that wouldn't have looked out of place in Blackbriar Keep. Somewhere there was probably a button. Nudge the right picture or sniff the right flower and the wall would swing open like something out of Scooby-Doo. I didn't have the time.

I reared back and smashed my head into the wall. It tickled.

Dust fell like fine snow. I thumped it again. The whole world shook. I kept head butting and the house kept shaking until I thought the whole place might come down. Myantha just stood there watching me make a fool of myself until, on the twelfth try, the wall caved in.

"Whaddaya know," she said. "Your head is good for something."

Skull aching, I cleared the rocks and stepped through the door. There was a torch. I lit it and walked on down. The stairs were slick with gunk. The music drifted up, a jingle from another world:

If you are a hungry boy
A grumpy boy
A grumbly boy
You'd better reach for Joll-E Boy…
Snack cakes!

The words meant nothing.

The stairs ended. I fit the torch into a sconce and nudged open a heavy wooden door. It swung open to reveal LB's teenage bedroom, twisted and stretched to a scale fit for a god. There were no windows. The lights were dim. The walls stretched up infinitely and the floor peeled away into the dark. It was as big as an airplane hanger.

No. It was much, much bigger than that.

"We should leave," said Myantha.

"Go ahead."

I had to see what else was here.

She waited by the stairs as I walked the length of that long, sickening room. It was a goddamned mess, just like you'd expect, crowded with oversized versions of everything my brother had ever thought might be cool. A model train that put Jett Creek's bus system to shame. A collection of action figures—half mint, half ready for play—that no toy store could match. A shelf the size of a building that seemed to contain every comic DC had ever published, another for Marvel, a third for indies. A tower of LPs that disappeared into the gloom and a turntable that had the song about the drugstore on repeat. A bed the size of a swimming pool swaddled in oversized X-Men sheets. A wall of televisions playing cartoons and pornography that was too gross, even for the nameless one to stomach. A long line of cages.

Cages.

What for?

There was none of LB's art, nothing of Odette or his family or friends—nothing except for what turned him on when he was fifteen or twenty years old. I didn't blame Myantha for being scared.

At the end of the room, I found the only thing there that was human sized: a little wooden desk that LB used in grade school, that I'd inherited from him, that still sat in Mom's office at the flower shop, waiting for her kids to come after school and do homework once again. There was a 3x5 card on it, covered with incoherent symbols that seemed weirdly familiar. I stared at it for a while and tossed it aside.

I opened the desk. Inside was a notebook. I touched it.

Sirens screamed.

The door slammed.

Purple gas sank to the floor.

It smelled like Mom's shop. Everything it touched, it burned.

I ran for Myantha. She ran for me. My big lungs must have been sucking more wind than hers, because the poison hit me first and it hit hard. My knees buckled. I crashed into a row of action figures and hacked blood all over a mint condition Princess Leia, in her costume from Hoth, which probably wasn't great for the resale value. My neck seized, twisting my head until I saw Myantha gasping and falling to the floor.

My eyes drooped once, twice, then slammed shut. There was a moment of clarity, just like when I'd leveled up, and the fog of stupidity lifted long enough for Callie to recognize what I'd seen on the 3x5. Those strange shapes were called letters, and they spelled out a message: "Don't Open the Desk. It's Full of Secrets and IT'S A FUCKING TRAP."

Anyway, that's how the nameless one died.

14

In the black I saw Myantha, eyes flickering and out of sync, clawing grooves into her neck, gulping toxic air. She was trying to talk. No words came.

How long can you leave someone trapped in the instant of their death? How long would I have to watch Myantha sucking deadly air because she'd been stupid enough to worship me? How long would I see LB roasting like a marshmallow in the dirt? How long would Matty be trying to smash out the fire crawling up his leg, that awful terror on his gentle, trusting face? How many more friends would I watch die?

Those questions echoed around the great empty cavern of my mind, and I realized I was coming to. The sickening tang of mothballs stole into my nose. My tongue stuck to the roof of my mouth. I felt nothing else.

"I don't know what the hell is wrong with her!"

It was a woman. At first I assumed it was Mom, but no, it was Odette. I was on the couch in her dim, cluttered office. I'd never heard her so close to panic.

"I found her on the table, face down, cold as a fucking snow cone. Her heart is beating. She's breathing, barely, but she won't wake up."

"I'm up," I groaned. She didn't hear.

"It's the game store on Carriage Street, at the entrance to the park, right next to the funicular. Yeah. 106 Carriage."

I kicked off the blankets and tried to stand. It didn't work. I rolled onto the floor.

"Fuck!" screamed Odette. She dropped her phone and pulled me off my face. I forced a thumbs up and tried to smile.

"I'm awake."

"God damn it," said Odette. She found the phone and put on the sweetest voice she had. "It's all right. Totally fine. She woke up, she's all good. I can tell because she gave me a thumbs up. Thank you—goodbye."

She slammed down the phone. I wouldn't have blamed her for kicking me in the face, but instead she offered her hand.

"They might send an ambulance anyway," she said. "They're stubborn like that."

"I'm sorry."

"I get the feeling you've been saying that a lot lately."

My stuff was piled on Odette's desk: notebooks, maps, my bag. The monocle rested on top. I lurched across the floor and tried to put it all away, as if that would stop her from seeing what she'd definitely already seen. She pushed me back onto the couch.

"Quit trying to move. I'm making you peppermint tea."

I'd never thought herbal tea could sound like such a threat.

The kettle rumbled. Odette dropped a teabag into a stained thrift store mug that said, "Horse Show Mom," poured the water and handed me the cup. I'd gotten used to how in my hands, it didn't even feel warm.

"Thought you were dead," she said. "So thanks for that. I've already had my husband and one of my favorite customers burned alive, but what this store really needs is clerks dying in the back room."

"This is good tea."

Odette rubbed the monocle like she was testing a swatch of fabric.

"You remember when LB had that heart thing?" she said.

Three years before. He collapsed at home and made a big deal out of how the doctor told him he was one chicken tender away from a quadruple bypass. Until quite recently, it had been the scariest thing that ever happened to me.

"He quit eating fried food and red meat," I said. "He went nuts on fiber. For like, six months. After that, I didn't hear any more about it."

"It wasn't his heart."

"Oh?"

"I found him in his office, notebooks and D-Rings scattered everywhere. He was flat across the desk, half frozen, same as you. The doctors kept saying it seemed like exposure—exposure in an eighty-three degree room!"

"What'd he tell you?"

"That he had no idea what happened. I think he did. I think you do, too. And I figure it's gotta have something to do with this stupid fucking monocle that you stole off my husband's body an hour before we dropped him into his grave."

She pelted the monocle into the garbage can. I lurched off the couch and dug it out of the trash. Cracked, but not broken.

"Did he tell you anything else?"

"That even though he liked being a medical mystery, it would be simpler to tell everyone it was just his heart."

"Mom lost sleep for a year."

"You think he gave her a thought? You think he cared what it did to me, finding him?"

"No."

"And do you?"

She sat on a box of paper napkins and cupped my hands. I could not feel her warmth. I forced myself to look her in her eyes, whose whites were apple red. She looked as tired as me.

"I've had a shitty couple of weeks, y'know?" she said. "I thought you were gone, Callie. I couldn't...that would be the end of me."

"I'm sorry," I said again, wishing I had other words.

"You're enough like your brother that I don't think you

are."

She said it like she wanted me to get out. I didn't think I could stand, so I asked the only question I could think of.

"Did LB still read comic books?"

"What? No. He said it was a dead medium, kids shit."

"Did he collect action figures, model planes, stuff like that?"

"LB wanted to be a grown-up since before he could walk. He thought people who hung on to that stuff were pathetic. Why?"

"The night he died—you saw him storm out. Did he say anything to you, anything about why he was going to the studio?"

She picked at her cuticle, couldn't get it where she wanted, and bit it instead.

"He told me he was going to bury the Queen of Skulls."

That almost made her laugh, but her little flare of mirth was extinguished when she saw that I didn't think it was funny at all.

"Earlier we were talking about my suspects…" I said. I put enough spin on the word suspects to make it sound like I was joking, even though nobody on earth would have believed I was.

"Yeah?"

"What about Karina?"

"Karina the clerk? My Karina?"

"She wasn't here the night of the fire."

"She's off Thursdays. So what?"

"She's always wanted to be a part of the game. She was the one who printed that character sheet you found—I thought it was somebody in my group, but—"

"Stop, okay? Please just stop. There's no reason she'd—there's no reason anyone would kill LB."

"Sure there was."

"What, then?"

I drained my tea. I untangled the leather strap on the end of the monocle and dropped it around my neck.

"Because he was the kind of guy who would nearly die and not tell his mom why. Because he fudged die rolls, because he set fires, because he was just smart enough to be good but too lazy to be great. Because he thought he was a god."

She didn't answer. Just sat on the desk, rubbing her hands.

"If you fuck up," I said, "if you do something unquestionably evil—like a hit and run, only much much worse—is there any coming back from it?"

"Why? Are you thinking of taking up hit and runs?"

"I'm just wondering."

She chewed on her thumbnail, checked her work, and chewed some more. It's what I loved about Odette. No matter how dumb the question, she answered like she gave a shit.

"I think," she said. "I think no. If you fuck up, you fuck up. There's no fixing it."

"That's what I was afraid of."

"But that doesn't let you off the hook. No matter how hopeless it is, you've gotta try."

Odette started folding the blankets I'd knocked on the floor. I reached for one, but she made a face that said she didn't need the help.

"Please go home I love you so much and...I think you'd really benefit from twenty or thirty hours' sleep."

I opened the door but didn't leave. I wanted to take her advice, to go home and pass out and forget, but it just wasn't going to happen.

"The night he died, I killed the Queen of Skulls. Except I didn't. He cheated to tell me I had. Why would he do that? Why would he warp his own game just to give me, like, a moment?"

"He thought rules were for other people. To him, that was the whole point of being a GM."

At the bottom of the stairs I stopped to breathe beside a chest filled with foam weapons left over from the high school LARPing summer camp. Odette opened her door and called after me: "Whatever's going on here, I want you to stop. But if you're going to kill yourself, for god's sake, don't do it in my store."

"You got it, boss."

In the front, the first customers had arrived. Diego was

helping them find something to play. He watched me unlock the case of miniatures and root around on the bottom rack—the shit that never sold. Behind a pair of singularly uncool wizards and a dopey looking dragon, I found the least exciting mini that had ever come through the shop. The box called her, "Peasant." She had no muscles, no weapons. She just sat at a table, waiting for the world to pass by.

"Smart lady," I said, and charged it to my account.

A trio of teenage boys huddled around a board game, arguing fiercely about a minor point in the rule book. They looked ready to flip the table and start swinging, but I figured they probably wouldn't. I had spent a lot of my life having arguments precisely that stupid.

I didn't regret a second.

I stepped onto the street and felt the welcome kiss of cold air. I wondered if I this would be the last time I ever passed through the door.

Outside, the funicular inched down the mountain, carrying a half-dozen tourists back from their little adventure on the peak. A zipline would be faster, I thought.

The shit I let you idiots do.

Since the minute I stepped into Winterwind, I'd been trapped by the rules. But I was a GM now—I'd been one since the minute I snatched the monocle off my brother's corpse—and if LB never gave a shit about the rules, why should I?

When I got home, I was shaking. I wanted to charge up the stairs and dive back in, but I forced myself to take it slow. Myantha wasn't going anywhere. She'd be dying for as long as it took for me to do this right.

I ate a bowl of raisin bran. I poured a cup of coffee, but my stomach lurched at the sight of it, so I dumped it out without taking a sip. I didn't need it. It would be years, I figured, before I could sleep.

I turned on every light in my room and set out my paints. I clicked the model together and forced myself spend a minute or so running my fingers over the grooves in the plastic—the droop of her shoulders, the arch of her nose—thinking about

217

how much better this would look if it were carved from wood. I found an old mix tape, made sure it had been made by Jill and not LB, and popped it in. Gentle distortion filled the air. I started to paint.

I gave her a primer, a first coat, a second coat, a wash. I pulled out every trick I knew to make her look alive, because soon, I figured, she would be. Rather than match the earthy brown color scheme suggested by the box, I put her in black jeans, a gray sweatshirt, and blue Chucks. The Plateau wouldn't know what hit it.

I painted until the sun was gone, lingering over every brushstroke, because as long as I had a brush in my hand, pain was banished and grief went with it. It was only when I finished the work that my hands started shaking again. I drained a glass of water, sketched a map of the gigantic bedroom where the nameless one had died, and set her on it.

I pulled on my best sweatshirt and got ready to return to the Plateau, hoping this adventure wouldn't end with Mom finding me dead on the floor.

WHEN I STEPPED OUT OF THE MONOCLE, PURPLE GAS WAS STILL falling. The nameless one was twisted into a ball beneath my feet, even uglier in death than in her short, pointless life. Myantha's fingers unclenched. She'd probably never seen torn black denim or a stained gray tank top, and the hoodie must have been a novelty as well. She'd never imagined I could be so human-sized, so soft, so scared. She'd never really seen Callie Myles.

I wrapped my sweater over my mouth and held my breath. It didn't help. The gas hit harder this time. Before I realized, I was on my knees, then flat on my face, trying to figure out why my lips were moving without making a sound. Finally, I croaked something out.

"You're in a bedroom. A weird bedroom."

I coughed blood onto the floor.

"There's gas. It's brutal."

My eyes slipped shut. Sleep wrapped me in a bear hug.

"The gas stops."

My voice dropped to a whisper.

"The gas stops."

Pressure built behind my eyes.

"The gas stops."

My head felt like it was going to explode.

"The gas stops."

Silver light danced around the edges of my vision. Everything else drifted away.

"The gas stops."

The gas stopped.

For a long time, I just breathed.

My eyes still closed, I scratched another rule onto my imaginary list:

7. *The GM can use her words to change this world. It hurts like hell.*

A hand gripped my shoulder. I forced my eyes open. For the first time in a while, Myantha looked happy to see me.

"You again," she said, helping me up. I leaned against a rack where thousands of green and tan army men squatted, screamed, killed, and died. "I mean, it is you, right?"

"One hundred percent."

"Got a name this time?"

"Callie Myles. Nice to meet you."

It was a cheery moment marred only slightly by the gnarled corpse on the floor. I twisted open the nameless one's hand and tugged off the Ring of Wayfinding. It had barely fit those muscle-thick fingers. On me, it was dangerously loose. I snapped the adventurer's bag off her hip—those things are handy—but the rest of her gear I let her keep. Even if I'd thought it would fit me, I was done with that golden mail.

I led her to a part of the room that didn't have a dead body in it, in front of a bank of free-to-play arcade classics. The toxic greens of the Teenage Mutant Ninja Turtles glinted off her eyes.

"How did you stop the gas?"

"I say how I want things to be, same as my brother used to do, same as you do when you play your Gray Game. It hurts like crazy, and the world does what I need."

"Show me."

"Can't go on faith?"

She didn't think that was funny.

I pointed at the gloom overhead. My palms sweated. God, I needed this to work.

"It begins to snow."

The pressure built. I kept my eyes open and invited it on.

"In the cloudless dark high above Myantha and Callie, soft white flakes fall like flour from a sifter."

The pain built and built and built, and those silver sparks flooded my vision, but I kept watching her until the pressure stopped and downy snow drifted down from the ceiling. Myantha caught it in her hand. She laughed and it was beautiful, and I did not mind when, just for a moment, she looked at me like I was a god.

"What now?" she said.

"I've tried doing this gentle. I've tried being rough. No matter what I do, it keeps getting me killed."

She crossed her arms, massaging the image of Arabeth. What a disappointment I must be. She nodded at the monstrosity on the floor.

"Why did you take that form?"

"I've made mistakes. Horrible ones. I'm trying to atone."

"What mistakes could be so awful that you'd turn yourself into that to make up for them?"

Her gaze was soft. Her lips turned up slightly, gesturing at the idea of a smile. This was the most she'd ever liked me, and I was about to ruin it. Oh well. It's not like there's ever a good time to sell someone you accidentally murdered their mom.

"The poison in Glittermore was an herbal toxin," I said. Her expression hardened. She said nothing. "Zircon made it from plants in the woods outside of town."

"Why would he do something like that?"

Now came the shitty part.

"Because I asked him. He smeared the poison on my arrow. I fired it at a chipmunk. I missed."

"Oh my god."

"It flew into the woods. I never thought about it again. Apparently, it—"

That's when she punched me in the nose. No wind-up, no nothing—her fist leapt up from her side and slammed into my extremely mortal face. Something went crack, blood poured everywhere, and I dropped to my knees.

I tried to get up. She kicked me in the head. It hurt like, well, like getting kicked in the head. A whole universe of pain exploded across my skull, and I went sprawling across the shag. I had no strength to call her back, and no reason to try.

A long time later, I stepped out of that impossible house into the dark of the swamp. I had toilet paper stuffed up my nose and a punishing headache that throbbed worse every time I breathed. I deserved it, but it still sucked. I was halfway down the driveway when a figure drifted out of the dark. I reached for my weapon, remembered I didn't have any, and was preparing myself to die some more when I realized who it was.

"Please don't kick me any more," I said. "Or do, if you want. Really, you probably should. I deserve it."

"You're a real fucking bitch, you know that?" she said. I nodded. I didn't think she wanted more of an answer than that. "It's not just what you did, or that you killed her, or that you hid it from me, although my god all of that is really something—it's that you could have the power to create a poison so deadly, shoot it into the woods, and not even bother checking where it lands."

"I know it isn't anywhere near good enough, but I didn't know what I was doing."

"How could you not know?"

"I'd been lied to."

"By who?"

"By the Gray Lord."

"I'd like to hit you some more. I'd like to hit you until the bones in my hands shatter, and then I'd like to stand on your windpipe until you stop wasting this world's air."

"I wouldn't stop you."

"I don't think you could. But it wouldn't fix anything."

"Probably not."

"Then what are we going to do?"

I smeared my hands across my face, pressing back tears. Once I was reasonably under control, I said, "There's something waiting for us at the Edge of the World. I don't care what it is. I don't care if it kills me. I just want this story to end."

"Make it happen. It's not like I have anywhere better to be."

I squeezed Myantha's hands. She did not squeeze back. I let them go, and resigned myself to never touching her again. It didn't matter. It was time to say the magic words. I sure as shit hope they worked.

"You stand near a lonely white church on a windswept hill at the Edge of the World."

The pain hit.

Silver burst across my vision as bright as an atomic bomb. I'd never had somebody jam a rusty nail into my eye, but I figure it felt like this.

And then I felt the wind. It pressed against me like a wall, pushing me one step and another and then a third. I would have kept going, because I was too weak to stand up to it, if Myantha hadn't smacked me hard across the back of the head. My vision cleared and I saw my feet hanging off the lip of a cliff. Far below—so far I couldn't even hear the waves exploding on the rocks—was the sea.

"That's a hell of a trick," she said, screaming over the gale.

We were a few hundred yards south of the salt-stained little village where Arabeth made her first bloody mark on this world. If anyone lived there, they were smart enough stay inside. Along the cliff, the ground sloped into a steep, rocky hill. At the top was my ending, the white church I'd been dreaming of all this time.

We climbed, saying nothing, focusing on not getting blown into the sea. I went numb instantly—it turns out a thin hoodie and worn denim are not exactly cut out for winter at the ass end of the Plateau—but I kept moving. I wanted to know who was inside that church.

I wanted to wring their neck.

In this whole gray place, the church was the only white thing. It looked solid, like it had grown right out of that barren earth. As we got closer, I saw its windowless façade was covered with intricate carvings. It wasn't until we were outside the door that I realized the material wasn't marble.

"It's bone," said Myantha. "Right down to the foundation, it's all bone."

The delicate structure of some dead bastard's hands and feet were arranged into a relief of a screaming face, as neat as macaroni art. Above the door, a dozen femurs formed a blooming white rose.

"Yeesh," I said, and went inside.

The door was unlocked, like always. The floor, a mosaic fitted together from bits of flattened skull, was empty. The wind whistling through the slits in the wall sounded like someone murdering a bagpipe. But there was no table at the front, no people, no dice, no smoke, no fire. There wasn't anything at all.

The door slammed. The echo died fast.

I stood in the center of that useless room, waiting for a monster to jump out or a hidden panel to swing open, but nothing came.

"Are you cold?" said Myantha.

"I'm fine."

"You look cold."

She sounded like my mother. It suited her.

She tapped on the wall. Nothing happened.

"What are you doing?" I said.

"What you do. Looks pretty stupid, doesn't it?"

"It does."

Together, we tapped on the walls.

As we went, I inspected the decor. The walls were covered with interlocking spirals of carefully-chosen bones. But the end of the room, where my brother usually burned to death, was a yellowed mess of shattered ribs, cracked hips, and unidentifiable shards.

"What do you think?" I said. "Was this wall done later? Had they run out of good bones? Is there a pattern? A code?"

She ran her hands across the jagged bone, thought for a while, and said, "It might just be a shitty wall."

I should have been heartbroken. All that blood had added up to fuck all. But, lucky me, I was too cold to feel much at all. I was trying to shake some feeling back into my fingers when I turned and saw the picture on the floor.

From the entrance, the mosaic on the ground had looked abstract. At this angle, it formed a woman's face. Her lips were thin. Her eyes were black. Her hair looked as coarse as a pine cone. A border ran around the mosaic, from her neck to the top of her head: vines studded with thorns bursting into flames.

"Mean anything to you?" said Myantha.

"Not a goddamned thing."

When we got outside, the wind slammed the breath from our chests.

"Fuck!" shouted Myantha. "Are you okay?"

"I'll manage."

"Bullshit. We need to get you in front of a fire before your fingers turn black. I'm not done with you yet."

I tried to form a snappy comeback, but my teeth were chattering too hard for me to talk. She thrust her cloak at me and I took it without arguing. We made our way down the hill to the inn. I sagged against the rough wooden door and fell into the warmth.

It was, unquestionably, an inn. Long dead animals adorned the walls; recently dead animals filled the sideboard. The ceilings were low, lime-washed, and stained with smoke. The windows were barred against the weather. I had a sudden craving for pulled pork, and wondered if it was worth the trauma to magic myself up a barbecue plate. A fresh stab of pain split my skull and I decided it would be better to let that dream go.

I crashed into a fur-covered chair beside the fire. I peeked around the room, trying to remember how LB described it the first time I'd come here. It was shittier than I'd imagined.

Myantha piled furs on top of me. I squeezed my cold hands

between my cold thighs, trying to convince some part of me to get warm.

"I'm getting us food," she snapped. "Don't bother trying to move."

"I wouldn't dare."

She went to find the proprietor. In the chair opposite, a squat man with pink cheeks and a sagging red beard peered out from behind a mug of hot beer. He looked like Yosemite Sam on a bender. He was the only customer there.

"No way to dress for this weather," he grunted after a while.

"I'm learning that."

"The hell you doing here?"

"Sightseeing."

He coughed out a laugh that sounded like he'd never tried laughing before.

"Just what sights did you come to see?"

"The church on the hill."

"The ossuary?"

"I guess. What's its deal?"

"It's a memorial to a woman, dead woman, name of Summer."

"The woman on the floor?" He nodded. "How'd she die?"

"Her house caught fire. She was in the back, working on her garden. Tried to get out, but the rose bushes blocked her way."

"Did you know her?"

A scowl formed underneath his beard.

"Just how old do you think I am?"

"I'm sorry, I—"

"That woman died two, three-hundred years ago, if she ever existed at all. Nobody here ever heard of her until a few winters back, when a ship pulled up at the cliffs. Gang of workmen rigged a winch and hauled up basket after basket of those awful bones. Started building a church. They were northerners, same as you, and strange. We told em to get the hell off our cliffs, and they gave us a heap of silver to shut up. Said take it or die. Wasn't much of a choice."

"They just built the church and left?"

"They did."

"Why?"

"The hell should I know? Northerners. They're odd."

He tilted his cup, found it empty, and grimaced.

"Another round, Lena?" he called to the innkeeper.

"Get it yourself!"

He got up and patted me on the head. I was having such a shitty day, I didn't even mind.

"Any idea who sent the builders?" I said.

"Maybe. Bastards left a heap of trash for us to clean up. At the bottom of it, my cousin found a sketch, a plan of what the church was meant to look like. Had a name in the corner."

"What did it say?"

"Lomella."

Lomella. The Queen of Skulls. I tried to figure out what that meant, but my head was just too cold.

He waddled off to pour his drink. Myantha was up there beside the innkeeper, who had a broad back and a long curved knife that she was using to carve paper thin slices off a roast. This must have been the woman who dumped the tankard in Fausto's lap. By the look of her, he was lucky she didn't do worse.

Myantha dropped a tin plate on the arm of my chair. I picked up one of the slices of meat, rolled it into a tube, and ate it. It was salty, and with the headache I had, salt was what I craved.

"This is good."

"Eat as much as you can. I booked us a room. The innkeeper thinks we're rich, and she's going to rip us off, so when you're feeling up to it you'd better conjure up a shitload of gold."

"Gimme a few more plates of this meat and I'll give you the whole world."

"You'd better. Being next to you is making my skin crawl. I want this to end fast. What's your plan?"

I didn't have any fucking idea. I'd already performed one

miracle that day, halfway cracking my skull open to save her from a room full of poison gas, and now I just wanted to eat my roast in peace. But I had committed too many crimes to deserve such a blessing.

"I hear somebody in my inn is cold," said Lena, voice booming down from above my chair. "I can't stand that."

I looked up and she looked down. Her arms were as dark and powerful as oak trees. Her ponytail fell heavy across her neck.

And a white patch hid her left eye.

I'd like to say I did something cool. I'd been looking for this woman for god knows how long—you'd think I'd have had something clever prepared. But instead I grunted, "Oh shit!" and tried to scramble to my feet.

She pushed me right back down.

"It's you," she said.

"It sure is."

She broke into a huge smile. I saw every tooth, her tongue, her throat. She looked ready to devour me.

"You won't be running away so quick," she said. "I've waited so long to meet you, Callie Myles, and you'll have to forgive me—I'm an innkeeper. I like to chat with my customers."

She slipped the knife out of her belt, sat on the lip of the hearth, and rested the blade on her leg. Little motes of gold flickered out of Myantha's fingertips. I held up a hand for her to wait.

"Chat," I said. "Okay. I can chat."

"So what the fuck brings you here?"

"I want to know why you killed my brother. I want to know why you killed my friend."

Lena leaned in close. Her breath smelled like old dog.

"Oh, it started a long time ago. You remember the first time you came to my place?"

"Quite well."

"That thief of yours made a pass at me. I answered him with a pint of ale. And then the cliff-men attacked and you ran outside. Do you remember, by chance, what happened next?"

"We fought them off. We saved the town. We tracked them to—"

"Slow down! Please, please. Before that. When the cliff-men ran, when you sheathed your swords, what did you do?"

She grabbed my face hard enough that I thought she might crack a tooth. The furs slid to the floor. I strained to remember more of the session. LB had been in top form that day. He made me smell the hot blood steaming on cold ground. He made me feel the pull of an arrow as I ripped it from a corpse.

"I retrieved my arrows," I said.

"And then?"

"We looted the bodies."

"Whose bodies?"

"The cliff men."

"And…"

"And the victims, too."

She let go of my face and leaned back against the hearth. I got it now. I'd have thought I had no room for more guilt, more shame, but nope—I felt this too.

"There was a boy there, a smith's apprentice named Weston," she said. "He was poor, honest, funny, the type who never quit smiling no matter how hungry he got. He was my little brother and he had nothing in the world except a knack for making armor and a ring that always helped him find his way home."

I felt Arabeth's ring on my finger. A level one trinket. A souvenir.

"You wrenched it off his body," said Lena. "I was too shocked to stop you. I don't suppose…do you remember his face?"

"What?"

"Tell me something of his smile. His eyes. Tell me the color of his hair."

She smacked me across the cheek. I wanted to give her what she wanted, but no matter how I scoured my memory, there was nothing there. LB never described his face.

"I'm sorry. I don't—"

She slammed her fist against my left hand, flattening it against the arm of the chair. I pulled against her, but she was far too strong. She ran her thumb across the stolen ring.

"This isn't yours," she said.

"Lena—"

She whipped down her knife.

It made the slightest crunch as it severed the bone.

15

THE FINGER FELL TO THE FLOOR. IT LOOKED SMALL. FAMILIAR AND alien at the same time.

My finger. The one I used to flip people off. I'd never thought it would be so far away.

It twitched.

And then I felt hot blood spilling across my palm and heard the ragged screams ripping from my throat, and I knew shit had gone really wrong.

White light filled the room. Myantha pressed an arrow of light to the innkeeper's head. Skin sizzled where it touched her temple.

"Lose the knife," said Myantha.

"No."

They held there for a moment, each waiting for the other to break. It took Yosemite Sam to break the stalemate. He appeared behind Myantha and pressed a steak knife into her back. By the way he was sweating, I could tell he'd never threatened anyone before.

I pressed a wad of fur against the wound, trying to ignore the pain, trying to remember that I was in control.

"The bearded man drops his knife," I said. A thousand pinpricks started behind my right eye. Yosemite Sam looked at me, fist squirming on the hilt of his knife. "He drops his knife and gets the hell out."

He started for the exit, looking like he didn't know what he was doing or why. My other eye started to burn. Lena flicked her knife. The lanyard split. The monocle fell to the ground, taking with it the pain in my head and whatever power I might have had. Yosemite Sam relaxed.

"Put the arrow away," said Lena.

Myantha lowered her fists. The arrow disappeared. Sam shoved her against the hearth, his knife shaking against her hip.

"What the hell was that?" he said.

"What did it feel like?" said Lena.

"An iron fist, squeezing my brain."

"The power of a god. The power to reshape the world without getting out of her chair."

She pushed me onto the ground and planted her boot on my sternum. She picked up my finger. She shook it until the ring dropped into her palm, then tossed the severed digit into the fire. The pain roared like a jet engine.

"If all you wanted was the ring," I said, "why'd you cut off my fucking finger?"

"Because you deserve to bleed."

I didn't know where I was going, but I hoped that if I kept her talking, the pain would fade enough that I could think my way out.

"How did you find us? How did you kill LB?"

"After you defiled my brother's corpse, I started hearing stories from the north, all along the middle road, of Heroes who appeared whenever there was trouble, who saved villages from unknown evils and killed anyone who got in their way. People called them champions. I knew better. I thought I was the only one who understood until I started having dreams about the church on the hill, the Gray Lord dying in fire, and all his little Heroes dying with him."

"I had those dreams too."

"Do you know who sent them?"

"Tell me."

"A long-lost daughter of this town. Lomella."

"The Queen of Skulls."

"I don't know how she found us, I don't know how she slipped into our sleep, but she called to dozens of us up and down the Plateau—anyone whom the Heroes had wronged. The mothers of guardsmen you crippled. The sons of bandits you killed. She offered us revenge."

"She called to me too. Why?"

"To offer a chance to make amends for what you did. Don't you wish you'd taken it?"

"A bit. What did she have you do?"

"Weston wasn't the only one in the family who could work iron. Before I bought this inn, I was married to a smith. Working in his shop, I learned what he knew and quite a bit more. The Queen came here, right to this inn, and told me about a spell called Astral Leap. Said she needed special iron for it—Gorham's Iron. Old magic. I hadn't been near a forge since Weston died, but for her I cast a twenty-sided die. She gave it to someone from your world, and they gave it to your brother, and that was how he died."

"Which person from our world?"

She picked me up by my throat. As it happens, this is not the most comfortable way to get picked up. She pressed her knife against my belly button.

"Ask another question and I'll gut you. It's rather addictive, watching gods die."

Lena clenched tighter. I clawed at her fingers and closed my eyes and tried to think of something more constructive than, aw, damn, I'm going to die.

"Put her down!" said Myantha.

"I think you aren't supposed to talk," said Sam.

"That's right," said Lena. "Open her up."

He dragged the knife hesitantly across Myantha's side. A thin stream of blood dripped down her robes. Myantha said nothing.

"Cut her like you mean it," said Lena.

"I can't, I can't," muttered Sam. He did not drop the knife.

"There's no reason to hurt her," I said.

"Remember Weston. You taught him to hunt. He called you uncle. They tossed his body aside like it was trash."

He closed his eyes and tried to bury his knife in Myantha's stomach. Either he was too sweet or too slow. She wrenched her hands away, held them over his eyes, and barked the incantation for Blinding Glare.

He exploded backwards across the rug. There were scorch marks where his eyes had been. He whimpered and crawled.

Myantha reached for his knife.

Lena threw me down like a dancer smashing a plate in a Greek restaurant. My spine snapped across the chair, leaving me a bruised, throbbing pile.

Lena kicked the knife away and grabbed Myantha by the shoulder.

"Do you know what your demigods do when they aren't here?" Lena said.

"No one does," said Myantha.

Lena slammed Myantha into the hearth. A flaming log tumbled down her back and fell onto the floor. Its light caught a piece of glass under the chair nearest me. The monocle.

"They play a game," said Lena. "They call it *Winterwind*. They sit around a table in a dark room, drinking and eating until their guts hang over their belts, laughing at our pain. They clap for whoever kills the most, steals the most, tortures the most. They roll dice. We live or die."

"Bullshit."

"My queen told us you were from Glittermore. Your town, your people—they died because of her."

"I know. She fucked up."

"No. She botched a roll. How many dead—all for the sake of her game?"

There it was, the last of it. The truth I'd been holding back from Myantha since I met her. I don't know what she made of it, because before she could say anything Lena slammed her against the stone. Myantha went limp.

I stretched out my good hand. I touched the monocle. Lena put her boot on the glass. She picked up the knife.

"You didn't have to kill Matty," I said. "He wasn't a monster. He was a kid from the mountains with a big heart and a talent with iron. Isn't that the kind of guy your brother would have liked?"

It was the wrong thing to say.

"That was your last question," she said.

She kicked me onto my back and pressed the knife against my shirt. I waited for my chance to dodge or make a reaction roll or a saving throw or anything the rules could give me, but the rules had gone out the window some time ago, and I did nothing but watch as she buried that long knife in my chest.

I suddenly felt quite heavy.

Ever open the dishwasher before it's done running and water dumps out all over everywhere? That's what happened all over my legs, but instead of water it was blood. Viscera is probably a better word—in the torrent that spilled across me, across the floor, there were shapes faintly familiar from freshman bio. I was watching myself from a long way off, wondering which blob might be my liver, when the snap of bone brought me back.

Lena looked up. In the reflection of her knife, I saw Myantha swelling and twisting and growing in directions people are not meant to grow. Her head twisted to reveal a long slobbering jaw and a tongue covered with black and oozing sores. From deep within her came a sound as horrible as the cry of a dying child.

For a moment, Lena forgot about me. I tried to stand up and the pain ripped through me and I sank back down onto my ass.

The beast roared.

"Come on," said Lena. "Try."

She raised her knife and took a step backwards.

I had just enough in me to lift my leg. My foot caught Lena's ankle. She tripped and tumbled backwards onto the floor.

She did not drop the knife.

Which was too bad, because her neck fell right on it.

Skin split. Blood sprayed.

She was dead the instant she hit the rug.

I wanted to believe that was the end, but as long as the Queen of Skulls was out there, I could not exhale.

The beast that was Myantha leaned over me. I raised a finger to touch it, as gentle as popping a bubble, and she snapped into her true form.

"Thank you," I croaked, trying to push myself up on hands slick with blood. "That's a hell of a trick."

"I'm sorry I wasn't quicker."

"Get me the monocle and I can heal us both."

She picked it up. She tossed it in her hand, enjoying its weight. She tied the strap around her neck. She held her face to it and squinted into another world.

"Myantha's wounds heal," she said, and threw her head back as the pain hit. The cut on her side hissed shut. Her burnt hair regrew. Even her clothes repaired themselves.

"Hurts like a bitch, doesn't it?" I said.

She nodded. She smiled.

"So you really don't have any power?" she said. "Just one handy trinket?"

"That's right. I'm as human as they come. Now please..."

She took my hand. She pulled me halfway up and let me dangle. Pain, unthinkable pain, erupted along my ruined body.

"What did you roll the day my mother died? What did the die say?"

"A one."

"You rolled a one, and I lost everything.'

"Please, I'm hurt, I'm so hurt, and I can explain if you just stop the pain."

She dropped me to the floor. I settled like a quilt kicked off the bed. She leaned down and talked slow.

"When we met, I could tell you thought I was dumb, pointless, weak. All I do is save your fucking life, and all you do is lie. I didn't complain because I thought there was something in you that was divine. You're no god. Not even a half god. Just a stupid girl with power she doesn't understand, treating me like an NPC."

"I'm sorry."

She kicked me in the face. It was a pleasant distraction from bleeding out across the floor.

She tugged the Ring of Wayfinding out of Lena's hand and slid it onto her middle finger. My bloody stump ached.

"I'll see for myself. Your paradise, your friends. If it's how the innkeeper said, all of them really should die."

She pressed the button on the monocle and vanished. There was no sound but the fire and the slow drip of blood out as I lay trapped and dying in a world that wasn't mine.

I SHOULDN'T HAVE SURVIVED. WITHOUT THE MONOCLE, I WAS only human, and this was a world where humans did nothing but die.

I figured I'd get sleepy or numb, that the pain would fade and death would become tempting, like how two a.m. turns a gas station burrito into a really good idea. It never happened. The pain got worse than anything I'd ever felt, and I only got more awake.

After spending I don't know how long sucking dust on that ragged old rug, I got my ass up. More of me tore. The flesh looked like frayed ribbon. I looked away, vomit rising in my throat, for some reason feeling it would be deeply embarrassing if I threw up. I squeezed the fur across my abdomen, trying to hold the wound shut. It didn't help much.

I took a step.

All of me screamed. I tasted blood.

I kept walking.

I thought I'd already maxed out the pain, but with each step, more of my insides seeped through my fingers, and new parts of me joined the agony party. My vision blurred; my head got heavier, but I was still on my feet when I got to the counter. I wanted to breathe for a minute or two, but if I quit moving that would be the end of me, so I forced my way behind the bar, trusting in the power of cliché.

This was an inn in a fantasy town, and inns always have four things:

1. A vacant room

2. Big goddamned roasted legs of meat

3. Hot booze

4. Shitty knickknacks for sale

In a chest above the bar, I found a rusted dagger, three warped arrows, a cracked buckler, a few extremely sad level one spells, and a corked vial of noxious black goo. I didn't have any money, but the proprietor was busy being dead, so I didn't think she'd complain if I helped myself. I choked down half of the goo. It tasted like Craig's juice. I rubbed a dollop on my finger stump and smeared the rest over the wound in my chest, then bit back a scream as the flesh shuddered closed.

Fatigue hit. I locked the front door, stuffed my pockets full of meat and lurched downstairs in search of that empty room. The guest rooms were underground—the better to escape the lashing wind—along a straw-lined hallway low enough to scrape my head. The first three doors were locked. The last opened onto a cell with no window, an overflowing chamber pot, and the shittiest, most inviting bed I'd ever seen. I was asleep before I remembered to be afraid.

Dreams came. Dreams of forgotten sessions: the rampage in Godin Woods; the incident below the rookery; the ambush at the Lonely Falls. I heard my victims scream, tasted their blood, smelled their shit. On the wind floated the laughter of Callie and her friends, a universe away.

They were not the best dreams I'd ever had.

I woke up starving, stuffed some meat into my mouth, passed out chewing and was sucked back into dreamland. My knife tore through the ribcage of a frightened monk. An arrow split a Hordesman's skull. This went on for a while. Finally, I woke with no pain but the aching thirst in my throat. For a few luxurious seconds, I forgot where I was. Then I smelled the shit in the corner and the whole thing flooded back. I made for the stairs.

This was gonna suck.

Lena's body had started to stink. Trying to keep my back to her, I grabbed a tankard and opened the keg. Brown ale sloshed in. Without thinking, I tilted the mug to beat back the foam, and for a moment I was back in Critical Hit, pulling a pint for a *Magic* nerd with a fake ID, pulling a pint for LB.

I didn't know what was going on back in Jett Creek. I had no idea if I was still up there rolling dice, sacrificing a few seconds with every toss of the d20. Maybe I'd vanished from that world—maybe I was stuck in a coma. Or maybe time had simply stood still.

It would take more than one beer to find an answer. If time in Jett Creek was frozen, my friends were alive. If the hours I'd slept had passed there, too, then Sondra, Craig, and Doc were all dead. Maybe others too. In Winterwind, Myantha was low level, but in Jett Creek, an Arrow of Light goes a long way.

I drank. It helped.

When the mug was empty, I pulled the key off Lena's hip and unlocked the rooms downstairs. I found some winter gear that more or less fit. I staggered upstairs, unlocked the front door, and searched for the right way to say goodbye to a corpse.

"I'm sorry. It doesn't matter, but I am."

I felt like an idiot, a killer, a fraud. I decided there wasn't any point in saying more.

Outside, the wind roared like a leaf blower. The air was cold and heavy with salt, which stung like hell against my dry skin. For a moment I dreamed of moisturizer, and then I remembered there wasn't a drop on this entire screwed up continent, and that made me want to cry.

I crossed the town square, where the grass was blown flat by the wind. This was where Arabeth first rolled dice, first drew blood. The doors to the meager shops and houses were drawn tight, but there were slats in the windows and behind some of them I thought I could feel eyes.

I walked faster, my too-big boots slapping hard on every brick, until the path grew steep and the town fell away. I reached the ossuary and walked on to the cliff, to the sea. I dangled my legs. Far below, in perfect silence, gray water abused jagged rocks.

Someone in Jett Creek had learned my brother's secret and killed him, either for what he'd done here or for reasons unknown. He deserved it. They were also responsible for what happened to Matty, and that was bitterly uncool. And they were, indirectly, the reason I was stuck here. I wanted to know who it was. The rest of the party had shut me out, and called me crazy, but they were still the closest things I had to friends in that world or any other. I was their GM and I would do what it took to keep them safe.

Problem was, this prison was perfect. It had taken the Queen of Skulls hundreds of years to master Astral Leap, and she was an extremely magical bitch. I had no books, no money, no food, no friends, no hope.

There was nothing to do but jump.

I scooted forward until I was nearly off the edge. I told my hands to let go.

They didn't.

"I am going to die in this place. Dysentery will kill me, or highwaymen, or some kind of super gross medieval plague, but I will definitely die here. I am not a survivor, never have been, and I don't think I can change that now.

"Or I die today. It would be much more efficient, much less painful. I've spent a short lifetime taking the easy way out. Why stop?"

Far below me, a pair of gulls swirled over the surf, gray birds against gray water. If I jumped, I wondered, would they get out of the way?

"Caledonia Elizabeth Myles! Knock this shit off!"

Her voice cut through the wind, so sharply that I spun around to see if she was really there.

She was not. But I listened to her all the same. I backed off the cliff, I walked back down the hill, I resigned myself to an inconvenient death because Mom had already lost one kid this month and didn't need to lose anymore.

I did not look back at the sea.

I had a new quest. For the first time ever it was one I'd given myself.

Step one: Figure out how LB got here in the first place

Step two: Get the fuck out

This would be an adventure, I told myself. Adventures are fun.

I spent that night in a ditch, too cold to forage, too hungry to sleep. Like that awful white lady in *Gone With the Wind*, I promised myself that the next night, I wouldn't go hungry, but night arrived and food didn't, and I decided I would have to learn how to starve.

I spent weeks trudging across the highlands, where nothing grew but brush and whole days ground by without anyone passing me on the road. The war had not come this far south. The few people I saw weren't refugees. They were travelers, traders, hunters, bards. Some of them gave me food and didn't complain when I gave nothing in return. One—a woman whose bag was heavy with the pelts of weird creatures—gave me a crash course in trapping, and after that I was hungry less. Another, after laughing hysterically at my extremely fucked skin, gave me some invaluable tips on natural moisturizer, which was nearly as welcome as the food.

Winter came.

I survived it.

When the earth thawed, I found myself on the edge of a swamp. I walked through the muck, turned up the driveway, and was back at the Ranchettes. The patio was cracked worse than ever. The weeds that sprouted through the concrete were dead. I put my hand on the doorknob and tried to believe I would find answers inside.

It smelled like sage and ginger, fresh flowers and garlic and perfume samples torn out of magazines. It smelled like home, and I let myself pretend it was.

The first thing I did was take a shower, hot enough to blast my skin raw. I found a cabinet full of Bugles, Ripples, Hershey Kisses, Chocabloc, Reese's Cups, snack cakes, and countless other gas station snacks: sugary, salty, and in between. I ate until I made myself sick, which didn't take very long. When I finished barfing up chocolate, I figured I deserved another shower. As the water scoured my skin, I remembered LB giving me baths in this tub. We'd splash each other with lukewarm water, sink and raise and sink my boats, and laugh until my fingers pruned. I stayed in the shower until the hot water ran out and my fingers pruned again. I shut off the stream, toweled off, and took a long nap in a bed that smelled like Mom.

I woke to the stink of swamp. The illusion was gone. It was time to make myself do what I'd come here for.

Deep below the house, in a room whose size still made me reel, the gas was gone, the snow was melted, and the alarm lights flashed. Heavy carpet muffled my footsteps. The desk waited at the end of the room. I flipped over the 3x5 LB had left as a warning and found no instructions for disarming the trap. Wires crept down the desk's leg into the floor. I was no electrician, so I left them alone, wondering what else I'd failed to notice before.

I started with the cages. There were six, and they weren't for animals. Before, I'd been too icked out to step inside. Now I forced myself inside. The bars were gold-plated iron, thick as a sausage and close together. There was no blood, no shit, no claw marks, no sign that anything had ever been held here at all, until I looked closely at the floor. At the base of six of the bars, scratched small enough that you couldn't see them from outside, there were names—Jhyia, Phesia, Villosa, Berra, Flara, Caghayn—each etched in a different hand. I had met enough people on the Plateau to know them for women's names.

I stepped out of the cage, wanting another shower. I didn't know what had turned the boy that gave me baths upstairs into the man who built these cages, but I was more certain than ever that he had deserved to die. In hopes of pushing past how extremely fucking sad that made me, I kept looking around.

The room was packed with collections. CDs, LPs, cassettes. VHS, LaserDisc, DVDs, and a whole shelf of what I assume was Betamax. Magazines, zines, books, comics, newspapers. All of it ruthlessly catalogued. None of it shit I cared about.

I picked over the arcade games. There were dozens, from *Soulcalibur II* all the way back to *Space Invaders*. I played a couple rounds of *Street Fighter*, getting my ass kicked each time, and considered that it would be just like LB to force me to beat the whole game in order to open that goddamned desk. But he sucked at fighting games—he wasn't patient enough—and that would lock him out, too.

That brought me to the final resting place of the nameless one. She looked worse than ever, and didn't smell great either. I tugged my shirt over my nose and, without really meaning to, started reshelving the action figures she'd toppled when she died. Once a clerk, always a clerk. I was straightening the last of the *Star Wars* figurines when I glanced at the DC shelf and saw Daredevil where he should not be.

Safe in his plastic, whip in hand, Stan Lee's blind superhero was flanked by Green Arrow and Green Lantern. I had never been a comics head, but I knew enough to spot a Marvel character behind enemy lines.

I rescued him. The rack of Marvel figures was at least fifty feet high, and the only way up was by ladder. Squeezing the toy under my armpit, I scaled it slowly, glancing down rows of costumed heroes and sinister baddies in search of whoever took Daredevil's spot. On the highest shelf, I spotted Wonder Woman, first lady of DC comics, far from home. Trying not to look down, I swapped her for Daredevil, descended the ladder, and put the Amazon where I'd found the Man Without Fear.

The lights stopped flashing. The fluorescents flickered on. The Joll-E Boy jingle started playing again. At the end of the room, the desk popped open.

"LB, you fucking asshole."

I ran to the desk. I picked up the notebook. I didn't die, which was a welcome change. I sat on the nearest chair—a fat green beanbag—and flopped the notebook open. The first page caught fire. I flung it across the floor. The book burned.

"Fuck!" I shouted, and scrambled up the beanbag. Smoke plumed. I was ready to make another hopeless sprint for the exit when the smoke twisted into the shape of a man.

A big man.

A jerk.

A god.

LB, skin and clothes and face a shifting fabric of gray, was about to speak when he bent double coughing and nearly fell down. I tried to help him, but my hand went straight through his wrist. The smoke parted and reformed. Finally, he stood straight. Smoke snaked out of the still-burning book to join his form.

"Sorry," he said. "Gotta quit smoking."

I laughed. I couldn't help it. He pulled a little gray rectangle from the front pocket of his flannel, withdrew a textureless cigarette, and lit it. He took a long drag and asked me, "So what the hell's going on?"

"Are you really him?" I said. I wasn't sure what I wanted his answer to be.

"Nope. Just his notebook. How is the big man?"

"Dead."

"Fuck." A long drag. "Welp, how can I help?"

He tried to lean against the wall. When he put weight on his shoulder it dissolved into fog. Panicked, he straightened up and tried not to touch anything else.

"What is this place?" I said. The smoke man looked around and shrugged.

"Looks like my old bedroom but, y'know, freaky big. Kind of excessive, if you ask me."

"What's in the notebook? A confession? An explanation? A will?"

"It's a story. I like telling stories—liked it, anyway. This one's from when I was in college. It's about how I first came here. Wanna hear it?"

"Yeah."

"Thank god. I've been waiting a long time, y'know?"

His voice dropped. His gut hung loose. His shoulders slumped. He pulled hard on his beard, and really looked like my brother for the first time.

"Sophomore year I didn't do anything but fuck around in

the forge and play *Those About to Die*," he said. "Those sessions were the stuff of myth. We'd play two, three days straight, so cranked up on speed or coke that time melted by. We'd spend a week on a single battle—armies of thousands cascading across the desert. We felt sand under our feet and blood in our mouths. College, y'know? It was fucking fun."

The book burnt down to cinders. The smoke grew thin.

"I get it," I said. "You were really cool in the eighties. What about the monocle?"

"It was near dawn on a Monday. We'd just wrapped one of those marathons and my heart was going too fast for me to lie down. I got a fifth of scotch and went to the forge."

"What did you do?"

"I lit the fire and drank the scotch."

"And then?"

"I couldn't fucking tell you."

"You dick."

"I blacked out! What do you want? I came to and the fire was cold and the bottle was broken and there was that god-damned monocle cooling in the water."

"Did you write anything down?"

"Kinda? There was a notebook next to me. I'd written a whole lot of chicken scratch under the heading, 'Gorham's Iron.' Don't ask what it means. I got nothing."

The fire stopped. The smoke began to clear. LB noticed it. Fear crept across his face. He tried very hard to stand still.

"When you came here for the first time," I said, "did you think it was a game or did you know it was real?"

"At first I figured it was just a choice hallucination, like I'd punctured a hole in my consciousness and ascended to a higher plane. I ran a couple of sessions using the monocle and it was fucking great. Then one night, after the game was over, I went for a walk on the Plateau. I decided to walk as far as I could, see how far the fantasy went. I passed through Blackbriar, went north into the lands I'd never even dreamed of, and saw that the detail never stopped. I realized it was real."

"How'd that hit you?"

"It fucking wrecked me. My players had been killing real people, and I'd made it happen. I just shut down."

"And then what?"

"I vowed to make it right."

"How?"

I held my breath. I needed an answer here, something useful, hopeful. Something worth believing in.

"Dunno," said smoke boy. "The notebook stops there. Do you think I turned things around?"

"There are cages over there, human sized, with women's names carved into the bottom."

"I guess I didn't. Damn."

His face turned from gray to white, either from embarrassment or because he was running out of fuel. I picked up the pace.

"If I lose the monocle, does time in Jett Creek keep going, or does it stand still?"

"I don't know. I always figured the smart thing to do would be to not lose it."

"How do I get home?"

He shrugged and I grabbed for his shoulders. My hands sliced through him. He tried to shove the smoke back where his upper arms had been, but the more he moved, the more he dissolved into the air.

"You fucking bastard!" I said. "You ruined this world. You ruined me. You have to get me back."

I might have been right, but it didn't matter. He was gone.

I slumped onto the beanbag and spent a little while feeling sorry for myself. When that grew stale, I kicked over the nearest rack of children's toys and stalked out of the long, awful room. Upstairs, I filled my water skin and emptied the snack cabinet into my adventurer's bag. I was about to leave when I decided the nameless one deserved a proper barbarian funeral.

The kitchen drawer held screwdrivers, a hammer, a heap of nails and bolts and anchors and a tangle of wire and twine. There was also an unopened box of candles. I lit one and placed it on the kitchen counter. I blew out the pilot light and cranked up the gas, then shut the windows tight.

I was hip deep in swamp water when the house exploded: a pyre for a nameless brute. For the first time since LB died, I felt free. I had no brother, I had no past. Everything I'd done was my fault and nobody else's. I had a long way to go.

I walked north, toward the war, toward the Queen, wondering where the fuck I was going to learn to cast Gorham's Iron.

16

I SPENT SEVEN YEARS LOOKING.

War settled over the Plateau like a lead blanket, suffocating everything. Once, I'd have fought it, but I wasn't a Hero anymore. I wore no armor; I carried no sword. When I had to go somewhere, I walked. When I got hungry, I ate. When I was broke, which was always, I worked in taverns, bakeries, smithies, barns, fields, stables, and all the anonymous little pits of enterprise that kept this world humming, war or no.

I walked high roads, low roads, and nameless trails; scaled mountains and crawled along valleys; explored every hamlet and village and settlement on the Plateau. I went to places so dull that the Heroes never could have imagined them—places untouched by adventure, where nothing had ever happened and nothing ever would. I asked everyone what they knew about Gorham's Iron.

No one knew a damn thing.

I met thousands of people. I saw them kill and steal and blaspheme and rape. I saw them heal each other, help each other, feed each other, roll their dice, and love. Every day I was shocked that in a land so ugly and ruined, the people could be so gentle—those people the Heroes had always passed by. I was embarrassed that, given an opportunity to explore this limitless world, we'd never come up with anything more clever to do than kill.

The worse the war got, the warmer the Heroes were remembered. Once, at a campfire on a path too muddy and meandering to be called a road, I heard a teenage girl tell her siblings about the time Fausto stole the sun.

"The sun is wise, but Fausto is clever, and clever wins. He knew the sun can't see behind a shadow, and so he tricked his shadow into trading places with him. He snuck into the sky, hidden in his own darkness, and grabbed the sun with both hands."

"Wasn't it hot?" asked her little brother.

"Scalding! Fausto burned himself terribly, but he tore off a piece of light and slid back to earth before the sun even knew he'd been there."

"What did he do with it?" I asked.

She pointed at the moon.

"Hung it where the sun could never find it—in the night sky, that travelers and thieves could always have light to work by. Haven't you heard that story before?"

I shook my head. In the stories I remembered, Fausto was a thief who killed for fun and stole for no one but himself. I never told those tales. I'd learned early on that if you're sharing someone else's campfire, sad stories don't get you fed.

I went back to Glittermore and tried to understand the magic Fisher had worked at his forge. I found nothing but corpses. I left them to their tomb. The rest of the town had been razed. I'd have liked to see LB's statue toppled and buried in the sand, but that would have been too poetic. It was just gone.

I climbed the mountain to consult with the librarian of the Ronastery, the only man on the whole Plateau who'd ever bothered to sit down and read. As Arabeth, I'd danced up those awful slopes. As Callie, the climb nearly broke me. The third time I fell, I split my lip on a hidden rock and spluttered blood across the snow. I tried to stand. My legs had other ideas. I sank onto dangerously cold ground.

"Rainy afternoons under a blanket. Strong black tea. Good beer. The way Sondra cackles when she casts a spell. The way Doc laughs at her own jokes. All of Craig's bullshit."

I got myself cross-legged. I pressed my mouth into my sleeve until the bleeding slowed. I was still too tired to stand.

"Peanut butter and jelly sandwiches. Cold cider. Hot cider. Apple cider donuts. Any donut, really. Christ I want a fucking donut."

I spat, staining the pure white with a mouthful of blood, and reached for the only thing that really mattered.

"Mom. Mom. Mom."

That got me to the top.

Black stained the Ronastery walls. The gate hung loose. The main building was a smoldering wreck. The zipline was cut.

The library's door had been ripped off its hinges. The shelves were empty, the chains that held the books slashed through. Torn pages fluttered out the door and off the cliff. I grabbed a few. Trying to chase another down, I rounded a corner and nearly stumbled into a pit. Inside were the monks, stacked face up in an open grave.

The pages in my hand held recipes for nettle tea, gooseberry wine, lentil soup. I scattered them across the bodies and turned away.

There were days I felt every person who died in this war had been killed by my hand. There were others that I remembered Mom's maxim, "Guilt is a wasted emotion," and told my feelings to fuck off. Today, no amount of swagger would dispel that guilt.

Screaming wind slashed my face, hard enough to start me bleeding again. I tried not to turn away. The mist blew away and I saw Blackbriar Keep, far below, a toy castle swarming with the minions of the Queen of Skulls. I had a vision of myself decked out like a ninja, scaling the uneven walls of her fortress, slipping into her penthouse and challenging her to a duel to settle this once and for all. But that was just daydreaming. My enemies were back in Jett Creek.

Before the mist clamped back down, I looked past the keep, through the pass. I saw an entire world out there. I saw how much farther I had to go.

"Well, shit," I said, and started back down.

For a party of Heroes, entering Blackbriar would have been suicide. But I wasn't important any more. I faded into the background better than Fausto ever managed and slipped through the fortress in less than two hours, leaving through the Spur Gate, which had never been rebuilt, since the Queen of Skulls was certain no enemy would ever come this way again. I passed over the spot where Zircon died. His blood was long gone. The forest closed over me and I realized I was farther now than the Heroes had ever gone.

Out of the mountains, out of the woods, across a prairie where purple grass stretched to the horizon under a perfect blue dome. Through villages, hamlets, towns, and cities whose sparkling towers made Winterwind look like the backwater I suppose it had always been. The diversity in language, architecture, mindset, and everything else astonished me, and made me embarrassed that I had once believed all of this had sprung from the mind of my shithead brother.

Here there were no statues of LB, no legends of the Heroes. This was the domain of Lomella I, the vengeful, the all-seeing, the eternal, the Queen of Skulls. Her enemies had been crushed decades before, and there was no need for the viciousness that characterized her war in the south. Every citizen was watched. Every official was corrupt. No one cared about me.

I slept in stables, in inns, and beneath the stars. I woke one morning under the gaze of a ten point buck whose mossy antlers stretched as wide as my arms could reach. It was so beautiful that for a long time, I could not breathe.

"Hiya," I said. It did not startle. "I don't suppose you know anything about casting Gorham's Iron?"

It kept mum. I packed up my meager campsite. The buck watched me walk away.

Slowly, by asking every smith in every town the same question, I picked up fragments about the legendary iron.

"Back in the old days, they used to melt rubies and mix em in before puddling. Made it glow like fire. Royals liked that, back when we still had that type of royal."

"Had to cook it up under a full moon. No, a new moon. No, I was right the first time: a full moon. The moonlight would get caught up in the mix and made the iron glow in the dark."

"Right as it's cooling, you gotta sing to it. Saddest song you know. That's all it took, and you had a piece of metal that could banish despair. That's what my grandmother said, anyway, but she was generally full of shit."

When they'd finished their stories, I'd nod politely and move on. I wrote down what they said, even though none of it was ever worth a damn, except what I heard from three different smiths in three different towns, who all spoke of an ironworker named Randall who once wandered the countryside asking the same questions as me. And so, rather than search for Gorham's Iron, I looked for him.

Problem was, there were a shitload of Randalls. Every town had two or three, and none were even remotely wise. I walked and walked and walked, accomplishing nothing besides building up calf muscles a gym rat would kill for. I found so many false Randalls that I considered giving up, but every time I considered settling down and starting a life here, I thought about Mom and kept looking instead. Finally, in a seaside city far to the north, where equatorial heat slicked every person, beast, and stone, I found the man.

He was stringy, from his lean muscles to his long, coarse hair. He was dirty and wet, which is what happens when you sleep underneath the pier. And he was younger than I expected—in his fifties, maybe, or a hard-lived forty-five. But the biggest surprise was that he knew my name.

"Holy shit!" he said when I smacked him awake. "Callie, right?"

"Excuse me?"

"Callie whatshername—Callie Myles! Callie Myles from

Critical Hit! Tell me I'm wrong."

He was chipper for a homeless drunk. Loose, too, in a way people from this world never were. The way he said my name, it was like he was like he was begging me to come out for ultimate frisbee. I knew where I'd met him before.

"Randy Randy."

"As randy as ever."

I pulled him up. The surf rose around our ankles. We leaned on the pilings, preferring wet feet to the brutal sun.

"What the hell are you doing here?"

"Duh. I got trapped."

"How?"

"That fucking monocle, man! I was cleaning up the back room after a late session and LB fell asleep on the couch. He was snoring like an idling truck and he'd fucked my character up really bad during the game and I was basically just sick of his shit. I lifted the monocle off his neck and I was going to throw it out the window, strictly to be a dick, y'know, and I found the little button on the side. I've always said that buttons are for pressing, yeah? So I pressed it and blammo, I landed smack in the middle of the battle we'd just hit pause on. I was saying to myself, 'Whoa, this world looks like a giant model, that's pretty cool,' when I saw the big motherfucker on horseback ready to cut me in two."

"What did you do?"

"What anybody would do—I pissed my pants and smashed the button and went right back to good old planet earth."

"LB was still asleep?"

"Yeah, even though I was screaming like a little bitch. That guy could sleep through Ragnarok. So I kicked him in the shins pretty hard and threw the monocle at him and was all like, 'What the fuck, man?'"

"What did he say?"

"Not much. Basically he punched me in the face and put me in a headlock and dragged me right back to that battlefield. But he wasn't dressed like himself there—he had these gray robes. It was all very Lord of the Rings for a guy who always said he 'considered himself above the clichés of high fantasy.' Also he could fly."

"What a dickhead."

"I know, right? He jumped up in the air and flew me halfway around the world and dumped me in a tree and said, 'Don't fuck with my stuff,' and that was the last I saw of him. How's he doing, by the way?"

"He's dead."

"Cool."

The surf tickled my knees. It was time to go.

Randy followed me up the ladder. Masts and ropes cast a lattice of shadows that provided absolutely no relief from the heat. Around us, sailors and longshoremen worked as slowly as their masters allowed. Scowling at the sun, Randy patted his pockets until he found a small flask. He did not share, which was fine by me.

"You've been looking for Gorham's Iron," I said.

"A long time now."

"How did you know that was what you needed to get home?"

"'Cause I was there the night he made that shit up!"

"You remember how it happened?"

For the first time in ages, hope flickered in my chest.

"I remember it better than him, I bet. He was cranked up on so much speed—we must have been playing seventy hours straight. Late in the session, one of us wandered the wrong way down some underground mine—we went on a lot of tangents back then—and LB cooked up this whole crazy scene with magic smiths having an orgy and casting black magic and brewing up a huge pot of this special iron. He said it, over and over, 'Gorham's Iron, Gorham's Iron, Gorham's Iron,' and he pretended it was in his notes but I knew he was just pulling it out of his ass, y'know, the way that when he was really going he could make shit up and it was like it had been real all along."

"Yeah."

"So after we wrapped, LB's head was still back in that cave. We were walking all over campus and the sun was coming up and he kept saying, 'I could make that shit, you know? I saw the whole ritual, right there in my head. I know what it takes. I could cast Gorham's Iron.'"

"And did he?"

"Shit yeah!"

"How?"

"Mixed up a bunch of garbage that is not supposed to go in iron."

"Like what?"

"If I knew, do you think I'd have spent, shit, I don't know how many years walking around this fucking continent trying to figure it out? We were pretty drunk."

I yanked him off the barrel. It wasn't hard. I shoved him to the edge of the pier.

"Tide's in. Water's high enough that you won't break your neck if you fall. Probably won't drown, but you'll get really goddamned wet. Do you want to get really goddamned wet?"

"No."

"So tell me everything you learned."

"Gorham's Iron is bullshit."

"Why?"

"Because the shit you need, you can't get here. Crazy stuff like thiamine mononitrate and sodium caseinate. Try asking for that shit in the general store. They'd burn you as a witch. Even stuff you'd think would be simple, like it calls for beef fat? Well they don't have cows here. Ever notice that? No cows. Just those jacked up pig-looking critters, so where are you getting the beef? You're not, that's where. You're fucked."

I let go of his collar. He sucked on his flask and made a face when he found it empty. He sat on a barrel and closed his eyes to the sun.

"Anyway, I've got a pretty good set-up. I'm sick of wanting to go home. How is life back on earth, by the way?"

"Shitty."

"Figures."

"Where did you find the recipe?"

"In a library."

"A library where?"

Without opening his eyes, he pointed across the sea. The sun was low and the water rippled like fire. I'd heard stories of people sailing across that water. I hadn't heard many of people who came back.

"I don't suppose, just by happenstance, you hung on to the book?" I said.

"You think I'd steal a library book? What kind of scum do you think I am?"

I didn't answer that question. He told me the name of the city where I'd find the library, and I spent my last bit of cash to get a spot on the next westbound ship. We sailed when the tide turned. The last I saw of Randy he was dangling his legs over the dock, waiting for the water to drain.

The library was a small brick building that overlooked a harbor halfway around the globe. Inside, I found underground stacks containing all the knowledge this world had to offer. After weeks searching every dark corner, I found *Being an Exploration of the Planes of Life, From High to Low and Elsewhere, and Theories on the Beings that Walk Between*. It explained Astral Leap. It gave a recipe for Gorham's Iron, and I saw how impossible this would be.

"Using a forge rooted deep in the earth, prepare your iron in the ordinary way. At the pivotal moment, incorporate into the mixture one measure of mono and diglycerides, sodium acid pyrophosphate, soy protein isolate, calcium and sodium caseinate..."

And on and on and on, a relentless list of unpronounceable chemical compounds that would have been hard to find on Earth, land of the future, and was beyond inaccessible in a place where fire still felt cutting edge.

"Fuck!" I shouted. My voice echoed down the dark stone halls. Far away, someone shushed.

I kicked something. It didn't make me feel any better. I sat down, rubbing the stump where my finger had been.

I'd spent years pretending I was on the quest to end all quests, that a door home was right around the corner. I'd been lost the whole time.

If you are a hungry boy

I was going to live the rest of my life here. It would probably be short. I could spend decades trying to drag this continent into the age of 21st century science in order to invent the wild array of chemicals found on that list, or I could do like I should have done at the start and fucking give up—either by throwing myself off the handiest cliff or just admitting that this was where I was at, and trying to build a new life.

A grumpy boy

I'd spent years acting like a job selling board games was all I'd ever want, that Critical Hit could be my whole life. That lie led me here. If I couldn't get home, I'd have to do the thing I'd been fighting against for so long. I'd have to get my shit together. Nothing scared me more than that.

A grumbly boy

At least they have RPGs here, I thought. Maybe I could get together a regular game.

And then I noticed what I was humming—the idiotic jingle that had been bouncing around my head, off and on, since I burnt my brother's fortress of solitude to the ground.

You'd better reach for Joll-E Boy...

"Snack cakes," I shouted. "I know what this is. I know what this is!"

The guy at the end of the hall shushed the hell out of me. I didn't care. I ripped open my adventurer's bag and dumped out a lifetime of armor I couldn't equip, weapons I was too cowardly to wield, and spells I wasn't qualified to cast. I pawed through stale rations and rancid potions, dirty homespun underwear and quite a lot of unidentifiably rotten food. At the very bottom, beneath the greasy old Doritos bags and chocolate-stained Reese's wrappers, I found the one treat from LB's snack cabinet that I'd never been hungry enough to eat.

Joll-E Boy Snack Cakes.

Strawberry flavored.

A two pack.

I ran my finger down the ingredients list and saw everything

Randy Randy had never been able to find: thiamine monitrate and sodium caseinate and beef fat and soy protein isolate and everything else that made snacks on Earth so creamy and perfect and sickeningly American. Serving size: two cakes.

I had everything I'd need.

I shoveled the mess back into my adventurer's bag. I wrapped the snack cakes in my softest rags and put them on top of the pile. For good measure, I stole the library book, too. Randy Randy would have been disappointed. I didn't care.

I cinched the bag until it sank back to pocket size and made for the exit.

Now all I had to do was learn to make iron. How hard could it be?

BIG SURPRISE—IT WAS REALLY FUCKING HARD. SMITHS IN THAT part of the world were not particularly friendly, and they had no interest in sharing the secrets they'd spent a lifetime accumulating with a ragged-looking woman whose accent matched no place they'd ever been.

After months, I talked my way into an apprenticeship with an ancient woman named Serafina whose good humor and absolute commitment to her art reminded me of Doc. In a year, I knew everything she knew. For the next two years, I pushed us both to learn more, until we were able to compel iron to do things no one on this planet had ever dreamed of. The whole time, my Joll-E Boys were sweating themselves to death inside the wrapper, and I prayed the precious chemicals inside weren't breaking down.

When there was nothing else for us to learn, I spent half my savings on two small round pieces of glass—the finest this world could provide—and the rest on a ticket back across the sea. I told Serafina goodbye, wrapped my lenses in as many layers of fabric as I had, and set out for home.

It was harder to get back to the Plateau than it had been to leave. I was somewhere in the neighborhood of thirty-five by then, and in a country shattered by war, that is too old. I had a cough that wouldn't quit and a fever, too. When I was too weak to walk, I lay down. I lost days that way. Probably I was dying. I didn't really care. My head was far away, in a mythic land of paved highways and convenience stores and cable TV. I saw my friends. I saw my mother. I wanted to know if they had survived.

In the flattened waste that had been Glittermore, there were peonies on Myantha's mother's grave and rubble where the workshop had been. I shifted the rocks by hand. I grew sicker. Coughing blood as thick as raspberry syrup, it occurred to me that I could die now and no one in this world would miss me. A Hero can make herself a legend in a few hours. What had I'd done with my seven years? Nothing but stay alive.

Finally, I pulled away a brick that revealed the darkness of the mine. Strength fluttered back into my shoulders. When I'd cleared enough to get through, I wriggled into the darkness. I lit a torch, and thought of the light that bloomed from Myantha's hands. Down the tunnel, I fancied I smelled corpses, but that simply couldn't be.

It had been so long since Arabeth committed her atrocity here, but I'd had enough nightmares of this tunnel to remember every turn. During my travels, I'd lost a lot of my old self, but I'd never figured out how to escape that guilt.

"If I make it home alive," I said as I stood at the threshold to the cavern, "I'm going to need a shitload of therapy."

The corpses were where I'd left them. They were skeletons now. Mushrooms and weeds spiraled through gaps in ribs and the places where faces used to be. I made myself look at them for a long time. When they didn't frighten me any more, I lit the forge.

I dropped pig iron into a bucket and set it melting. Once it was simmering I unwrapped the snack cakes. Age had left them pale, so squishy they were almost liquid.

"I guess I don't look much better," I said as I dropped them into my bubbling brew. They caught fire, hissed, and dissolved. "I really hope I didn't fuck this up."

I poured the iron into three molds. It cooled. It hardened. I dropped it into a bucket of spring water. When it was safe to touch, I fitted the pieces together, then secured them with the tiniest screws this world had ever made. My frames were ready.

I'd never really considered making another monocle. In this world and every other, they were only for assholes, so I made glasses instead. They were chunky squares, partly because I wanted them sturdy but mostly because that's what suited my face, and even when she's stranded in another universe a girl has a right to look good. They folded up nice. I felt proud.

I unfolded the many layers that protected my lenses. A nail-thin line stretched across each one: an innovation whose simplicity made the woman who cut them smack her knee and smile. They were bifocals.

I dried sweaty hands on my fur and popped them gently into the frames.

"Don't break these, you idiot."

I didn't break them.

"Thank fuck."

I put them on. They were so heavy they slipped off my face. My hand shot out and caught them before they hit the ground.

"Note to self: get a croakie," I said. "Note to self? When the hell have I ever said that? I'm blathering. I must be stalling. I must be fucking terrified. Makes sense. These took seven years. If they don't work, if they don't work..."

I couldn't say it, but I knew there would be no second attempt. After this, there was nothing but the cliffs, if I could even make it that far.

I took a deep, useless breath, and pushed the glasses back on. When they were as snug as I could get them, I reached for the button.

17

Roses drifted in on the breeze, as rich as heavy cream. The night was not cold.

My hand reached for a bedpost. It was right where it was supposed to be, which was good, because my knees were buckling. I tumbled onto a wadded comforter that was softer than anything I'd felt in years. The glasses were heavy on my nose. I folded them carefully and slid them into my pocket. I pressed knuckles to forehead and found ten perfect fingers, which I appreciated like I never had before.

I rolled over to look at the clock. The detail of this world, the way everything looked so hard and rich and real, made my stomach turn. Once I was reasonably certain I wouldn't puke, I finally noticed the time.

7:15.

I hadn't lost a minute. Seven years of life, but without the dice rolling back here, not a moment in Jett Creek had passed.

Except that when I left, my window had been closed.

Something scraped against the shingles outside. I scrambled over on shaking legs and thrust out my head. Silhouetted in the orange streetlight, I saw the woman who'd left me behind.

"Stop!" I shouted. "Please."

She didn't. She slid down the roof and leapt over the gutter into my oak.

I grabbed my backpack and went after her.

My roof was never the fun type of roof, the sitting around kind where high schoolers climb out to get high. It was the other kind, the steep kind. When I was younger, Jill always snuck out here to smoke, but I stayed on the windowsill, too chicken to even put my feet down.

I was different then.

I leapt out the window, skidded across the shingles and found that no matter what I told my feet, they had no interest in slowing down. I flopped onto my face. I rolled once, twice, three times, and stopped with my nose in the gutter and my feet in mid-air.

"Yikes," I said. Real cool, Callie.

Myantha dropped softly onto the grass. I stepped awkwardly onto the nearest branch and tumbled forward into the trunk. I inched down one branch, another, another, moving so slowly that I thought this must be a nightmare, until I reached the ground. When I caught my breath, Myantha was gone. I jogged to the corner and saw no one. The air was too warm, and the chirp of crickets made my skin crawl.

"This is stupid. This is so extremely stupid. I have a car. Next to a car, magic fucking sucks."

My beat-to-hell Acura was in front of the house. Dust fogged its windows; bird shit was splattered across the hood; Wendy's wrappers filled the back seat. It looked like it had been sitting there for seven years, but nope, that's just how I kept my car. I fumbled for the key. The streetlights were giving me a headache, and I felt naked without my furs. I squirmed in my seat, squeezed the wheel and yanked on the gearshift. Nothing happened.

"You gotta turn it on," I said.

I turned the key. Noise exploded from the stereo: the distortion and misery I'd once considered music, but that now sounded like a heart attack. I jabbed buttons and twisted knobs and finally managed to shut off the noise. I wanted to scream or cry. I'd spent so long trying to get back to my home. I hadn't considered that by the time I got here, it wouldn't be home any more.

I tried to breathe. When it was clear that was impossible, I threw the car into drive and pulled down the street, as tentative as a fifteen-year-old virgin, trying not to think about what I was doing, trying to focus on the fact that it was Saturday night and everyone would be at Critical Hit.

"She doesn't know where she is," I told myself. "But she's got the ring, and she'll figure it out."

At the first intersection, I blew through a stop sign, then slammed on the brakes and tried to slow my heart.

I smacked down the sun visor and inspected myself in the warped little mirror. There was no gray in my hair, no gaps in my teeth. All my scars were gone.

"Don't fall for it. You're not some piece of shit 21st century girl. You're the nine-fingered wanderer of the Plateau. You mastered Gorham's Iron. You've seen things no one on this world can imagine. You can—"

A screaming horn interrupted my inspirational speech. I wanted to crawl under the dashboard and die. I drove on.

I cruised down Broad with my arms shaking, head snapping at every shadow. Unable to get a feel for the gas pedal, I veered between driving stupid slow and stupid fast. I swung through a red light onto the last block of Carriage. There, glowing brightly at the end of the cul-de-sac, was the thing I'd fought so hard to return to. My once and future home. Paradise with plastic dice.

Critical Hit.

Naturally, there was nowhere to park. The law-abiding thing would have been to cruise until I found a spot, but it seemed a lot easier to leave my car on the sidewalk.

"Life and death, right?" I said as I slammed the door. God it felt weird to be back on these streets, back in these clothes.

"Hey scumbag!" shouted a passing wizard. "You can't park there."

I flashed a middle finger and pushed past him before I realized there were not to supposed to be wizards here. I glanced
at his long brown cloak, his sallow face and patchy beard. He
looked like a refugee from the Ronastery. My stomach lurched
as I remembered that mass grave.

I looked through the front window, past the miniatures and
new board games, and saw a shop full of people dressed up like
it was the middle ages, or the far-off future, or a fighting game,
or some kind of anime bullshit.

"Cosplay Saturday," I said. "You've gotta be fucking
kidding."

The sidewalk wizard grabbed my elbow.

"Are you going to repark your car or am I going to have to
make you?"

"Jesus, you're an asshole," I said. From my back pocket I
snatched my employee ID. I shoved it in his face. "This is GM's
business. Get the hell out of my way."

It was so stupid that it actually worked. I jerked open the
door. Inside, close to a hundred superheroes, cartoon characters, and giggling blue-haired twerps were rolling dice and
sucking down milkshakes and beer. Amateurs. Anybody who
counted knew the serious action was in back.

Behind the bar, flanked by Diego and Karina, Odette finished drawing a pint of red ale, which she set on a tray with
four others. In her trademark white sweater and sweats, she was
more striking than any of the costumed nerds there. Throwing
elbows and stomping toes, I fought across the crowded floor
and slipped under the railing at the end of the bar.

"Heyo Callie," said Diego. He looked waxier than normal—like the inside of a potato.

"Not fucking now, man."

He started to say something. I ducked under his arm, crept
up behind Odette and hugged her hard enough to spill the beer
in her hand.

"Shit!" she said.

"I missed you," I said, not caring how stupid I sounded. "I
missed you so much."

"It's only been like eight hours."

"The longest of my life."

I watched the door for visitors from other worlds. It was hard to tell with everyone dressed like extras from Blackbriar Keep, but I was pretty sure I didn't see Myantha come in.

Odette set the spilled glass in the sink, picked up a clean one, and filled it to the brim. The ale looked crisp and cold. My throat ached.

"What are you doing here?" she said. "You almost died this morning. I feel like that rates a day off."

"I wanted to apologize. For real, no attitude. I've been a fucking mess, and if I let you down at all..."

"Don't worry about it. But thanks."

"Yeah. Of course." I tapped the tray of red ale. "For the back room?"

"Indeed."

I lifted the tray. My hands were steady. I didn't spill a drop. Odette followed at my elbow all the way to the door of the back room.

"I'm GMing tonight. They, uh, they asked me to step in."

"No kidding."

In that moment, if the floor had dropped out from under my feet, I wouldn't have cared. It wasn't that my players had asked someone else to GM that hurt—although let's be honest, that hurt fucking bad. It's that I hadn't played in one of Odette's games since I was a pimple-scarred teen. When she was in form, which was basically always, she ran the table like a master weaver sweeping together a tapestry from so much useless thread. (I think that's how that works? Add weaving to the long list of things I don't know shit about.) I'd have given anything to be part of her game.

"Whatcha playing?" I said, trying to remember how casual sounded.

"*Space Pirates*. It's about space pirates."

"Mind if I sit in?"

"There's no room."

"Craig, Sondra, Doc...that's a full table?"

"And your friend, too."

"Since when do I have friends?"

She paused outside the curtained doors.

"The girl with the freaky colored contacts. She said you told her to come play."

Maybe I should have run, or looked for a weapon or someplace clever to hide. I certainly should have done something to prepare for Myantha, but seven years of anticipation left me flatfooted. By the time I realized what was happening, the door was always swinging wide.

It hit the table, which had always been too small for the space. In the middle were dice, chips, unpainted minis, and a stack of blank character sheets for an unfamiliar game. Sondra, Craig, and Doc leaned back in their seats. I didn't remember the last time I'd seen them so relaxed.

Myantha sat in LB's chair like she owned it. I wonder if she knew it had belonged to her god.

I'd always wondered how she'd look without a hint of plastic or paint. She was sturdy, bigger than I expected—the kind of person whose arms scare the shit out of the other people at the gym. She gave me a little wave. I waved right back.

I'd spent seven years imagining this confrontation. I'd written speeches in my head—of apology, of rage. I'd fantasized about beating the shit out of her, or letting her beat the shit out of me. I'd expected adrenaline, terror, fury. Instead, I felt like I'd fallen into an underground lake: still and cold and certain that whatever happened next, I could take it.

Probably.

My players took their drinks. They did not meet my eye.

"You're finished with me, right?" I said. No answer. "I get it. It was my job to take care of you, to entertain, and I didn't do either. But just a heads up—Myantha is here to kill all y'all."

"Listen, Callie," said Sondra, "it's getting old."

"Just wanted to let you know. Y'all play your game. I'm gonna eat some chips."

Craig and Sondra looked to Odette, waiting for her to throw me out. Instead she handed me a bag of Fritos. I leaned in the doorway and ripped them open. They tasted better than anything I'd ever eaten. Myantha stared through me. I tried to pretend it didn't hurt to see the hate in her eyes.

"You were telling me about the game," she said.

"Basically, it's a conversation," said Odette. "A group improv, only not as viciously uncool as that sounds."

"Is there an element of prayer?"

Doc and Craig snorted. Sondra sat straight, stretching out that pool noodle spine.

"How you mean, prayer?"

"We play games like this where I come from. We take them seriously. We act out our dreams, confront our horrors, build a story with nothing but quick wit and dice. Where I grew up, nothing is more holy than that."

"And just where are you from?" said Doc.

"Somewhere weird," said Craig. "Florida?"

"Not quite," she answered. "If there is no prayer in your game, what is it for?"

"A good time?" said Doc, with that skittish look people get when they're talking to someone who's either lost their mind or come from another planet, or both.

"And what makes it a good time?"

"We solve problems with our friends, tell bad jokes and drink good beer. What could be better?"

"And do you kill?"

"When we have to."

"How often?"

"Basically all the fucking time," said Craig. "Your point?"

The smile snapped off Myantha's face. I dumped the rest of the chips down my throat. This was going to be awful.

"What do you kill?" she said.

"Monsters, critters, beasties, standard animals, soldiers, guards, creeps, bullies, and basically anybody who gets in our way," said Sondra, ticking each one off on her fingers. "And guards. Did I already say guards? There are so many guards everywhere and we kill all of them."

"Why?"

"What else would you do with a guard?"

Myantha's hands twitched.

"What are you getting at here, honey?" said Doc.

"Is it to protect yourself? To protect the weak? To survive? Why do you kill?"

There was a long pause as everyone at the table considered this patently stupid question. I knew how they'd respond, and I knew how Myantha would react. My friends still thought they were playing a game. Part of me looked forward to the faces they'd make when they learned they were wrong.

Finally, Craig gave the group's answer:

"We kill for fun."

"For fun?" said Myantha.

I glanced around for a weapon and saw nothing but rapidly warming beer.

"Yeah," said Craig. "I mean, it's a game."

Her hands snapped up like slingshots. I threw my elbow over my eyes a half-second before she unleashed her Blinding Glare. In that little room, the scream of trumpets was louder than I'd ever heard. Blood trickled down my earlobe. I uncovered my eyes and saw my friends curled into balls, hands over their ears, screaming words I couldn't hear. Myantha was on the table. Her arms glowed from elbows to fingertips. The range of colors was vaster than I'd seen in the other world: pale yellow and orangey gold on her arms, scalding white around her fingernails. The light swirled into the air, spinning her bow. She pointed it at Craig's head. He looked up, still blind.

I grabbed Doc's beer.

Myantha drew her bowstring taut.

I whipped the pint at her head. She ducked, firing her arrow straight into the ceiling. It burst through the roof of that cramped little room. Fire poured through the hole.

The ringing in my ears faded. I heard a roar that I assumed was a burst eardrum, but turned out to be rushing flame. Someone screamed, "Holy shit!" I couldn't tell who.

Myantha drew back to fire again.

I grabbed Odette and Doc by their collars and dragged

them out of the room. I smashed my elbow into the fire alarm. White lights strobed. A mechanical shriek split the air.

A shop full of cosplayers lurched out of their seats, muttering variations on, "What the fuck?" They couldn't see the smoke; they couldn't see the fire. All they saw was one out-of-breath clerk who didn't even bother to put on a costume.

"All you motherfuckers out! Single file. Like grade school."

A shoulder hit me in the back of the neck. I slammed into mildewed carpet, wind knocked out of me. I looked up and saw Craig's Birkenstocks fleeing.

What a bastard.

Strong hands hoisted me up—Doc on one side, Sondra on the other. Odette pushed around us to take charge of the evacuation.

"Get out front," I said. "Stop Craig. We need him."

"Why?" said Sondra.

I shook my head and wheezed out: "Run!"

They didn't like it, but they nodded. Doc took a last long look at me. She ran.

I stuck around to cover their retreat. I didn't have long to plan. Fire swept along the ceiling of the main room, dumping black smoke that stung my lips and scorched my eyes. I backed into the wall. My neck touched glass. The LARPing case. Inside was an armory carved from duct tape and foam. Some of it was straight trash, but there were a couple of pieces that had been painted with enough care that, through a wall of smoke, they might look real. I grabbed a rubber mace in one hand and a styrofoam ax in the other, crouched low enough to get away from the worst of the smoke, and waited to die.

Myantha crashed through the doors, eyes like tarnished silver, and pointed her arrow at me.

"This is bullshit. You could have killed me back at the inn."

"I had to see it for myself."

"So you saw it. So kill me. Nobody else has to die."

Without taking the arrow off me, she relaxed just long enough to glance down that long, lovely room, its scarred wooden tables, its racks of beautiful cardboard games. I looked with her. I'd lived a whole life there and fire was swallowing it whole. But I'd lived another life someplace else, and I wasn't really sentimental anymore.

"All these games," she said. "All these worlds. How many are real?"

I had no answer. The fire kicked up another octave. Something popped like a string of Black Cats and chunks of the ceiling began to fall.

She drew back her string.

I took one last breath of truly shitty smoke-filled air.

She took her shot.

I threw the mace underhand, like a bowling ball. It met the arrow in mid-air and exploded into a shower of sparks that knocked me right on my ass. When I opened my eyes, she was gone.

Coughing like hell, I crawled to the front of the shop. By the register was a bowl of miscellaneous dice, 25¢ each. I grabbed a fistful and threw myself out the door.

Cold hit me like ice water. It was very hard to breathe. Sondra and Doc had Craig trapped between them. Odette was in the street, watching her place burn.

"Did you see Myantha come out?" I said.

"No," said Doc. "She must still be inside."

"Illusions are her specialty. She could have gotten out without anyone seeing."

"Then what are we going to do?"

"Run."

Sirens floated over the crackling wood. My car was right there—amazing how convenient parking on the sidewalk can be—but the street was jammed with cosplayers and passersby who'd stopped to watch the fire. There was no way out but up.

"Come on, y'all," I told Doc, Sondra, and Craig—my three suspects, my three friends.

I ran up the hill. I didn't have to say anything to make them follow—they just did it, and for once they asked no questions. At the top of the street, the long wooden funicular car sat closed for the night. The door was locked, but it was flimsy, and I only had to kick it twice before it snapped open.

Inside stank of sawdust and old leather. I flipped on the lights and made for the front. There was one button and one lever. The button started the engine, and the lever began the slow climb to the top of Mount Jett.

18

THE CAR RATTLED, EVERY WINDOW SHAKING IN ITS FRAME. WE looked back at the burning shop, at the sky glowing orange, at the ribbons of smoke twirling into the night.

"So..." drawled Sondra. "What's the deal with your friend?"

"Later," I said. "Everything you want to know, ask it later. For now, these are the rules. *Winterwind* is real. All of it. LB stumbled on it in college when he was so high he could hardly see. He had power there, power like a god, and instead of using it for good he used it for fun. He did horrible shit and we're being blamed for it. We did horrible shit, too."

I'd been rehearsing this speech for seven years. I hadn't planned on rushing it, but now I talked as fast as I could. Out the window, maybe a hundred yards down the hill, white light glowed.

"Everything we did there, everyone we killed, that was real. We all have blood on our hands."

"But we were Heroes," said Craig.

"On a good day. Most of the time, we were killers. War criminals, just like Matty said. Reckon with that later. I came back to save you—"

"Came back from where?" said Doc.

"Later. Myantha, the mage, is following us. When she catches us she will kill us. I don't really blame her, but—"

And that's when Sondra shouted, not quite helpfully, "What the shit is that?"

It was light. Light that swept up from the foot of the mountain to break across the trees like a tidal wave. It wrapped around the car, bright enough that it was almost blinding. It hissed like steam. Everyone but me threw themselves to the ground. Craig kind of yelped.

"It's just light!" I said. "It can't hurt us."

It dripped from the windows and pooled on the floor, then separated into puddles the size of dinner plates. One by one, figures rose up from them: the Gray Lord, Arabeth, Zircon, Fausto, Phælandro, Billiam. One by one, they were swallowed by flames.

"Shit," said Sondra.

The light receded, pulling back to dance along the slowly-rising car like dolphins beside a ship.

"Forget it," I said. "She's trying to scare you."

"She's got a knack," said Sondra.

Craig kicked the front of the train car. It didn't accomplish anything.

"Doesn't this box go any faster?" he shouted.

"No. It's the slowest, stupidest train in the world," I said. "We've got twenty-one minutes before we hit the observation area. We're going to get to the park, find someplace safe, and lock the fucking door. By the time she gets there, I hope, this will be over."

I scattered dice on the wooden floor. From my backpack, I pulled three minis: Phælandro for Sondra, Billiam for Doc, Zircon for Craig. When Craig saw what I'd given him, tears pooled in his eyes.

"Cry later," I said. "It's time to play."

"In the game we can kill her?" said Craig.

"It's not a game, and no we can't. But I'm hoping we can

prove we deserve to live. That work for you?"

Doc and Craig nodded. Sondra cackled.

"I just found out magic is real and it's trying to kill me," she said. "I've never had more fun playing this stupid game."

I sat in front of my players and perched my iron specs on the tip of my nose.

"Oh, and one more thing. We're not killing anybody any more. Not if we can help it."

Before they could argue, I pressed the button on the side of the frame. Time stopped. Iron flowed from the glasses and sucked me into the world I fought so hard to leave behind.

AND ONCE AGAIN I WAS UNDERNEATH A DEAD MINING TOWN, standing before a burning forge with my back to a garden of bones. The world was flimsy and plastic, I was short one finger and my lungs were fucked, and I felt right at home.

I looked through the bottom of the bifocals and saw the funicular, the dice, and three terrified players waiting for me to tell them what they saw.

"You stand at the gate to Blackbriar Keep," I said.

My skull split in half and my words came true. Blackbriar reared up like a middle finger. From every parapet dangled the hideous banner of the Queen of Skulls. In front of the main gate were fifty of the most chiseled, vicious guards I'd ever seen. They had swords and armor and bad attitudes, and I was wearing Chuck Taylors. For a moment, they were surprised to see me. Then they reached for their blades.

"No one knows I'm here," I said.

Blood trickled out of my ears. The guards forgot all about me. The nearest stood slack jawed, trying to figure out what had just happened, and then the sky tore open and quit worrying about me.

Three figures drifted down from the tear in the heavens: a walking corpse in shit brown robes, a guitarist wearing the world's fakest beard, and a half-naked brute whose hammer was so long, he just had to be compensating. It had been a long time since the Heroes split the Blackbriar night. Was there anyone left who remembered that sound? Or did they not tell those stories any more?

They settled on the ground in battle stance, pretty as any mini I'd ever painted. The guards charged. Time slowed.

Fifty armed men was more than these three could handle. Luckily, I was not through changing this world. I pointed at the guards.

"You're at home with your families," I said. Pressure built in my much-abused skull. "You're with your wives, your husbands, your parents, your kids."

The guards raised their weapons. The Heroes just stood there.

"You are happy. You are safe. You are far from here."

The nearest guard got ready to bury his short sword in Phælandro's gut. I clapped my hands in front of his face and invoked every ounce of authority granted by my birthright as a GM.

"You are at home."

The pain hit so hard that I fell to my knees and puked. I looked up and watched the guards wash away like ice under warm rain. Every part of me was cold. My head felt like a soft, rotting melon. One more trick like that and I'd pass out.

"Phælandro," I said, somewhere far away. "There are no guards, but the gate—"

"Mudball," Sondra answered. The crack of dice echoed across the heavens. Phælandro dropped to one knee, threw out their hands and spat a huge wad of sodden earth that blew a hole in the portcullis.

"Direct hit," I said. "An open door."

Sondra gave a little yip of pleasure.

"Let's fucking move," I said.

I guided them through the shattered iron gate, telling them everything I saw. Through the bottom of the glasses, I saw my players checking their sheets, moving their minis, asking questions. I heard my voice answering, saw my hands reaching for dice and rolling and rolling, all automatic, all perfectly in sync. I checked their faces for hesitation, still wondering which one had betrayed us. There'd be time to figure it out if any of us survived.

"You're inside the castle. Alarm bells clang. The whole place shakes. An army wakes up."

And I won't be able to protect you from them, I thought, as I dragged my hands over the rough stone, looking for what LB's map had said would be there.

"Notice anything?" I said.

"Huh?" said Craig.

"Billiam—do you notice anything?!"

"Oh!" yelped the bard. "I search for traps."

"Not a trap."

"Hidden doors?"

"Roll for it."

Billiam ran his hands along the stone until he found the seam. A tiny door popped open. I leapt through it and they followed. We hurtled up a twisting set of secret stairs. The castle was breached and we weren't dead yet.

I heard myself charging through a description of the mossy stairs, the flickering shadows, the footsteps of guards. I had a foot in each world and it didn't just feel okay—it felt correct. My narration was seamless. I was good.

The stairwell stopped at the great hall, where a heap of crushed trophies and torn banners were all that remained of the glories of Blackbriar's dead Duke. It was dark. The air was dry and cold, and the room was empty save for the four armored men at the far end straining to hear what was happening in the rest of the castle.

"Where now?" grunted Zircon, sounding just like always.

"The old chapel," I answered, trying to shake the feeling that I was talking to Matty Barber. "Through the high doors. Right past the four gigantic guards."

"They're not a problem," said Phælandro.

"Remember, buddy—non-lethal magic only."

"But that magic sucks."

"So does murder."

"Ugh. Fine."

Phælandro strutted across the floor, hands over their head, snapping like a flamenco dancer until they had the guards' attention.

The guards didn't attack. That was a mistake.

"What the hell are you doing here?" said the man in charge.

"This," they said.

They dropped, growling, and slammed their hands onto the ground. When they made contact with the stone, the floor tore open and lava belched out of the crack. Two of the guards took it in their eyes. They fell, blinded and screaming. The third guy's cloak burst into flames. He hurled himself backwards into a tapestry and tried to use it to smother the fire. The fourth guy dodged the lava and was about to call for help when Phælandro opened their fist. Mud poured from their hand, slopping all over his feet, climbing his body until he was buried up to the neck.

It should have held him, but this old bastard was tougher than mud. His face turned tomato red as he flexed every muscle in his body. Cracks appeared on his shell. It exploded, spraying dirt everywhere. He pulled the knife from his belt, flipped it around, and buried it in Phælandro's side. They fell, blood everywhere. The guard picked them up with one hand, like he was hoisting a sack of groceries, and prepared to toss them into the glowing fissure.

Phælandro glared at us and said, "Little help?"

What they got was a song.

Billiam unslung his guitar and began to hum. The bard's voice was as smooth and strong as polished oak. It blended with Doc's country rasp, which drifted tinnily out of my glasses, in a kind of hellish harmony, and raced up the scales until it became an unbearable buzzing.

The guard dropped Phælandro and opened his mouth. He tried to scream, but there was no room for sound to pass. A swarm of mosquitoes poured from his lips and swept across his body.

The air filled with red mist.

He staggered back, eyes wide. Even for him, this was too

damn much. He sprinted away down the hallway, insects blocking his screams.

Billiam's song stopped. The mosquitoes disappeared. The guard who had so recently been on fire emerged from the tapestry, picked up his sword, and stalked toward the dying mage.

"Your turn, Zircon," said Billiam.

Zircon looked around, uncertainty clouding his sweet, dumb face.

"What do I do?"

"What do you mean?" said Billiam. The guard with the sword pressed his blade to Phælandro's throat.

"Do I hide in shadows? Try to sneak or backstab, or—"

"You're Zircon, idiot," yelled Phælandro. "Zircon crush."

"Oh. Yeah."

Zircon's brow relaxed. He raised his hammer above his head and charged down the hallway, bare flesh shining in the light of the bubbling pit. He slammed his hammer into guy's chest.

Zircon crush, but he did not quite kill.

The hall was still.

The injured guard moaned horribly. I watched the two blinded guards push across the floor, calling to each other through the dark.

In the funicular, my friends cheered, and my voice told them to shut up.

"Y'all still aren't through the door."

Billiam loped across the floor and knelt beside Phælandro. He tipped out half a vial of healing gunk and massaged it into their flank until the wound healed.

"Badass," Phælandro said. "Thanks."

"Those men you blinded," I said. "They're hurting and scared. And the other guy is about five minutes from dead."

"Good."

"Nope. It ain't. What are you going to do?"

Phælandro scowled at the men writhing on the floor. Through the glasses, I saw Sondra frowning, too.

"Those fuckers are really real?" she said.

"With moms and dads and little babies, hopes and dreams and a past and—if you do the right thing—a future."

"Ugh. Boring. I help them heal."

Phælandro dumped most of what was left in the healing potion down the throat of the man Zircon had crushed, stabilizing him. He was still passed out, but his breathing no longer sounded like onrushing death. They yanked the blinded men to their feet and slopped a fistful of gunk across their ruined eyes. The guards blinked, rubbing their faces. When they saw the mage, they cowered like beaten dogs.

"Really sorry about that," Phælandro said. "But, y'know, it's a war."

"What are you going to do to us?" said the younger of the two. His voice was very thin.

"Just get the fuck out of here."

They obliged, sprinting down the nearest flight of stairs. Their footsteps died away. It would not be long before they sounded the alarm. Mercy was not convenient.

Billiam twisted the knob on the great wooden door. It rattled, but didn't open.

"Door's locked, y'all," he said. "Can't believe I'm saying this, but I wish Fausto were here."

"Fausto was weak," said Zircon. "This is how you open a door."

He reared back on one foot and kicked the door as hard as he could, which was plenty hard. The wood turned to sawdust. Our path was clear.

As the Heroes admired his destructive handiwork, I stepped over the obliterated wood into a darkened chapel where the air froze my breath. Moonlight filtered pink and blue through stained glass. At the end of the hall waited the woman we'd come to see. But before I could introduce myself, our railway car shuddered to a stop.

I tapped the button on my glasses and leapt back to Jett Creek, where Craig, Doc, and Sondra stared at me like I was a visitor from another world.

Which, I guess, I was.

"We're at the mountain top?" I said.

"Yeah," said Doc. "Where the hell have you been?"

"All over the place."

"When you put those glasses on, you went into the game?"

"I keep telling y'all, it's not a game."

Pins shot through my hips as I got to my feet. I swore that if I survived this night, I'd start doing yoga or something. But first we had to find someplace to hide.

I jerked open the door and stepped onto the gangway that led to the visitor's center. The walkway rattled. Below, the mountain sloped abruptly away. The gangway ended at a chain-link door.

Locked.

Not just locked but padlocked, held with a heavy chain. Beyond it, the park was closed. Every light off, and no sign of security or anyone else. I pulled harder, pointlessly. It didn't budge. I went back into the car.

"Who can pick a lock?" I said.

All eyes turned to Craig, who blushed the color of the bandanna that hid his thinning hair.

"I was never actually a thief!" he said. "You can't just roll a die and open a locked door. I mean, you can't, right? I don't really know what the hell's going on."

Sondra, Doc, and Craig squeezed their way onto the gangway. Sondra raged against the lock. She made a hell of a lot of noise, but it didn't get her anywhere. While they argued, I looked out the car's back window. The smoke was high, blown far enough by the wind that the orange glow of the fire seemed to spread across the entire town.

But that wasn't the only light I saw. Halfway down the mountain, Myantha's glow bobbed like a lantern, making its way up the slope. Shit, she was fast.

Behind me, Sondra and Craig were close to strangling each other. Doc was on the gangway, banging on the locked door. I pressed the button to start the train. A buzzer screamed.

"What is that?" said Craig. "It sounds bad. Is it bad?"

"It means we're going back down," said Doc.

"Fuck that," said Sondra. "Everybody on the gangway. We'll take our chances up here."

"Nope," I said. I grabbed Doc's wrist and pulled her back into the car. I slammed it shut.

"What's this now?" said Doc.

"I'm not going to die at a goddamned tourist trap. Get ready for the return trip."

The train lurched so hard that Craig nearly fell down.

"I thought we were running away," he said. "I was really on board with running away."

"Running got us nowhere. We're going back."

"Hold on though," said Sondra, grinning, "isn't she going to kill us and stuff?"

I looked out the window. Myantha's light had disappeared.

"She's gone."

"Where?"

"I don't know. But look for yourself—her light is out. She could be anywhere, but she's not climbing this mountain."

It was a lie. Myantha had seen us turn around. She was planning something, and it was going to be brutal, but I was through running away.

"All y'all sit down," I said.

"If she's gone, why keep playing?" said Doc.

"Because we've got shit to settle with the Queen of Skulls."

I didn't wait for her to answer. I pressed the button on my glasses and vaulted back into Blackbriar Keep.

The chapel was dark save for the glittering moonlight and a single dying candle. The floor was slick. The pews were gone and the walls were bare. The altar had been swapped for a simple wooden throne. There sat the Queen of Skulls. She was so still, she might have been asleep. The mammoth Greene Blade leaned against her throne.

But I didn't have time to tell my players anything more than, "It's a church. She's got a sword. What do you do?"

They argued, using time we didn't have. While I waited for them to decide to charge in headlong—the same thing they always did—I took advantage of my invisibility to inspect the Queen, getting close enough to see the faded lightning scars trailing out from under her golden eye mask, down her neck, and beneath her silver plate mail. She really did look like Danny DeVito. I flicked my finger across the blade. Sharp as hell.

I was about to tell my players to make up their fucking minds and attack when the Queen turned her eyes to me.

"Hello," she said. Her voice was as cool and smooth as the light of the moon.

"You can see me."

"I can."

"Well…shit."

Without any strain, she hefted the huge sword and pressed it against my side. I didn't care for it.

"So you're not gonna believe it," I said, "but we didn't come to kill you."

"That's awfully stupid."

"We were going for merciful."

"Mercy requires power. You have no power here."

"Even so. We'd like you to leave the Plateau. Please."

She laughed so hard her shoulders shook and tears welled up at the corners of her eyes. It would have put me at ease if it weren't for the sword nestled against my chest.

"That is quite a request from an unarmed little girl," she said. "I spent years readying my war machine to seize the Plateau. I sharpened my army to a razor's edge. I shattered Blackbriar. I will take my reward."

"Nobody else needs to die."

"That's just the kind of thing people say when they're on the wrong end of a sword."

"I've seen your home town. The church for your mother. You've got a sentimental side, don't you?"

Her smile went out like a burst light bulb. Her voice dropped to a snarl.

"If that's what you saw at the church, you've understood nothing at all. My army will not rest until my banner flies above the Edge of the World. If there were anything you could do to stop me, well, you'd have done it by now. Your brother wasn't smarter than me, Callie Myles, and neither are you."

"Did you kill him?"

"He thought I was part of his game, just another mini to nudge across the table. He didn't notice when I turned the Plateau against him. When he finally realized I was a threat—"

"He cheated to make you die."

"It didn't stick. Thanks to you."

I glanced at the trio of bickering idiots on the other end of the room.

"Which one of them helped you?" I said.

She chuckled. I didn't think that was a good sign.

"Do I look like a woman who needs help?"

"All right," said Phælandro. "Let's charge in and fuck her up."

The Heroes bolted down the chapel, looking as heroic and useless as three people can be.

"Callie?" said Billiam. "What's up?"

"Well?" said the Queen, smirking. "Aren't you going to answer your friends?"

"The Queen of Skulls is on her throne. She's got her sword pressed against a young woman—a really good looking young woman who happens to be me."

"Let me at her," said Phælandro. "I've got something nasty I've been saving."

"I can't. The Queen moves first."

"Do I?" said the Queen.

I wanted to lie, to cheat, to change it, but I felt pressure building behind my eyes just thinking about it. Bend the world once more and I'd pass out or worse, and that would be the end. I nodded at her. Her lips spread, revealing silver, pointed teeth.

"Then for my move, hmm...I believe I shall cut you in half."

I started to answer. I didn't get far.

She dragged that sword across my stomach. My abdomen split like a water balloon, spilling far too much of me across the chapel tile. I'd like to say the pain was like nothing I'd ever felt before, but it was actually pretty similar to the last time I got disemboweled.

She sneered, disappointed by how easy I was to kill, and pushed me onto the floor. She stalked down the hall, sword screaming across the marble, to finish the Heroes. I was colder than the stone, I thought, as I felt the quite familiar sensation of life slipping away.

I focused on the Queen of Skulls. She'd made her move. The Heroes had a chance.

She'd made her move.

She'd made her move.

The more I thought it, the slower she walked, until she was hardly moving at all.

"Callie?" said Craig. "You good?"

Through the glasses I saw them staring, gray with concern. I was so tired of people looking at me like that. I was tired of everything, really, and I had been for a long time. Sleep beckoned.

"No," I said. "I'm extremely not."

"Can you come back here?"

"That's not a bad idea."

It was silly of me to come back to the Plateau. I died so readily here. I could go home, I could stay at home. I could forget about this entire universe and just wait for the Queen to kill me there.

I could go home.

My hand drifted toward the button on my glasses, the button that would take me away from this cold chapel. It never made it.

Back on the funicular, a golden arrow exploded through the windows. The ceiling erupted in flame.

Myantha had made her move, too.

The car rocked sideways. The world flipped upside down. The train was off the tracks.

You know when you're catastrophically drunk, right on the verge of blacking out, and you trip or something and it's like watching the world through someone else's eyes as they tumble to the ground? That's what it was like watching this disaster through the glasses. Doc and Craig slammed into the ceiling. I landed between them. Sondra dangled from a bench.

My sluggish brain was trying to work out if I was in more danger in Winterwind or Jett Creek when Sondra's bench tore away from the ceiling/floor.

It landed on my chest.

I heard little popping sounds. I think they were my ribs. My friends pulled on the bench, but they couldn't get it to move more than an inch or two. I guess it was crushing the breath out of me, because my view of Jett Creek started to dim.

"Jesus Christ," said Craig, "this is so fucked."

"Shut up and let me think," said Doc.

Sondra stroked my cheek, more tender than I'd ever seen her.

"Callie, baby. You're gonna be fine."

I heard the words through my glasses, and I heard them in Blackbriar, too—hissed through the teeth of the cadaverous wizard standing right in the path of the waiting Queen of Skulls.

I mumbled something. Sondra didn't hear. She got closer.

"Phælandro," I said, "it's your turn."

"You're a crazy bitch, you know that?"

"What's your move?"

"Am I allowed to I kill her?"

I thought of Lomella, the young woman whose life story I'd skimmed over, who had left home to seize power in a far away country, but made a point of sending builders back to her home town to build a church in her mother's honor. I had no reason to hurt that woman, but I did not know how much of her was left. So many had been broken beneath the army of this Queen.

"Yeah. I think that's the only way."

"When in doubt..." She reached under an upside-down light fixture and dug out a d20. "Mudball."

She rolled. In Blackbriar, things got fast fast. A sticky brown orb exploded from Phælandro's fists. If the Queen of

Skulls had been average height, it would have taken her head off, but her DeVito-esque stature saved her. The mudball sailed over her head, ripped a hole in the priceless stained glass, and vanished into the night.

"You missed," I said.

"Who's next?"

"Craig."

Everything in the funicular was either slightly on fire or extremely on fire. While Doc continued straining against the bench, Craig quit helping, hopped over a burning gum ball machine, and tried to rip open a window.

"We have to get the fuck out of here!" he said.

Before I could think of something inspiring to say, Sondra answered for me: "Shut the fuck up and make your move."

"Are you nuts?"

"Just do it."

"Uh, uh…Zircon crush!"

Sondra slapped the die into his hand. He tossed it over his shoulder and didn't bother watching it land. He slammed a sandal through the window and knocked away the glass.

Zircon leapt through the air and brought his hammer down. The Queen's armor cracked. Maybe some of her bones did, too, but when he tumbled to earth she was still standing.

She was hurt—she had to be hurt—but I couldn't tell how bad.

"Doc," I said.

"Let it fucking go," she answered. Thick smoke and on-rushing tears made her voice snotty. She turned her back on me. I wasn't sure if it was in search of a better grip on the bench, or because the smoke was making her retch.

I was very, very cold.

"Mr. Fakebeard," I said, "your audience awaits."

Doc quit working on the bench. She picked up the d20 Craig had thrown away, bounced it in her hand and said, "This feels like our last session."

"Yeah."

"I've got something I've been saving."

"Oh, god," said Craig. We all knew what was coming.

"Wailing Ax."

"Hit it," I said. My words were wet and my mouth was, too. I tilted my head, trying not to choke on the blood.

Doc rolled the die. I didn't see it land. I was too busy watching Billiam Fakebeard make the move he'd been waiting for his whole imaginary life. Fingers dancing on his guitar like a shithead virtuoso, he did a back flip off the nearest column and hung in mid-air. He whipped his guitar over his head, long hair and fake beard fluttering as the instrument morphed into a flaming crimson ax. History's most masturbatory guitar solos echoed around that ancient chapel, shattering the stained windows. As colored glass rained, Billiam brought the ax right onto the middle of the Queen of Skulls', well, skull.

Doc showed off the die.

"Hey," she coughed. "I critted. Did I kill her or what?"

Nowhere close.

The Queen of Skulls wrenched the ax out of her head and hurled it across the floor. Blood streamed through her hair, making red waterfalls across her eyes, pouring into her laughing jaw. She was hurt, but she wasn't finished. This wasn't just any beastie. She was a campaign boss, and they don't go down in one round. She rubbed her hands together, ready to kill us all.

"I guess that means it's my turn?" she said.

"It should be," I groaned, "but this is no time to play fair."

She whipped around, giving me a glare as cold as the tile. She'd thought I was dead, or close enough that it didn't matter. She raised her sword high, ready to decapitate me.

"She's weaker than she used to be," I said, and agony surged through my head, and my words became true. The Queen's biceps atrophied. The sword clattered out of her hand.

"She never recovered from our last fight."

Her back hunched. Her limbs twisted. Every fiber of my two broken bodies sang out in pain.

"Zircon's hit caught her right in the spine. She's crippled."

Pressure built in my head. The world faded away.

"Billiam," I said, "your Wailing Ax sliced her in half."

The Queen split down the middle and splattered to the floor. Pain cut through me like I'd hugged a buzzsaw.

In Winterwind, I died.

In Jett Creek, I died, too.

AN ARCHER STANDS AT A CROSSROADS IN AN ANCIENT FOREST, NOT sure if she should make for the water or the mountains, the town or the keep. Wherever she goes, she will find adventure, have fun, draw blood, and perpetrate terrible crimes.

After fourteen years, a few thousand die rolls, and too many dead to count, her hit points run out. As black sweeps over, her brain's final flashes ask if this last death means anything at all. She's killed the nastiest baddie this world had ever spat forth. Lomella is dead, and because of that, innocents will live. That's good, probably, but is it enough?

Probably not, but fuck it. You do what you can.

19

THANK GOD FOR FIREMEN.

Three of Jett Creek's paunchiest volunteer firefighters were taking a break from battling the inferno at Critical Hit when they saw smoke pouring up from the funicular. While we waged glorious war against the Queen of Skulls, they clambered up the tracks of the ruined train. They kicked in one of the car's windows, dragged Craig out, shouted for the others to follow, and came back for me. They got the bench off and pulled me to safety, like saving my life was nothing at all.

That's what they told me, anyway. I was too dead to care.

I coughed awake, feeling lots and lots and lots of pain. Shifting, I heard the crinkling of a space blanket. I opened my eyes and saw I was just a few feet from the funicular, which was burning down to the struts. Even that couldn't make me warm.

The firemen looked at me like, well, like I'd come back from the dead. One was an extremely moustachioed old man—the guy who owned the hardware store across from Mom's shop. The others were younger—soft bodied boys grinning through soot. One of the young men patted me on the head and walked away to check on Craig, Sondra, and Doc, who were huddled under trauma blankets of their own. They stared. I tried to give a cheerful wave, but I don't think I sold it.

"Well shit," said the boy who stayed behind. "She's not dead anymore."

"That so?" said the old man.

"You saved my life," I croaked out.

"Maybe a little bit. We got the bench off you, we hauled you out, but not for any particular reason."

"You were fucking gone," said the kid.

"Don't be swearing in front of victims."

"I don't mind."

The old man shrugged, unimpressed.

"You were cold as cold. We didn't do nothing because there wasn't nothing to do, 'cept put a blanket on and wait for the EMTs to take you away. Then the—what's the nice way to say it? Nerd?"

"Geek," said the kid. "I think they like geek."

"Whoever it was, the girl with the freaky eyes, she slipped past and put her hands on you. There was this glow, kinda purpley. Heard your ribs snap back together. Next thing I know, you're breathing again."

Healing touch. A stalwart. 2d6 hit points. I wondered how many HP I had left.

Enough to stand. Enough, in fact, to make it look easy. I hopped to my feet, pretending there were parts of me that didn't hurt, and clapped my hands.

"Damn," said the kid. "You're not dead at all."

"Where did she go?"

"Hard to say," said the old man. "We were kinda focusing on you."

"And thanks for that. I've gotta go."

"Like hell! EMTs'll skin me if I don't hold you till they get here."

"They'll take me to the hospital."

"No doubt."

"Tell 'em I can't afford it. You boys are doing god's work—I'll see you around town."

I tried to bypass my players, but they threw their crinkly blankets to the ground and surrounded me as I made my way down the hill. The path was steep, and walking along the tracks only made it a little easier. I stumbled a few times, but they did not let me fall.

"Way to come back from the dead," said Sondra. "Next to you, Christ is a chump. No way he could pull off that hoodie."

"Thanks."

"I'm sorry we couldn't, y'know—" said Craig, imitating what I guess was supposed to be someone pulling a railroad bench off their friend.

"It's all right. You had fun being Zircon, huh?"

"Best session of my life."

"I guess it would be stupid to tell you to sit down," said Doc.

"Yes."

When I got tired, they helped me keep going. As their fingers wrapped around my aching arms, I remembered I still had to get to the bottom of whole, "Which one of my friends is a murderer?" thing. At the moment, just breathing was hard enough.

After a while, we made it back to the cul-de-sac, where the fire was dying down. The store was in cinders, but the buildings beside it were only scorched. Two fire trucks cast frothing water into the sky, tamping down whatever flames remained. The ambulances were gone. I hoped they'd left empty.

"Lotta good games in there," said Doc.

"So many tiny cardboard people," said Sondra.

"What a waste," said Craig.

I saw my car. The windows had exploded; the metal was scorched; the stained upholstery had burnt away. Even the Wendy's wrappers were gone. I tossed my keys through the broken glass.

"I guess that's why you don't park on the sidewalk," I said.

"There's a lot of reasons not to park on the sidewalk, dear," said Doc.

Diego loomed out of the smoke.

"If I could just grab you for one second, Callie—"

"You know what, man," I said. "Why not? I'm living on borrowed time."

His eyes went wide. It was nice that there was someone on this planet I could still surprise. He walked me away from the group. His hands were shaking. Every inch of him looked clammy. I thought I'd do him a favor and get this over with quick.

"You're asking about a date, right?"

"How did you—"

"I am so extremely flattered, but there's a big pretty big age difference here and I keep dying and I just don't think it's going to happen."

"What?"

"I'm saying no. You asked me on a date and—"

"Whoa!"

"Huh?"

"I did not ask you on a date. You're my coworker, and you're way younger than me, and—"

I bent double laughing. It hurt a ton, but it had been seven years since I had a really good chuckle, and man did it feel good. He didn't know why, I don't think, but he laughed too.

"Then what the fuck is going on?" I said.

"I was trying to ask if Doc is seeing anybody."

"Doc?"

"Of course Doc. She's smart as shit and super sexy and, yeah. Doc."

"She's all yours, dude. But I should warn you—there's a one in three chance that she's a super powerful dark wizard and a murderer to boot."

"Cool. Thanks for letting me know."

He disappeared into the darkness, shaking his head. I bet it'd take him a year to get up the nerve to ask her out.

Odette sat on the sidewalk opposite her ruined building, watching the smoke. The flashing emergency lights made her look pale, even sick—as sick as me. For a second I couldn't tell what looked off about her and then I realized that for the first time since I remembered, she'd taken off her sweater.

"Cool tattoos," I said. They were lovely, just like her. Mostly floral—lilies and tulips and roses and a lot of others I wasn't smart enough to recognize wrapped in the most delicate looking fire.

"Thanks," said Odette.

I stood next to her, wanting to sit down but knowing that if I did I might not be able to get back up, so instead I offered her a hand.

"I'm sorry," I said.

"Fuck it. I'm insured. Are you going after the woman who did it?"

"Unless you need me here."

Odette shook her head.

"You're off the clock. I'll call you Monday. Figure we'll have some shift changes."

I nodded and walked away. I was halfway down the block when I realized I'd forgotten to say something important to Sondra, Doc, Craig and everyone else who had hung around to watch the shop burn, everyone who had ever rolled a die.

"I love you!" I shouted. "I love all of you!"

I don't know if they heard me. They didn't turn around.

A FEW BLOCKS OF COLD AIR DROVE THE SMOKE OUT MY LUNGS. I stopped once or twice and tried to enjoy the night, since I was pretty sure it was the last I'd ever see, but my feet couldn't stay still.

Someone waited on the creaky old glider that'd been dying on our front porch since before we moved in. For a second I thought it was Mom. Because human beings are the stupidest things in the universe, I was actually relieved when I saw that, no, it was the woman who was trying to kill me instead.

I pretended I didn't see her, because no amount of death can stop me being petty, and walked to the front door. I reached for my key and remembered I'd chucked it into a burning car. Oops. Not like I'd need it, anyway.

"You knew I'd be here," said Myantha. The moonlight

dripped off her like mercury.

"You didn't seem the type to, like, go to Sonic for a cherry lime-aid."

She chuckled, even though what I'd said couldn't have possibly made sense, and patted the cushion. I sat down. The swing sagged almost to the floor.

"You left me to die back at the Edge of the World," I said. "I didn't."

"Well done."

"Tonight you tried to kill me. You missed. You tried again and just about managed it. And then, instead, you saved my life."

"Why do you think I did that?"

"At first I figured it was because you wanted to kill me yourself, but that's stupid supervillain shit, and you've never been one percent stupid."

"Why, then?"

"I think that, before you have your revenge, you want to know how the hell I made it back and what happened to your world along the way."

She pushed on the floorboards. The tortured joints of the glider screamed.

"So tell me."

I told her. I wasn't shy about stretching it out. It was nice on that glider, nicer than I'd remembered, and I wanted the moment to last a little longer before every moment was done. So I gave her the whole seven years—pulling myself off the floor of the inn, burning LB's house, slipping through Blackbriar, meeting Randy Randy, mastering crafts I'd never had patience for in my own life, and realizing that freaky plastic world actually felt a lot like home.

"I didn't know what happened when you took the monocle," I said. "If time were passing here or not. I didn't know what kind of world would be waiting when I got back."

"But you kept on."

"If there was a chance to save my friends, I had to take it."

Another hard push on the swing. When we slowed, she

asked: "What kind of world will be waiting for me?"

"You missed seven shitty years. A lot of burnt crops. A lot of mass graves. But now the Queen of Skulls is dead."

"Hrmph."

She stalked down the porch. When she came back, her eyes were red and dry, like a clean wound. She wrapped her hands around the arms of the glider and squeezed until it came to a stop. She growled.

"I worshiped you."

"I didn't deserve it."

"But you did! You were magnificent. You had power. And you used it for nothing. When a god gives you the strength to save worlds, and you use that strength to play games, you are worse than a fraud. You are a monster."

I nodded. She wasn't wrong.

It had taken most of what I had to walk back here, to sit beside her, to fake patience as I waited to see what she was going to do. I didn't have the energy to argue for my life. I wanted this to be done.

"You still going to kill me?"

She lifted her hand. Deadly light surged into her fingertips.

"Would you like me to?"

"I deserve it. I'm through pretending I don't. I killed people, real people. Some of them I didn't know what I was doing. Some I did."

"Yes."

The light in her hand glowed brighter. I had to work to keep my eyes open. Her bow scribbled itself in the air.

"But I don't want to die. This world is a paradise. I'd like to enjoy it. So what I want is for you to absolve me so that I can sink back into my stupid, regular life, but after what I've done... The rules demand justice. So go ahead."

The arrow rested, weightless, against my forehead. The flesh burned.

"Would you really just go back to your old life?"

"What do you mean?"

"The Plateau is fucked, and it's your fault. You spent seven years there. You saw how bad it is. Would you really leave it alone?"

I tried to picture myself watching television, doing laundry, reading the newspaper, checking my horoscope, scowling over a crossword. It didn't fit.

"Nope. I lived there. I died there. I can't let it go."

I tensed my jaw, waiting for that gorgeous arrow to end my life.

And then, poof.

It disappeared.

"Where I come from," Myantha said, "justice is not simple. You don't get to repent; you don't get to die. You have power and you are going to use it. Start a new campaign. Rebuild your party. Rebuild my world. Call it a game, if that's what makes sense to you, but play like every choice means life or death."

"That's better than I deserve."

"If you were your brother, maybe. Scum like him would see this as an easy way out. But you have a conscience, Callie Myles, and this will be your hell."

She squeezed my shoulder. Her eyes flashed red, then settled back into a nice soft green. She raised the monocle to her face.

"I'll be watching."

"We'll give you a show."

She took one last look at her fallen god. She pressed the button. She was gone.

Another friend lost. Another layer of guilt. She was right. Death would have been a relief I didn't deserve.

I sat for a while, marinating in my shame, until that rusty glider's creaking started to drive me nuts and I realized the pit in my stomach wasn't just misery. I was hungry, too.

I tore away the duct tape that hid the spare key under the stoop and opened the front door. The house was warm. I tore off the hoodie and tossed it onto the stairs. Tomorrow I'd burn these clothes. Tonight I needed a goddamned snack.

In the kitchen I found potato bread. I found jelly. I found a fresh jar of crunchy peanut butter. I smacked the sandwich together and was licking the knife clean when Mom walked through the door, frayed bathrobe cinched tight, an empty water glass in her hand.

"Saw the weirdest light outside just now. Like a transformer exploded. Or maybe it's a UFO. That'd be cool."

She didn't quite finish that last sentence, because as soon as I saw her I stuffed half my sandwich in my mouth and wrapped myself around her hard enough to knock the wind out of her chest. I chewed and cried and chewed and cried until she pried me off.

"Oh, sweetheart," she said, kissing my forehead. "I miss him too."

That wasn't even close to what this was about, but I didn't argue. There were worse hells.

THE HOUSE WASN'T MINE, BUT I HAD A KEY. I LET MYSELF IN AND walked down the scuzzy carpet to the kitchen, the only room where the lights were on. Every cabinet was open. The counters were piled with mixing bowls, scratched teflon pans, and "As Seen on TV!" gadgets whose plastic had gone yellow. Odette hunched over the sink scrubbing the drain. An untouched mug of chamomile tea cooled beside her. I watched from the dining room, through a window sliced into the paneled wall.

"I came to make you tea. Like I should have done weeks ago. I guess I'm too late."

"Tea doesn't help. Want some?"

"Sure."

I lowered a pile of kitchen junk onto the floor and sat on a creaking barstool. She twirled the knob on the electric range and set the kettle on a coil beginning to glow orange.

"How's the shop?" I said.

"Total loss, but we knew that. Nobody got killed, which is good. Insurance is already showing signs of being a pain in the ass, but they'll pay me every fucking cent."

"You're rebuilding?"

"What the hell else could I do?"

We were quiet until the kettle boiled.

"When did you create Lomella?" I said.

Odette turned off the burner. The whistling died.

This woman had been there my whole life, a mentor, a friend, teaching me how to play games, how to teach them, how to work. She had never demanded anything more than that I show up on time and with a reasonably good attitude, and for that she had given me everything. And here I was, trying to get her to confess to murder.

I was turning into a real bitch.

"A long time ago," she said.

"I thought you didn't play."

"I don't, not with customers or staff. But LB was running me a solo campaign. We'd been doing it for years. One has to find ways to keep the romance alive."

She walked out of the kitchen. I followed her to LB's office. The books, the desk, the boxes, were all gone. The only thing left was the old rotary phone, which sat, cord tied around it like a noose, on the peeling laminate tile. A wad of paper towels occupied one corner, next to a squirt bottle of Windex. The big square window glowed, a perfect black mirror.

"I found your campaign books," I said. "Lomella's life story. I thought it was just background material for our game— LB over-preparing, like always. I'd forgotten he could still run other campaigns."

"She was our baby. I created her as a level one orphan, a child of the Edge of the World. She fought her way up the Plateau, through the pass, on into the wider world. She leveled up so many times that LB had to keep inventing new ways to make her more powerful. She founded an empire. She crushed everyone who got in her way."

"But why did she look like Danny DeVito?"

"I've always used charisma as a dump stat." She laughed, and a little light came into the room.

"Why did you quit?" I said.

"I found those notebooks, his 'plan' for the campaign."

"All sins, no sins, all sins, no sins?"

"That's the one. I confronted him and he broke down. I'd

never seen him cry so ugly. He said the game was trying to kill him. I thought he was being hyperbolic. He called me an idiot, threw the monocle at me, and told me to look for myself. So I did."

"What did you see?"

"Fucked up shit. A world my husband twisted and abused because it made him feel like a god. I found that weird fucking house in the swamp."

"The cages."

"The cages. I walked all over the Plateau, went north, too. Saw that the most evil person there, the one who'd killed thousands and oppressed an entire continent, was my character. He made a murderer out of me."

"You were the one who chose to play evil."

She slammed her fist on the window. Our reflections wobbled.

"It was supposed to be a game! How the fuck was I supposed to know that every person I executed had a family, that every village I burned had a past?"

She leaned on the window and glowed against the dark. Her skin looked gray, her lips pale. Ever since LB died, I'd been trying to find ways to cross the space between us, but she kept getting farther away.

"When I came back, I tore into him. Told him he was a fucking sociopath. That didn't hurt him the way I thought, so I said his art was shitty, and that made him blow up."

She smiled. She'd always known how to get under LB's skin.

"What did he do?" I said.

"He took Lomella away from me. Told me that if I wouldn't keep playing, he'd make her an NPC, use her in y'all's campaign, have her do worse shit than I'd ever dreamed of, just to prove that he could. 'I'm not playing god,' he said, 'I am god.'"

"What a dickhead."

"Yeah."

"When he first realized what was happening on the Plateau, he tried to fix it. What changed?"

"He couldn't control his power, but he kept trying until it stopped his heart. After he got out of the hospital, he gave up. Decided if he couldn't atone, it would be a lot more fun to go full bastard."

"How much time had he spent in the game?" I said.

"Hundreds of years. Maybe more. Being alive for that long would fuck anybody up."

She slid down the glass to the floor. I sat too, and dug my fingers into the shag.

"I wish someone had told me what was going on," I said.

"What would you have done?"

"Nothing, probably. That's most of what I do. But I'd have liked to know."

"If anything like this happens again, you'll be the first person I call."

I took a long breath and asked the ugly question.

"So how did you kill him?"

"By the end, he was mostly sleeping at the studio, but one night when he was here, once he'd put back enough beer to pass the fuck out, I lifted the monocle off his gut and stole Lomella's mini out of his bag and went back to the Plateau as the Queen of Skulls. I knew I had one shot, but that I could stay there as long as it took, which ended up being about a year."

Her face contorted at the memory of that lost time. I knew how she felt.

"I flew that kickass bone monster of mine right over Blackbriar Keep and landed it on the Plateau, way behind enemy lines. I disguised myself as a merchant. I found people y'all had hurt. It wasn't hard. There are thousands."

"I know."

"And I lay the seeds for a conspiracy. I built the church at the Edge of the World. I found the innkeeper and told her about Astral Leap and Gorham's Iron. I gave her a Joll-E Boy snack cake and she gave me a d20 that could travel through space and time. I corrupted Brother Fisher and the monks and taught them to use the die as a kind of homing device for a fireball. It was all kinda involved, but when you've got level 30 magic and all the time in the world, you can get a lot done. And then I came home."

"Did he know what you'd done?"

"He knew I'd been fucking with his pet universe, because the next time he paid the Plateau a visit the calendar had jumped ahead a year and he didn't know why. That's when he broke. He sensed my little conspiracy, but he couldn't stop it, and no matter how much he begged me to tell him what was going on, I just pretended I didn't know what he was talking about. It was kinda cruel, I guess, but he deserved it. Again, the cages, y'know?"

"And then he used me to try to kill the Queen of Skulls."

"Yeah. You did it just the way he wanted. He pitched that fake tantrum and when he was storming out, I decided I'd seen enough. I gave him the iron d20 like it was an apology, a make-up gift. He believed me. That was it."

She said it like it was nothing, but she looked very, very sad. There was nothing really for me to say.

"How did you figure it out?" she said, finally.

I tapped my shoulder. She shrugged off her sweater and glanced at her tattoos.

"Shit," she said. "You know, I forget I even have these?"

"The floor of the church you built at the Edge of the World had the same design. As soon as I saw you without your sweater, I knew."

"He deserved to die."

I took her hands. They were awfully warm.

"He did," I said. "Would it make a difference if I said I forgive you?"

"I don't fucking care if you forgive me or not. I did the right thing. It was the hardest thing I've ever done; it's left me broken in a way I didn't know people could break, but it was right. That's enough."

She closed her eyes and breathed away her rage.

"Anyway, that's what I've been up to. What happened with you and the woman who burned down my store?"

"She let me live so that I could mend the fucked up shit LB

left behind."

"You're going to keep running the game?"

"New campaign starts Thursday. You want to play?"

AT SEVEN SHARP, CRAIG SHOOED THE LAST CUSTOMER OUT OF Loose Joose and flipped off the open sign. He spun a knob beside the door and the lights dropped to a soft white glow.

"Nothing like a little atmosphere."

"Don't be an idiot," I said.

"I can't even see my sheet," said Sondra. Craig hung his head and turned the lights back up.

We dragged three tables together to make one long one. I sat in the middle and passed minis to Sondra, Craig, and Doc. Odette rolled up an astral mage named Annila. She described her as, "Like the Queen of Skulls, but not so evil." And after an hour of slightly infuriating hand-holding, we were able to produce a fighter named, sigh, Crusherella for our newest player, Detective Leah Sparks. She clutched her grayish-green juice like it was a lifeline, staring frozen at the papers, maps, and dice smeared across the table.

"Y'all are going to take it easy on me, right?" she said. Doc slapped her on the back.

"Relax," she said. "It's like losing your virginity. It's ridiculous and embarrassing, but you only have to do it once."

I put on my iron bifocals. Leah didn't know their secret, but we'd tell her soon enough. Behind my cardboard screen, I had two sharp pencils and a sheaf of notes. I'd spent two weeks on the Plateau prepping for this session, getting a sense of the chaos left behind when the Queen of Skulls' army fractured into competing bands of warlords and raiders. I found a village that needed our help, people we could save.

They waited for me to speak. I sipped my juice, which was disgusting, and reached for the twenty-sided die.

ACKNOWLEDGMENTS

As always, pride of place goes to the magnificent Sharon Pelletier, who worked tirelessly on this book for over a year. Without her counsel, Callie Myles' adventure would hardly be an adventure at all. Thanks as well to David Pomerico and the team at Harper Voyager, as well as Kathryn McConnell, Brandi Varnell, and the good people of Squeaky Bicycle. Their unflagging support for my work made Critical Hit possible.

The beautiful maps at the front of the book were created by Ryan S. Thomason, and the paucity of typos can be credited to ace proofreader/copy editor/all-around cool person Adele Ciccaglione. I recommend hiring them both.

This novel is dedicated to anyone who ever played a game. I would like to single out a few regulars at my table, whose incredible imagination taught me everything I know about RPGs. Nate Jones, Kate Eastman, Robert Norman, Blake Lowell, Timea Hopp, Brian Whitton, Lauren LaMack, Tomás Nazal, Patrick Over, Casey Matteson—it has been an honor to play with you, and I hope we get to do it again soon.

A special thanks is due to the fans of my games, including *Deadball*, *Lost Ship*, and *Comrades*. Many of those players appear as NPCs in the following pages, and I would like to extend particular thanks to Patreon backers Jake Smith, Craig Harris, Alfred Dobradi, Colin Ross, Kris Herzog, Lachlan Jones, Dom Guido, and Todd Ellis. Y'all know how to play.

This book is also dedicated to my brother and parents, but because those are people one cannot thank enough, I would like to say again: Thank you Caldwell, Mom, and Dad.

And of course, I would not have been able to write a word without the support and affection of my family. Yvonne, August, and Dash—you are the reason I exist. The love that animates this book is the love I feel for you.

FAVORITE NPCS

Drawn from LB's notebooks, these are some of the most memorable characters to grace the tables of Critical Hit. Use them in your game, or see them in your dreams.

AKRONDA THE BLUE	A wickedly-funny monster hunter who specializes in killing gigantic beasts. Dreams of avenging her long-dead parents.
FOX EMBER	A non-binary redheaded wizard gifted in illusion and trickery. Uses laughter to cast spells, and laughs all the time.
HARUKU	An enigmatic diviner employed by a group of traveling merchants who uses his foresight to keep them safe on the road.
HE'YU	A marksman, prankster, and "doctor" with an unfortunate habit of launching into flute solos in the heat of battle.
JAMES MCINNES	A lanky, bearded country boy, his calloused hands disguise the best education money can buy. Lives for the open road.
JASON WEITZEL	The owner of Weitzel's Roadhouse, a legendary inn where the beds are soft, the food is hot, and the ale is icy cold.
KATINKA	A cat-like performing arts instructor as skilled with an insult as she is at training the bards of Blackbriar Town.
LUCIUS COITELO	A pint-sized bureaucrat with ties to the underworld. Yearns for respectability, but cannot escape his criminal past.
LUCRETIA DRO	A superstitious noblewoman who believes the Gray Lord speaks to her directly through her divination stones.
MAGNUM PARNASSUS	A famed monster hunter, now owner of Parnassus' Weirdities & Oddities, whose gruff demeanor conceals a warm heart.

MAGPIE	A fixture of the Blackbriar night, distinguished by their mysterious countenance and birdlike black and white hair.
MAISIE	A brilliant cook whose signature almond soufflé has inspired madness, brawls, and at least three epic poems.
MATIKUS THE UNHOLY	A sorcerer tired of being interrupted by do-gooding adventurers. Maybe immortal, maybe undead. Definitely cranky.
MERVIN SPOOR	A brilliant tracker whose secretive nature has prompted rumors that his talents are the work of sinister magic.
MICHAEL DEAN	A disabled veteran employed by the Blackbriar postal service, he lives to sip beer and roll dice at the tables of the Gray Game.
MR. CALVIN COOPER	A pastoral poet whose passion for his art has been undermined by the demons that lurk deep within his mind.
NIKLAS VILD	The towering leader of the Yellowstockings, a fearsome mercenary gang locked in a death-struggle with their rival Grackles.
R.K. DAWLEY	A wandering brute who loves brawling, knives, and being alone. Always has something useful in his pocket.
SELENEYE WYRBEL	A middle-aged beauty whose silver hair and gray eyes have a way of coaxing the truth out of strangers.
WARKITTEH	A colossal green-eyed cat blessed with the powers of magic. Can walk on two legs, but prefers all four. Probably napping.
YARDENNE	The finest poet on the Plateau, a wandering bard attended to by an impish creature known as Orion the Chaos Lord.

FURTHER READING

IF I'VE DONE MY JOB CORRECTLY, THIS BOOK HAS WHETTED YOUR appetite for tabletop gaming. Whether you are new to the hobby or simply looking to get back into it after a long break, the landscape of tabletop roleplaying games can be daunting. But fear not! With the exception of some of the miscreants in this novel, tabletop gamers are a welcoming bunch, and it will not take much work to get you rolling dice, having fun, and laughing until your face hurts.

If you and your friends are looking for the classic fantasy RPG experience, I have had wonderful success running David Black's *The Black Hack*, which offers an ultra-streamlined version of old school roleplaying in the vein of *Winterwind*. For solo players interested in exploring a realm like the Winterwind Plateau, Shawn Tomkin's *Ironsworn* is exceptionally well made, and was one of the inspirations for the world of this book.

Not interested in swords and sorcery? Explore the halls of a monstrous high school in Avery Alder's exquisite *Monsterhearts*, drop bombs on Nazis in Jason Morningstar's thrilling *Night Witches*, or fight for your patch of the wasteland in D. Vincent Baker and Meguey Baker's *Apocalypse World*, whose brilliant rules engine was the basis for most of these games. (As well as for my own *Comrades: A Revolutionary RPG*.)

These recommendations are based on my own narrow experience, but there is no need for you to follow my trail. The absolute best way to learn about tabletop gaming is to pay a visit to your local games store. Ask what they recommend, and if they have any regular games that are looking for players. It may take a bit of work to find the right system and the right group, but once you do, I promise you will have the time of your life.

THE AUTHOR

W.M. AKERS IS A NOVELIST, PLAYWRIGHT, AND GAME DESIGNER. He is the author of the mystery novels *Westside, Westside Saints,* and the forthcoming *Westside Lights.* He is also the creator of the bestselling games *Deadball: Baseball With Dice* and *Comrades: A Revolutionary RPG,* and the curator of the history newsletter *Strange Times.* He lives in Philadelphia, but hasn't traded in his Mets cap yet. Learn more about his work at *wmakers.net.*